Gihli,
The Chief Named Dog

A CHEROKEE NOVEL

Also by Courtney Miller

Cherokee Chronicles

Book 1: The First Raven Mocker
Book 2: The Raven Mocker's Legacy

White Feather Mysteries

Ludwig's Fugue
It's About Time

Gihli,
The Chief Named Dog

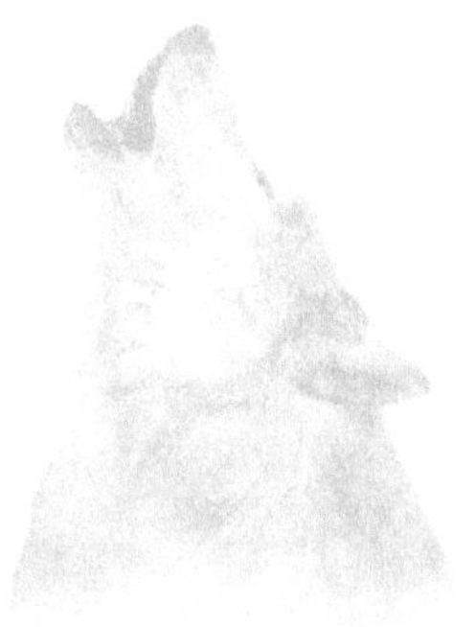

Courtney Miller

Popul Vuh
Publishing

www.PopulVuhPublishing.com

*Dedicated to the Cherokee People and
to preserving the memory of the ancient culture.*

Acknowledgments

I AM GRATEFUL TO the team that helped put this book together. K. T. Hutke Fields, Principal Chief, has been so helpful and supportive. My wife, Lin's help was steadfast. Dr. Judith Briles' selfless dedication to the success of authors was vital. I want to thank Margaret Ireland, my editor; Nick Zelinger for the fantastic cover; and Ronnie Moore for the creative layout of the book.

Main Characters

Gihli (gee-hlee) "Dog", Tagwa Chief

Alihelitsidasdi (ah-lee-hay-lee-chee-dahs-dee) "Happy One", Long Hair Clan

Atselvdi (ah-chee-lew-deh) "Impersonator/Mimic", Long Hair Clan, Apprentice Priest

Adanvdo Alsgida (ah-DAH-new-doh alls-GEE-da) "Spirit Dancer", Paint Clan, Uku

Kalona Ehlawei, (cah-low-nah eh-lah-way-eee) "Quiet Raven", Long Hair Clan, Peace Chief

Kalanu Ahkyeliski (Kah-lah-noo Ahk-yee-lee-sss-key), "Raven Mocker", Deer Clan, Witch

Sali (sah-lee) "Persimmon bark", Paint Clan, Paint Clan Priest, Uku's Assistant

Waya Usti (wah-yah oos-tee) "Wolf Puppy", Wolf Clan, Tracker/Scout

Amadohi (ah-mah-doe-hee) "Peaceful Waters", Wild Potato Clan

Tawodi Gvnage (tah-woe-dee Gew-nah-geh) "Black Hawk", Bird Clan, warrior

Sudalegi (soo-dah-lay-gee) "One Thing" , Forest People

Wananahi (wah-nah-nah-heh) "Tender Woman", Wild Potato Clan, Beloved Woman

Tlomeha Usdi (tloe-mee-ha oos-dee) "Little Bat", Bird Clan, Tracker/Ball Player

Wahuhu Adawehi (wah-hoo-hoo ah-dah-way-hee) "Wise Owl", Bird Clan, lead warrior, Chief Red Wolf's Assistant

Waya Gigage (wah-yah gee-gah-gee) "Red Wolf", Wolf Clan, War Chief

Saloli (sah-low-lee) "Squirrel", Long Hair Clan, Wispy Woman

Prologue

Dealing with archaeological finds is one thing, dealing with people is another. We must move closer to the Cherokees as human beings who have had the same talents, hopes, dreams, needs, emotions, conflicts, and accomplishments that are common to all of humankind.
—Thomas E. Mails, The Cherokee People

It was the sense that there was a subtle imbalance in the world that morning.

THEY ALL AWOKE WITH foreboding. This was a family accustomed to optimism, determination, and resolve—a family that had achieved great things in their lives.

He was born Ugidahli Unega, White Feather, and had earned the name Kalanu Ahkyeliski, Raven Mocker. He was the patriarch of his family, living alone as an outcast because he had chosen the dark path and perhaps had discovered the secret to immortality. For what reason would he awaken with dread?

He was born Ugugu, Snow Owl, and had earned the name Adanvdo Alsgida, Spirit Dancer. He was the good son, the wise father, and grandfather who had risen out of fear and shame to become the village Uku, the high priest. For what reason would he awaken feeling fear and apprehension?

She was born Kalona Ehlawei, Quiet Raven. She was the granddaughter, daughter, and grandmother who had risen above her difficult childhood to become a Beloved Woman and the Peace Chief of her village. For what reason would she awaken with a dire premonition?

She was born Alihelitsidasdi, Happy One, a teenager living a happy, innocent life with a bright future. Her close friends and family just called her Ali. For what reason would she awaken with anxiety?

He was born Atselvdi, Immitator, a teenager already far along the white path to becoming a priest and probable successor of his grandfather's position as Uku. For what reason would he awaken with ill portents?

It was in the air that was not as crisp as it should be. It was in the colors that were not quite as bright as they should be. It was in sounds that seemed somehow slightly muffled. It was in the odors that seemed subdued. It was in the bed that felt harder and the covers that felt heavier than usual. It was in the sour taste of their morning saliva. It was the sense that there was a subtle imbalance in the world that morning.

Perhaps, they all sensed the omen of evil that was lurking in their future.

*The dog had barked
incessantly for two days and
was grating on her
exceptional patience.*

In the heart of the Cherokee nation, in the land of the ancient Ani Yun Wiya, the Real People, a small, unassuming village sat nestled among tall trees on the side of a mountain. The river they knew as The Long Man flowed next to the village they knew as Tsikohi. It was a typical village inside tall, palisaded walls with daub and waddle houses arranged neatly along orderly streets.

On the north side of the village, a large, regal, seven-sided Council House faced east atop a large, rectangular mound overlooking a ball field and dance field. On a tall pole, the white flag of peace danced in the breeze.

Not far away, in the heart of the village, Kalona Ehlawei lived in a three-room home with her father, the Uku, the high priest, and her teenaged twin grandchildren.

A welcomed breeze blew back the door cover and moved through the room disturbing the smoke from the fire in the stone hearth. Kalona Ehlawei straightened her back, wiped sweat from her brow and swiped her hands on her skirt. The breeze felt good but Kalona shook her head in disgust. With the door cover blown back, there was nothing to block the sound of a gihli barking in the distance. The dog had barked incessantly for two days and was grating on her exceptional patience.

Kalona Ehlawei was a tall, stout woman of uncommon presence and stature. It was said that she had shown extraordinary peace and resolve all of her life and even in the face of a violent and horrific birth. Consequently, the name they had given her at birth was Quiet Raven and nothing in her life or character had occurred to change it.

She, of course, did not remember her horrible birth day, but had overheard the story whispered many times. It was a day the residents of Tsikohi would never forget.

It had promised to be a joyous day. Her father had recently been ordained the village Uku and he and his priest friend, Sali, sat guard outside the house, the house she still lived in, waiting for the birth of his first born. Her mother's sister was also pregnant, but not quite due yet. Her mother was surrounded by family and birthing was going well.

Outside, Kalona's father had been surprised by the arrival of his mother who had come from far away. It was a momentous reunion since he had not seen his mother since he was a young boy.

This hopeful setting was cruelly interrupted by a sibling from her father's past—his evil brother, Tsisgili, a raven mocker witch, son of Kalanu Ahkyeliski.

Tsisgili had suddenly swooped in at the moment of birth and tried to seize baby Kalona from her mother's arms. The shock had prompted the premature birth of her mother's sister's baby. Kalona's grandmother and her mother's oldest sister lost their lives battling the witch. The shock of the event left her mother in a coma.

Kalona's father reportedly put up a valiant fight against his evil brother and chased him into the valley beyond the village stockade, but were it not for the appearance of her father's father, her grandfather, the evil witch, Tsisgili, might have prevailed.

Her grandfather, Kalanu Ahkyeliski, was an enigma himself. He was a legend. He was the first raven mocker witch. And although he had once used his extraordinary skills to save a village from the monster, Nunyunuwi, a cannibal witch, the villagers feared Kalanu and had tried to burn him alongside Nunyunuwi as a witch. Kalanu had escaped and tried to start a new life in a far away village raising twin sons. Ugugu, Kalona's father now known as Adanvdo Alsgida, had followed the white path. Adanvdo's twin brother Tsisgili had followed the dark path becoming a raven mocker like their father. But unlike their father, Tsisgili was pure evil. It had taken the skills of the father to defeat his evil son and save his good son, Adanvdo, and his granddaughter, Kalona.

When Kalona's mother died seven days after her birth, according to custom, little Kalona was given to her mother's surviving sister to rear. Although emotionally damaged by the incident, and burdened with a newborn, her mother's sister was the last of the Ani Gilohi clan in the village and it fell upon her to raise Kalona along with her own infant.

But, in a strange twist, not long afterward, Kalona's fragile aunt tossed Kalona and her own baby in the river and disappeared never to be heard from again.

Kalona never learned what happened to her aunt or her cousin. If anyone knew, no one wanted to speak of it. Alone and with no other maternal family left to raise her, Kalona was taken in by her father.

Her reminiscing was interrupted by the dog barking again. Kalona's dutiful granddaughter was humming as she stirred the mixture of corn, beans, and squash, the soup they called the three sisters. It reminded Kalona of something.

"We will need to gather more sisters this morning," she said with a smirk. Her granddaughter, Alihelitsidasdi, did not respond. Kalona could see that her happy granddaughter was lost in a daydream. Ali's independence and zest reminded Kalona of herself. But, unlike her granddaughter, she had never had a real childhood and had never known the freedom and happiness of little Ali. As an only child, Kalona had been forced to grow up quickly to take care of herself and help her father.

She knew that the death of her mother had left an unhealable wound in her father's heart. Adanvdo had been a good father, but as the Uku, the high priest of the village, he was very busy and had little time for household chores or looking after a child. So, the lonely, little Quiet Raven had learned to do the household chores, look after her father, and raise herself.

It was a curse he had brought upon himself when he chose the black path of witchcraft.

THE BURDEN A MAN carries in his heart weighs heavier and can break him sooner than any weight on his back. It is a load that cannot be shrugged off to give the muscle a rest. It must be borne until lifted by a countering emotion, a counterweight that returns the heart to balance or lifts the heart to euphoria.

Kalanu Ahkyeliski had long been excommunicated from his tribe and forgotten. Tossed aside like worthless trash unworthy of life among the principal people, the Ani Yun Wiya; unworthy of love or compassion; a feculent, distasteful bite to be spit out and washed away.

It was a curse he had brought upon himself when he chose the black path of witchcraft. He could not blame others for his fate, nor could he seek absolution for his sin. There was no council where he might seek forgiveness, and no remedy for the curse he had cast upon himself.

His amazing perception enabled him to understand the powers inherent in the physical world and tap those powers to achieve what no other man or witch had ever achieved before him. Kalanu Ahkyeliski knew how to capture the askina, the four souls, of a human being or an animal and consume the essence to make it his own. This incredible knowledge enabled him to extract the remaining life of a person and transfer the number of years he or she had left to live on to his own life, or to extract the souls of an animal and shape-shift into that animal at will.

He was a brilliant but lonely man with no one to talk to; no one to share his special genius with; no one to admire and encourage him; no one to appreciate his wisdom. Although it had enabled him to extend his life, it had left him old, isolated, remorseful, and empty.

He lived secluded on a mountain, concealed atop a rocky crag overlooking a deep canyon, not far from the small Cherokee village of Tsikohi. A small seven-sided hut nestled against the rock face beside a small, sterile pond provided him shelter. Above the pond, water from a spring poured out of a crack in the rock face and fell unobstructed into the elongated depression that cupped the icy waters of the crystal clear pool and poured the excess into the canyon below.

In the summer, the spilled water mostly turned to spray and evaporated into the fog that perpetually hovered over the valley below. The rest consolidated into large drops that crashed into the tiny tributary that would join the larger river known as the Agusa Jisdu.

In the winter, the water would freeze and form massive curtains of ice from the hole in the rock to the frozen pond and eventually down to the canyon floor.

The lonely old wizard stoked the last link he had with the Ani Yun Wiya—the sacred fire that he kept perpetually burning in the hearth centered in his small hut. He had acquired the fire's original flames from the sacred fires that burned perpetually in a pit beneath the large Council House in the village where he once lived.

Seven-sided structures were meant for council houses, rituals and religious centers, but Kalanu Ahkyeliski had never built a traditional house to live in, preferring only his small, seven-sided hut.

In the winter, he would live in the hut to stay warm. In the summer, he hardly slept in it, spending most of his time sitting in the shade next to the waterfall where the spray kept him cool, or perched on the edge of the crag watching the sky vault rotate around him.

There had been a time when studying his dark craft had been enough. Not anymore. Now it defined the boundaries of his loneliness.

Satisfied that the fire would continue without him, he walked to the L-shaped rock that he had named Edoda, meaning sit with me. It was a sad joke. Nothing but a rock would invite the old witch to sit anymore.

He slid his body into the familiar groove and waited for Grandmother Sun to start her climb in the east. The Edoda sat on the edge of the crag with a canyon below carved out by centuries of erosion. It afforded the lonely man a throne in the only world he was now safe to live to view the world that had banned him forever.

This morning, thick, pinkish clouds filled the gorge and the surrounding valleys. As the emerging sun began to brighten, the lonely witch's eyes focused on his bluing feet and gray-white, rotting legs.

He knew he could no longer put it off. It was simple—to live or not to live. His time on earth was running out and if he wished to extend his years, he would have to invade the Tsalagi, the people he was once a part of, soon and steal the souls of an unfortunate victim.

But even though he was a despised and notorious witch, he was not an evil man. His mind wrestled with what he would have to do to extend his life, and time and again, he had decided that he would just let his life expire.

But when he felt his strength wane and nausea filled his stomach, when his muscles ached to the bone and cramped, dark thoughts crept back into his mind.

He had only done the deed twice in his life. The first time was in a moment of desperation to save his old mentor. It was still distasteful; it was still his worst nightmare. It was still the moment in his life he most regretted because it had marked the turning point.

The second time he had stolen the souls of an evil man, saving mankind from a murdering plague, he had rationalized. But deep within he had not accepted the rationalization and even this act remained distasteful.

So, how could he do it again? How could he take another's life without remorse? He reasoned that there were evil people that deserved to die. People whose lives served no useful purpose and who clung to no purpose for living. But did anyone really deserve to die? And, where would he find such a person?

Behind him, he heard a snap! A raven squawked desperately. The decrepit wizard's blue lips smiled and his red eyes sparkled. He had caught a raven in his trap. "Soon, I shall taste your souls!"

*"The great apportioner has
indicated that I may be able
to help you."*

The gihli began to bark again. Kalona sighed with a huff and shook her head. Someone needed to do something about that pup. She decided to step out, greet the morning sunrise and cool off. She tied back the door cover and stepped out to find a thick, soupy fog drifting past the house. As she stepped out, she was startled when something moved next to her!

She shrieked and stepped back as she watched the murky image of an old man duck and throw his arms up to cover his head. The motion launched a small pouch over his head that Kalona reflexively snatched out of the air. She could feel two round beads in the pouch telling her that the old man had brought a gift for the Uku to exchange for his services.

"Ulasedena Uyotsvhi! You old fool, what are you doing sitting by my door? Are you lost?"

The old man whose deformed ankle had prompted him to be called Crooked Foot, struggled to stand and bowed his head timidly before the village Peace Chief.

"Oh... we-we-well, ... no, Chief." The stammering old fool cowered before the hefty woman who was glaring at him with her fists pressed against her hips.

"I wish to ... uh-uh ... well, I nee-nee-need to ... uh-uh-uh ... see the Uku!"

Kalona realized that she had scared the poor man. She handed him the pouch and took his arm. "Come inside. The Uku is not up yet, but maybe we can rouse him."

"What's going on?" Kalona's grandson, Atselvdi, shouted as he came running to the door.

"It's okay, Atselvdi. Crooked Foot has come for the Uku. Come sit, Crooked Foot." The gracious host extended her hand to indicate where to sit by the hearth. "Have you eaten?"

"Oh-oh-oh-oh ... oh, yes, thank you. I mean ... na-na-na-no ... well, I've ee-ee-ee-eaten, that is."

Adanvdo Alsgida appeared in the doorway of his bedroom rubbing his face with the palms of his hands. Kalona introduced Crooked Foot to her father and added, "He seeks your medicine."

Ali looked up and offered, "Would you like to eat something? I have Three Sisters cooking on the hearth."

The old man looked at the pretty young girl with alarm. She giggled sweetly and explained, "You know . . . corn, beans, and squash."

The old man's face reddened and he nervously chuckled at his gaffe.

Kalona addressed the Uku, "I didn't hear you come in last night, Father. Were you out late?"

The weary father smiled at his daughter and then to the worried looking visitor, "Let us smoke."

Adanvdo sat by Crooked Foot and grabbed the pipe and tobacco pouch that always lay next to the hearth and began to prepare it. "How can I help you, old friend?"

Outside, the gihli began barking again causing Adanvdo to flinch, close his eyes and grind his teeth. His attentive grandson, Atselvdi, sat across the hearth from his grandfather and Crooked Foot.

"Well ... uh-uh-uh ... it's a-bou-bou-bout my grand-daughter."

The Uku forced a smile, "Your granddaughter?"

"Yes ... well ... uh-uh-uh-uh ... she ... uh-uh-uh ... has the pain."

Adanvdo lifted the tobacco-filled pipe, picked up a splint lying on the hearth and held it over the flames of the fire pit to light it. He began sucking on the pipe as he placed the lit end of the splint over the barrel.

Soon smoke began escaping from Adanvdo's mouth. He blew out the splint and drew deeply on the pipe, then handed it to his timorous friend.

Clumsily, Crooked Foot dropped the little pouch from his hand and grasped the pipe. He popped it into his mouth and sucked hard. The nervous old man coughed, expelling billows of smoke, and then bashfully handed the pipe back to Adanvdo.

He coughed again and cleared his throat before continuing, "She ... uh ... she has be-be-been ... losing her food. A-and ... well ... uh ... her face is too warm ... a-and she ... uh-uh ... sleeps ... well ... she usually da-doesn't ... I mean ... na-not this much."

The Uku pondered the words of the nervous man and inhaled on the pipe thoughtfully. Then he spoke, asking, "Where is the pain?"

"Oh, ... uh ... i-in her stomach."

"Is there swelling?"

"Oh! Um ... I ... uh ... thi-think so."

Adanvdo glanced at the pouch lying in Crooked Foot's lap and changed his demeanor into a somber, Uku mood. "I must consult the Great Apportioner."

Laying the pipe on the hearth, straightening his back, resting the back of his hands on his knees with his palms up, then closing his eyes, the old priest readied himself for deep meditation.

Kalona knew immediately that her father wanted to consult the beads. Crooked Foot became very uncomfortable again and gazed at the Uku in awe, then glanced nervously at Kalona. She could see in his eyes that he was at a loss for what he should do.

Kalona pointed to the pouch he had dropped on his lap. The old man with the crooked foot looked down at his lap and saw the pouch. Nervously, he picked up the pouch and held it up to Kalona questioningly. Kalona privately chuckled at the old man's ignorance. She nodded toward the Uku.

Sweat appeared on the old man's brow as he looked at the Uku. Ali could see that the nervous old man was afraid to interrupt the Uku's meditation. She slipped over and squatted beside the hesitant guest, gently took the pouch and dumped the two beads into her great-grandfather's extended palm.

Without opening his eyes, the Uku closed his hand around the beads. Ali winked at Crooked Foot and patted him on the shoulder. The relieved old man beamed gratefully at the considerate young girl.

Adanvdo placed the white bead between his thumb and forefinger of his right hand, and the black bead between the thumb and forefinger of his left hand. He held up his hands chest high and mumbled a chant.

After a few moments, he paused, rolled the bead in his right hand, the white bead, and then opened his eyes.

"The great apportioner has indicated that I may be able to help you."

"Oh, thank you, Uku."

Adanvdo looked at his great-grandson and nodded. Atselvdi nodded back and rose to go retrieve the Uku's belt and pouches. Kalona left to retrieve medicinal herbs from her bedroom that she had prepared for just such an occasion.

Adanvdo explained to his friend that his great-grandson, Atselvdi, had gone for the spiritual things he would need and that his daughter, Kalona, had made special herbs he would use. The shy man's face lit up appreciatively. The Uku enjoyed his pipe as they waited.

"I'm sure your granddaughter will be fine, Grandfather," Ali offered, "she's so good to everyone and is always laughing and having fun. We are very good friends, you know."

The proud grandfather beamed at Ali. "Wado, child, my granddaughter speaks of you often. She likes you ve-very much."

Atselvdi returned wearing the belt and medicine pouches and draped his great-grandfather's beaded Spirit Belt around the Uku's neck. He then draped the Uku's cape around his shoulders.

Over the years, pudgy little Atselvdi had grown into a tall, lanky boy. His great-grandfather had proudly taken him on as an apprentice, certain that Atselvdi would someday be a great priest. And Atselvdi had gratefully devoted himself to his great-grandfather and to the study of the priesthood.

Kalona entered the room and handed a small pouch to Atselvdi.

Atselvdi took Adanvdo's arm. The Uku was old and rising had become very difficult. Ali helped Crooked Foot to his feet as his deformed foot made it especially difficult for him. They chuckled at their bones crackling and Adanvdo patted his guest on the back congratulating him for the accomplishment.

Now Adanvdo put his hand on Crooked Foot's shoulder to reassured him. "I will need to examine your granddaughter and ask her about her dreams. Atselvdi has my medicine. We will accompany you home."

Kalona informed him, "Granddaughter and I are going to the gardens this morning. We may not be here when you return."

Adanvdo led his grandson and the old man out of the house. He stopped to sniff the air and smelled a sad foreboding. He looked about. The color was wrong. Something was not right with this foggy, dreary morning and in his heart, he felt a sadness, a loneliness.

It had been many years since he had carried this feeling of anxiety inside him. Years ago, it was ever present like a piece of him he could not get rid of. For years he had carried the dread and fear that his twin brother might someday find him and he would be confronted with pure evil. His fears had been fulfilled when Kalona was born and Tsisgili had returned. After his father, in a fierce battle, had entombed his evil brother into stone, over time his heart had calmed.

He drew in a generous helping of the chilly, damp air and reached within his consciousness for logic, for a rationalization that would explain away his eerie feelings of dread.

Perhaps these feelings were remnants from his dream —one he could not quite remember. It was lost when external voices had snatched him away from his dream this morning. Perhaps the haunting memories of his long dead, evil brother had visited him in his sleep. These were the familiar portents that had dwelled in his heart when his brother had been alive and ever threatening him from the dark shadows. But now that evil creature was locked up in the bowels of the stone megalith rising up like a spire in the meadow outside the village, marking the spot where evil had been defeated.

Perhaps his sweet wife had visited him from the Nightland and touched his heart with her kind and loving presence. She was the love of his life and no one since had touched his heart the way she had. His heart ached with the thought of her and her untimely death at the hands of his evil brother.

So much of his life had been fouled by his brother's foreshadowing threat. Just his threat had stolen happiness from him the first twenty-five years of his life.

"Grandfather?"

Adanvdo's mind leaped back to the present with the sound of his great-grandson's questioning voice. He blinked and cleared his throat and shivered as the contradiction of his feelings were engulfed by the reality of the moment. His innocent, loving grandson was standing by his side, looking up to him as his mentor, while his old friend Crooked Foot was needing his medicine.

*The disintegrating fog
revealed a shadow moving
rapidly toward her.*

A CHILLING BREEZE FLOWED down the mountain and followed the Long Man River into the valley dissolving the low-lying fog as it approached the small Cherokee village of Tsikohi. In the fields beyond the stockade that surrounded the village, the white cloud blanket concealed the village women and girls scattered about with their baskets gathering corn, beans, or squash.

Feeling isolated amidst the dense fog, petite, pretty Alihelitsidasdi dropped an ear of corn into her half-filled basket and paused to listen to the roaring in the trees as the breeze grew nearer. She felt uneasy.

The thick air muffled most sounds, but like faint echoes, she could hear the gihli barking in the village and then a lone raven cawed from somewhere above the fog, perhaps in the trees near the edge of the cornfield. But the fog was so thick that she could not see the raven or the others in the field around her. In fact, she could only see a few paces ahead.

Ali heard the raven call again and looked up to see a glow passing over the fog dome. Like a bright light encircled by a radiant rainbow, the raven circled above her.

The brittle corn stalks began to rattle as the breeze pushed into the cornfield. The disintegrating fog revealed a shadow moving rapidly toward her. The ghostly figure materialized into a massive, muscular man with a deformed head.

As the force of the breeze hit her in the back, a sense of horror sent a chill through her. Before Ali could scream, the hideous predator scooped her up without even breaking stride and raced through the cornfield past the backside of the stockade and into the forest beyond.

The captor's large hand that was clasped over her mouth smelled of dead fish and dirt and his body stank from sweat and war paint. The struggles of the fragile girl had no effect on the strong abductor.

She felt as if she might break in half as shocks of pain bolted through her dangling legs and up her spine each time the warrior's feet pounded the ground. As they raced through the thick underbrush, the branches and thorns tore at her skin and clothes.

She became aware that there were others running with them. Two other warrior-like men with deformed heads were also carrying struggling girls on their hips!

Suddenly, her captor slung her to the ground and brutally wrapped a leather strap around her mouth. She sensed the same thing happening to the two other hapless girls. She wondered if her best friend, Amadohi, was one of the captives. She struggled futilely to see the others.

Ali had heard stories of warriors whose heads were deformed at birth by tying boards to their foreheads. It left their foreheads flattened and swept back and made their eyes appear to protrude and their long noses extend out to a point. But her imagination had not prepared her for the horror of how a Tagwa warrior actually looked—evil, fierce, not human.

With their captives muted and bound, the warriors slung the girls recklessly over their shoulders, knocking the breath out of Ali, and raced off again.

She desperately gasped for breath but as her frail body bounced on the hard, muscular shoulder of her captor, even more air was forced from her lungs. Lack of oxygen and fear left her weak and faint.

The evil men carried their delicate cargo over the rolling hills and through the dense forest as ominous clouds were building above. The party broke into the open and Ali recognized the boulders that marked the edge of the deep Agusa Jisdu canyon.

The warriors paused for only a moment before darting to the right and leaping off the escarpment onto a rocky trail leading to the bottom of the canyon. The blow to Ali's ribs from the jump knocked the last remnants of air from her lungs. The pain, horror, and lack of oxygen teamed to grant her temporary relief. She passed out.

*She was standing, almost
floating under a tree; her
hair and face so pale that she
could be a ghost.*

As they walked through the fog-filled street that led to the house of Crooked Foot, the irritating yelps of his gihli disturbed the muffled silence. "Perhaps the gihli senses something," Adanvdo commented. "Was he like this before the thing was put under your granddaughter?"

The old man took some time to consider this before answering, "No, ... uh-uh ... Uku. He ... uh ... da-DID get a-a-agitated about the s-same time!"

This curious exchange caught Atselvdi's attention. He knew how much the dog irritated his great-grandfather and he admired him for putting aside his contempt for a nuisance to try to understand it.

When the domesticated coyote pup saw his master and the two strangers emerge from the gray cover, he raised his level of intensity and wagged his tail happily. But when Adanvdo fearlessly approached the pup, it began prancing back and forth yelping loudly.

When the stranger was undeterred, the poor gihli lowered its head and tail and began half-whining, half yelping as if begging the stranger to be afraid. But Adanvdo was not afraid and reached behind the gihli's head, grabbed a handful of the mutt's neck hair and skin and pulled the gihli's head up to his face. The gihli licked its nose profusely and gulped for air.

The skilled Uku spread open one of the gihli's eyes and then the other and studied them carefully. He then examined the gihli's teeth and gums and smelled his breath.

Now Adanvdo ran his hands down the gihli's side and felt its stomach. Then he grabbed the gihli by the tail and lifted up its rear to examine its hind end.

Adanvdo let go of the gihli and crossed his arms in contemplation. The gihli whined pitifully and ran to its master. Crooked Foot looked more and more concerned as time passed.

An owl hooted softly from a nearby tree. Adanvdo's heart leaped and left him short of breath. He squeezed his eyes shut and fussed at himself privately.

It's just a little hoot owl, he reassured himself. Your brother has been dead for thirty-six years. Get ahold of yourself.

Then he spotted her, just a flicker from his periphery vision like a wisp of smoke. She was standing, almost floating under a tree; her hair and face so pale that she could be a ghost. Her yellowed white dress wafted like a cloud drifting around her body. Startled by the strangeness of her, Adanvdo gasped and jumped back.

The owl hooted again above her. The hushed wind moved to push a mist in front of her. A raven cawed in the distance. Adanvdo searched the sky but could not find the bird. When he looked back down, the fog had dissipated, and the woman had vanished. Adanvdo was left doubting his eyes and feeling chilled inside. Yet, the wispy woman had looked eerily familiar.

Adanvdo shook his head resignedly. "Let's look at your granddaughter."

Crooked Foot raised his eyebrows and led the Uku and his apprentice into his house. The small, rectangular house had only one big room. The hearth was in the center and cots were stacked like bunk beds against the north wall opposite the entry.

Crooked Foot's wife was placing a log on the fire. The air in the room was filled with stinging smoke, heavy with heat and smelled of burnt oak. Crooked Foot's daughter sat on the floor next to her daughter lying on a cot, and was washing her face with a wet cloth.

Adanvdo stood in the doorway and allowed his eyes to adjust to the dark room. He took a moment to study the room as if looking for clues and then walked slowly across to the young girl. She was curled up on her side. He guessed her to be thirteen or fourteen summers old—about the same age as his great-grandchildren, Ali and Atselvdi.

She was shivering and sweating at the same time. The girl's mother moved away. Adanvdo bent over and brushed back the girl's hair noting the fever. He greeted her kindly in the traditional manner, "Osiyo, Granddaughter."

The girl attempted a smile and whispered, "Siyo, Grandfather."

"Do you have pain?"

The girl nodded and placed her hand gingerly on her stomach. Adanvdo placed his hand beside hers and felt the tautness of her swollen stomach. Adanvdo took the damp cloth, wiped the sweat from her face, and stroked her forehead. "It is necessary that I ask some questions; you must answer truthfully."

The girl nodded tentatively indicating that she would try.

"Have you broken any taboos?"

The girl's eyes widened and she glanced desperately at her mother. Adanvdo realized that his question was too broad to ask of an innocent young girl. He clarified, "Have you done your need, defecated, in the yard or in a trail?"

The frightened girl rigorously shook her head no.

"Have you had bad dreams? ... say, of snakes or fish or the like?"

She paused to consider this question. She appeared to be digging into her memory for anything of note. Finally, she whispered, "I don't remember anything like that."

The wise old Uku thought to himself, *I like this young girl.* He believed that she was sincere. "Do you ever play with the Little People?"

"I've never seen one," she admitted.

Adanvdo addressed his next question to her mother, "Do you know of anyone of a different mind than your daughter or your family?"

The young mother gasped and placed her hand over her mouth. Crooked Foot's wife stepped forward to intercede for her daughter. The old woman looked sternly at the Uku. Adanvdo guessed that she was wrestling with whether or not to mention something or someone that was troubling her. Adanvdo took a chance. "Who is the person?"

"Well, Uku, I don't know if he is of a different mind, really. But right before my granddaughter felt the intruder, I heard the gihli start barking. Assuming it was just someone passing by on the street, I waited. But when the pup persisted, I listened and could hear someone stirring behind the house. I looked outside just in time to see him duck behind our neighbor's house and I later saw him shuffling down the street heading for his ... clan house."

Clan house? Then Adanvdo thought of the one person in the village he knew who actually lived in a seven-sided clan house instead of a traditional rectangular house. The remark about shuffling also fit. Not mentioning the suspect by name to avoid evoking his magic, Adanvdo whispered, "An elder priest, perhaps?"

The distressed grandmother nodded nervously. Adanvdo found this amusing, but did not let on. Old Sali had that effect on people. He just looked suspicious and even a little creepy.

"Does she pass the yellow?"

The young mother acknowledged and appeared surprised by the clairvoyance of the Uku. Adanvdo instructed the young girl to lie flat on her back. He removed the beaded belt that hung from his neck and laid it over the length of the feverish girl's body.

The beaded belt was as wide as the length of a man's forearm and almost as long as Adanvdo was tall. It had the geometric design of a person's body running the length of it. Down the left side were various stylized plants. Down the right side were animals or birds. To everyone except Adanvdo and Atselvdi, the beautiful beaded belt was a magic belt endowed with sacred powers.

The Uku and his apprentice knew that the belt was actually an elaborate code. The beads arranged in plant designs indicated the medicine used for the adjacent part of the body. Beside the yellow navel of the body, six trees were stylized. They were the alder, common persimmon, sycamore, chokeberry, poplar, and cucumber tree. This told the Uku that he should use the bark from these trees to treat swelling in the navel area.

Below the six trees were seven white squares representing rocks to be heated. The barks would be laid over the heated rocks and then cold water poured over them to produce a healing steam for the patient to breathe.

To the right of the yellow navel, a black raven, a black buzzard, a brown eagle, and a white raven indicated the spirit animals to be addressed in the conjure. These spirits would be asked to carry the intruder out of the patient and deliver it to the Nightland to die.

Adanvdo requested the pouch Kalona had prepared for them from Atselvdi. It would contain the six barks. Kalona knew the treatments as well as any priest after assisting him for so many years.

He opened the pouch to find a smaller pouch lying on top of the six barks. This would be the herbal powder to mix with water to be drunk by the patient.

Atselvdi handed the smaller pouch to his great-grandfather. Adanvdo motioned for the family to gather around the girl. With somber faces, they stood stiffly next to the girl's bed. The young girl trembled, partly because of her fever and partly out of fear.

Adanvdo Alsgida, their trusted Uku, looked into each one's eyes. "The treatment will not be painful."

There was a collective sigh of relief. "We must perform the treatment four times."

Adanvdo paused, looked out the door, then looked at Crooked Foot. "We will need the gihli to be present."

The old man briskly limped out to retrieve his dog. Adanvdo addressed Crooked Foot's wife. "I will need for you to boil two pots of white water."

The stern woman looked confused. "WHITE water?"

"Go to the Long Man where the water dances over the rocks and is made white. Fill three pots. Bring them back here and heat two of them on your fire. Atselvdi will accompany you and gather the seven white stones I need."

Crooked Foot's wife handed one pot to her daughter, one to Atselvdi and grabbed one for herself. As they started for the door, Adanvdo asked, "Is this a sacred fire?"

Again, the old woman looked puzzled, so Adanvdo explained, "Did you restart the fire using flames from the sacred fire of the Council House?"

The old woman nodded yes. Adanvdo then asked, "Have you kept the fire going?"

The old woman nodded yes again. "You have a sacred fire; that is good."

As they departed, Atselvdi stopped, dropped his pot and looked out the door of the house anxiously. He then looked at his grandfather with wide eyes. The Uku felt a chill and shivered involuntarily. The foreboding he had felt earlier returned and left him feeling sad again. He stared at the door. Something was wrong and Atselvdi sensed it too.

A low rumbling noise drew Kalona's attention away from her reminiscing.

KALONA EHLAWEI WATCHED THE dark clouds building above her as she dropped a handful of beans into her basket. The stout old woman grumbled to herself as she observed that her basket was almost full. She knew that it usually took longer to fill a basket with beans than with ears of corn.

She looked toward the cornfield thinking that her granddaughter should have joined her by now. The fog had thinned and now she could see the stalks of the corn shaking as if trembling in the cold breeze. "That girl!" she thought. "She and Amadohi are probably off playing again."

She shook her head in mock disgust. Ali had always been a delightful child. Her name meant Happiness, and this happy child had brought her much happiness.

On some level, though, Kalona was jealous of her grandchildren. They had grown up in a peaceful world devoid of struggles or war. Kalona's life had been hard. She had never experienced the blissful joy and freedom her twin grandchildren were enjoying. From birth, she had been her father's helper and caretaker. These responsibilities had denied her a childhood.

Kalona had waited until her nineteenth summer to marry. Finding love so late in life had made it that much more precious and euphoric. Her husband had been strong, tall, and reserved and of the Ani Waya, the Wolf Clan. For eight moons after they married, they shared a peaceful, blessed life together. For a short time, she had been deliciously happy and they looked forward to the birth of their first child. But war brought their euphoria to an abrupt halt.

During the months while her husband had been off in war, she had grieved and felt overwhelming dread and worry deep in her stomach. Then, when she learned of his death, she had fallen into deep depression. She was certain it had affected poor little Tsi-la in the womb. She had named the baby Tsi-la, Flower Blossom, in hopes that she would bring to her the freshness, the beauty, and independence that she had yearned for in her own life. But, Tsi-la was a sickly child who stayed inside most of her life and avoided playing with other children. Kalona blamed herself for her daughter's poor health.

Tsi-la's self-imposed seclusion had worried Kalona. She feared that her daughter would never find love, or that love would never find her daughter, always hidden in the house. When Tsi-la reached her fourteenth summer, the current age of Ali, Tsi-la had married. Kalona had forced her daughter to accompany her to the Ball Play dances. It was at one of those festive affairs that love finally discovered her daughter and Tsi-la fell desperately in love with her first and only suitor.

The moment he approached her at the Ball Play dance, she became immediately obsessed with him. Kalona's greatest fear had been that Tsi-la would never find love, so when it happened, it was a complete surprise to her. And, even though she had actively pushed Tsi-la out so that she might at least have a chance at love, when it happened, she found herself being protective and defensive.

It was a short courtship and soon after the marriage, Tsi-la was blessed with beautiful, healthy twins. But Kalona had been very disappointed that her daughter never seemed to take to the mothering instinct and saw the twins as a distraction from her devotion for her husband.

When the Tagwas once again brought war against the Cherokee and Tsi-la's husband left to fight in the war, Tsi-la drifted into depression and neglected the twins completely, forcing Kalona to take over caring for them. Kalona understood her daughter's despair. She had felt it herself when her husband went off to war. But she had never understood nor forgiven her daughter's dispassion for her children.

But there was nothing she could do for her daughter. When word came that Tsi-la's husband had been killed in the war, Tsi-la disappeared and was not found until days later when her lifeless body was found lying in the field at the spot where she had last seen her husband.

A low rumbling noise drew Kalona's attention away from her reminiscing. She looked skyward at the heavy, dark clouds. But she realized that the sound was not thunder but voices in the cornfield. Sensing that something was wrong, she stood up straight and peered across the bean field and over the corn stalks. A crowd had formed at the edge of the cornfield near the stockade wall. Kalona grabbed her basket and rushed to join them.

As she approached, the crowd besieged her chaotically, all talking at once. Chief Kalona Ehlawei held up her hand and the frantic women hushed. Kalona's calm, strong character had won her the respect of the village which had bestowed upon her the title and responsibility of village Peace Chief.

Her eyes fell upon one woman who understood she had been recognized to speak. "Chief, the girls are missing! There are footprints!"

Kalona dropped her basket and placed her hand on the hysterical woman's shoulder to calm her. She peered sternly into her eyes. "Take a deep breath and tell me what you know."

A voice from behind Kalona spoke. Kalona recognized Chief Waya Gigage, the village War Chief, his primary assistant, Wahuhu Adawehi, and his tall, barrel-chested nephew, Tawodi Gvnagei, who was flanked by several village warriors.

The War Chief spoke, "Delagalis and Walelu have disappeared. The footprints suggest they've been abducted!"

Kalona understood the implication. Abduction was an act of war and would constitute a change of leadership.

A tall, slender, muscular young man of about sixteen summers ran up and waded through the mob to Chief Waya Gigage. "Father and I have found tracks behind the village leading into the forest. The tracks indicate there are three large men carrying heavy loads."

Kalona's stomach flipped. She frantically searched for her granddaughter. She spotted her granddaughter's best friend, Amadohi with her mother, Wananahi. "Have you seen Ali?"

Amadohi and her mother gasped and looked first at each other and then back to Kalona. Their faces betrayed the answer.

"Ali!" Kalona shouted.

"Ali, too?" someone whispered in the crowd.

Chief Waya Gigage raised his hands to quiet the crowd. "Has anyone seen Alihelitsidasdi?"

The crowd was silent. Kalona grasped her chest and dropped to her knees. Amadohi and her mother grabbed her arms and helped her back to her feet.

Chief Waya Gigage continued, "All right, then, we may be looking for three girls—Alihelitsidasdi, Delagalis, and Walelu."

Chief Waya Gigage addressed the tall, stalwart, older warrior standing next to him, "Wahuhu, you will lead the search party. Take six warriors, my messenger, and a ..." The wise war chief looked at the young tracker. He did not want to hurt his nephew's feelings. "Take Tlomeha Usdi and his son for trackers. A larger search party will slow you down and make too much noise and we may need warriors here to defend the village. Hurry! They may have a long head start."

Wahuhu quickly chose his warriors and raced off behind the tracker's son, Waya Usti.

Kalona started to join the search party, but Amadohi and her mother, Wananahi, held her back. "Where are you going?"

"I must help find Ali!"

Wananahi shook her head in amazement at her dear friend. "Good grief, old woman, you can't hunt. You can't fight. You can't even keep up with those young warriors. Come on, we must go find your father and see if he has a blessing."

"Now the gihli must carry the intruder to the Nightland!"

THE UKU REMOVED ONE of the heated pots and poured the bark powder into it. The pungent smells of the herbs quickly filled the room as he stirred the mixture and then set it on the hearth to cool.

He dipped his finger in the pot of cold water and allowed a drop onto each white stone nestled in the corner of the fire pit. The water hissed as it hit the stones indicating they were ready.

Adanvdo removed the beaded belt from the granddaughter, draped it around his neck and then instructed the mother to lift her daughter's head. He took up the simmering pot of medicinal powder mixed in the white water.

He motioned to the mother to position her daughter so she could drink the potion. "Take seven big gulps of the potion."

The girl did as she was told, but the bitter potion made her grimace and shiver as she drank it. As the Uku placed the mixture back on the hearth, his apprentice placed the six barks on the scalding white stones and then poured cold water on them to create a pungent steam. Adanvdo indicated to the girl that she should breathe deeply to inhale the steam as he fanned it toward her with his cape.

Adanvdo rubbed his hands over the flames of the fire pit to heat them as he spoke, "Sge! Daloni gatagei adoniga (Now then, the important thing has become a clayish yellow!)."

As he called upon the spirits, he rubbed his hands to keep them warm, "Sge! Kalono anage usanuli atonaniga (Now then, Black Raven, quickly thou hast come to listen!). Thou art staying in the Nightland, thou powerful wizard."

Adanvdo brought his outstretched hands around in a circular sweep imitating the raven's manner when hovering over its prey. He whispered to the mother to expose the girl's belly. "It seems it is only what has become clayish yellow. Quickly, come again and pull it out ..."

The Uku squawked like a raven as he placed his warm hands on the girl's swollen stomach, "Caw, Caw, Caw, Caw!"

He gripped her stomach as if grabbing the intruder and pulling it out and then he grasped the dog. "Thou hast gone to put it away in the Nightland, not for one night but forever!"

The whimpering gihli cowered before the Uku. Atselvdi was startled by this last piece of the conjure. The words were right, but grasping the gihli was new. The shocked apprentice looked at the Uku questioningly. But the Uku ignored him and returned to the fire, continuing the conjure by calling upon the Black Buzzard spirit to "eat the yellow thing and carry it to the Nightland forever ..."

Again, the Uku swept his hands in a broad circle imitating the flight of the buzzard over the petrified girl. "Swish, swish, swish, swish ..."

Adanvdo dropped his hands onto the swollen belly, grabbed the imaginary intruder and placed it again on the timorous dog.

A sudden flash came to Atselvdi. *It's an Exchange! He is using the gihli for an exchange!*

Adanvdo returned to the fire once again, and this time summoned the Brown Eagle spirit. He imitated the flight of the Brown Eagle around to the girl and hovered over her. "Thou hast come to bury it not in thy stomach, and not for one night, but forever! Gwa, gwa, gwa, gwa!"

Again, he dropped his hand onto her cramping stomach and wriggled his fingers as if the eagle were eating the Yellow. Again, he placed hands on the gihli.

Then he returned to the fire to call upon the final spirit's help. "Now then, ha . . . now thou hast come to listen, White Raven!"

He swept his hands over her like a raven gliding to its prey and held them hovering over her and then he dropped his hands gently on her stomach as he said, "Now they have let thee down. It is merely a ghost that has caused it. There shall only remain the traces of where thou hast passed."

Adanvdo moved his hands to the cowering dog and continued, "Now thou hast come to put him on his feet. Thou hast come to put the important thing into the gihli to carry to the Nightland to never return!"

The enthusiastic Uku slowly released the gihli and straightened his aged back. He solemnly walked over to sit by the hearth. As he rested, he closed his eyes and quietly chanted while wafting steaming vapors toward the girl.

The stunned onlookers waited for something else to happen. Atselvdi was the first to snap out of his trance. He glanced at the girl on the cot. She was staring up at nothing as a single tear crept down her temple. She appeared to be afraid to move.

Her mother was standing against the wall at the head of the cot rubbing her arms nervously. She looked at Atselvdi with pleading eyes. The grandmother stepped over and put her arm around her daughter to comfort her. Crooked Foot was staring at his beloved dog trying to understand what had just happened.

Adanvdo took a long drink from the cold water pot before rising to face the family. "When the stones cool, remove the bark, reheat the stones, replace the bark and pour cold, white water over them so that she may breathe the vapors. Give her the potion again when Grandmother Sun reaches the top of her journey across the sky vault. Seven big gulps."

The girl's mother just stared at the Uku with wide eyes. The grandmother calmly affirmed she understood what was to be done.

Adanvdo looked at Crooked Foot and then back to his great-grandson, then back to the bewildered Crooked Foot. "My friend, come sit with us."

The old man hobbled over to sit by the hearth with the priest and his apprentice. He stammered timidly, "I do not have tobacco to offer you." It was clear that he was embarrassed that he could not be a proper host to two such important members of the village.

Atselvdi glared at his great-grandfather. He could not believe that he was intending to sacrifice the poor dog. Was it really necessary? The conjure had always worked without an exchange. Just because the gihli was irritating was no excuse to sacrifice him unnecessarily.

Adanvdo stared thoughtfully into the flickering flames of the fire pit. "Sometimes the gihli understands things we miss or just don't see."

He paused as if considering what he had just said. "The dog feels a close connection to your granddaughter. When the Yellow was put under her, the gihli sensed it and was greatly concerned. His spirit has been in turmoil and he has done the only thing he knows to try to help her. He has tried desperately to drive away the intruder through his incessant barking. But instead of driving off the intruder, he has drawn the intruder in. His belly is starting to swell and he has been dropping little piles with the yellow in them."

Atselvdi and Crooked Foot jerked their head toward the sniveling gihli. Atselvdi tried to examine the pup's stomach with his eyes, but could not tell for sure if there was swelling.

"The gihli carries the intruder in him and now the intruder of your daughter as well."

The Uku looked at his apprentice with a look of dread and then gave the desperate man the diagnosis. "Now the gihli must carry the intruder to the Nightland!"

Crooked Foot was clearly confounded.

Atselvdi felt sorry for him. He doubted that Crooked Foot even understood what that meant. The Uku looked at him with a fatherly expression and explained, "Take him to the woods with you—like you are going hunting. Take him to the spot you found him. Show him that you appreciate his great sacrifice."

The confused old man's face contorted as he tried to concentrate. Adanvdo spoke slowly, "Kneel down and let him see the love in your eyes. Extend to him your love and then quickly send him to the Nightland!"

Crooked Foot appeared to still not understand. Adanvdo explained further, "Terminate him swiftly and with tenderness."

Adanvdo looked at his great-grandson. "Atselvdi will go with you and will say what needs to be said. He will show you where to bury him there in the mountains."

Tears ran down the old man's cheeks. Suddenly, the gihli began to howl as if he understood what had been said. He sniffed the air and began pacing back and forth yelping in first one direction, then the other.

Atselvdi and the old man looked down heartbroken. Adanvdo studied the dog's strange behavior. Something just did not fit!

*They were losing time and
a decision needed to be
made immediately!*

Waya Usti followed his short, wiry father through the woods and was followed closely by the rest of the search party. Tlomeha Usdi was born of the Ani-Tsisqua, the Bird clan, and was the best tracker in the village. His son, Waya Usti of the Wolf clan, had learned well from his father and was a good hunter and tracker in his own right.

The search was going well until they hit the rocky cliff overlooking the Agusa Jisdu River. Rabbit Creek was the name of the river and was also used to describe the canyon that had been gouged out by the river.

Tlomeha Usdi threw up his arm to halt the search party. He squatted at the edge of the rocks and studied the smooth surfaces where the trail disappeared. Tlomeha Usdi and his son began to scour the surfaces for clues. Four paces in, the rocks were scuffed slightly in several places, but the darkening sky and the smooth rock surface made it almost impossible to determine where the path led from there.

The tall, stern leader of the party, Wahuhu, grew impatient. "Tlomeha Usdi, maybe we should form a circle and fan out to look for signs."

Tlomeha Usdi's face did not conceal his contempt.

Waya Usti explained, "Picking up tracks on these smooth boulders is extremely difficult, especially with the overcast sky. If we fan out, the only traces could easily be wiped out."

As if to punctuate the young tracker's words, thunder rumbled through the dark clouds opening them up to dump their heavy load. As the rain poured down, the searchers looked up and then at each other in anguish. The significance was evident to all; the rain would wash away the trail.

Tlomeha Usdi stood and strode across the rocks to the edge of the cliff. He stared dejectedly in the pouring rain into the canyon below. "What have we done to merit the wrath of the spirits?" he muttered to himself.

Wahuhu studied the path they had followed from the village. It had been a wide arc first heading south and then curving more to the east.

At first, he had been convinced that the abductors were Kusa warriors from the Southwest. Now he suspected Uchee, maybe Yamasee. If he was right, they would be following the Agusa Jisdu, at the bottom of the canyon, east to the Tugalo River.

What bothered him was the nature of the raid. Typically, neighbor tribes raided the villages for goods or territory. Typically, raids consisted of substantially more than three warriors. And, typically, they raided outlying and bordering villages. The Tsikohi village was far from the border of any neighboring tribe. This had the feel of retaliation, but Tsikohi was a small village and Wahuhu knew of no one who had a grievance with his village.

They were losing time and a decision needed to be made immediately! Wahuhu called the party together. "We will follow the stream toward the Tugalo."

Wahuhu looked at Tlomeha Usdi as he spoke. He had given a command, but he waited for the respected tracker to agree. Likewise, the searchers looked to Tlomeha Usdi for confirmation.

He had been searching the stream below and the path from the cliff to the stream with his eyes. Tlomeha Usdi was contemplating Wahuhu's choice as Wahuhu shared his logic. "If the kidnappers had headed west, the stream narrows and the canyon deepens. To the east, the stream grows wider and the valley widens as it winds its way to the Tugalo. Once on the Tugalo, if they have boats, they can cruise out of Tsalagi territory quickly."

Tlomeha Usdi agreed. Wahuhu addressed the messenger. "Report our decision to the Chief!"

Kalona, trailed by Amadohi and Wananahi, and drenched by the pouring rain, rushed into her house. She found her father, Adanvdo Alsgida, snoring in his bed. Kalona shook him and he started snorting and smacking as he struggled to connect with consciousness.

"Father, wake up!" Kalona shouted.

Adanvdo blinked and tried to focus on his daughter. He mumbled in a questioning way.

Kalona exclaimed, "Ali has been kidnapped!"

Adanvdo's eyes widened. "Ali?" Kalona helped him sit up on the edge of the bed.

Adanvdo was struggling to break from his dream. Although it had been 36 years since his evil, soul-thieving brother had been entombed in the rock megalith jutting out of the meadow west of the village, his brother often visited him in his dreams. Fear gripped his stomach as visions of what the evil witch might do with his grand-daughter flashed across his mind!

"Yes, your little Ali has been kidnapped. A search party is looking for her and two others. They were taken from the cornfields."

The old grandfather rubbed his eyes with the palms of his hands and mumbled unintelligibly. It was not likely that his witch brother would have kidnapped three victims. His fear subsided as he began to push his dream from his mind and focus on his daughter. Kalona sat next to him and put her arm behind his back. "Is there a blessing?"

Rubbing his eyes again, Adanvdo began rocking back and forth, chanting. The old priest always mumbled his chants, his words seldom discernible, so it was hard for Kalona to tell this time whether he was chanting a sacred blessing or bemoaning the fate of his beloved great-grand-daughter.

It was no mystery to the best friend of Ali. Amadohi burst into tears and dropped to her knees in front of Adanvdo Alsgida, threw her arms around his waist and tried to comfort him and be comforted. The realization that her best friend was in mortal danger had finally over-whelmed her.

Adanvdo hugged the young girl and kissed her on the top of her head. Amadohi and his great-granddaughter were constant nuisances—always teasing him and treating him irreverently. But he loved it and loved them dearly.

Ali's twin brother, Atselvdi, came into the house, dripping and looking sad and dejected. "The gihli is in the Nightland." Then he stopped and glanced around the room. "What has happened?"

Kalona rushed over and hugged him. "Ali has been kidnapped! Wahuhu is leading a search party to find her. You must help your grandfather gather what he needs for the blessing."

Atselvdi stared in disbelief at his grandmother while her words registered in his mind. Finally, he blinked and pushed past his grandmother. "What do we need for the ceremony, Grandfather?"

The old Uku did not answer, but his apprentice did not need a response. He had earned his name "Immitator" as a small child when he had demonstrated his ability to repeat the stories told to him verbatim. Atselvdi's supple brain had drained the experienced mind of his mentor and teacher. Now he knew the blessings; he knew the medicines; he knew the dances and songs; and he knew how to diagnose and how to prescribe. He was a skilled priest in his own right, but had always operated dutifully in the shadow of his respected great-grandfather.

Atselvdi quickly gathered up the needed articles and led his great-grandfather out of the house and up the street to the old Clan Council House where they would fast and pray for Ali's safety.

As they approached the creaking, seven-sided clan house, thunder rumbled overhead and then rolled slowly to the southeast and the downpour changed to a gentle shower. The old Uku pulled the blanket off his head and glanced toward Crooked Foot's house. It was so peaceful without the gihli barking. "How did Crooked Foot handle the ..."

Atselvdi was startled by the question. He had pushed his trip to the woods with the old man and his gihli out of his mind and was deeply concentrating on the conjures to protect his sister. He looked at his great-grandfather blinking, "Oh ... he did all right. I kept reminding him that it was for his granddaughter."

Adanvdo glanced up to check Grandmother Sun's glow behind the heavy clouds. "It will soon be time for her next treatment."

*Wahuhu frowned. "Only
fools would go west."*

Reasoning that the abductors were headed for the
Tugalo River, Wahuhu had chosen the eastern trail off
the rocky cliff. Drenching rain had made the path muddy
and slippery but the enthusiastic search party descended
quickly.

The old tracker, Tlomeha Usdi, and his talented son,
Waya Usti, scanned the trees, rocks, and bushes on their
descent for confirmation that the kidnappers had also
gone this way but they found nothing.

When they reached the bottom of the cliff, Tlomeha
Usdi counseled Wahuhu, "If they had boats, there would
be deep marks on the shore where they pushed them into
the water. We should search for any depressions."

Wahuhu approved, but added, "We must hurry! If
they have boats, we may not be able to catch them at all."

Tlomeha Usdi motioned for his son to search upstream
while he searched downstream. Waya Usti broke off a
branch from a Birch tree and moved quickly beating back
the bushes along the edge of the stream but was finding
no evidence of any boats launched into the stream.

Waya Usti was concerned with how hastily Wahuhu and his father had decided on the direction they should pursue the abductors. There was no evidence to support their decision and if they were wrong, they might lose the trail forever. Waya Usti had felt that they should make sure that the kidnappers had not gone down the west side of the escarpment, but he had kept quiet. Now was his chance.

He practically ran along the bank hoping to reach the point where the western path connected with the stream. Before he even reached the halfway point, he heard his father shout, "Waya Usti!" But he kept running as though he did not hear.

Now Wahuhu yelled, "Waya Usti! We must go!" But Waya Usti still kept running and beating the tall grass along the shoreline as if he were searching for boat tracks. He only needed to go about one hundred paces more.

"Waya Usti, they're calling you! Where are you going?" The voice came from just behind him. He spun around to see his cousin, Tawodi, come running up.

"I just want to check the western path for tracks before we head east."

"Why would they go west? There's nothing up there but a narrow canyon and the springs that feed into the Agusa Jisdu."

Waya Usti knew that Tawodi's logic was sound, but his instincts told him to check anyway. "Yes, but what if they did? What if they aren't taking their captives back home, but looking for a hideout?"

Tawodi glanced up the canyon to the west and squinted. Then he glanced back toward the search party. Wahuhu and Tlomeha Usdi yelled again, "Waya Usti! Tawodi! We cannot wait any longer."

Tawodi hung his head and then looked at Waya Usti. "I fear you may be right, cousin, but it is Wahuhu's decision to make. The longer we delay, the further away they get. I'm sorry, but we must rejoin the search party."

Tawodi yelled, "We're coming, Wahuhu!"

Tawodi whispered to Waya Usti. "Let's go."

Tawodi and Waya Usti rejoined the search party. They stood respectfully before the village's second in command. Wahuhu glared at Waya Usti and inquired, "Where were you going?"

"I wanted to check the western path to see if there were any tracks." Waya Usti explained. Cousin Tawodi nudged Waya Usti discretely cautioning him to be silent.

Wahuhu studied the young tracker. Tawodi intervened, "Shouldn't we make sure there are no tracks on that side? Shouldn't we make sure they didn't go west before we rush to the east?"

Wahuhu frowned. "Only fools would go west."

". . . unless they were unfamiliar with that route." Tawodi paused and calmly stared back at Wahuhu. The weathered warrior-leader remained silent. Tawodi continued, "Or maybe they know the area very well and are counting on us going east."

Waya Usti was surprised by Tawodi's support and so was Wahuhu. Tawodi Gvnagei was a large-boned young man with a wide face and huge round chest. He was deceptively tall and stared down into Wahuhu's eyes. Wahuhu was accustomed to looking down on others.

But Wahuhu did not appear to be threatened by Chief Waya Gigage's giant nephew. Wahuhu was the main assistant, a tested warrior, and longtime friend. "Time is wasting!" Wahuhu stated. "We must keep moving or we will surely lose them. Soon, we will reach the point where they encountered the rain. There the wet ground will be our friend and the mud will hold their tracks."

The stern man turned a kinder eye to Waya Usti and explained, "If they went east, they could not go far."

Tawodi Gvnagei respectfully waited until he was sure that Wahuhu was finished. Then he offered, "Let Waya Usti and I go west and make sure we have not been fooled. Once we have checked the western trail, we will race to rejoin you with what we find."

"No!" Wahuhu retorted, "we must stay together to be strong for the encounter. If we find no tracks left in the mud, then we shall search the western path."

With that, Wahuhu nodded to Tlomeha Usdi. The skinny-legged tracker sped off downstream with the rest of the search party falling in behind. Waya Usti shook his head in disgust and fell in behind his huge cousin.

Sali, spoke. "This is the work of witches."

Near the riverside entrance of the village and within the stockade, the grand, seven-sided Council House rested atop its raised rectangular mound. The entrance was centered on the eastern side of the heptagon and was framed with a narrow, tall portico.

Beside the portico, the grieving Peace Chief lowered the white flag that had flown over the almost fourteen-year peace time. The War Chief replaced the white flag with his red flag and raised it up the tall pole signifying that the village of Tsikohi was now at war. Waya Gigage placed his arm around Kalona's waist and led her inside.

Inside the Council House, seven sturdy posts supported the cone-shaped roof. Several rows of benches for guests and the general public ringed the area outside the posts. Just inside the posts, a row of white benches reserved for the civil and religious leaders of the village encircled a row of red benches reserved for the war counselors and war leaders. The benches encircled the fire pit where the sacred fire always burned.

The benches were split allowing passage down the middle of the Council House. In front of the westernmost post, three white high-backed chairs faced the entrance. The center chair, reserved for the village Uku, was empty since Adanvdo Alsgida and his apprentice and great-grandson, Atselvdi, were fasting and performing the blessing for safe passage in the Ani Gilohi Clan House.

The Uku's assistant, Sali, sat in the chair to the left and in the chair to the right, the village Peace Chief, Kalona Ehlawei, slumped staring into space. She did not want to be there. She just wanted to be Ali's grandmother right now.

Several paces in front of the Uku's throne were three red high-backed chairs. The center of this set of chairs was reserved for the War Chief, Waya Gigage, with his main assistant to the right and his speaker and messenger to the left.

Chief Waya Gigage sat alone on his throne waiting for his council of warriors to assemble. His main assistant, Wahuhu was in the field leading the search party. He expected his messenger to be returning soon with news of the search.

Usually a rowdy group, the warriors were solemn as they took their seats on the red benches. This evening, the clan priests and the Beloved Women occupied the white benches. It was typical for this group to be quiet and reverent but today they were mumbling, chanting their sacred prayers, and whispering among themselves.

Distant shouting heralded the approach of the messenger. The occupants of the Council House collectively turned their heads toward the entrance expectantly. The shouting grew nearer and louder until the messenger burst into the Council House.

He stopped and bowed his head before the esteemed warriors, priests, and chiefs who stood to greet the skinny man. A crowd of villagers waited at the entrance for the messenger to approach the War Chief and then streamed in to fill the public benches.

Muffled greetings were exchanged and then the crowd hushed to hear the news.

"We followed the tracks south and then the trail curved broadly to the southeast. We lost the trail at the rock cliffs overlooking Agusa Jisdu. There the rain came and washed away the tracks. Wahuhu decided to follow Agusa Jisdu toward the confluence with the Tugalo and Tlomeha Usdi agreed."

Chief Waya Gigage nodded and the messenger took his seat beside him. The floor was now open for questions.

A warrior asked, "Any sign of who the abductors are?"

"Nothing so far," the messenger replied.

Another warrior conjectured, "If they are headed south, they are probably Kusas."

Another countered, "But if they are headed down to the Tugalo, they might be Uchee, maybe Yamasee."

Chief Kalona Ehlawei spoke. "Tagwa!"

All eyes trained on the Peace Chief. She commanded great respect in her village, but all knew that she had suffered greatly at the hands of the Tagwa. It had only been thirteen years since the peace was last made with the Tagwa nation, but not before Kalona had lost her husband, son-in-law, many friends, and indirectly, her daughter in the wars with *those despicable people.*

"The Tagwa are ruthless, ugly, heartless fiends!" Chief Kalona continued, "They live for war. They train their children for war. They strap boards to their little babies' foreheads to deform them and make them look fierce and evil." The thought made Kalona shiver.

Chief Waya respectfully waited to be sure Kalona had finished, then spoke. "The Tagwa have kept the peace with us for thirteen winters now. They are fierce but only a tiny nation now compared to the Ani Yun Wiya. Their nation is east, not southeast, of us."

"The headwaters of the Tugalo originate in their country," Kalona countered.

A warrior added, "They have kept the peace with us but they still raid their other neighbors—even their old Tuscarora allies."

The Uku's assistant, Sali, spoke. "This is the work of witches."

The room was quiet as everyone stared at Sali. There were those in the village who suspected that Sali might be a witch himself. He was a creepy old man. No one knew how old he actually was but some speculated that he had seen one hundred summers.

His eyes bugged out when he spoke and then sunk into oblivion when he was quiet. His toothless mouth disappeared into his deeply furrowed face, which became blobs of lumpy skin. His name, Sali, meant Persimmon Bark, and aptly described his massively wrinkled face.

Chief Waya took a deep breath and thought, *what is there to say after that?* What Sali said bothered him. This was not like a raiding party. It was more like an act of vengeance or a random act by individuals rather than a raid. But he was not aware of any transgression by any member of his village. But witches?

Ali's stomach knotted and she felt nauseous as she watched her hideous looking abductors.

THE SMELL OF THE wet, dank forest greeted Alihelitsi-dasdi as she awoke. She found herself bound to a tree near a small stream at one end of a clearing.

Two thin branches supported her like crutches with her hands tied behind the tree and her feet strapped to its base.

The kidnappers were busy gathering wood, building a fire, and setting up camp. Rocky cliffs rose up on either side of the narrow canyon. *They will never find us!* Ali feared.

She looked around and recognized the other two girls. Like her, they were bound to tall, thin birch trees. Walelu was tied to a tree about fifteen paces from her. The third girl, Delagalis, was further off, maybe twenty-five paces, tied to a tree that was across the stream from the campfire.

Ali's stomach knotted and she felt nauseous as she watched her hideous looking abductors. Fear was a cultured weapon of the Tagwa. The steeply angled foreheads, flattened from birth, made their heads look like a serpent's and it made their eyes menacing.

The warriors wore black paint on their bodies and faces with white and red designs around their eyes. She had heard that before battle, they often chewed on beets or red paint to make their teeth and mouth look bloody.

One of the warriors took a small bowl and dipped it into the stream. Ali's lips, tongue, and throat were dry. The cool water dripping from the bowl looked so good.

The warrior rose and took a drink from the bowl. Water ran down the corners of his mouth and dripped off his chin. He was larger than the other two. His long, black hair was pulled back and tied at the center of his deformed head making his head look like a fish with a long black tail.

Around his right eye he had painted a white circle, while red lines criss-crossed his other eye representing a star. The trunk of his body, his arms, and his legs had been scratched with a ceremonial, comb-like device called a kanuga. Crusted scabs lined the scratch marks where blood had once trickled to the surface. *A ball player,* Ali surmised.

The massive man carried the dripping container to Delagalis. As he approached her, he drew his knife from its scabbard. Delagalis's eyes grew wide as she flattened herself against the tree.

The Tagwa placed his knife through the leather belt gagging her and sliced it in two. The gag dropped to her shoulders freeing Delagalis's gut wrenching scream.

The Tagwa slapped her across the left cheek with the flat side of his knife blade and then back across the other cheek throwing her head to and fro violently.

Delagalis stood silent and trembling as blood collected along the shallow slice marks on her cheeks. Her attacker offered her a drink from the bowl full of water. Delagalis defiantly turned her head away.

The Tagwa tormentor placed the bowl in front of her lips and she threw her head to the other side. The warrior splashed the water into her face and then tossed the bowl to one of his colleagues as he stomped away.

In his turn, the second Tagwa went to the stream and filled the bowl with water. The second man was tall and muscular, but smaller than the first. He had painted one white circle around one eye and one red circle around his other eye, but otherwise, his paint and scratches were the same as the other two abductors.

It was Walelu's turn. Walelu stoically stood still as the ugly man cut off her gag. She allowed the warrior to place the bowl to her lips, but contemptuously pressed her lips tightly forcing the water to spill down her chin.

The fiend found this very entertaining and laughed heartily.

"Let us go," Walelu pleaded.

The fiend grew serious and glared into her eyes. His elongated head made his eyes appear to bulge out.

"Let us go!" Walelu continued as tears rolled down her cheeks.

The monster backhanded her across the face. Walelu slumped and wept quietly.

Ali struggled against her restraints and tried to yell at the warrior, but her words were muffled by the leather strap.

The monster frowned at her. His frown turned into a smirk as he advanced slowly toward her. As he walked up to the tiny girl, he lowered his head and slumped his shoulders in a hulking fashion. He slowly sawed the leather strap from her mouth.

"Brute!" she scowled.

He pushed the bowl to her lips. She decided to accept the water. Maybe cooperation would be better.

Her response drew cheers of approval from the third abductor. Ali felt guilty. She felt as if she had betrayed her friends so she did not swallow.

The warrior drew close to her and taunted her in his ugly Tagwan language. She spit the water into his face.

Her action gave the other abductors great fun, but it outraged her tormentor and he slugged her in the stomach. She doubled over and gasped for breath. Severe pain radiated through her body and she felt sick.

The warrior grabbed her hair, pulled her head back and poked his face into hers. She vomited into his face.

He staggered away wiping his face and coughing as his friends rolled on the ground with laughter. He dropped to his knees in the shallows of the stream to wash off the vomit.

The third Tagwa babbled something boastful to his friends as he stood and approached Walelu. He could have been the second Tagwa's twin except for his eye paint.

He had a white circle around each eye which made him look ghoulishly comical. Walelu suppressed her weeping, straightened up, raised her chin and gazed at him scornfully. The warrior and the maiden locked eyes as he drew his knife and placed it to her chest.

Walelu did not blink. The warrior's friends jeered him on. He sliced the leather ties on Walelu's blouse. The other warriors cheered as he hacked the blouse from her body slowly and methodically.

"Leave her alone, you animal!" exclaimed Delagalis.

"Let us go, cowards!" shouted Ali.

The second Tagwa emerged from the stream, stomped toward Ali and struck her in the head with his fist so hard that the blow left her unconscious.

13

*"If it is a witch, would it
not be better for our
granddaughters than
evil renegades?"*

THE MESSENGER FROM THE Tsalagi capital, Katuwa,
accompanied by the returning special messenger from
Tsikohi arrived in the village long after Grandmother Sun
had passed through the doors at the end of the world. A
special council was called.

The news from Katuwa was that there were no other
reports of raids. The Great War Chief had instructed his
messenger to learn more about the incident. The messenger made no secret that the Great War Chief did not
think that it was a raid, "... because, if it were a raid, it
was very unusual for a raiding party to pick a village so far
inside Tsalagi territory. The fact that young girls were taken
instead of food or goods, suggested that the abductors
could be anyone, even Tsalagi!"

The village Council House grew noisy with this remark, but Chief Waya raised his hand to quiet the crowd.
Slowly, he regained control of the room and spoke, "I do
not believe that anyone in our village nor in a neighboring
village would do this! And as for retribution, I know of

nothing that any of our villagers have done to offend anyone."

The crowd voiced agreement and resumed lively discussions among themselves until the oldest person in the room feebly pushed up to stand. The room quieted again and turned their attention to the old priest, Sali.

Suddenly, tiny, round, black eyes popped out of the wrinkled lumps of his face startling the messenger from Katuwa to the amusement of the crowd. Sali looked around the room in no hurry to speak, and then said, "The abductor does not seek war."

Sali studied the messenger and then Chief Waya. "The abductor does not seek revenge."

The scary old man stared at Chief Waya for a moment and then Peace Chief Kalona. "The abductor is a witch seeking to steal the purity and youth of our village, to steal their askinas and give himself long life."

Shock, rage, contempt! Kalona felt all these emotions almost simultaneously. Her flushed face deceived her. She struggled to control herself. She struggled to remember that she was the Peace Chief for the village.

She struggled to keep her role as mother/grandmother out of this situation. But, the shock of the tasteless brashness of the old priest caught her off guard. The rage that fired inside her upon hearing such a cruel prognosis for her granddaughter by that ridiculous, contemptuous old man was too much.

Kalona leaped from her chair. "Witch! ... Witch? ... What witch? If you know something, share it with us. What is your proof? What do you base your accusations on? ... Tell us!"

The old man's beady eyeballs grew large. He was not accustomed to being challenged. And Chief Kalona Ehlawei was a formidable foe when roiled.

Kalona was breathing hard and her fists were clinched as she glared at the quivering old priest. Deep regret began to well up in her. She began to feel pity for the elder priest who was her father's best friend. The gentle old man had been like an elder uncle to her for her whole life.

She realized how disrespectful she had just been. She could feel the quiet of the crowd. She sensed the shock that they must be feeling to see someone as prominent as herself attacking such a fragile old man. She wished she could take back her words. She wished she knew what to do to make things right again. How could she ever restore face for Sali. Tears welled up in her eyes. She opened her mouth to speak ...

Chief Waya swallowed hard. Sali's words had hurt the beloved Peace Chief deeply. It was her granddaughter he was condemning. The situation had exploded and he must calm nerves and try to restore face. He stood to speak ...

Sali spoke, "Your heart is afraid, Granddaughter. All of our hearts are afraid. Which one of us does not cherish beautiful Alihelitsidasdi? Which one of us does not love lively Delagalis? Which one of us does not cherish sweet Walelu? The loss of any one of our dear granddaughters would leave a hole in our lives."

Tears streamed down Kalona's cheeks. She began to tremble. A great sadness engulfed everyone in the Council House as Sali continued, "I wish that I had words to comfort you, beloved grandmother for whom I have only the greatest respect. But I ask you to think of this: If it is a witch, would it not be better for our granddaughters than evil renegades?"

Kalona gasped and drew back in disbelief. *What?* She thought, *What bizarre choice is that?*

Low murmurs traveled around the room as the confused crowd tried to grapple with Sali's conundrum.

Sali looked around the room and sensed everyone's confusion. He closed his eyes, took a long breath and just stood for a moment as if deep in thought.

Finally, he opened his eyes. Remarkably, the ugly old man's face appeared kindly and sympathetic as he spoke, "Would you rather Adanvdo Alsgida face a warrior or a witch?"

Sali stopped to let his words sink in.

Then he continued, "Which one is the Uku better equipped to defeat?"

Kalona got it. She looked at this pathetic old priest that only moments earlier she had had only contempt for and realized how wrong she had been. Just that quickly, her image of Sali had gone from contempt to deep respect ... maybe awe.

"We don't have to touch the witch to defeat him. The witch is a foe we can fight from a distance. We can reach the witch through the spirits. We can fight the witch with superior conjuring. The white way always defeats the dark way, does it not?"

Kalona placed her hands together and bowed her head, "Wado, Sali. Forgive my harsh words. Please, use your great wisdom and conjuring to keep our granddaughters safe."

Sali closed his eyes and solemnly walked out of the Council House chanting quietly. One by one, the priests of the other six clans rose and followed Sali, each mumbling the white way blessing for triumph over the dark way.

Kalona looked at Waya Gigage. The irony of the War Chief seeking peace with the combative Peace Chief did not escape her.

Waya raised his hand to silence the crowd and looked around the room before addressing the Katuwa messenger, "Our priest Sali is a wise man. His words must be heeded. You may tell the Great War Chief that a witch must be considered."

The representative appeared to be skeptical but diplomatically accepted the village chief's consideration. Waya updated the messenger with the news from the search party. And with that, all understood the council was ended and began to file out of the Council House.

*With renewed energy, the
desperate grandmother
rolled out of bed, slipped
on her moccasins, wrapped
a bear skin around her
and headed back into the
dark night.*

Waya Usti sat alone on the escarpment where the trail of the abductors had been lost. The valley below flickered with light from the search party's campfire beside the Agusa Jisdu. They had failed to find any sign of the kidnappers anywhere along the Agusa Jisdu all the way to the Tugalo.

Villagers living at the confluence were certain that no one had passed by on foot or by boat. A chagrined Wahuhu had ordered the search party to return to the escarpment to search for evidence to the west.

The journey back had continued after sunset aided by a full Duliidsdi, the Nut Moon, the September moon, which enabled the search party to reach the escarpment shortly after the moon set behind the deep canyons up the Agusa Jisdu to the west.

Now the searchers were sitting around the campfire telling their stories to take their minds off the disappointment of failing to find the missing girls. Waya Usti did not want to think of something else. He wanted to continue the search, but knew that nothing could be accomplished in the dark unless ...

Waya Usti stood up on the escarpment that gave him a sweeping view of the surrounding landscape and searched the darkness for another glow in the night—the campfire of the abductors.

To the east lightning flashed, momentarily illuminating the now distant rain clouds. There was no sign of a campfire in any direction.

The disappointed young man sat down cross-legged on the boulder and stared into the darkness hiding the mountains, valleys, and rivers. Somewhere in that black soup, three young girls were living a nightmare.

Waya Usti dangled his legs over the edge of the boulder and leaned back dejectedly, bracing himself on his elbows and looked up at the vast black sky loaded with billions of spirit campfires. If only he could speak to spirits. His father had told him many stories about the spirits in the sky sitting around the twinkling campfires. They could see all things on Turtle Island, the entire world. Surely they knew the whereabouts of Ali.

But this night he did not want to think about the many stories his father had shared with him about the night sky. His thoughts were solely of Ali. He thought about her happy smile, gleaming eyes, and abundant energy.

Her name, Happy One, could not have been more perfect. She was always that. But it was HIS name, Wolf Puppy, that had connected him to her. As a kid, he had been constantly made fun of, but never by Ali. She never joined in and even scolded her friends if they made fun of him. He admired her for that.

He knew that she had never really had an eye for him, though. Why would she? She was royalty. Her family was of the Ani Gilohi, the Long Hair or Twister clan. They were the keepers of the stories; the priests; the peace chiefs. They were the intellectuals of the tribe; they were better than the others.

They showed it in the way they carried themselves with a little "twist" in their shoulders as they walked; the elaborate hairdos; the way they raised their chin with almost arrogant pride to appear as if they were looking down on others.

Waya Usti's mother's clan (and therefore his) was of the Aniwaya clan, the Wolf clan; the clan of warriors. But having a mother in the Wolf clan and a father in the Bird clan had been a wonderful combination for him.

The warrior Wolf clan and the hunter Bird clan were a perfect complement of skills. He had often been recognized for his abilities. And his uncle, Waya Gigage, was the war chief for the village. Maybe that counted for something.

But the friendship that his uncle and Ali's grandmother had developed did not really extend to him. In fact, he doubted that Kalona Ehlawei even knew he existed.

Waya Usti lay back on the rock and sighed. He felt that he was a fool to think that Ali would ever care for him the way he cared for her.

Kalona sat outside the clan Council House and watched the smoke of the sacred fire from inside meander up into the dark sky to join the bright camp fires of the spirits. She knew the smoke would carry the message of the abduction to the spirits above. The smoke message from her father and grandson would implore the spirits to look after her granddaughter and the other girls.

She listened to the muffled sound of a drum beat and songs being sung by her grandson, Atselvdi, and her father, Adanvdo. Kalona mouthed the words she had heard so many times as a priest's daughter.

She held the herbs and plants her father had requested and waited until he was ready for them. She knew that her father and her grandson were doing everything they could to keep her granddaughter safe.

Kalona stood as the chanting from inside ended. Atselvdi poked his head out and blinked while his eyes adjusted to the darkness. She held out the bag full of herbs and plants and waited for him to see her. Her young grandson took the bag, "Are you all right, Grandmother?"

"Yes but I am tired."

"You should go home now and rest. Grandfather and I are connecting with the spirits and sending great powers to Ali."

Kalona smiled. She believed that the enthusiasm and faith of her grandson did carry great power. And no one she had ever known could connect to the spirits like her father. He had earned his name Spirit Dancer.

"I know you are. Your powers are strong, Atselvdi. Do not let the black spirits place doubt in your heart. Oh, and please tell Father that Sali suspects a witch kidnapped the girls."

Kalona brushed Atselvdi lovingly on the arm and nudged him back through the door of the Clan House. Atselvdi disappeared back inside.

The tired, sad, old woman crossed her arms and rubbed her shoulders and upper arms for warmth. The damp chill of the night air attacked her joints and made them ache.

The beat of the drum resumed as Kalona headed for home. As she walked the lonely street to her home, she relived the meeting at the Council House.

That crazy old moss-head, she thought, he's probably right. Only evil would want to harm my beautiful granddaughter. Ali brings happiness and laughter to everyone. She is kind to all things and all things love her. How could such a horrible thing happen to such a perfect child?

She remembered that Chief Waya's messenger would try to contact the search party in the morning. He would tell Wahuhu that the council believed that the kidnappers were not part of a raiding party but acting independently ... or possibly a witch! She chuckled. No one but Sali believed they were witches.

The messenger would return with whatever news there was, hopefully by afternoon. The Great War Chief's messenger would return to the capital city, Katuwa, and carry the message that the Tsikohi council agreed with the Great War Chief's assessment and would keep him updated on the status of the search.

Although it had not been said, everyone understood that the implications of this were worse for the girls. If they were captured in a raid, they would be taken back to the tribe to become slaves or wives or traded for something of value. But independent captors were probably wanting to enslave or, worse, ravage the poor girls!

Tears streamed down Kalona's cheeks as she reached out to steady herself against the front of her house. The heartbroken grandmother gripped her chest and took a deep breath. She forced herself to block out the black thoughts and silently prayed to the white otter to defeat the kidnappers' wits. She prayed to the white beaver, white rat, and white weasel to gnaw away the tenacity and resolve of the abductors.

As if the spirit world was racing to her rescue, a stiff breeze blew by. A raven screeched amusing her. She imagined the wind catching the sleeping raven by surprise and forcing it to flap its wings madly to keep from toppling from the branch.

She gazed into the tree across the street. She could not see the old raven but she sensed he was there. She had been told that when she was born, a beloved woman standing in for her deceased grandmother looked up to thank the spirits and saw a raven sitting quietly in a tree looking down on the newborn baby.

The surrogate grandmother was impressed by how silent the baby and the raven were in the wake of such a violent tragedy. Especially since ravens are notorious for being irritatingly noisy. And it was said that little Kalona never cried from the time she was born. Her surrogate grandmother believed that the raven was a guardian spirit that would look over her adopted granddaughter, so she named the baby Kalona Ehlawei, Quiet Raven.

Throughout her life, there would be times when Kalona Ehlawei was alone and would sense someone or something watching her. When she would look, she would see a raven sitting nearby quietly staring at her. She believed that each time it was that same quiet raven that inspired her name. As Kalona had gotten older, she assumed that the raven had aged with her and must be very old now, indeed, for a raven. But still she believed it lived on and continued to look after her.

She also believed that it was this same guardian raven that had pulled her from the river after her deranged aunt had tossed her in to be rid of her.

Kalona entered her house. The neglected hearth emitted only a dim orange glow casting strange, dancing shadows around the main room of the house. The chilled old woman stoked the fire and added several logs.

As she waited for the fire to rekindle and radiate warmth to her aching joints, she stared at the spot next to the hearth where her little Ali usually sat. Tears streamed down her cheeks.

She found her way to her bed aided by the brightening glow of the growing fire. She lay on her bed exhausted but unable to sleep. She felt helpless but she was determined to find a way to help her granddaughter. It was in this moment of desperation that she realized what she must do.

It was then that she remembered who had often helped her as a child. "It's what they do!" she said out loud. With renewed energy, the desperate grandmother rolled out of bed, slipped on her moccasins, wrapped a bear skin around her and headed back into the dark night.

The weird snake made grunting and snorting sounds and then tilted its head to one side and struck, sinking its long fangs into her armpits!

A SONGLIKE VOICE CALLED softly from the darkness, "Waya Usti."

Waya Usti sat up abruptly.

"Waya Usti."

His eyelids would not open so he rubbed his tired eyes.

"Waya Usti."

"Ali?" he called out realizing that it was her voice calling his name. "Where are you?"

The distant sad voice called again, "Waya Usti."

He leaped up and ran toward the haunting voice.

"Waya Usti."

The voice of Ali seemed to be moving away from him. He tried desperately to run faster to catch her. As he ran, the trees and thickets grew thicker and thicker and it became increasingly difficult for him to continue. He dropped to his knees and began crawling underneath the thickets but the ground was wet and the mud slippery. His arms were growing tired and heavy and his legs were exhausted.

And then he broke through into a clearing filled with a large lake. Ali was standing by the edge of the water facing him.

"Ali!" he cried out.

"Waya Usti," she answered softly.

Waya Usti crawled toward her but as he moved toward her, she appeared to float backward out over the lake.

"No! Stop! Don't be afraid. Come to me," he pleaded with her. "I will protect you."

She looked at him and his heart felt full and warm and excited. Waya Usti reached out to her. "I am here, Ali."

Suddenly, as she extended her hand to him, she dropped into the water and disappeared! Waya Usti ran to the edge of the lake where he could see her looking back at him from the depths. She appeared to be mouthing his name. When her bubbles burst onto the surface, he could hear the yelping of a wolf puppy.

"No!" he screamed, abruptly sitting up.

The startled young man was breathing heavily and sweating. He looked around him and realized he had been dreaming and was actually sitting on top of the boulder overlooking the Agusa Jisdu. The campfire below had burned down to glowing embers and was no longer flickering against the trees. The search party was quiet now and most likely all were asleep.

Waya Usti rubbed his eyes and searched the darkness again for signs of another campfire somewhere. "Ali ..." he whispered and placed his chin on his knees. "Ali ..."

Alihelitsidasdi's feet were tingling. She looked down to see a huge, black horned snake slithering past. She tried to move but remembered that she was bound to the tree. Slowly the horrible snake wrapped itself around her squeezing her hands and arms and making them numb.

The huge head of the snake came around from behind her and looked into her eyes. She tried to scream but she was gagged again. The entrapped girl struggled to free herself as the giant snake drew back and opened its mouth revealing giant sparkling fangs dripping with venom.

The weird snake made grunting and snorting sounds and then tilted its head to one side and struck, sinking its long fangs into her armpits! Excruciating pain fired from her armpits.

Ali gasped and bumped the back of her head on the tree. The world swirled around her. She looked down and realized she had had a nightmare.

Her armpits were raging with pain, not from a snake's fangs but from hanging on the branches of the tree that had been supporting her. She stood up against the tree stretching her tight, aching stomach muscles and freeing her armpits from the thin branches. The reality of her situation rushed back to her. She listened to the snoring Tagwa warriors.

As her eyes adjusted to the darkness, she could see the star glow reflecting off parts of the warriors' bodies producing patches of silver, shining skin. She could see Walelu slumping limply, still bound to the birch tree. Walelu was naked with many black shadows covering her body, but Ali could not see Delagalis in the darkness.

Slowly she realized that there were now four bodies lying on the ground around the fire pit. The forth was a naked Delagalis! She lay motionless, flat on her back with her arms and legs tied to stakes.

Ali's hands, fingers, and toes were numb and tingly. She tried to wiggle her fingers but it hurt like thousands of thorns penetrating them. Slowly the blood returned to her hands and fingers and she carefully tested the ropes around her wrists. The ropes seemed a little looser than before. After drying, perhaps the ropes had loosened. She worked her wrists back and forth, careful not to tighten the knots.

As she struggled to loosen the ropes, too soon her arms, fingers, and hands grew weary and started to cramp. Gingerly, she let herself back down on the branches and found new spots under her arms to rest on. After she rested for a while, she would resume working on the ropes.

Further up the Agusa Jisdu not far beyond the Tagwa camp and hidden by the canyon walls, spray from a waterfall drifted down onto the lush vegetation beside the stream making a hissing sound in the darkness.

High above, a rocky ledge was aglow from a fire where a decrepit old wizard lay beside it with his eyes closed and his stomach full. He was shaking a gourd rattle and chanting a mystical conjure. Kalanu Ahkyeliski was summoning the dark spirits to aid him in his quest.

He worried that perhaps he had put it off too long. Perhaps he would not find the strength to do what he must do. His life force would soon run out and if not replenished, he would die like a common, mortal man.

To assist him in his evil endeavor, the master wizard had first stolen the askina, the four souls, of a healthy raven. Shape shifting into a raven would give him the mobility to fly and enable him to approach his prey disguised as a raven.

Stealing the souls of the raven required almost the same ritual as stealing the souls of a man. He had to consume the askina at the proper times and in the proper sequence.

The first and most difficult was the soul of its conscious life. This soul left the body simultaneously with death as its last breath. As Kalanu punctured the heart of the raven, he had placed its head in his mouth and sucked out the dying raven's life soul.

The second soul was the soul of physiological life and was captured by consuming the liver within seven days of death. Consuming the heart within one moon cycle captured the soul of circulation. And finally, consuming the marrow of the bone captured the fourth soul. He had consumed them in sequence but all in one feast—all that night.

The weakened wizard pushed himself up from the fire pit and wiped raven blood and bile from his lips. He reached into his medicine pouch and pulled out the root Aholiyehvsgi, dipped it in the water, took a bite and chewed the juices out of it.

After spitting out the remainder of the root, he began the chant whose words were so ancient they were no longer spoken nor understood by the people. He waded into the frigid pond until he was waist deep and spread his arms overhead reaching into the night sky. He waited until he could feel the water settle and then dropped his head.

The crystal clear water reflected the campfires of the spirits above. Before him in the water, he could see the constellation of the Ani Tsutsa. The cluster of seven spirit campfires were those of the seven boys who long ago became so angry with their mothers that they danced and prayed to the spirits to help them escape into the sky.

Eight boys had danced around in a circle until they lifted off the ground and began to float upward. One of the boy's mothers managed to pull her son down, but the others rose into the sky to join the spirit world.

Ceremonially, he brought down his arms circumscribing a circle terminated by scooping up the water containing the reflection of the Ani Tsutsa and splashed it on his forehead and rubbed it over his face and chest.

Again, he raised his arms up to the Ani Tsutsa and called upon the boys to extend to him their powers of levitation. His eyes burned red and sparks began to spew from his arms as his head began to change into the shape of the raven's head.

The shape-shifting wizard's arms changed into black wings as he dropped them to his side and shot into the sky. Fire and sparks streamed from his arms and body as he extended his arms out and glided over the Agusa Jisdu, circled around and dove down between the deep canyon walls.

16

A branch snapped behind them. The startled teenagers jumped to their feet and spun around ready for combat.

THE STREETS OF TSIKOHI were quiet. Wisps of fog floated by like thin ghosts futilely searching for their ancestors. The rank smell of damp wood, dirt, straw, and plaster insulted her nostrils and the dank air chilled her tired and weak body. She pulled her bearskin cape tight around her neck as she passed by the hut of Wananahi, and daughter, Amadohi. Wondering if they were sleeping, she stopped to listen and could hear Wananahi snoring loudly.

Kalona chuckled. Nothing could keep that old woman awake after Grandmother Sun goes to bed. But then she thought about poor Amadohi, her granddaughter's best friend. Kalona guessed that worry might be keeping the child awake this night.

In the distance, she heard a muffled scream. She listened intently, but only silence followed. *It is understandable that mothers and grandmothers could be having nightmares tonight,* she thought.

With a heavy heart, the sad grandmother treaded on to the east exit. As she neared, she could hear chanting and the sounds of a gourd rattle. She stopped to listen. It was coming from Sali's hut.

Sali lived in a decrepit, seven-sided abandoned clan council house. It was not the custom for anyone to live in a clan council house, but somehow it seemed to fit the ancient priest.

Kalona recognized the song for protection. Once again, pangs of remorse filled Kalona's stomach. How could she have been so disrespectful at the Council House meeting? Clearly, Sali had a good heart and was calling on the white spirits to grant safety for Ali and the other girls.

Kalona was comforted knowing that her granddaughter had so many powerful priests praying for her. Perhaps she should return home and leave everything to the priests. Perhaps Ali did not need her help. Besides, what she was about to do was very risky.

Kalona looked over the vertical posts that formed the east wall of the village into the darkness where the mountain lay. Darkness shrouded it, but she could see it in her mind's eye. She knew she had to do this. She had to do whatever she could at whatever risk to help her beautiful granddaughter.

The tired old woman climbed the steep hill where she had come many times as a child to play with her strange little friends. She stopped to catch her breath and to listen for the happy drums and singing that she had not heard for so many years. Sadly, only the wind in the trees and her own hard breathing disturbed the silence this night.

It was forbidden for adults to seek the village of the Yunwi Tsunsdi. As a small child, the Little People had been great playmates. They looked like adults but were tiny like she was back then. They were well shaped and handsome with long hair reaching to the ground.

She loved visiting them because they seemed to spend most of their time happily drumming, singing, and dancing. She was told that they were wonder workers and especially helpful to children.

But they were not so enamored with adults. In fact, they shunned them and if annoyed by an adult, might cast a spell, making them disoriented or even crazy! But Kalona was willing to risk the consequences if they could save her granddaughter.

The wind whispering in the trees made it difficult to hear any subtle noises. Kalona tried to block out the whispers to no avail. Perhaps she was still too far away from their caves.

Joints aching, her head heavy from want of sleep, Kalona continued up the slope. She decided she would go to the huge boulder that rested below the caves where the Yunwi Tsunsdi lived. There she would wait and hope that her little friend, Nvwoti Atlisdodi Usdi, the Little Medicine Bowl, would sense her presence and come to her.

As a child, she had run up this mountain. But her age now made it an almost impossible journey for her. As a small, lonely child, dancing with the Yunwi Tsunsdi had been some of the happiest times of her life.

When she finally reached the boulder, she dropped to her knees and reached her hand out to the cold, damp stone for support. Even this close she could not hear the drumming and singing she had always heard when she had visited before. She reasoned that maybe they were quiet because they were sad about the kidnapped girls. Or, perhaps they sensed the presence of an adult.

Kalona rolled off her knees and sat back against the boulder. Her heart was pounding so hard she could feel it in her ears. She began to worry that the Yunwi Tsunsdi were angry with her—maybe that was why they were quiet!

She worried that they might cast a spell on her. She checked to make sure she was not disoriented and confused. She pictured in her mind the path back home to reassure herself that she was not disoriented, yet.

The exhausted old woman lowered her head and whispered, "Nvwoti, if you can hear me, I need your help. I mean no disrespect by coming to you, but I am a humble, desperate old woman who needs you more than she has ever needed you before. Please, understand that I do not seek your help for myself. It is my sweet, innocent granddaughter. Evil has taken her from me and she is helpless unless you can save her!"

Kalona broke down and sobbed uncontrollably.

"Waya Usti?" the quiet, questioning voice echoed in the deep canyon below. It was cousin Tawodi.

Waya Usti responded, "Up here."

"Where?" Tawodi asked.

"On the rock cliff above you," Waya Usti replied.

"What is it?" someone asked.

"Shhh! It's all right, I was just talking to Waya Usti. Nothing has happened."

Waya Usti stood and looked down at the barely glowing embers of the campfire. He could not see anyone in the darkness, but could hear Tawodi climbing up the path clumbsily.

Waya Usti greeted his huge cousin, "Osiyo," he whispered.

"Siyo," Tawodi whispered back as he climbed up onto the boulder and stood next to Waya Usti.

"Couldn't sleep?" Tawodi inquired.

"I was hoping to spot their campfire."

"Did you?"

"No."

The two young men sat down on the boulder and stared into the night. "They should've listened to you," Tawodi consoled.

"Maybe. We won't know until the morning whether there are any tracks on the western path."

"Waya Usti?" It was Tlomeha Usdi.

"Up here, Father. Go back to sleep."

The two cousins sat listening to the crickets and frogs singing along the stream below.

"Are you worried about Ali?" Tawodi probed.

Waya Usti was taken aback. He assumed that no one knew about his feelings for her. "I'm worried about all of the girls."

Tawodi snickered.

"What's so funny?" Waya Usti protested.

Tawodi was silent, which made Waya Usti even more irritated.

A branch snapped behind them. The startled teenagers jumped to their feet and spun around ready for combat. The tiny, nimble body of Tlomeha Usdi scrambled up onto the boulder and stood before them. When he saw their surprised looks, he bent over laughing.

Tawodi looked up at the sky in disgust while Waya Usti gritted his teeth and exclaimed, "We could've killed you sneaking up on us like that!"

Tlomeha Usdi reached up and patted the boys on their shoulders while he tried to regain his composure.

"Whatcha doin' up here?" the little man queried.

"Waya Usti thought he might be able to spot their campfire from up here," Tawodi explained.

Tlomeha Usdi thought about that for a moment and then replied, "Good thinking."

"I haven't seen anything, though."

Tlomeha Usdi was proud of his tall, strong, clever son. Waya Usti had always been smarter than the average boy his age. He had picked up hunting and tracking very quickly and Tlomeha Usdi feared that Waya Usti was almost as good at hunting as he was. Only experience and instinct separated them at this point.

Waya Usti was surprised that his father had come up to join him. His father was a no-nonsense man who kept his feelings and thoughts to himself. Waya Usti had never felt that close to his father, although they had spent much time hunting together.

He often wondered what his father thought about, but could never get him to open up. Anytime he had tried to discuss something with his father, his father had either shrugged, changed the subject, or walked away. But tonight, the stocky little man with skinny legs seemed unusually friendly and approachable.

"Will we find them, Father?"

Tlomeha Usdi shrugged.

As she watched them, she heard the rustling again and could see for certain that the Tagwas were not making the sound.

"**W**AKE UP, OLD WOMAN!"

Kalona Ehlawei jerked awake. She realized that she had fallen asleep from exhaustion. She looked nervously about trying to understand where she was and what just happened. As her eyes adjusted, she realized that a small round shadow was in front of her. It was her little friend, Nvwoti Atlisdodi Usdi.

"Oh, thank goodness, it's you!" she exclaimed under her breath.

"Who else?" quipped the little man.

"I have come to ..."

"I know why you have come and now you must go!"

A huge tear rolled down Kalona's cheek. "Oh, dear, I've angered you!"

"You must go now; I don't have time for this." Nvwoti said coolly as he stood and folded his arms.

Sadly, the broken-hearted old woman struggled to her feet. She wanted to protest; she wanted to argue. But she feared the power of the Little People. She feared he was angry with her. As she pushed up to stand, her aged knees made a popping sound. The little man giggled.

How cruel, thought Kalona. The proud woman stood up straight and gathered her strength to begin her return down the mountain. This had been a terrible mistake.

As she stepped forward to pass by the contemptuous little joker, she made certain she did not look at him. But as she took a step, she heard him whisper, "Did you not think that Alihelitsidasdi is a friend of the Yunwi Tsunsdi?"

The startled old woman grabbed her chest, fell back against the boulder and slid back into a sitting position. She shook her head and exclaimed, "What do you mean?"

But when she looked up, the Yunwi Tsunsdi she had once called her friend was gone!

"Nvwoti! Explain! Will you help her? Is she ... is she ... dead?" Kalona broke down sobbing.

In her dream, Ali's mind was racing while exploring all possibilities. Again and again in her mind she experimented with the bindings on her wrists. How could she keep them loose and then pick at them to loosen them even more? She needed to pick and tug gently, gently, over and over.

Ali awoke with alarm! Something had startled her, but she was not sure what. Somewhere, she heard a rustling sound. She stared into the darkness around the campfire. She could see one Tagwa lying between her and the campfire. He was not stirring.

Beyond the campfire, she could make out the other two by the glow from the campfire embers, but they were also still. As she watched them, she heard the rustling again and could see for certain that the Tagwas were not making the sound. This time it sounded like the rustling was behind her. She held her breath and listened intently. A panther, perhaps?

There it was again! She was certain that it was coming from behind her, then behind and to the left ... and then to the right. There were several creatures in the bushes behind her! Was it a bear with cubs? No, a mother bear would make more noise. Whatever it was, it was small.

Coyotes! It could be a pack of coyotes sneaking up to investigate, drawn by the smell of blood. She began to tremble. Alone, coyotes are more timid than rabbits. But in a pack, they are vicious, relentless killers.

But then the trapped girl heard something much more curious. Whispers. Villagers coming to rescue her? Ali's heart began to race with excitement! She listened acutely ...

"Alihelitsidasdi."

Someone was whispering her name. "Yes?" she whispered.

"Be still! I am going to untie your hands."

She recognized the voice of one of her little friends, the Yunwi Tsunsdi, the Little People.

She felt the tiny hands working on the ropes and tickling her wrists. She stood to relieve the pain under her arms. The rustling grew louder and came from all around. She could hear the little people fanning out around the camp. There had to be fifty, maybe one hundred of them had come to rescue her.

She felt the short, regular gusts of someone breathing in her face and smelled the foul stench. A raven squawked loudly from a distance prompting her to throw open her eyes. Dark eyes shimmered in the dim moonlight glaring at her. The deformed head of the Tagwa slowly materialized in her vision. He was close—right in her face. A morbid grin spread across his lips and his eyes glistened with menacing delight.

A flash of light momentarily glinted off the knife blade held in his dangling hand. He scooped up his genitals on the blade as if serving it up for her adoration. As if offering her this delectable meal to satisfy her sexual craving.

She shivered violently and felt the ropes slip away from her wrists. In a rush of rage she seized the knife and shoved it into his groin doubling over the assaulter into agonizing screams of pain.

Finding the knife now in her possession, she raised and forced it down into the back of his neck, then into his chest as he reflexively threw back his head. Again and again she thrust the knife into the ghoul of her worst nightmare.

Bound at the ankles, she fell on her face and quickly doubled over to slash the ropes. With emotion tweaked to its most violent peak, she jumped to her feet and lashed out stabbing and flailing with blind rage at whatever approached her.

In the background, she sensed an army of Little People and a dark, giant birdlike shadow battling the evil Tagwas with her and it gave her power and strength and determination she never knew she possessed.

Wahuhu gasped, "What horror has happened here?"

THE TRACKER, THE SON, and the young warrior sat on a boulder waiting for the sun to break the plane of the horizon. Soon they would have the light to search for signs along the trail leading west from the rocky escarpment. The squawk of a raven startled them.

Tlomeha Usdi stood and stretched as Tawodi Gvnagei and Waya Usti joined him. The three jumped off the boulder and walked up to the trail head. The beginning of the trail was a series of natural rock steps. The evidence of tracks, if there were any, would be beyond the steps where soil and vegetation took over.

Tawodi and Waya Usti followed Tlomeha Usdi down the stone steps. The transition point was in the shadow of the escarpment and therefore still very dark. Tlomeha Usdi squatted and waited for more light.

A panther like scream echoed from somewhere up the canyon. The three looked at each other urgently. Tlomeha Usdi spoke for all three, "Sounded like someone screaming."

The boys nervously agreed as they gazed up the canyon and waited for whatever it was to scream again.

Bright sunlight streamed across the trail ahead of them as the sun broke above the horizon. Tlomeha Usdi rose and began the search for evidence. They found nothing on the trail down to the river, but they were not surprised. They did not really expect to find good evidence until they reached the point where the rain hit. The rain would have washed away the tracks up to that point, but afterward the mud would hopefully preserve the tracks.

As they reached the Agusa Jisdu, the rest of the search party joined them. Wahuhu asked the obvious question, "Find anything?"

Tlomeha Usdi shook his head then continued up the trail scanning every twig, every rock, grain of sand, and every plant for signs. Waya Usti followed him repeating the same search. If there were evidence to be found, one of them would find it.

Grandmother Sun was rising fast and starting to warm the air. Waya Usti listened to the breath of the wind in the trees on the ridges above them. The breeze was picking up now and blowing from the southwest but he could not feel the breeze yet in the sheltered valley.

Far away up the valley, Waya Usti heard something! "Shhh! Listen!" he whispered. It was not a panther. It was a girl's agonizing scream echoing up through the canyon above!

Tlomeha Usdi and Tawodi looked at Waya Usti. Tawodi grabbed Waya Usti's shoulders expectantly as Wahuhu shouted, "They are up there!"

Waya Usti broke loose from his cousin and raced up the trail. He would not look back until he reached the camp of the abductors. Only his agile father could keep up with him, but not far behind the band of determined warriors raced after them.

Then there was silence.

Waya Usti stopped to listen, but there was nothing. Tlomeha Usdi hollered ahead to his son to continue. The two raced ahead fearing what they might find.

Finally, Waya Usti burst into the camp with his knife drawn and ready for battle. The first thing he saw was Walelu's blood drenched body slumping from a tree. She was clearly dead. Waya Usti's heart stopped.

Then he saw Ali kneeling over and cradling the bloody body of Delagalis. She was tugging futilely on the dead body bound to the ground with ropes tied to stakes.

"She is alive!" he shouted.

Waya Usti raced to her to wrap his arms around her. Ali screamed and with surprising strength, threw off the young man, jumped to her feet and lunged at him with a huge hunting knife! Waya Usti rolled to the side as her knife plunged into the ground where his head had just been.

Tlomeha Usdi dove on top of her and wrapped his arms around hers as they tumbled across the ground. Tlomeha Usdi struggled to hold her arms back as Waya Usti grabbed her wrist and tried vainly to wrestle the knife from her hand.

"Ali! It's okay! We've come to save you!" Waya Usti pleaded as he fought with the crazed, battling girl.

The search party approached the conflict and watched in amazement as the scrawny little girl kicked and punched the daylights out of the muscular young hunter and his father. Three stout warriors dived in to restrain the fierce little Ali as Waya Usti continued to talk to her and plead with her. The five men were no match for her.

Then, Wahuhu walked up and softly spoke her name. The little hellion looked into Wahuhu's eyes and seemed to recognize him. She broke down. The warriors released her as Waya Usti seized her and embraced her lovingly. She dropped the knife and slumped onto his shoulder, sobbing.

Tawodi picked up the bloody knife and knelt beside the blue-gray body of Delagalis. He felt her bloody neck but was not surprised that he could find no pulse. He cut her bindings and then stood and walked over to Walelu to cut her loose. He gently lifted the stiffening, lifeless body and carried her over to lie beside Delagalis.

Wahuhu covered Ali with his feathery white cape. Assured that Ali was in capable hands, he scanned the campsite. He walked to the river where several of his warriors were standing, dumbfounded by what they were seeing.

Wahuhu had been in many wars and many battles but he had never seen so much blood. Floating in the shallow stream were two dead, mutilated Tagwa warriors with blood streaming from their massive bodies changing the waters downstream to crimson.

The stiff, bloating bodies were held in place by a fallen tree preventing them from floating further downstream. They had hundreds of gaping knife wounds all over their bodies. And then he saw what his warriors were staring at.

Submerged in the middle of the stream was a third Tagwa warrior. His eyes were frozen in horror at something that once faced him as Wahuhu was facing him now. His mouth gaped open, there was a huge hole in his chest, and his intestines coiled around his lifeless body.

Wahuhu gasped, "What horror has happened here?"

Wahuhu turned away from the stream visibly shaken by the macabre scene. Behind him, one of his brave warriors began to vomit. Wahuhu had felt nauseous from war. But this was different. It was not the sickness brought on by fear, remorse, and exhaustion. It was a sickness induced by a shocking, grisly, sadistic scene of cruelty and brutality.

Wahuhu looked at the traumatized little girl who had somehow survived this horrible experience. "How?" he questioned with disbelief. This fragile little girl he had known since her birth. How does a happy, innocent child find the courage and strength to not only kill but to savagely mutilate three ferocious Tagwa warriors?

Waya Usti rocked back and forth comforting the trembling, cold, intense Alihelitsidasdi. "It's all right, Ali. You are safe now. No one is going to harm you anymore."

The young tracker/hunter stroked the distressed, fragile girl's hair tenderly. As he desperately tried to comfort her, his eyes panned the horrific campsite. The images of the ravaged dead girls flashed into his head.

It could have also been Ali! Waya Usti shivered and his eyes filled with tears. The long shadow of Wahuhu flowed before him. Respectfully, Waya Usti stood holding the exhausted girl in his arms and faced the tall leader.

Wahuhu caressed her head, but she did not respond. She was quiet now and he could see that she had retreated to somewhere deep and safe in her mind.

As his eyes scanned the carnage, he shuddered and lamented, Mama Gigahai Usati. Wahuhu wondered if they would ever know what happened in this small clearing that would forever be remembered as Water with Much Blood.

*His face was frozen in a
scream and his eyes still held
the horror of what he had
last seen in death's throes!*

THE FIRST HINTS OF morning light found Kalona Ehlawei fast asleep in her bed. She was physically exhausted from the arduous journey up the mountain and back. And she was mentally fatigued from the abhorrence, the apprehension, anxiety, and tension that had debilitated the energies of thought exercised after the news of the abduction.

She did not hear the loud thump on the house the first couple of times. Again, something hit the house! In her heavy dreams, the image of a large, black bird crashed into her house. The vivid picture of the crumpled wings and broken neck stirred her heart and evoked deep feelings of compassion. The dying bird opened its beak and uttered muffled squawks urging her, begging her for pity.

As it slid down the wall chattering its urgent cries, Kalona's eyes cracked open, fluttered, and then closed. Another thud on the wall startled her awake. Kalona's adrenaline powered her out of bed and to the front door where she could hear the squawking growing louder. It sounded like fighting birds and then another loud thud!

She pulled back the fur door covering. It was not a raven squawking. Instead, it was an old woman. The grieving old woman heaved another stone at the house as a younger woman tried to pull her away. She was begging the old woman to come home with her, but the old woman was hysterical.

As Kalona's eyes adjusted, she realized that the woman was old Crooked Foot's wife. When the old woman saw Kalona she began screaming, "Dog Killer! Man killer! It's your fault he's dead!" then hurled a rock in the direction of Kalona.

Kalona started toward the old woman when a tall, lanky young boy raced down the street and subdued the old woman by wrapping his arms around her. The younger woman began pounding on the poor boy yelling, "Let go of my mother! Don't hurt my mother!"

Crooked Foot's wife continued screaming hateful words. "It's your fault! You made him kill the gihli ... the poor gihli! You made him kill our protector!"

Suddenly, Adanvdo Alsgida approached. As the old Uku neared, the manic widow stopped struggling and shouted at him with madness in her eyes, "My husband is dead because of you!"

Adanvdo gasped! The daughter confirmed, "Father died last night. She blames you, Uku."

Adanvdo was stunned. He motioned for Atselvdi to turn loose the now quiet widow.

The struggle had left the boy's hair disheveled and his clothes appeared to be on sideways. As Atselvdi shifted his clothes and pushed his hair back from his eyes, his great-grandfather addressed the widow with tears in his eyes, "May I see my old friend?"

The deep sadness in Adanvdo Alsgida's eyes melted the anger of the widow and she began sobbing.

The daughter took her mother by the arm and led her toward their house. Atselvdi took his grieving great-grandfather by the arm and followed, still pushing and poking at his unruly coiffure with his free hand.

Kalona was stunned. She started to follow but her weary body protested. The overwhelmed old woman dropped to her knees, rocked back on her heels and put her head in her hands. *What's next? Do more tragedies await?*

What was the world coming to? Abductions. Death. Rage. The harmony and balance that had made Tsikohi a paradise for so many years had suddenly been disrupted. What had they done? Maybe there was someone who had transgressed and brought on the wrath of the spirits.

Her weary mind's eye rolled through the town's roll: searching for a suspect; searching for a troublemaker; searching for a heretic. She began to doubt even herself. Perhaps the citizens of Tsikohi had grown complacent and the great Apportioner was sending them a message.

Kalona fell forward clutching her face as the back of her hands dropped onto the gravelly street. She felt utterly powerless.

Adanvdo was in shock. How could this be? He had not sensed anything wrong with Crooked Foot. Besides, whatever might have been placed under him should have been transferred to the gihli in the ritual.

Had Atselvdi not remembered the words? Maybe he had said a curse instead of the sacred words. *I should have gone with him, he thought. No, Atselvdi knows the words. Perhaps Crooked Foot succumbed to his sadness.*

Adanvdo entered the bedroom of Crooked Foot with the aid of his great-grandson. He found the corpse not on his bed, but lying on his back, curled up on the floor. His face was frozen in a scream and his eyes still held the horror of what he had last seen in death's throes!

The old Uku knelt beside the dead man and looked into his horror-laden eyes. A film was starting to dull the once vivid gaze. The old man's mouth was open wide with strange discoloration encircling it.

Adanvdo recognized the pose. He had seen it many years before on the body of Dalala, the vivacious girl who had been his friend and companion before he left the trade caravan to settle down in Tsikohi. It was the face she wore after his brother had murdered her. He had seen the horror stricken pose on his wife's face after the birth of their child, Kalona. Both had felt the horror of his evil brother seeking them out to steal their lives, to sequester their souls for his treasury.

The dead man's shirt was bloody and sunken with a suspicious crease in it. Adanvdo pulled up the shirt to reveal a gaping hole in the dead man's chest. The stunned Uku shook his head in dismay and sat back. It was the same wound he had seen on Dalala.

Atselvdi knelt beside his mentor and studied the strange corpse. He had never seen anything like it, nor had his great-grandfather ever told him about anything like it.

"What happened to him, Grandfather?"

"Witch!"

Atselvdi's heart skipped a beat and fear gripped his stomach. "A witch?"

Adanvdo looked up at his innocent grandson. He knew his grandson had never seen a witch nor had he ever discussed the dark side with him. He had never told him about his brother, Tsisgili, the evil witch that had killed Dalala, his wife, his wife's sister, and his mother so many years before.

"A witch did this," Adanvdo clarified.

The priest and his apprentice sat in silence allowing the gravity of the event to sink in.

At last, Adanvdo closed the eyes of Crooked Foot, forced his mouth shut, and pulled down his bloody shirt. With his grandson's help, they managed to pick up and lay him back on the bed. Atselvdi recited the blessing for safe passage to the upper world as Adanvdo drew a blanket over the deceased man. He retrieved a sacred necklace from his pouch and placed it on the victim's chest and then hung sacred beads over the door.

The old Uku patted his apprentice on the back sympathetically as the apprentice finished his chant. Atselvdi hooked his arm under his great-grandfather's and supported him as they exited the room.

Adanvdo and Atselvdi greeted the dead man's survivors outside. Adanvdo addressed his widow, "His death is most foul. A great curse was put under him and no one should enter his room. I will personally take care of the cleansing and burial."

The widow's eyes grew large and she grasped her throat and began to wail loudly. Her daughter and granddaughter physically supported her and joined her lament.

The priests shuffled out leaving the family to grieve. They were both completely devastated by what they had seen. As they stepped outside, a voice whispered from the shadows, "Tsisgili!"

20

*"I felt confident that the
barking gihli was keeping
away the witch."*

Adanvdo Alsgida stopped but did not face the whispering shadow. A quiet voice whispered the name of his evil brother again, "Tsisgili." He recognized the voice of Sali. Adanvdo nudged his grandson. "Go see about your grandmother."

Atselvdi stared into his grandfather's eyes silently protesting. But he could see the resolve in Adanvdo's eyes, so he reluctantly trudged off. Adanvdo asked his long-time colleague, "Have you checked the tomb?"

Sali shook his head no and started up the street toward the western exit. Adanvdo joined him. "How did you hear about this?"

Sali took a deep breath, "I had not heard the gihli barking since yesterday morning. I decided to check on him."

Adanvdo did not understand. Sali explained, "I fed him the witch's tea."

"You fed the gihli the witch's tea?"

Sali's silence answered the question. Finally, Sali confessed, "When the gihli stopped barking, I assumed it meant that the witch had given up and had gone."

The Uku shook his head. The irony fed his grief and a tear ran down his cheek as a pang of remorse gripped his heart. No doubt, the dog had managed to keep the witch away from the old man until ... until he had sent the dog to the Nightland."

"How did you know there was a witch stalking our old friend?"

Sali was quiet for a long moment. Then he whispered, "I didn't know who he had come for ... I thought it might be me."

Adanvdo huffed in disgust. "Did you even know there was sickness placed under the family?"

Sali shook his head and then looked up to the sky. "It was the dark night before the new moon. I was walking home from the Council House very late. As I approached our old friend's house, I heard a raven squawk and looked up to glimpse sparks trailing off in the distance!"

Sali glanced at Adanvdo to see if he understood the significance. "The gihli must have heard my gasp, or perhaps he saw the flash of light. At any rate, he began barking compulsively and it gave me the idea. The gihli could provide advanced warning if the witch returned."

Adanvdo felt a pang in his stomach. Often mistaken for a falling star, the witch left a trail of sparks when he flew across the sky in the shape of a raven. Has the most evil witch of all returned?

Sali continued, "I felt confident that the barking gihli was keeping away the witch."

Adanvdo nodded but he was angry! The old priest should have come to him with such important information. Now a friend had exchanged his life for the evil benefit of the witch.

As the two old priests trudged across the meadow, they could see in the morning light that the megalith was intact. But they continued up to it and walked around it to make sure.

Adanvdo was confounded. "Do you think he managed to escape without leaving a sign?"

Sali closed his eyes. Adanvdo had another question, "Why the old man?"

Sali considered the point before answering. "If you were looking for a weak man and a healthy man, who would you choose?"

Adanvdo conceded the point. Sali posed the only plausible conclusion. "Only the Raven Mocker knows how to steal a man's souls to add their years to his own. Only your brother, Tsisgili, mutilated his victims to steal their souls. We only know of two Raven Mockers. If Tsisgili is still entombed in this stone that leaves your father."

Adanvdo was stunned. He had not even considered his father—the original Raven Mocker witch. There was no doubt that his father could do it. He knew how to do it. And he had to be nearing the end of his life and needed to do it to extend his years. "There is no one else, is there?"

Sali shook his head and started back to the village. Adanvdo trudged along beside him deep in thoughtful remorse. He whispered his doubts, "I can't believe he WOULD DO IT."

Sali paused. "It doesn't sound like him. Perhaps he got desperate."

"But why would he pick a kind and harmless man?"

Sali offered, "Instead of some cruel, deserving person?"

Adanvdo flinched at Sali's satire. He waited for Sali's explanation. Sali rubbed his chin. "Why don't you ask him?"

Adanvdo's stomach started spinning. His memories flashed back to that summer day when he was pacing in front of the house waiting for his wife, Wadulisi, to give birth to their first child. Sali was sitting next to the covered porch studying his fire for signs of lurking evil.

He had glanced up the street and immediately recognized the formidable hulk, his cousin Big Elk, and beside him an old woman that turned out to be his mother whom he had not seen since he was a small boy.

His memories jumped ahead. Big Elk had just congratulated him for becoming the father of a beautiful little girl when Sali's fire exploded flattening the old man on his back. Two flashes exited the side windows of the house and streaked to the west meadow. He had raced inside to find Wadulisi pressed up against the wall behind her bed with horror frozen on her face. His mother lay crumpled on the floor like a discarded rag and Wadulisi's older sister lay on the floor on a pallet of blood.

His friend, Gray Wolf, was battling Wadulisi's younger sister trying to retrieve the baby from her grasp. Her just born baby lay beneath her on the floor still in its bloody birth coat.

His memories now took him to the meadow where his father in his raven-feathered cape was battling his evil brother dressed in his black, speckled owl-feathered cape.

His father hurled his stone spear into his evil son and the magical spear had engulfed Tsisgili and entombed him in a great stone megalith.

After the great battle, Adanvdo and Big Elk had tracked his father to his Cliffside abode. It had been a poignant meeting that had left him yearning for more. But subsequent visits had been hurtful battles between father and son, between priest and witch.

His father had beseeched Adanvdo to seek immortality and could not understand his son's reluctance to use his knowledge to prolong his life. Adanvdo had argued that the consequences of witchcraft were not worth the price of a purloined life. Adanvdo had beseeched his father to give up the life of the witch and turn to the white path.

In time, the bitterness of their irreconcilable differences separated them and Adanvdo stopped visiting his father. His father cherished his privacy and he had not disturbed his father in years.

Conflicting thoughts were spinning in his head. He was emotionally devastated, but there were so many unanswered questions. How was the mysterious death of the old man connected to the kidnapping? He remembered that Kalona had told him Sali blamed a witch for the kidnapping. "Why would the Raven Mocker attack an old man when he has three young girls to feast upon?"

Sali paused again and stared up at him with questioning eyes. "Is HE one of the three kidnappers?"

Adanvdo blinked rapidly. "Three kidnappers?"

"Tracks." Sali resumed walking. "There is not likely a connection."

*The witch felt no remorse
for his victim whose life he
had stolen.*

THE HAGGARD OLD WITCH sat next to the crackling flames and trembled as his rotting stomach digested the sweet tasting, tender meat he had just consumed. Almost immediately he could feel the healing effects of the delicacy as his rejuvenated blood carried new life throughout his body.

He sat for a moment experiencing the feeling of his energy rebuilding. He mumbled the sacred words—some of the words so archaic that not even he remembered their meaning. But, words so powerful and absolutely necessary for the transfer to work.

It was the most evil of all conjures—the transfer of a victim's remaining life to the witch. The transfer involved capturing the askina, the four souls, of the victim. First, the essence of the person's individualism, personality, and consciousness, and the first soul to leave the person that escapes with the person's dying breath! To capture this part of the askina, he had sucked out the last breath of the victim.

The witch must consume this soul since it is the catalyst that energizes the other souls to coalesce and revive the witch's decaying askina.

E:hihyvga tsada:nvdo
[Bring me your soul!]
Tsi:sgili gv:hnage:i
[I am the black owl of the night]
Sv:no:yi ditsado:ida
[Night is your name.]
Tsana:hwi u:hyoha
[The owl hunts your heart.][...]

He reached over and squeezed fresh bile from the victim's liver over the victim's heart roasting on the spit above the firepit. The succulent juices from the heart and bile spewed as they dripped into the fire.

He breathed in the wonderfully sweet smell of the burning juices. As he let the basted heart roast, he scooped marrow from the crushed rib bone lying on the hearth and placed his two fingers into his mouth to suck off the sweet marrow.

Then he carefully sliced off another piece of the heart with his knife and held it with his thumb against the knife blade. He raised it to his mouth and chewed and smacked and slurped on the delicious slice of meat.

With each bite, he could feel the individual souls energizing his waning body. He could feel the second soul of the liver cleansing and expelling the poisons of his aged liver.

He could feel the soul of the heart surging through his bloodstream. He could feel the fourth soul from the bone marrow, filling him with strength and energy. His life was renewing and his skin color changing from bluish-gray to healthy bronze.

The witch felt no remorse for his victim whose life he had stolen. He was not haunted by visions of the fear the horrified man had experienced when he was attacked by the flaming raven. He remembered the joy of shifting his shape from a raven into a panther and then into a hideous wolf and then into a ferocious bear. All he cared about was that his victim had many years left on his life, and now those years were his.

Atselvdi found his grandmother lying on her bed. She looked years older and tired, too tired to speak. He slumped on the bed beside her unable to decide whether to share with her the shocking discovery of the murder or not. His grandmother had always been the one he could turn to for comfort and for plain and simple explanations.

He knew that she would not hold back; that she would shoot straight; she would share with him what she knew about witches. He took a deep breath and phrased his question carefully, "Grandmother, have you ever seen a witch?"

His question was answered by the rattle of her gentle snore. Atselvdi chuckled. He would let her sleep. She needed the rest.

He trudged back into the main room and sat beside the hearth. The crackling fire looked lazy and melancholy. It was sending only trace smoke messages to the sky, such a striking contrast to the fire raging in his head.

As a kid, he had heard fanciful stories from his little friends about witches and their amazing powers. But, his grandfather had avoided speaking of them. When he had asked about witches, his grandfather had seemed uneasy and had reluctantly promised to discuss it with him someday. Perhaps today was finally that someday.

No one had ever said that witches were violent or mutilated people. They were supposed to be mysterious, or clever, or sinister. They played tricks on people, or put the sickness under them, or conjured a curse, or mixed up potions for nefarious purposes, or hung around sick people as harbingers of death.

Strange old women or reclusive old men were the witches that had been pointed out to him by his enlightened friends. They were weird and sometimes a little scary, but no witch he had ever seen or heard of was capable of the evil he saw that morning.

*How could Atselvdi
comprehend such a bizarre
history after having lived
his whole life in an idyllic
world of peace and harmony?*

Adanvdo pushed back the door cover and discovered Atselvdi sitting by the hearth. The young boy looked at him with expectant eyes. That subject he had most dreaded discussing with his great-grandson could not be put off any longer.

Adanvdo shuffled across the room and took up his usual place by the fire. How to begin? He pulled his pipe from the hearth and picked up a pouch filled with sacred tobacco. He wanted to impress upon his grandson the dire anathema associated with witchcraft. The consequence, the curse associated with the decision to go down the dark path.

He tamped down the tobacco in the bowl of the pipe and then retrieved a splint to light it. Perhaps he could use his father as an example. He had even entertained taking his grandson to see the lonely, desolate life his father was forced to live because of his life choice. But he feared his father would try to convince his grandson as he always did with him that immortality was worth the curse. No, he was not yet ready to share with his grandson the awful shame hiding in his roots.

He puffed thoughtfully on the pipe. To young people who have not learned of the consequences of bad decisions, witchcraft can seem attractive and desirable. Youthful minds filter reality through porous sieves of naiveté. Inexperienced brains fail to detect the nuances that painful experiences embed in our comprehension. Immature reasoning focuses on fanciful benefits overlooking the cause and effect of undesired consequences.

The reluctant teacher let smoke find its way out as his subconscious alerted him of the glaring eyes of his anxiously waiting student. "Are you troubled by what you saw this morning?"

"Yes, Grandfather."

Adanvdo drew on his pipe again. He could not continue to put off his great-grandson, but it was a delicate matter and he must be careful.

"Witchcraft is a dark path lined with temptations that even intelligent men sometimes fall for. It takes a wise man to see through the evil seduction."

He could see that his grandson was bursting with questions, questions that posed a barrier to the lessons and cautions he was so thoughtfully framing. He passed him the pipe. Atselvdi took a quick, token puff. "Why would anyone want to murder another so cruelly? Was he angry?"

The curious boy returned the pipe impatiently. Adanvdo took a deep breath, grasped the pipe by the stem and dumped out the tobacco on the hearth. This was not going to be a counsel; this was to be a training session.

"He was not angry. Our crippled old friend had something so coveted by the witch, that he was able to set aside his humanity."

Atselvdi's face contorted, expressing without words his confusion. Adanvdo looked into the dwindling fire and reached over to add a log. "This witch is on a level all his own. I know of only three that have developed the skill of stealing a man's souls."

Atselvdi's eyes widened. Adanvdo continued, "A man has four souls. When a man dies, the conscious soul departs the body immediately. It sometimes lurks nearby until it can get its bearings. It may even expose itself as a spirit."

Adanvdo had his grandson's undivided attention. "That is why we do not speak the name of the dead. If he hears his name, he might come back instead of searching for his ancestors in the Nightland."

"Have you ever seen a spirit, Grandfather?"

Adanvdo paused to recollect. "Yes, but the spirits I have seen and called upon were not lost. They came to me knowing their place. They understood their powers and their situation."

Atselvdi fidgeted impatiently while his grandfather spoke. He was ready with another question: "Who were the three witches?"

Adanvdo frowned. The three witches? He was deceived by the question because of his discussion earlier with Sali. Had Atselvdi heard the abductors were witches? Then he remembered his comment about knowing only three witches capable of stealing souls. "Oh, the first was Nunyunuwi. He was a giant that feasted on hunters who lost their way and found themselves in his forest."

"What happened to him?" Atselvdi prompted his grandfather when he paused to remember the legend.

Adanvdo looked into the eyes of his eager grandson. "Your ... a young boy, about your age, discovered Nunyunuwi's secret. That boy ..."

Adanvdo did not want to disclose to his grandson that the young boy was his father and Atselvdi's great-great-grandfather. "That boy had chosen the dark path. He wanted to save an old couple, both witches, from dying. They had taught him all they knew, but they could not teach him how to live forever. He had learned that Nunyunuwi knew the secret of immortality so he went to him to uncover his secret."

Adanvdo could see that Atselvdi was eager to hear more. Had he opened a world to his grandson that would lure him in? He added another log to the fire then continued the story. "The young man had also learned that Nunyunuwi had a weakness. The cannibal witch's powers were drained in the presence of a menstruating woman."

Atselvdi's face contorted as if tasting a bitter fruit. Adanvdo continued, "The young boy, using the knowledge he had acquired from the two old witches, concocted a potion for his girlfriend and used her to neutralize Nunyunuwi and forced him to reveal his secrets."

Atselvdi's face stared back in disbelief. Adanvdo had shared with his naïve grandson an incredible tale that sounded more like a fantastic children's story than a depiction of real life events. As he reviewed this tale in his mind, it even seemed unbelievable to him.

How could Atselvdi comprehend such a bizarre history after having lived his whole life in an idyllic world of peace and harmony? How could Atselvdi know that his experience during his short lifetime was more abnormal than the extraordinary, grotesque and chaotic world that had proceeded?

"That really happened, Grandfather? That's really possible?"

Adanvdo felt nauseous. He sensed that his grandson was intrigued by the story, perhaps even excited by the prospect. He had to show his grandson the consequences. He had to tell the rest of the story. "Yes, it sounds fantastic. One might be tempted to find it enchanting, mysterious, and wondrous. Many have been drawn into traveling down the dark path expecting marvelous and phenomenal rewards."

He paused and engaged his grandson's eyes with his most dire and portentous stare. "But only disaster and tragedy await the protégé of the dark powers. Nunyunuwi was captured and burned in a blazing inferno lit from the sacred fire. The young boy was condemned by his village, his family, and all of the Ani Yun Wiya, the real people for choosing to become a witch. He has lived a dismal and lonely life of solitude and shame."

Atselvdi looked down at the ground. It was a lot for a virtuous child ignorant of the dark path, raised in the light; only cognizant of the white path; only exposed to harmony and balance and the right way. "Who was the third?"

The third! Adanvdo shivered with the thought. Even though his brother was dead and entombed in a stone megalith, he still brought fear and dread to him. "He was the most evil of all men, of all witches. He was incapable of remorse. He was incapable of love or compassion. He brutally mutilated his victims."

"Like the old man?"

Adanvdo was startled by his grandson's connection. "Yes."

"So, he is the witch?"

"He is the witch entombed in the megalith in the meadow."

Atselvdi gasped. "He has come back from the grave?"

Atselvdi's questions were too much for his grandfather. He did not have the answers. The boy was asking the questions he was searching for answers for himself. "No. He is still in the tomb."

The astute apprentice presented the only logical conclusion. "So, it is the boy who defeated Nunyunuwi?"

Adanvdo looked at his perceptive grandson. "I don't know. I don't think so. But I don't know who else it could be."

"Where is he, Grandfather? We must track him down. He must pay."

Adanvdo snapped back, "We do not know that he is the one. It is not his style."

Adanvdo did not want to admit that his grandson's simplistic reasoning had merit. He tried to rationalize that it was more complex. There was more to it than his grandson could understand, but he could not convince himself. "Grandson, we must not speak of this to anyone."

Atselvdi looked questioningly at his great-grandfather. Adanvdo explained, "We do not understand the connection to the abduction, or even if there is a connection. We must not add to the grief already being suffered."

Atselvdi stared away in thought. Reluctantly, he agreed.

"Return to the Clan Council House and resume the blessings for our kidnapped girls. I will join you soon, but first I must consult with Chief Waya."

"But Grandfather ..."

Adanvdo did not answer. Atselvdi watched his great-grandfather trudge away. He followed him up the street.

As Atselvdi topped the hill to return to the Clan House, he glanced back down the street toward his house. He stopped abruptly. Chief Waya Gigage was talking with his grandmother! She grasped her chest and the War Chief grabbed her arm to steady her. Atselvdi knew instantly that he had brought news about the abduction. He turned to shout at his grandfather, but Adanvdo was already nearing the Council House.

The whole village watched silently as the search party emerged from the woods.

Wᴀᴇɴ Aᴅᴀɴᴠᴅᴏ ʀᴇᴀᴄʜᴇᴅ ᴛʜᴇ Council House, he found it buzzing with news from the search party. Clan Priests, old warriors, and many concerned citizens were crowded around the messenger listening intently to his account of the bloody scene he found at the Tagwa's camp. Everyone hushed when Adanvdo entered.

Adanvdo was facing the room full of pitying faces, and his pulse quickened. "Tell me what you found."

The crowd stirred uncomfortably until the messenger approached their anxious Uku raising his hands, "Alihelit-sidasdi is alive. She has been through a harrowing ordeal and ... well, she is unconscious."

"The other girls?"

The messenger lowered his head and whispered, "Murdered."

"Kidnapper?"

"Three Tagwa renegades. They were brutally stabbed to death and dumped into the river before the search party arrived." He looked up into the eyes of Adanvdo. "Ali was found with the bloody knife. One girl had been staked to the ground. The other was tied to a tree."

Adanvdo frowned and studied the messenger. "You think Ali killed the Tagwas?"

The messenger shrugged and exhaled as if exasperated. "Who else?"

Adanvdo looked into space trying to understand. The messenger offered another theory. "Unless the Tagwas got into a fight and killed each other?"

Adanvdo felt his body go numb. "Chief Waya?"

"He has gone to your house to inform you and Chief Kalona."

Adanvdo stumbled out of the Council House. He felt the strong hands of sacred fire tender, Stoker, grasping his arm, "Shall I help you home?"

Adanvdo took a deep breath to regain his strength. "I can make it. I should go inform Atselvdi."

Stoker reluctantly released his fragile Uku and watched him walk off.

Halfway up the grand avenue, Adanvdo spotted Chief Waya striding down the hill. His stern, determined demeanor changed to concern when he recognized Adanvdo. He rushed up to Adanvdo and declared, "Adanvdo Alsgida, I have been looking for you."

"I have heard the news."

"The search party should be returning at any time. I have informed Kalona. She has headed out to the meadow to greet them."

Adanvdo glanced about nervously then moved closer to the Chief. "There is a matter I must discuss with you."

Waya waited. Adanvdo glanced about again, and pointed to the house of the deceased Crooked Foot. "The old man has been murdered."

Always in control, Chief Waya's expression remained unchanged. He waited for Adanvdo's explanation. "He was visited by the witch."

Waya adjusted his head slightly to one side, "THE witch?"

Adanvdo continued, "Remember the girl from the caravan years ago? The horror in her eyes, the gaping mouth ... the chest wound?"

Waya stared at the house of the murdered man. "But, wasn't that ... your brother?"

"I have always thought so."

Waya looked toward the meadow. "The megalith?"

"The megalith is intact."

"Where is the old man now?"

"He is in his room. I have placed the beads over his door and told the family to stay away. I handled the cleansing myself last night."

"Who knows about this?"

"Sali, Atselvdi."

Waya grabbed Adanvdo's arm. "Take me to see him."

As they walked, Adanvdo repeated, "The megalith is intact."

Waya did not respond. Adanvdo did not offer further explanation.

The whole village watched silently as the search party emerged from the woods. The village's top warrior, Wahuhu Adawehi, led the way stoically, looking at no one and trying to hide the pain in his heart. Chief Waya and Adanvdo approached him. Waya asked, "The Tagwas?"

"I left guards with them at the camp."

Waya waved him on. He and Adanvdo looked at the procession as it passed. Two warriors trailed along behind Wahuhu carrying the corpse of Walelu on a make-shift carrier followed by two more with Delagalis.

Behind them, Tawodi Gvnagei trudged along with his head down and his hands grasping the poles of Alihelitsidasdi's carrier. She lay motionless, curled up in a fetal position covered by Wahuhu's bloody white-feathered cape. She appeared to be in a trance. Waya Usti held the other end of the poles and stared sadly at the girl. Tlomeha Usdi followed some distance behind, clearly saddened and forlorn.

Kalona burst from the crowd and dug her arms in around her little Ali. The traumatized girl did not respond. She appeared to be completely oblivious to the world around her. The heartbroken grandmother stroked the comatose girl's face as she looked up at Adanvdo. Tears flowed down the cheeks of Kalona as the old Uku began to chant a song.

Agonizing screams revealed that the mothers of the dead girls had discovered their daughters.

Chief Waya touched Adanvdo's shoulder. "We will speak of the other matter another time."

Adanvdo nodded without stopping his song. Waya approached Kalona and whispered, "Let them continue, Kalona. They will carry her home for you."

Kalona walked beside the carrier holding Ali's hand while Tawodi and Waya Usti carried her into the bedroom in the back of the house. They set the carrier down gently in the center of the floor and then Waya Usti lifted the unconscious girl from the carrier and placed her onto the lower bunk as directed by Kalona. He moved aside to allow the grandmother to sit beside her granddaughter and comfort her.

Tawodi watched for a moment and then looked at Waya Usti and gestured toward the door. Waya Usti looked at Tawodi, then at the girl who held his heart and then back at his cousin. Tawodi understood, gathered up the carrier and left.

Waya Usti stood quietly, protectively, at the end of the bunk and watched his love who appeared tranquil as if in a peaceful, deep sleep. Kalona seemed unaware that he was there as she sat caressing the poor girl's hand and weeping.

Outside the house, Tawodi saw a tall, slender girl standing with her mother across from the house. Tawodi approached the sobbing girl. "You are Ali's friend?"

The pretty young girl attempted a smile as her mother looked sternly at the brash young man.

Tawodi felt inexplicably and completely inadequate in the presence of these two beautiful women. He tried to put on his very best manners. "I am Tawodi Gvnagei. My mother is Tawadi Aji. We are Ani Tsisqua."

The young girl gleamed. Her mother glared.

Tawodi explained, "I was with the search party."

The Mother let her scowling face relax into a more grateful, yet sad demeanor. She looked down and dabbed her eyes and nose with a cloth yielding to her daughter. "My mother is Wananahi, Ani Gotegewi clan. I am Amadohi. How is she?"

Tawodi looked down and thought for a moment, then answered, "Well, she was not injured physically by the abductors."

Tawodi looked at Amadohi and her mother for their reaction. They forced thankful smiles. Then they looked at him questioningly, waiting for the rest of his report.

"Yes ... well ... she is sleeping now. What she witnessed and experienced was more than anyone should ever have to experience. I guess her mind has sort of shut down temporarily."

The mother and daughter stood silently for a moment. Amadohi admired the eyes of Tawodi and he thought he may have actually felt her eyes twinkle! The mother looked at her daughter and registered a new concern on her face. The worried mother grabbed her daughter's arm. "Wado, Tawodi Gvnagei." Amadohi smiled sweetly as her mother scowled at the huge young man and led her away.

"She was amazingly strong and violent. If the other warriors had not helped us, I am sure she would've killed Father and me."

The house where Alihelitsidasdi slept soon filled with friends and family bringing food and potions and well-meaning advice.

There was much whispering about what might have happened at the fateful campsite. No one could believe that the frail little Alihelitsidasdi could have taken on three massive Tagwa warriors and conquered them.

Some theorized that the three girls surprised the warriors and managed to kill them but not before Walelu and Delagalis were killed in the attempt. Some theorized that the Tagwa warriors killed each other in a deadly fight over the last surviving girl.

Some theorized that a combination was possible. Perhaps, one Tagwa killed the other two and Alihelitsidasdi got the jump on him while he was distracted with Delagalis.

And so it went. But no one got it right.

Atselvdi entered the crowded house and pushed through leading his frail great-grandfather. Adanvdo's face was filled with apprehension as he shuffled along behind his great-grandson.

When Kalona saw her father, she burst into tears again. She pushed through to her father and hooked her arm into his. Adanvdo looked at his daughter with eyes that indicated he needed reassurance.

"She is still sleeping. She has no serious physical wounds, and I think she has found a safe place in her mind."

Adanvdo looked down for a moment. Kalona knew that he was considering what blessing would be appropriate for this very unusual circumstance.

When he looked back at her, she knew he had decided and led him to his great-granddaughter. As they moved across the room, a hush followed. Respectfully, one by one the speculators and well-wishers departed.

Adanvdo whispered instructions to his great-grandson and apprentice who obediently went to the old Uku's room to fetch the articles he requested.

Adanvdo was startled by the shadowy figure standing at the end of his great-granddaughter's bunk! Kalona gasped when she also spotted Waya Usti!

"Forgive me, Grandmother," the nervous, young sentinel stammered using the term for respect. "Forgive me, Grandfather. I did not mean to startle you."

The old Uku and his daughter stood dumbfounded. Waya Usti explained, "I offer myself to guard your granddaughter. I will protect her with my life!"

"Who are you?" Kalona demanded.

"I am Waya Usti, son of Waya Agisi of the Wolf clan. I was with the search party and it was I who first found Ali."

"What's going on?" Atselvdi demanded as he entered the room and found his grandmother and great-grandfather appearing to be alarmed by the presence of Waya Usti.

"Help your grandfather, Atselvdi. I must have a talk with this young man."

Kalona led Waya Usti to the next room.

Adanvdo removed his cloak and gently examined the sleeping girl. A tear rolled down the side of his nose and collected in the corner of his mouth. He ignored the tear as he began murmuring a chant.

As he muttered, he waved his hand across her body and bounced slightly. Atselvdi placed a gourd rattle in his hand and began chanting with his great-grandfather.

In the main room of the house, Kalona invited Waya Usti to sit with her by the hearth.

"Tell me what you saw," she implored of him as she placed wood on the fire.

"Yes, Grandmother," Waya Usti began respectfully. "It was very early this morning and we were heading up the canyon following the Agusa Jisdu when I heard a girl's scream. It was coming from up the canyon, so I ran toward the scream. When I reached the campsite, the first thing I saw was ..."

Kalona looked at the young man who had paused so abruptly. She could see in his eyes that he was remembering something horrible.

He stared into the fire as he continued, "... Walelu was tied to a tree and was naked and covered in blood and hanging limp. Her face and ... body ... had been hacked to shreds."

The old woman gasped! Waya Usti looked up at a tearing Kalona with painful eyes. "I could tell that she was ... dead."

Kalona touched the young man's shoulder. He continued, "I drew my knife and ran into the campsite looking for Ali. She was sitting on the ground with ... the other girl in her arms. That girl was tied to stakes in the ground and Ali was desperately trying to pull her free."

Waya Usti looked at Ali's grandmother again. "She had been hacked to death, also."

Kalona clasped her mouth and squeezed trying to hold on to her emotions.

"I ran over to Ali and tried to hug her and comfort her, but she must have thought that I was a Tagwa warrior returning to grab her because she threw me off her and dove at me with a huge knife. I barely moved out of the way in time. Father grabbed her from behind and tried to restrain her arms while I grabbed her wrist and tried to wrestle the bloody knife away from her."

Kalona began to sob quietly. Waya Usti did not notice. His eyes were fixed on the hearth, and his mind was reliving the episode. "She was amazingly strong and violent. If the other warriors had not helped us, I am sure she would've killed Father and me."

Waya Usti paused again as the visions of that encounter ran through his mind. He shook his head in amazement at the strength of delicate Ali.

"Truthfully, she was whipping all five of us until she recognized Wahuhu."

Kalona looked puzzled. Her silence brought Waya Usti back and he looked at the questioning old woman.

"When Wahuhu walked up and spoke to her, she recognized him and realized who we were. She stopped fighting and broke down. I held her and reassured her and she started trembling so Wahuhu gave her his owl-feathered cloak. ... I'm sure it's ruined."

Grave concern showed on Kalona's face as she asked, "Was she ... naked, also?"

"Yes ..." Waya Usti confessed sheepishly, "and covered in blood. I've never seen so much blood!"

"Oh!" Kalona Ehlawei shrieked.

Waya Usti assumed that she had jumped to false conclusions and quickly added, "But all of the blood on Ali was from the others!"

Realizing that the boy had misunderstood her concern, she asked, "Where were the Tagwas?"

"They were all three floating in the river, dead. The river was red with blood. It made some of the warriors sick."

"And you think Ali killed them?"

"She must have. The one girl was tied to a tree and the other tied to the ground."

After a long, thoughtful pause, Kalona confessed, "I just can't imagine it."

"I wouldn't have believed it possible, either, but I felt her strength and determination."

Waya Usti reflected upon this as Kalona studied him. He sensed that she was not convinced.

Kalona looked away. There was only one rational explanation. Her granddaughter had gotten the help of the Little People after all. She quietly whispered, "Wado, Nvwoti."

In the bedroom, the blessing for healing had begun. But the real blessing was that Alihelitsidasdi's mind hid from her the memory of that horrific day she spent in Tagwa captivity.

In time, it would be revealed to her in little pieces through her dreams and nightmares. Perhaps exhaustion; perhaps familiar surroundings and the comfort and safety of her own bed; perhaps the calming sound of her great-grandfather singing to her in his soft, calming manner; perhaps the warm, motherly feeling of a grandmother's loving caress; but for whatever reason, the young girl with extraordinary survival instincts just slept.

*"The wounds appeared
to have been inflicted
by the bloody knife
Alihelitsidasdi was
holding when we arrived."*

As Chief Waya, Wahuhu, and Adanvdo walked up the street toward Sali's hut, Adanvdo directed Waya's attention to the unsuspecting Wahuhu with his eyes. The Chief reassured him, "I trust Wahuhu completely. I want him to know everything."

Wahuhu jerked his head around questioning the comment. Waya stopped and addressed his assistant confidentially, "Do you remember long ago when Tsikohi was visited by the two witches and they battled in the meadow?"

Wahuhu glanced at Adanvdo. "I remember that Adanvdo's family was attacked by an evil witch, the one called Tsisgili. I remember that a mysterious witch rescued the village and entombed Tsisgili in the stone megalith. That is what I remember."

Waya continued, "A witch may have visited us again."

Wahuhu's face reflected his concern, "The Tagwa? You think the Tagwa were witches?"

Waya paused before explaining, "While you were away, Sali warned us in counsel that witches were involved in the kidnapping. We were skeptical."

Waya glanced at Adanvdo and then continued carefully, "But, here in the village, Adanvdo believes that the old man living over there," Waya pointed at Crooked Foot's house rather than say his name which might call him back from his search for the ancestors, "was killed by a witch."

Wahuhu considered the new information and stated, "He died while we were in pursuit of the Tagwa."

Then he frowned. "You believe they are connected?"

"That is what we want to discuss with Sali."

They found Sali sitting by the fire in his hut appearing to be sleeping in his usual prone position. Adanvdo took the initiative to speak, "Osiyo, old friend. Chief Waya Gigage, Wahuhu Adawehi and I would like counsel with you."

Without opening his eyes, the placid old priest nonchalantly gestured for them to join him by the fire.

As they sat, Chief Waya took over. "I want Wahuhu to describe for you and the Uku the mutilation he witnessed at the Tagwa campsite."

Adanvdo Noticed that Sali was making no attempt to prepare a pipe. The contrary old priest loved to smoke in private and occasionally shared his tobacco with a friend, but he rarely participated in the ritual of smoking during a counsel. In fact, the ancient priest hardly acknowledged their presence.

Wahuhu shifted nervously and then began, "First, I found two Tagwas floating in the stream. Their bodies were punctured by many knife wounds. The wounds appeared to have been inflicted by the bloody knife Alihelitsidasdi was holding when we arrived."

The old warrior respectfully turned to Adanvdo to assure him he meant no disrespect and then continued, "The river was red with blood, but I saw a third Tagwa submerged in the water. His face was contorted in a permanent expression of fear. His chest had been ripped open and he was entangled in his own intestines."

Sali's eyes popped open and he stared at Adanvdo. Adanvdo's eyes were wide as he glared back. They muttered their response in unison, "Another victim?"

Wahuhu blurted out before thinking, "Another?"

Waya summed it up for him. "It appears that the Tagwa, like our old crippled friend, was a victim of the witch."

Adanvdo explained, "The witch is after the souls of his victim and acquires them, partly, by extracting the heart, liver, and rib of his victim."

Waya added, "So, the wound to the Tagwa's chest would suggest that he was not just stabbed, but that perhaps he was gutted, as well."

Adanvdo added, "The Tagwa's wound is consistent with the old man's wounds."

There was silence as the four men contemplated the significance. Wahuhu asked, "So, you think a witch visited our village and the Tagwa campsite?"

Sali responded, "It is not likely a witch would pursue two victims that closely together."

Wahuhu showed alarm. "You think there are two witches?"

Waya looked at Adanvdo and appeared to be asking for his opinion with his eyes. Adanvdo watched Sali as he answered, "It would appear so."

The normally patient, quiet Wahuhu now appeared to be brimming with questions. "Where did they come from?"

Sali replied, "THAT is the question."

Wahuhu continued, "Why now?"

No one fielded this question. Wahuhu posed another question, "Will they strike again?"

Adanvdo thoughtfully answered, "It is not likely."

The head of the village military forces got to the point. "How do we defend ourselves?"

Adanvdo paused in hopes that Sali might offer a suggestion. His thoughts turned back to many years before when he and Sali and the previous village chiefs had devised a plan to prepare for a possible visit by Tsisgili. Adanvdo's stomach tensed when he remembered that their plan had failed miserably. They had neither detected Tsisgili's return nor been able to deal with him. It had taken the extraordinary skills of Kalanu Ahkyeliski, the first Raven Mocker, Adanvdo's father, to confront and defeat the evil witch. Adanvdo could think of nothing he had learned from that encounter that would help them now. He was eager to hear what Sali might have learned.

Wahuhu, seeing Waya's and Adanvdo's eyes trained on Sali, addressed the old sage, "It appears that the Tagwa were not witches, but victims of a witch?"

Sali grimaced and agreed. Adanvdo stared at the fire. He shared his concern, "I don't want Kalona to know about this. I have not told her much about her birth or the witches in the meadow."

Waya also expressed his concern, "No one should know about the witch or witches for now. Sali, I think you should declare that the Tagwa are not witches to allay any fears our friends may have. We will clean and enshroud their bodies and turn their fate over to the Blessed Women."

The room grew quiet. No one had any more to say, but their minds were full of questions and their hearts full of anxiety.

*"I don't know, but the
idea of burning them is
pretty popular."*

WAYA USTI HAD DECIDED to take a walk. He needed time alone to wind down and digest the last few days. He had exited the village through the east exit and strolled through the corn, bean, and squash fields, then down by the Long Man and was nearing the north exit when he could hear voices raised in argument. He stopped to listen and realized that the voices were coming from the village Council House. He decided to investigate.

The Council House was filled so he stood at the entrance to search for a place to sit. There was no order in the room. Heated discussions were occurring everywhere and all at once. Chief Waya Gigage, Wahuhu, Tawodi, and several other warriors were huddled around the Chief's chair.

Waya Usti spotted his father, Tlomeha Usdi, sitting all alone so he slipped unnoticed down the aisle and sat next to him.

"What's happening, Father?"

Tlomeha Usdi motioned toward the center of the Council House, "They are arguing over what to do with the Tagwa bodies. Before we knew who kidnapped the girls, the old priest, Sali, had convinced some that the abductors were witches and now they are insisting that he be asked to exercise the bodies and perform the burning ceremony. Some think that they should be treated as enemy combatants. The Chief wants to return the bodies to the Tagwas and to their mothers and fathers. But that idea isn't getting much support."

"Does Sali still believe they are witches?"

"I don't know, but the idea of burning them is pretty popular."

Chief Waya Gigage stood and waited for the crowd to get quiet. "The evil that these abductors have displayed is beyond the normal behavior of even a Tagwa warrior. But, our Uku has something to share with us."

Chief Waya sat and Adanvdo stood. "Sali and I have discussed this matter. We do not believe the Tagwa are witches."

The crowd in the room erupted. Clearly, most of them needed more reassurance. Adanvdo raised his hand and slowly the room quieted. "Has anyone ever heard of a Tagwa witch?"

There was grumbling among the crowd but no one offered an example. "Witchcraft is evil, there is no doubt, but the conjures and the wizardry require some degree of intelligence."

The crowd hushed, contemplated the implications, then erupted into laughter. Adanvdo sat down.

Chief Waya stood. "The three Tagwas that attacked us are renegades. The Great Chief in Katuwa does not consider their actions to be representative of the Tagwa people. I agree with him. We agree that they should be brought before our Blessed Women for judgment."

The crowd grumbled again, many in disagreement, hoping the young Tagwas actions would prompt a war against the Tagwa. Remembering the wars from years before, they wished for the annihilation of the Tagwa.

And there were those who felt they should be burned as witches. Those who agreed with the War Chief were few.

But the Chief had spoken and his word would be final and with that, Chief Waya Gigage asked for the general public to clear and called for a private session of the priests and distinguished warriors.

Chief Waya, Adanvdo, and Sali had decided to keep secret their concerns about a witch or possible witches. They were worried that if word got out that one of the Tagwas and Crooked Foot were victims of witchcraft, it might create a panic. They suspected that once people believed a witch was involved, it would be almost impossible to relieve their fears.

Tawodi Gvnagei was chosen to lead six other young warriors back to the Tagwa campsite to retrieve the bodies. As village Uku, Adanvdo Alsgida would normally accompany them on such an ominous duty, but, he was old and, understandably, wanted to remain in the village beside his granddaughter. Sali was next in line, being the elder priest in the village and the Uku's assistant. But he was much too frail for such a journey.

So the duty fell to the next in line, Ulogidv Unega, the priest of the Paint clan. But Ulogidv Unega surprised everyone by refusing! The priests silently waited for his explanation, but instead he nominated the Uku's apprentice, Atselvdi, to go in his place proclaiming that it was a job for a younger person.

The priests were shocked, but decided to honor Ulogidv Unega's request. They did so partly because Atselvdi was a good choice and partly because, although they would never admit it, it relieved them of the responsibility. So the Uku's apprentice was chosen to accompany Tawodi and the six other young warriors to retrieve the dead Tagwas.

After the council meeting, the War Chief received countless visits at his home by citizens concerned about Sali's statement that the abductors were witches. Adanvdo's declaration that he and Sali were convinced that the Tagwas were not witches had not appeased the masses. Sensing that the matter would need to be addressed more conclusively, he called in Sali, Adanvdo, and Wahuhu to discuss the matter again. They agreed that directing everyone's attention to the Tagwas and proving that they were not witches might dispel the worries about witchcraft. Then they could deal with the actual witch matter secretively. They also agreed that the Uku should incorporate protective measures and assurances for the retrieval party.

*Sali chuckled, blinked
his eyes, closed them and
answered, "Do the rabbits
challenge the foxes?"*

Gʀᴀɴᴅᴍᴏᴛʜᴇʀ Sᴜɴ ᴡᴀs ᴊᴜsᴛ rising when the chosen warriors arrived at the Council House. The Uku and his apprentice were already there. Atselvdi was stoking the sacred fire. His mentor had raked burning coals to one side of the hearth, formed them into the shape of the seven-sided Council House and was intently studying the smoke. The Uku reached into his medicine pouch and pulled out sacred tobacco. It was a special blend grown in secret and strengthened by its exposure to illuminating rays from the eastern sun. He sprinkled the tobacco over the fire. As the flakes of tobacco floated down over the symbolic hut constructed of glowing embers, the Uku muttered:

"Gha! Usv:i asgaya gvhnage:i!
[Listen! Black Man of the Night]
Galvladi Tsa:hlidho:hi:sdi.
[Who resides above.]
Nigv:nadv:na higo:lodi:sgi.

[The one who foresees everywhere]
Gohu:sdi tsadehli:do:hi nige:sv:na.
[You see everything.]
Ale hna:gwo doyu:ghodv ditsa:notsa tsadi
    tsadv:hnv:hi!"
[And you have stated that you tell the truth!]"

Atselvdi watched as the flakes of tobacco gently ignited as they floated down and settled beside the mound of embers. Half settled nearer the southwest corner, the other half collected at the northeast corner. Adanvdo muttered,

"Wado, Usv:i asgaya gvhnage:i!
[Thank you, Black Man of the Night]"

He then struggled to his feet with the aid of his apprentice. The Uku's knees creaked and popped and, as if mocking him, the large Council House creaked and popped as a gust of wind pushed by.

The Uku looked up at the ceiling of the Council House and slowly searched around the room.

When no more creaking and popping occurred, he quietly explained the significance of his small fire ceremony. "The gentle burning of the tobacco flakes indicates that there are no witches in the Council House. If witches were present, the flakes would have flashed or popped as they ignited. Where the ashes tend to congregate indicates the direction of a witch, if one exists."

The wise old man waited for his clever apprentice to comprehend the significance. Atselvdi marveled at his great-grandfather's depth of knowledge. In his lifetime, he had not seen his great-grandfather ever have to deal with witches. He wondered how he knew what to do. Where had Adanvdo gained this type of knowledge?

Atselvdi whispered, "The ashes fell to the southwest in the direction of the Tagwa warriors and to the northeast in the direction of the land of the Ani Tagwas."

Outside, a raven squawked to punctuate Atselvdi's answer. The Uku seemed alarmed by the raven's call. Atselvdi had not noticed the ugly bird's squawk and stared at his great-grandfather questioningly. Atselvdi's answer to the test was surprising. He had intended for him to conclude that the Tagwas were not witches. But his clever grandson had made an interesting connection: Witches are often born of witches.

He noticed that his grandson was staring in the direction of the Ani Tagwas as if he could see something. Then he saw that Sali and Ulogidv Unega had appeared in the doorway of the Council House. Ulogidv Unega carried a large bundle of black cloth and rope. The black cloth would provide shrouds for the corpses and the two-stranded apocynum cord would be used to bind the shrouds to the bodies. Sali shuffled over to sit on the white bench rather than his place on the white thrones. Ulogidv Unega greeted Tawodi and whispered a request.

The warrior leader commanded two warriors to go to the woods to obtain locust wood for the carriers.

"Why locust wood, Grandfather?" Atselvdi quietly questioned.

"Because he is of the Aniwodi, the Paint clan, which is also my clan, and we consider locust sacred."

"I know it is the traditional wood for the Ani Wodi, but is it the proper wood for this?"

The old Uku smirked ruefully. One of the reasons his great-grandfather was so well-loved was because he knew when to be strict and when to be flexible.

Normally, the Uku would sit on the white throne at the back of the Council House, but today he chose to sit on the white benches with his colleagues. He and Atselvdi took places around the hearth next to Sali. Sali sat erect and smacked his lips as if waking up. With his eyes apparently closed still, he spoke quietly, "Did you feel it?"

Feel what? Atselvdi wondered. Adanvdo did not respond directly to the question but, instead, began to discuss the details of the blessing to protect the warriors on their mission.

Adanvdo addressed Sali, "Some say that the root [Sagittaria latifolia] is good medicine for giving one the ability to see witches."

Atselvdi found this remark curious. Earlier, his grandfather had taken him to gather a mixture of moss, wood, and insect plants and had told him that it was for the witch's tea.

Sali shook his head. "The root is no good!" As he spoke, he pulled a small leather pouch from beneath his cape. "I have mixed moss from rocks in the mountain stream with phosphorescent wood from a putrefied stump and two types of insect plant." Sali turned to Atselvdi, "We'll need pure white water from the Long Man."

Atselvdi looked at his grandfather to see his reaction to this arrogant old priest. To his surprise, his grandfather replied, "I agree."

Atselvdi dutifully went to the back of the Council House to take a sacred pot from an old chest. He then left for the stream. He would collect pure white water from the rocky portion of the river where the white water flowed.

Adanvdo checked to make sure they could not be heard. "What do we do if the clan priests figure out the purpose of the tea?"

Sali chuckled, blinked his eyes, closed them and answered, "Do the rabbits challenge the foxes?"

28

He pushed the crystals into the pounding waterfall and watched with amusement the dancing images in the glassy formation.

ATSELVDI RETURNED TO THE Council House with the sacred pot half full of white water from the Long Man. His great-grandfather was standing with Tawodi and his six charges discussing something very intense. Several priests stood just behind the Uku with very intense looks on their faces as well, occasionally nodding supportive approval.

Sali was still sitting upright on the white bench, but he appeared to be asleep. It was hard to tell since none of the features of Sali's face were actually visible beneath the wrinkles. His eyes, his mouth, and even his nose were buried somewhere behind blobs of wrinkled skin.

Ulogidv Unega was bending over the ancient priest and examining the pouch that Sali had earlier shown to Atselvdi and his great-grandfather.

Ulogidv Unega was startled by Atselvdi's approach and wheeled around to face the young intruder. Atselvdi looked at the pouch in the suspicious priest's hand and then at his wide, guilty eyes. Ulogidv Unega looked down at the evidence in his hand and then back at the young apprentice.

He explained, "You surprised me. I guess I am a bit jittery with all this business. The Uku is explaining the protective potion to the retrieval party and he asked me to fetch the mixture from Sali."

Atselvdi looked at the sleeping old priest. Ulogidv Unega also glanced at him. "I didn't want to wake Sali. He's getting very old and cranky."

With that, Ulogidv Unega joined the Uku and handed him the pouch. Adanvdo looked at Sali and noticed his great-grandson. He motioned to his apprentice to place the pot over the sacred fire to heat.

Tawodi tried not to show his concern about his assignment to lead the retrieval party. The instructions he had just received from the Uku on the administering of the protective potion to him and his men as a precaution did not help. Nothing in his life had prepared him for dealing with dead bodies.

Some time was spent building the carriers out of the proper materials as instructed. When the warriors were taken to water by the Uku and the priests, they were given the protective potion to drink. Only Adanvdo, Sali, Atselvdi, and Chief Waya knew that it was to enable them to "see" witches and thus be protected from them. Only they knew that the witch can shape-shift into predatory animals or even birds, but with the aid of the tea, the drinker can see the witch as he really is. Seeing a witch in this manner strips the witch of his powers and leads to his demise.

The priests shared their suggestions with Atselvdi on how to conduct the retrieval of the corpses and the ceremonies to keep the retrieval party safe and uncontaminated.

Then it was time ... time to return to the campsite! As the retrieval party marched out of the village, the priests stood by solemnly. Adanvdo and Sali exchanged knowing glances. The clandestine allies held back as the other priests headed for home. They found a small boulder beside the Long Man to sit.

Adanvdo sighed grandly and then commented, "No one questioned drinking the potion for protection."

Sali snorted and shook his head. "Maybe we'll get lucky and the witch will fly over them out of curiosity!"

The two conspirators laughed at the irony. Adanvdo sobered up. "If we are lucky, old friend, the witch has moved on and will not return."

Sali huffed, "humph. I heard him pass over the Council House, didn't you?"

Adanvdo shook his head dejectedly and admitted, "I think I may have."

Not far upstream from the fatal Tagwa campsite and at the top of the Agusa Jisdu Canyon, the Raven Mocker, Kalanu Ahkyeliski, sat on the rock he called Edoda gazing down into the deep canyon below. A deer and fawn had left the safety of the thick forest to wade into the Agusa Jisdu River for a drink. They waded into the middle of the stream and faced east. *Proper Tsalagi deer!* he muttered.

It was as if they were going to water just as the Tsalagi do for cleansing and inspiration or for special occasions.

His heart warmed by the sweet memory he began to nod off in the warm morning sun. Once again, his mind returned to where it all began; where he first committed to following the dark path; back to his childhood when he was known as Ugidahli Unega, White Feather. He reminisced about how he had journeyed into the forest to find the old woman and old man that had once given him shelter and fed him after his failed attempt at hunting. He remembered how marvelous all the plants and animals that they had collected seemed to him. He remembered his fascination with the preserved entrails and skins, the myriad of insects, and the odd-smelling potions.

"Osiyo!" he had yelled as he approached. The startled old woman had spun around dropping her basket of vegetables. He was astonished at how old she looked. It had only been one summer since he had visited her and yet she looked ten summers older. And her face had a yellow hue to it.

"It's you!" she exclaimed bitterly, obviously not happy to see him. "You have laid the curse under us. You must go away!"

She had alarmed him and he could not believe that he was the cause of her sickness. "How did I bring a curse to you?" he had exclaimed.

The old woman did not answer. She moved feebly toward her hut. As she approached, she called to her husband and he came out to help her. When he saw White Feather, he had the same reaction as the old woman. He, too, looked much older and was very sickly.

"You said you would not return! You accepted the necklace," the old man retorted.

"I'm sorry, Grandfather, but I could not forget about you and your wondrous medicines. I am returning your beautiful necklace and I want you to teach me your medicine."

The old couple looked at each other. The old man said, "Let us be alone now. We will consider it."

The old couple disappeared into their hut and he walked back into the forest and rested against a tree. Grandmother Sun climbed high into the sky before the old man came out of the hut and called to him.

The old man confessed, "My wife and I are not Kuni-akati as we had told you."

The old man looked down and paused for a long time. "We are witches."

His stomach had tightened as fear engulfed him. The old man looked into his eyes. The old man's eyes were yellow where they should have been white and red where they should have been brown. He continued, "We have followed the black path for too long and dark spirits have poisoned our askinas."

"What do you mean *askinas*?" he had queried.

The old man looked down in thought, then looked up into his eyes. "It is your essence, what makes you who you are, your life's connection."

"Do you not have a medicine for yourself?"

The old man chuckled at his naiveté but then grew very stern. "We need more than medicine to heal us now."

"Tell me what you need and I will get it for you. Tell me what to do and I will do it for you," he had cried desperately.

And so began the new path for him that would eventually isolate him from the real people, the path leading to becoming a witch. And not just any witch, but THE witch—the original Raven Mocker!

His reminiscing was interrupted by a rumble from deep within the canyon. He opened his eyes and looked up at the sky. There were no clouds anywhere.

Again he heard it, low and distant—rumble, rumble, rumble, rumble.

"They've gone to water!" He shuddered involuntarily at the realization that the recovery party was now at the campsite where the Tagwas lay dead. He rolled off the Edoda stone, retrieved his crystals from his Council Hut, and waded into the frigid pond.

The old wizard no longer went to water like a normal Tsalagi. It no longer had the power to inspire him to the white path or cleanse him. He was too far along the black path. The ties were broken. The white spirits turned their back to him. He was of the darkness now.

He approached the column of water flowing out of the rock face into the pond. He pushed the crystals into the pounding waterfall and watched with amusement the dancing images in the glassy formation.

*"Do you have a fly conjure,
Little Priest?"*

Adanvdo returned home to find Kalona cooking on the hearth. She helped him remove his medicine belt and cloak and delivered them to his bedroom while he looked in on Ali.

She looked so peaceful in her sleep. To look at her one could not believe what she had just endured. He muttered a prayer for her.

The tired old man shuffled back to the hearth and sat by the fire. He pinched tobacco from the small leather pouch and stuffed it into the pipe that always resided by the hearth. He reached over to pull a splint from the stack and held it over the reddened coals until it ignited.

"How did the preparations go?" Kalona inquired.

"Very well." The old Uku drew thoughtfully on the pipe.

"Where is Atselvdi?"

Adanvdo blew clouds of sweet smoke into the fire as he answered, "He was chosen to accompany the retrieval party."

Atselvdi's grandmother stopped and glared at her father. "Atselvdi? Why Atselvdi?"

"It is all right. He is ready. It will be good for his training and reputation."

Kalona shook her head and lifted the warmed pot from the hearth. As she raked three sisters into a bowl for her father, she questioned, "Wouldn't he be last in line for that?"

Adanvdo shrugged. "Well, it should have been me, but ..."

Kalona set the pot back on the hearth. "Then Sali, who is too old, of course, but what was Ulogidv Unega's excuse?"

Adanvdo blew smoke across the hearth and lowered the pipe to his lap. He stared blankly into the fire for a moment. "He did not say."

Adanvdo laid the pipe aside and realized that his daughter was not satisfied with his answer. "Before we could question him, he nominated Atselvdi. We were all surprised, but the other priests seemed pleased with the choice."

Kalona handed the bowl of soup to her father and dipped more into a bowl for herself. She shook her head. "Everyone knows that Ulogidv Unega has aspirations to be Uku. Why would he turn down this highly visible opportunity? And why would he nominate Atselvdi? Perhaps he is a coward!" she exclaimed.

Adanvdo ignored his daughter's comment, but she was probably right. It probably was cowardice on Ulogidv's part.

The protective grandmother appeared to be considering the issue further. "Perhaps Ulogidv Unega sees Atselvdi as his least threatening rival?" The old woman was pleased after all. This could be a good break for her grandson.

It was almost noon when the retrieval party arrived at the campsite. The bodies of the dead Tagwas were already bloating and blue and beginning to stink. The clearing was buzzing with happy flies drawn by the delectable opportunity. Even if the retrieval party had not been fasting, no one was hungry, so the distasteful business began immediately.

Atselvdi instructed the wary crew to go to water. The six warriors, their leader, Tawodi Gvnagei, and the two guards followed the young priest into the small, shallow stream.

They all faced east as Atselvdi began the ceremony. "We return to the water, and sing of thunder!"

The warriors answered with, "Ohanadu! Ohanadu! Ohanadu! Ohanadu!" [Thunder! Thunder! Thunder! Thunder!]

The young priest continued, "At the water, we bathe if we do not desire to be bothered by conjurers."

Atselvdi scanned the faces of the small congregation as he continued his prayer to keep them safe from witches. They seemed unconcerned, even unaware, of the peculiarity of his song. No one even reacted to the ending. "Tsigili! The black boxes will be your resting place. Your souls have just come to fall, never to return!"

As Atselvdi finished the blessing, he instructed the seven warriors to submerge themselves in the water and swim to the bank. The warriors looked at each other quizzically. The water in the stream was too shallow to submerge themselves. Some chose to splash the water over them, one rolled comically in the muddy water. The shallow water made swimming more like crawling.

Atselvdi led his reluctant muddy crew from the small stream and instructed them to stand around the Tagwas. He draped the black shrouds over the carriers and instructed the warriors to place the first Tagwa on a carrier, face down.

Tawodi approached Atselvdi. "Do you have a fly conjure, Little Priest?"

The levity broke the gloomy tension. The warriors and even the priest buckled over with laughter.

Atselvdi forced himself to continue the process amidst giggling spurned on by the infectious chortles of his comrades. He folded the shroud over the body and tied it with the double twined rope.

He moved to the next body. The corpse was entangled by its own entrails. Atselvdi felt a jolt to his system! Visions of the mutilated corpse of Crooked Foot flashed into his head. He waved off the warriors about to lift the body while he examined its trunk. He felt dizziness and profound foreboding as he studied the grotesque opening in his chest area. Atselvdi forced himself to kneel beside the body and examine the wound. As he feared, the breastbone was missing as was the heart and liver—the victim of a witch!

The stunned priest rocked back on his heels and squeezed his stomach. He feared he was going to be sick. Tawodi rushed to him and picked him up. "Are you okay, Atselvdi? You shouldn't be so curious. Let's just get these thugs loaded and back to the village."

Atselvdi agreed and staggered away from the others to regain his composure. Tawodi ordered resumption of the enshrouding.

Now he understood why his grandfather and Sali had inserted the witch's tea and the witch conjure into the ceremony. They knew!

Once the Tagwas were shrouded and secured, Atselvdi stood and nodded to Tawodi. Tawodi commanded the warriors to pick up the carriers. They followed Atselvdi back to the village as he sang the blessing for safe passage, "Get out of the way! Get out of the way! Listen! From the farthest mountain over there, I arose. Ha! We travel on the white pathways. Ha! It was the terrapin at the earliest sun rising! Ha! He has come to chop up the pathways in the center of your soul, enemies along the road!"

Hiding in the shadows of the dense leaves of an oak, the old shape-shifted wizard, Kalanu Ahkyeliski, watched the retrieval caravan trudge through the forest on their way back to the village. He had watched the young priest examine the corpse and knew that Atselvdi knew! The ceremony was laced with witch conjures so he knew that Adanvdo Alsgida knew, also.

*The shadow moved back
to watch the old man
pass by.*

THE DARKNESS OF THE night, the darkness of the soul, the darkness of evil enshrouded the mysterious witch as he stretched out his rotting arms and raised his reddened, dying eyes to the heavens. His blue-gray body began to glow luminescent green. Orange hairs sprouted and grew into fiery feathers covering his body. He parted his cracked and bleeding lips and shrieked the rakish caw of the raven that he drew out as if teaming in pain. The fiery feathers of his outstretched arms and of his lower body burst into flames propelling him upward as the witch shape-shifted into a raven.

The huge black bird rolled over as it reached the apex of its upward flight to glide over the dark forest turning to follow the Long Man down the mountain to the village of Tsikohi. The raven cackled as if laughing at the sight of the sacred fire across the Long Man from the village where six priests and the Uku encircled three corpses.

While their attention was focused on their ceremony, one of the most vile witches to have ever come from the Ani Yun Wiya glided over them and landed silently in the shadows of a nearby tree. Careful to position himself so that he could not be seen, the witch, posing as a raven, peered through the dark leaves at the seven strangers performing their morbid ceremony.

He did not know that of the handful who knew of the powers he was capable of, two of them stood before him now.

The chanting priests hushed. After ample time for private meditation and introspection, the apparent Uku led the six priests to the Long Man for the final cleansing ceremony.

Nausea engulfed the evil raven. His body quaked. His energy was draining rapidly. He cursed the diseased soul of his previous victim—an old crippled man who otherwise looked healthy—whose body was eating itself, a victim of cancer!

He had tarried long enough. He must seek out his next prey now. He had already chosen his victim. It was someone weak and vulnerable but with many years of life left. His body was shivering as he extended his wings and lifted off the tree branch. He flew a wide arc to avoid being seen by the priests. His coveted next victim was comatose nearby in the village. She would be easy prey. As he banked over the village and spotted his target, his stomach convulsed and he vomited the putrid bile of his last victim.

As he approached the window where his victim lay sleeping, someone entered the room! He feared a possible Seer! He squawked and pulled away. It would be fatal for him to be seen not as a raven but as a witch. His deception unveiled would lead to his demise. He flew into the cover of a leafy tree where he could wait.

Having fed her exhausted grandson, Kalona returned to her bedroom to sit beside her comatose granddaughter. She did not notice the pitiful squawk of the raven outside the window. As she stroked the hair of Ali, she sang a quiet song, "Sleep my little Ali. Your grandmother will protect you."

A tear trickled down the old woman's cheek. In her mind, she knew that she was not to blame for the abduction, but guilt gripped her heart and she felt she had somehow failed her wonderful granddaughter. She watched her lay motionless, just a shadowy form in the dark room.

Finally, the old woman dragged herself across the room to her own bed. Although she was near exhaustion, she could not sleep. She worried about whether Ali would ever wake up and if she did, would she be the sweet, playful, happy granddaughter she knew or a fractured, brooding, shell? Her innocence had been stolen by three vile, disgusting degenerates. *The Tagwa are a worthless disease on earth and should be wiped out!* she thought to herself.

She reminisced about the wonderful, kind, and brave relatives she had lost at the hands of the despicable Tagwas. Then she felt guilty. This was no attitude for a Peace Chief. This was no way to think as a Beloved Woman of the tribe. She challenged herself to clear her mind of such thoughts. She must expel all of her black thoughts for soon she would have to meet with the other Beloved Women of the tribe to decide the fate of the Tagwa warriors and, consequently, the fate of the village and perhaps the nation.

Her thoughts were interrupted by a raven call, which drew her attention to the wind rolling by. The image of the startled raven flapping frantically to keep his balance in the tree made her giggle. Despised as a vicious and haughty bird by most, the raven she was thinking of was her namesake and guardian.

Her father had often told her of the quiet raven that sat in the tree above her when she was born. It was probably not the same raven that now resided in the tree outside her window, but for all of her life it seemed that some raven was always nearby looking after her. She chose to believe it was the same one and that it was now very old and frail like her and, therefore, capable of being blown out of the tree by a passing breeze.

The breeze might be bringing a change in the weather, she thought. She listened for thunder. "What if it rains? Father doesn't have his cape!" she exclaimed out loud.

The raven cawed lazily. The old black friend was probably telling her that her worries were unwarranted. She had often found it comforting to talk to the raven when they were alone. Tonight she felt the need to talk. She rolled off her bed, trudged over to the window, draped her forearms across the sill, rested her chin and gazed sleepily at the massive tree.

"I wonder when father slept last? Probably not since the abduction and he probably won't sleep tonight. The old fool should turn over the Uku priesthood to someone else. He's getting too old."

The raven cackled. "Yes, I know he is still in good health for his age, but you have to admit he is visibly weaker than he was even last summer."

The raven purred like a resting panther. Kalona shifted, "It's not safe for a frail old man to be out so late."

She heard the thrashing of the raven's wings taking flight. She tried to catch a glimpse of her old raven friend. Outside in the stillness she heard the shuffling footsteps of her father returning home. Movement in the dilapidated house beside the tree caught her eye. She glimpsed a shadowy presence, a lurking, vigilant presence watching the house of Alihelitsidasdi. The shadow moved back to watch the old man pass by.

Atselvdi was very tired from his trip and had left the ceremony before his grandfather. He assumed that his grandmother had already retired because he could hear her muffled voice through the wall talking to his comatose sister. The room was too quiet without his grandfather's noisy snoring. Oddly, he found it hard to get to sleep.

After tossing and turning until his body was finally relaxing, he heard the familiar shuffling sound of his grandfather's footsteps coming into the room. He lay very still and listened as the old man tried to get undressed and slip into bed without disturbing him. He waited while his tired mentor fussed with the covers and finally breathed a relaxing breath, smacked his lips, and grew quiet. Atselvdi whispered, "One corpse was visited by the witch."

He could feel his great-grandfather's eyes staring at the bottom of his bunk! His grandfather whispered, "Are you sure?"

"Yes, Grandfather. His heart, liver, and rib bone were missing."

He could hear his grandfather take a deep breath. The old man was quiet for a moment. Atselvdi waited hoping that his grandfather might share more, but when he did not, Atselvdi asked, "You knew, didn't you?"

Adanvdo took another deep breath. "Yes. I did not want to worry you."

"That's why you added the conjures concerning witches."

It was not a question, just a confirmation. "So, the witch struck twice in one night?"

"It would seem so."

Atselvdi felt like he would have to pull the information out of his grandfather. "Do you know what happened to the Raven Mocker?"

He sensed that Adanvdo was stung by the question. He waited patiently. It would be impolite to force his grandfather into answering.

"Father, did you eat something?" Kalona whispered from the door.

Adanvdo's stomach growled. Obviously his grandfather was hungry, but it was Atselvdi's mind that was hungry, not his stomach.

"Come on, I can heat something for you. Want anything, Atselvdi?"

Atselvdi combed his fingers through his long, loose hair. "No thanks."

As his grandfather crawled out of bed and shuffled toward the door, Atselvdi clasped his hands behind his head. The vision of the mutilated Tagwan corpse flashed in his head. His thoughts carried him back to the corpse of the old man whose granddaughter was his age and his friend. She was a sweet girl who grieved over the sudden death of her grandfather, unaware that it was not from the thing put under her family, but a vile and vicious witch.

He vowed to learn all that his grandfather could teach him about the witch. He vowed to himself and to Crooked Foot's granddaughter to avenge the old man's death.

"With such a dismal existence, why would he want to prolong his life?"

GRANDMOTHER SUN'S MORNING LIGHT was casting long shadows over the house of Kalona Ehlawei.

"Osiyo," greeted a voice from the door.

"Siyo, come sit," answered Kalona.

Amadohi and Wananahi entered the house and hugged Kalona.

"My, don't you look important in your white dress?" Wananahi exclaimed.

Kalona danced around in a circle as the three laughed. "And what about you, dear? You look beautiful in your dress, too."

Wananahi blushed and timidly danced in a circle as her daughter and best friend applauded and laughed.

"How is she, Grandmother? Can I see her?" Amadohi questioned as she looked tentatively toward the bedroom of her best friend.

"Yes, of course." Kalona watched the young girl leave and then turned to Wananahi. "Let's sit by the hearth."

Wananahi looked at Kalona in earnest. "How is she, really?"

"She just sleeps. I suppose it is good that her mind has retreated to a safe place for now. I can't imagine what horrors the poor girl has endured."

In the next room, Amadohi sat next to her best friend on her bed. She awkwardly reached over and touched her traumatized friend's arm. Ali did not respond. Amadohi cried softly, "My friend! Where are you, Ali?"

Beside the hearth, the two close friends were silent. As members of the Beloved Women of the tribe, they were responsible for judging prisoners of war and it would be up to the Beloved Women to determine the fate of the Tagwa corpses. Each was waiting for the other to ask the question that both knew the other wanted to ask. Kalona placed her hand on Wananahi's hand. "Have you decided?"

Wananahi stared at the burning embers of the hearth. "I don't know. I want to hear what the others say."

Kalona hissed skeptically and shook her head. She wanted to be critical of her friend's indecisiveness, but how could she? She was conflicted herself. Her head and her heart were at odds with each other. The hatred in her heart wanted revenge. The hatred in her heart remembered the losses she had suffered at the hands of the Tagwa: her husband; her son-in-law and consequently her daughter; that giant, funny cousin with a raven tattooed on his head that often came to visit her father; and now her little Ali.

But, her mind told her that war was not the answer. She knew that supporting vengeance was contrary to her role as Peace Chief of the tribe. Balance and harmony had been upset for some reason. Whatever she and the other members of the village had done to bring on this great tragedy had to be rectified to restore the balance.

Taking the dark path could never lead to the white path. And her sensible side was empathetic for the family of the dead renegade Tagwas.

Wananahi broke the silence. "This has to be very hard for you."

Kalona shook her head.

"Can you be objective?"

The tough old woman could not suppress tears welling up in her eyes. "I'm not sure I can be, Wananahi!"

"That's understandable, dear. No one can fault you however you lean."

"How do the others feel about it?"

Wananahi seemed reluctant to answer. "The other Beloved Women have been very quiet about this very difficult decision."

Kalona answered, "I guess that most are like me—hoping that one of the Beloved Women will come to council with a convincing argument. I suspect that the vote should be in support of Chief Waya's and the Great Chief's desires." Then Wananahi smiled.

"What are you smiling about?" Kalona was clearly irritated with her friend.

"Oh, I'm sorry, Kalona. It's just ... oh, you know ... the irony that the Peace Chief may support war while the War Chief supports peace."

The old Peace Chief thought about her friend's observation and then burst out laughing. The two Beloved Women embraced in laughter and tears.

Amadohi returned to the main room where her mother and her best friend's grandmother appeared to be laughing and crying at the same time.

"Are you two all right?"

The friends released each other and tried to regain their composure. "Thank you for watching Ali. Hopefully, we won't be long."

"Thank you for asking me, Grandmother."

Kalona stood. "We should be going now."

Adanvdo and Atselvdi entered the smoky hut of Sali and joined him at the hearth. They found Sali slumped and apparently napping, as usual. Adanvdo placed his hand on the tired old priest's shoulder. Sali looked up at the Uku with tired, blood-shot eyes.

"Walk with us," Adanvdo implored of the ancient wizard and helped him stand. The two priests and the apprentice left the hut, arm-in-arm, heading down the street toward the western exit and the meadow.

Adanvdo made small talk. "Are you ready for your trip to the mountains, Grandson?"

Atselvdi beamed. "Yes, Grandfather."

Sali inquired, "Going to the mountains?"

"Yes, Grandfather, there are people who need me ... my medicine."

Sali closed his eyes. There would be no more small talk from the tired old man. Adanvdo winked at Atselvdi who grinned happily.

Slowly they made their way to the exit.

Atselvdi helped the priests through the switchback and paused to survey the meadow. He was anxious to learn why his grandfather had asked him to join them. He hoped it involved further discussion on witchcraft.

To their surprise, it would be Sali that would break the long silence as they waded through the tall grasses. "What do you think of the Tagwa mutilation, young priest?"

Atselvdi was not expecting to be asked his opinion. He was expecting to be learning from them.

Atselvdi countered with a question, "How many witches are there?"

Sali and Adanvdo studied the young priest. Atselvdi glanced back and forth tentatively at the two perplexed old men.

Adanvdo grinned proudly at the bewildered old sage. "He's right! There could be two."

Sali shook his head defiantly. The trio continued walking. Sali commented, "The old man wasn't a proper victim in the first place."

Adanvdo had to admit, "I have been troubled with the witch's choice, also. The young, strong Tagwa made so much more sense. Two witches acting at the same time is a stretch, but why would he claim two victims ... and the same night?"

Sali shook his head. "Why indeed."

Assured by the prolonged silence that the priests had nothing more to say, Atselvdi had more questions. "What does the witch do after he acquires a new life?"

Sali was impressed by the insightful question. Adanvdo accepted the challenge. "He probably lives in isolation and studies his dark medicine."

Atselvdi pondered this information which left him wanting. "With such a dismal existence, why would he want to prolong his life?"

The old priests looked at each other and Adanvdo raised his eyebrows as if to say, "You want to take this one?"

Sali started to place his hand on the boy's shoulder, but realized that he could not reach that high, so rested his hand on his arm instead. "He could feign a normal life in the meantime. He could walk among us and we wouldn't even know!"

Atselvdi jumped back and stared wide-eyed at Sali. He could not ask the question that had jumped into his mind—*could Sali be the second witch?*

The old priests continued on. Atselvdi sensed they were taking him somewhere specific. He looked beyond them at the huge stone spire poking up from the meadow— the Tomb of the Witch!

As they approached the huge tombstone, Adanvdo asked, "What do you know of this spire, Grandson?"

Atselvdi had heard fantastic stories. "Just that a great battle between great witches occurred here and the loser is buried inside the spire."

Sali glanced at his old friend as if curious to hear Adanvdo's version. Adanvdo squeezed his chin, rubbed his cheek, and then wrinkled his brow. "Do you remember our discussion about the three witches who had the power and knowledge to steal souls?"

Atselvdi stared blankly then raised his eyebrows and looked at the spire. "This is one of them's tomb?"

"Yes. And he was put here by ... by the one who con-quered Nunyunuwi."

Atselvdi was getting excited. "He was the other witch in the battle?" Then the young priest grew very somber. "He is a good witch?"

Sali chuckled but Adanvdo seemed to be finding an answer difficult. Sali interceded, "A man cannot be judged good even when his evil powers produce a good result. The result does not excuse the method."

Adanvdo studied his grandson's reaction to Sali's eloquent rejoinder. Atselvdi was reflective as he tried to register Sali's answer and fit it into his paradigm. "Even if his intention is good?"

Sali's eyelids were closed, but they appeared to be blinking as he smacked his lips in preparation to speak. "If a man's intentions are truly good, he will choose the white path. He cannot walk the black path and be judged good."

Adanvdo appeared to be struck by Sali's comment. "Sali is right. A man might do good things, but if, in his heart, he still clings to the dark ways, he cannot be judged otherwise until he turns his back on the dark path."

Atselvdi studied the tomb of the witch. "How can you be sure the evil witch is still in there?"

Sali's eyes popped open.

Adanvdo shook his head. "We assume that because the tomb is undisturbed, he has not passed through."

*"I'd like to fry their little
butts and let the Long Man
carry them home."*

Tʜᴇ sᴇᴠᴇɴ Bᴇʟᴏᴠᴇᴅ Wᴏᴍᴇɴ representing the seven clans of the village sat alone in the huge Council House. Kalona was filled with dread. This would be one of the most difficult councils she had ever attended. Not only was she carrying the burden of her conflicted mind and heart, but also, as the Peace Chief, it was her responsibility to lead the council.

The women took their places on the benches around the sacred fire. Each one sat on a blanket died in the sacred color of their respective clan. Kalona walked over to the hearth and picked up the pipe and tobacco. She stuffed sacred tobacco into the bowl and lit a splint. She carried the pipe and splint to her yellow blanket and sat down.

She reflected on the wisdom of the pipe. The sacred tobacco enabled the mind to better see justice and wisdom. Also, this important part of all councils gave the smoker something to occupy the hands while his or her mind contemplated the matters at hand. The pipe enabled Kalona to delay her words ... and settle her nerves.

The elder Beloved Woman sucked on the pipe to get it started. Soon whiffs of gray smoke puffed out and swirled around the barrel of the pipe. Kalona blew out the splint and inhaled deeply on the delicious tobacco. The moment had arrived! The elder distinguished woman exhaled slowly.

"We are the Beloved Women. We are the heart and soul of the village. We carry the traditions and passions of our tribe and of our clans on our shoulders. We call upon our white thoughts for guidance. We chase away our black thoughts. It is through the wise council of the Beloved Women that the people of Tsikohi may achieve the seventh level."

The emotional old woman's eyes teared and her voice trembled as she completed her opening remarks. Thankfully, she turned to the pipe for support and for time to summon her courage to continue. After a long draw from the pipe and an even slower release of the smoke, she resumed, "The tribe looks to us for our compassion; for our wisdom; and for our motherly instincts. What we must decide today affects not just the fate of the Tagwa prisoners, it affects not just the fate of our village, but it affects the entire Tsalagi nation and the Ani Yun Wiya!"

The Beloved Leader took another draw on the pipe. As she held the smoke, she gazed at each of her colleagues, one-by-one. Then she looked down and exhaled the smoke.

"The balance of our lives has been upset. I do not know what we have done to cause the imbalance. We have been taught that goodness is rewarded and evil is punished. It is the way of the Ani Yun Wiya to follow the white path. The white way always triumphs. Now it is up to us to find the white path to restore balance and harmony to ourselves, our families, our clans, our village, and our nation. Duyuktv."

"Duyuktv," the Beloved Women repeated in unison.

The old woman put the pipe to her lips and pondered her words. She remembered the teachings of her father that she had heard so many times. It had consumed her thoughts many, many times over her lifetime. And so many times she had questioned the fairness of life. Although she did not always understand it, it had always proven to be true and balance was always restored somehow. She exhaled slowly. "I beseech you for your thoughts."

Kalona passed the pipe to the Beloved Woman from the Deer clan. The tiny old woman accepted the pipe with disgust written on her face. She examined the pipe as though looking for a flaw. The muscles in her jaws were writhing. Finally, she took a quick puff of the pipe and spit out the smoke contemptuously. She shoved the pipe to the Beloved Woman to her left.

The Beloved Woman from the Bird clan rolled her eyes and smirked. She was an ample woman whose proportions spread out from a small top to a wide, bulbous bottom. A thin, hook-shaped nose protruded from the sagging jowls of her cheeks. Kalona mused to herself that if the woman WAS a bird, she would be a fat turkey.

The proud turkey-woman held the pipe daintily in her hand and placed only the very tip against her lips. Her lips pursed indicating that she was inhaling. The sophisticated turkey coughed violently several times and wiped her mouth distastefully. "No matter what we may think of the Tagwas, it is OUR peace we must be mindful of."

The other women shifted. It was no time to be laughing at their beloved friend. They tried to concentrate on her words. She finished with, "I'd like to fry their little butts and let the Long Man carry them home."

It was too much. The grim mood busted up into giggles.

The turkey-woman nodded confidently, clearly satisfied with her statement. She passed the pipe to the round, jovial woman representing the Blue Holly clan whose eyes squinted when she laughed. It was an infectious laugh that consumed her and made her shake all over. She kept her lips tight as if trying to suppress what she clearly could not. She reached for the pipe without looking at her friend from the Bird clan and placed it in her lap as she waited for her giddiness to subside. The other Beloved Women could not help but laugh with the happy little woman with the round face and body who possessed an innocence that made her very lovable.

"What can I say after that?" she questioned and then giggled again kicking off another round from her friends. The laughter felt good on such a grim occasion.

The sweet little lady pulled herself together. "Well, I think we would all like to fry their little ..." she hesitated and her eyes squinted as if that unmentionable word would trigger her again. The others laughed for her. "But this is a very serious affair. Whatever we do will not change what's happened. Nothing will make us feel better about it. Nothing will bring back ..." her eyes teared and her face grimaced. She passed the pipe and put her hands over her face as her body shook.

The tall, slender Beloved Woman from the Paint clan sat very erect and very stern. Her unwrinkled face disguised her advanced age. She was a no-nonsense woman who rarely participated in levity. She placed the pipe in her mouth and sucked air several times.

She frowned at the pipe, rose and walked over to the hearth for more tobacco and a splint. She stood by the sacred fire as she lit the pipe and tossed the splint carelessly into the sacred fire. She crossed her free arm and placed her hand in the crook of the other elbow. That arm stood erect supporting the graceful hand clutching the pipe. She exhaled the smoke and stared into space as if unaware of anyone in the room.

She appeared to be deep in thought. She took another draw on the pipe. She had the undivided attention of her peers. Finally, she exhaled a huge cloud of smoke and began, "IF we fry their little ... butts, it will not matter that we have every right to do so. The Tagwas will feel they must avenge the desecration of their sons. If we bury them and send a messenger, they will be insulted and answer with a raiding party. If we return the bodies, how will we explain that we are not expecting restitution for the deaths of our beautiful daughters? They will be suspicious ... I know I would be. There may be no solution that will bring peace."

The elegant old woman returned to her bench and handed the pipe over as she passed the Beloved Woman from the Wolf clan. The stout old woman puffed on the pipe nervously. She was clearly agitated. "She's right. There is no peaceful answer to this. Those evil renegades murdered and mutilated our sweet, innocent daughters! Their death is NOT retribution. We have every right to demand the death of their brothers, mothers, and fathers. We should insist they mutilate them the way their evil sons mutilated our girls!"

She jammed the pipe into her mouth and puffed furiously before continuing, "They aren't the big, powerful nation they were when we fought them years ago. We made sure of that. This time we should wipe them out completely! Murder every one of them."

Everyone understood her fury. No one had lost more at the hands of the Tagwa than the woman of the Wolf Clan. The sons of the Wolf clan were the warriors of the tribe. Four of her sons died in the Tagwa war. And now she had lost her granddaughter, Delagalis.

Kalona walked over, sat down, put her arm around her and comforted her. The poor woman broke down and cried uncontrollably. The other Beloved Women came to her to comfort her. Kalona realized that this council would be even more difficult than she had thought. But for her, the answer was clear. Now, she just had to convince her beloved friends. Tenderly, she took the pipe and handed it to her best friend, Wananahi of the Wild Potato clan.

Wananahi enjoyed the pipe and the taste of the sweet tobacco used for council. She had often told Kalona that she liked the way the warm smoke filled her lungs and the feeling of calm that it produced. She kept some of this tobacco in her house for special occasions or for when she was feeling down or lonely. It was one of the benefits of being the best friend of the Uku's daughter.

She was feeling very sad and lonely now. "I lost my husband in the Tagwa war."

Her quiet, vulnerable words drew the attention of her friends away from the agonizing sobs of the Beloved Woman of the Wolf clan. Kalona shifted and reached out a hand to her best friend. Wananahi squeezed the hand of Kalona and then released it. "I remember the fear and anxiety I felt waiting to hear news back from the war. And I remember the pain and anguish that I felt when I learned that my husband wouldn't come back to me. And then the anger that I felt toward the Ani Tagwas for taking away Amadohi's father."

Wananahi returned to the pipe. The memories filled her heart and tears filled her distant eyes. "I wouldn't want to go through that again. I wouldn't want anyone to have to go through that again."

Again, she enjoyed the pipe. Quietly, others remembered their pain and sobbed. "Some say that we have done something that has brought this evil upon us."

The graceful old woman drew on the pipe, closed her eyes, breathed deeply and then let the smoke curl out of her mouth elegantly. "I don't believe that. I don't believe that Une-lanunhi, the Great Apportioner, sent these men for retribution. I believe that sometimes bad things happen to good people."

The thoughtful woman raised her hands, palms up, and hunched her shoulders. "I believe that good things come of good deeds. I believe that to follow the white path, we must be strong and not let the dark ways tempt us to follow a dark path. Retribution is a dark path. Retribution may punish evil but what does it do for the victims? Does it really make us feel better to do evil upon others, even when they've done it upon us? Good actions are rewarded, not bad actions. I believe that we must do what is good for us. Let the Great Apportioner reconcile the anomalies. Let us maintain our course along the white path."

The Beloved Women were silent. Kalona was profoundly moved by her friend's eloquence. *What a peaceful world Wananahi lives in!*

It was again Kalona's turn to speak, but as she passed the tiny, bashful woman of the Deer clan she reached for the pipe. Clearly the little old woman was agitated. She took four quick puffs, shifted, and fidgeted with her blanket as she spoke, "The deer follow the white path."

Everyone looked at her curiously wondering where she was going with this.

"They harm no one. They peacefully raise their family and go about their lives with no malice."

The other Beloved Women looked at each other wondering if they were the only ones confused.

"Then a hunter comes along and kills one of them!"

The tiny woman looked around the room at her colleagues. "If the hunter is providing for his family and he does it properly—asking forgiveness from Awi Usti, the little spirit deer that looks after the family of deer— then he is forgiven and there is no retribution. The deer are sad for their loss, but they understand that it is the way of life."

The nervous little woman sucked on the pipe ignoring the fact that it had lost fire. "But, if a deer is killed maliciously and improperly, Awi Usti will lay the arthritis or worse under them."

Kalona was impressed. *What an interesting analogy.*

The little woman summed up, "We, the Beloved Women, are the Awi Ustis. It is up to us to watch over our families and make sure that injustice is dealt with."

Kalona sat in silence. She looked around the room. The Beloved Women were very divided. It would be a long, long council.

She was pleased with the final decision.

Kalona Ehlawei had dragged herself home with her exhausted best friend and equally exhausted father. They found Amadohi asleep beside her comatose friend. Nothing was spoken even in parting. Wananahi roused her daughter, Amadohi, and quietly left to go home while Kalona helped her father to his bed. She noticed that Atselvdi had already risen and left the house. Night had passed and it was early morning now.

After checking Ali, she peeled off her dress, plopped on to her bed, rubbed her face with her palms, rolled to her side and waited for the much needed sleep that would not come. She tossed and turned searching for a comfortable position as Grandmother Sun journeyed across the sky vault to peek over the tree line. Golden rays flooded through the window and provided a pathway for dancing particles. The troubled, famished woman got up, slipped into her tattered house moccasins and threw on her favorite, well-worn, deer skin dress stained from use in the kitchen and working in the garden. The soft, brain-tanned hide, was a very plain sleeveless straight dress draped over her portly body loosely and hung down to just above her knees. A bone hasp hung from the "V" neck unfastened most of the time unless she was going outside in which case she might add the waist belt. It was not proper attire for a village chief, but Kalona was not a vain woman and saved her more colorful and formal wear for ceremonies and council meetings.

Yawning broadly, she trudged into the main room and put a couple of logs on the glowing embers of the hearth. She set a pot of corn mush on to heat and as it was warming, she shuffled through the house to her father's room.

Cautiously, she looked in to make sure he was all right. She could hear his quiet snoring. He needed the sleep; she would not wake him. She returned to the hearth and dipped mush into a bowl.

As she ate, she mused. The Beloved Women had discussed, argued, cried, and comforted each other through most of the night before reaching a decision. The Uku, War Chief and his assistants and the clan priests had stayed up waiting in the chief's clan house. Many villagers had congregated at the dance field to await the verdict.

She was pleased with the final decision. She felt it was the only real solution capable of restoring peace in the village and keeping the peace between the Ani Yun Wiya and Ani Tagwa. She had advocated for the solution feeling that it was essential that the Tsikohians remain steadfast and not let the dark actions of the Tagwa renegades draw them off the white path.

"We have reached our decision after much discussion," she had told them."

She took another bite of mush and remembered the anxious looks of the people waiting to hear their decision. She had tried to be brief. "We will not be deterred by the evil that has provoked us. The Tagwa will have to face the Great Apportioner in the Nightland. We shall be strong and be steadfast on the white path we have chosen for ourselves. We believe that the renegade boys should be returned to their mothers for burial. We believe that they acted independently and do not represent the Ani Tagwa, therefore retribution is not required. They have paid for their actions with their own lives."

She fixed a bowl for Ali and trudged back to her bedroom. She cradled the sleeping granddaughter and tried to coax her to eat. She wiped the corn mush from her granddaughter's chin, but, as usual, only a small portion was actually consumed by the comatose girl. The loving grandmother laid the girl's head back down and covered her tenderly. Ali slept on.

Too tired to return to her bed, Kalona lay down beside her granddaughter and slept.

He had to admit that the fancy hairdos and exotic clothes looked great on beautiful Ali, but the exotic clothes and hairstyle just made poor Atselvdi look silly.

ATSELVDI SLIPPED QUIETLY OUT of bed. Even though Grandmother Sun was still sleeping, he had been awake for a long time and he could not wait any longer. The burden of tragedy had been lifted from his family and they had slept through most of the previous day and now slept mercifully sound in their beds. The next chapter of their lives might visit them in their dreams, but was not in their consciousness yet.

But, the next chapter of his life was now upon him and he was excited and anxious to engage it. Today, he would be traveling up the mountain on his own to bring his medicine to the forest people. He had respectfully lived his life in the shadow and under the direction of his great grandfather. He had never thought that he wanted anything more.

But the pride and gratification he had felt leading the retrieval party had left him wanting more. And now, this journey to administer his medicine independent of his mentor was all he could think about—all he desired. It was a welcomed change in his life.

Quietly, stealthily, he slipped on his clothes, his belt with its many pouches, his jingling necklace and his bulging pack while listening to the steady snoring of his grandfather. He had trained for this all his life and he did not need his grandfather this morning. In fact, he relished the feeling of independence.

And he would let his grandmother sleep. This morning he would style his own hair and fix his own breakfast.

As he wrapped and clipped the last braid to his head, he placed the empty bowl of mush on the hearth, wiped his sticky mouth with the back of his hand, slipped on his heavy back pack and stole quietly up to his great grand-father's bedroom door. He leaned against the door jam and said goodbye silently.

Adanvdo snorted, smacked his lips, gasped and yawned broadly as he rolled over on his back. Atselvdi froze hoping he would go back to sleep. Adanvdo opened his eyes widely then blinked. He stared at the bottom of the bunk above him, frowned, then turned to look at Atselvdi with a furrowed brow. The loving great grand-father strained to rise up. Atselvdi rushed over to help him sit up on the edge of his bed. "I'm ready to leave, Grandfather."

Adanvdo leaned forward and stood with the help of his attentive apprentice. The old Uku shuffled across the room and snatched up his sacred beaded medicine belt, carried it back and draped it around Atselvdi's neck. When Atselvdi tried to protest, Adanvdo hushed him with his uplifted hand.

The two crossed the main room and out to the porch. The old Uku bid his apprentice farewell, sending him on his mission to attend to the people of the forest in the remote areas surrounding Tsikohi who had requested their medicine.

Atselvdi puffed up proudly, put his hand on his mentor's shoulder to reassure him and then strode purposefully up the street.

Adanvdo watched his great-grandson strut past the Clan Council House, turn right and disappear. He was very proud of the remarkable boy.

However, no one but Atselvdi and his grandmother appreciated the eccentric style of the young priest, not even other Long Hair clansmen, the Ani Gilohi, a clan noted for eccentricity and arrogance that takes style to the extreme. Atselvdi's unique look begins with precisely coiffed hair—two tight buns swirled on either side of the tall, skinny boy's head. The long hair in each bun is first braided tightly and then wrapped round and round until the major sides of the priest's head are covered.

The swath of hair left on the top of his head is braided into seven thin braids and pulled through a richly ornate, hollow deer leg bone producing a spray of hair shooting up like tufts of grass. A long, white owl feather tops off the coiffure by sticking straight up through the deer bone and the spray of hair. A small red and white medallion dangles from the end of a leather string tied to the base of the feather.

Atselvdi's crane like neck supports an over-sized necklace made of alternating hollowed bird bone and eagle claws. At the center of the necklace, thumb-sized turquoise beads are strung in three strands terminating into a loop formed at the top of a fist-sized owl's scull.

A brain-tanned leather vest is decorated by conch shells on the shoulders and on each breast. Red beads on leather strings drape across the gaping vest, cascading down the front. A wide leather belt covered by a rattlesnake skin supports numerous rabbit fur pouches and a long, dangling, beaded belt. And, of course, the wide beaded medicine belt hangs from his neck.

Leather straps are tied just above his knees with deer tails dangling in front. The eccentric priest's long, spindly legs terminate into enormous, round, furry white moccasins.

Adanvdo laughed to himself, "He looks like a fat-footed whooping crane."

Adanvdo had never criticized nor even commented on Atselvdi's appearance to anyone. He left the boy's appearance up to his daughter. He suspected that she overcompensated for not having been around her mother nor spending much time with her clan relatives. After her mother and older aunt died and her younger aunt disappeared, Kalona was the only person of the Long Hair clan still living in Tsikohi. All she knew about her clan she learned during brief visits to other villages.

Adanvdo had not spoken to his daughter about the details of her birth and Kalona had mercifully never asked him about it. He had always intended to talk to her, but over time it just never came up.

The event had shocked and unsettled the village more than wars or sickness ever could. It disturbed the village as only a great catastrophe could. It was an event so far beyond the realm of normal human experiences that it traumatized the entire village and left it reticent. Adanvdo suspected that Kalona had learned a great deal about her birth from idle gossip in the village.

A birth can be an amazing event; dual births can be extraordinary. But the almost simultaneous births of Kalona and her cousin were but a whisper next to the tempest that almost devastated Tsikohi that day.

Adanvdo shivered with the memories of his life up to that event. Fearing his evil brother, he had fled from his home to join the Kokopelli Trade Caravan for over fifteen summers. The caravan traveled the world trading goods with the dominant cultures of Turtle Island and provided him with a perfect cover.

But he grew tired of the travel and unstable life and quit the caravan to settle in Tsikohi. The town had appreciated his great medicine and had adopted him and even made him their Uku. He had met the most wonderful woman he had ever known before or since, Wadulisi, and married her. For a time, he was as happy as any man could be. He thought that he had escaped his brother. He even came to believe he was ready to face his brother should he ever find him. But he was wrong.

Unbeknownst to him or anyone in Tsikohi, his evil brother found Wadulisi's younger sister. Saloli was a timid soul who lived alone and aloof. Adanvdo never understood what attracted his brother to her, but the physical and mental trauma of rape took its tole on her.

Saloli was very pregnant and was holding the just born Kalona when Tsisgili appeared and tried to wrench Wadulisi's baby from Saloli's arms. In the battle, Saloli dropped her own baby prematurely.

The event had been that last straw that had driven Saloli into complete madness. Despite her condition, she was the last of her clan and therefore it fell upon her to not only raise her own baby, but to raise Kalona, as well.

Seven days later, Saloli had disappeared and they had found little Kalona washed up on the banks of the Long Man. Saloli's own baby's blanket was found further downstream but his body was never found.

With no clan mother in the village to step forward and no mother bold enough to risk the curse of the child, Kalona was left to be raised by her father.

With moist eyes, Adanvdo remembered Kalona's childhood. She had been a faithful, loyal daughter and had given up her childhood to take care of him. He now regretted stealing his daughter's childhood. But at the time, his own grief for the loss of his wife had stolen his attention from little Kalona Ehlawei. She had never complained. And he had never suspected that she missed her mother or the benefits of a loving clan.

But now, he could see that she was reliving what she missed through her grandchildren and dressing them in the Ani Gilohi style brought her much pleasure. He had to admit that the fancy hairdos and exotic clothes looked great on beautiful Ali, but the exotic clothes and hairstyle just made poor Atselvdi look silly.

*Knowing the secret code had
not diminished Atselvdi's
respect for the belt.*

Tʜᴇ ᴍᴏʀɴɪɴɢ ʜᴀᴅ ᴘᴀssᴇᴅ quickly for the three-boat Tsikohi flotilla cruising down the Long Man to the confluence with the Chattooga and Tugalo Rivers. Tawodi Gvnagei looked at the tightly wrapped body lying in the bottom of his boat. He wondered if the rotting bodies would actually stink worse than the herbs and medicines smeared on the bodies of the dead Tagwas to prevent them from stinking and decaying. He dreaded riding in the boat with this stench for such a long trip and envied the Chief's messenger sitting in the front of the boat.

There had been very little paddling while flowing with the current of the Long Man, but paddling up the Chattooga required everyone to push their oars deeply into the waters to propel their boats upstream. It would make this part of the journey agonizingly long.

To Atselvdi, his exotic style was his source of confidence and beauty. The proud Ani Gilohi strode with a lilt in his walk and sassy twist in his shoulders that made his ensemble dance up and down and to and fro. And he interpreted the sparkle in the eyes and the beam on the faces of his beholders as adoration and respect—not scoffing or ridicule.

As Atselvdi strode proudly up the mountain trail, his thoughts were on the horrific corpse of the old cripple he had witnessed with his grandfather. This encounter with witchcraft had abruptly upset his idyllic view of the world.

His grandfather had taught him about the white uses of medicine and ritual all of his life. It had never occurred to him that evil men could or would corrupt the good purposes and twist it into dark uses. *What kind of person would desecrate the sanctity of a person's askina for his own evil purposes?*

Atselvdi felt a pang of fright in his stomach. He realized that he had left his grandfather alone to go to patients' houses. This was the first time that Adanvdo had restricted his services to the village compound and transferred his remote, rural patients to his great-grandson.

There had been no complaints from the messenger of the Ani Yvwi Adohi, the People of the Forest. They had watched Atselvdi grow up at his great-grandfather's side learning the priesthood so most had every confidence in his ability. And he had every confidence in his own medicine, but that was before the witch murdered Crooked Foot for his souls.

When Atselvdi had left that morning, it seemed natural and he had not had second thoughts about it when they had decided upon the plan. Now, he realized, everything had changed. *I must learn more about the witch from Grandfather. But how can I learn from him if we are separated?* he muttered to himself.

Atselvdi stopped in his tracks. "What now protects Grandfather?" he asked out loud as he felt the beautifully beaded sacred belt his great-grandfather had loaned him for his trip. The wide belt made of many colored beads had belonged to Adanvdo's father who had designed and made the belt. Everyone believed that the belt possessed extraordinary powers and it was known about and recognized far beyond the village.

Atselvdi removed the belt from his neck and studied it. The background of the belt was black with a white and red border. Down the center, red beads formed the geometric design of a man. Rows of multi-colored beads contrasted with the black background along both sides of the man and were also above the head and below the feet.

The rows on the left were stylized plants and leaves. The rows on the right were animals and birds. Everyone believed, since that is what Adanvdo had told them, that the designs represented the spirit world, protecting man from the dark world.

But Adanvdo had taught Atselvdi that the designs were actually codes. The colorful plants and leaves represented a potion or medicine. The colorful animals and birds represented a blessing. Adanvdo had taught him as a young boy how to read the belt. His grandfather had told him that if a person has a stomachache, the codes on either side of the stomach indicates what medicine and blessing to use.

It was amazingly simple in its concept, yet used skillfully by the priest could appear mystical and miraculous to the patient. Knowing the secret code had not diminished Atselvdi's respect for the belt. He believed that the belt was truly powerful and played an essential role as a protector of the priest and a healer of the afflicted.

Now, Atselvdi was in a quandary. His instincts told him to race back to his great-grandfather and give him the protection of the belt. His logical mind told him that he was overreacting and that he should continue to the aid of his patients. In fact, returning to his great-grandfather to give him the belt might actually be an insult to his great mentor.

Atselvdi climbed down into the ravine where a small stream was meandering its way down the mountain to join the Long Man. The conflicted priest kicked off his furry moccasins and waded into the cold waters and faced east. He reached into his pouch and pulled out a white and a black bead. He would let the Great Apportioner, Asgayagalunlati, reassure him.

Adanvdo stirred the mixture of oganagotagi (groundhog forehead) in the small clay pot and then handed it to the young mother to give to her sick child. Adanvdo pulled a rattle from his pouch and started shaking it. The bashful child rolled his fists over his face and giggled at the antics of the silly priest.

Adanvdo began to sing, "Treat the little one's stomach when they defecate the green and white. Drink the plant called groundhog forehead."

As Adanvdo danced and sang to the rhythms of the rattle, the distracted child unconsciously drank the awful potion offered by his mother. He shivered from the bitter taste. The genial old man held out his hand to the child. With encouragement from his mother, the child took the priest's hand and joined him in a happy dance.

The relieved mother laughed and clapped her hands as the jovial old man and her giggling child danced around the hearth. After a few trips around the hearth, the old Uku stopped and patted the child on the head. He was getting too old for such frivolity, he thought.

The child ran and jumped onto his mother's lap and hid his face in her bosom. Adanvdo put away his rattle indicating to the proud mother that the treatment was finished. As Adanvdo stepped outside, the grateful father offered the Uku a slab of venison. Adanvdo accepted the offering and started the short journey back to his home.

As he shuffled along the street, he dropped the venison into a cloth sling with a large pouch draped across his body and looped around his neck, careful not to damage the corn from the previous patient. It was a generous payment for a simple case of diarrhea. *First born*, he chuckled to himself.

Adanvdo felt a pang of fear in his stomach. He was worried about his beloved great-grandson alone in the woods with nightfall near. It was not safe even for an experienced priest if a Tsigili was on the prowl. Although Crooked Foot apparently had been healthy, the witch had picked him as an easy victim because of his immobility, shyness, and insecurity.

Adanvdo figured that the askina of the old man may have extended the witch's life by at least ten or fifteen summers. So, his fears for his great-grandson were probably unwarranted. There was a good chance they would never be visited by that witch again in his lifetime.

*"If you leave, the witch
will put the sickness under
him again."*

GRANDMOTHER SUN WAS PAST the midpoint in her
journey across the sky vault. As Atselvdi approached the
house of the old man known as Doya, Beaver, elderly
twin sisters sat cross-legged leaning back against the front
of the small, one room hut. They did not attempt to rise
as the young priest neared. He greeted them in the traditional way, "Osiyo, Grandmothers."

The old women scowled.

A young girl, roughly Atselvdi's age, came out the door
and stood, shyly, looking at the young priest. Atselvdi's
eyes fixed on the girl's large, dark eyes, round, babyish face,
soft lips and thin nose. He glanced at the twins searching
for some resemblance. The young girl was the right age to
be a daughter or granddaughter except that, in his opinion,
she was much too pretty to be related.

"Grandfather is inside," the young girl whispered.
Atselvdi followed her, past the staring eyes of the twins,
and began asking about his illness and symptoms.

The girl explained, "He claims a snake bit him in his
sleep four nights in a row ... in his dreams."

Atselvdi recognized the symptom. He had been taught that dreaming of snakes was related to something the person had eaten that had spoiled his saliva. The treatment required boiling a decoction of great bulrush, common or soft rush, vetch, with inner bark of poison oak growing on the east side of a poplar tree added. The prayer called upon the two Thunder Boys to take away the important thing that is under him.

According to legend, Thunder gave his sons snakes to wear as jewelry—the crooked nature of the snake relating to lightning.

The young girl led Atselvdi to a bunk on the back wall. Atselvdi slowed as he watched her long black hair blow backward slightly as she strode across the room. As she walked, she placed her foot in line with the other twisting on the balls of her foot causing her narrow hips to swivel slightly with each step. There was a dancelike rhythm to her stride. Sensing that he was not with her, she glanced over her shoulder and Atselvdi stumbled forward, blushing.

Old man Beaver lay on his side in a fetal position with his hands folded across his stomach. Atselvdi knelt next to the old man and began his examination. "Osiyo, Grandfather ..."

After interviewing the old man, Atselvdi was confident that he needed the anticipated decoction and explained to the young girl that he would have to gather the necessary ingredients.

He asked her to draw fresh water, build a fire next to the stream and be ready to boil the water on the fire. She escorted the young priest to the porch and bade him tell the old twins what he required. The old women pushed themselves up shrugging off his offers to help them. They waddled off into the woods and he could see that they knew exactly where to acquire the things he needed.

Atselvdi noticed that the granddaughter was cradling a heavy clay pot. He relieved her of the burden and asked her to direct him to the stream. He wanted to go to water and consult the beads for his own peace of mind.

Atselvdi poured the steaming liquid out of the pot into a small bowl and handed it to Beaver. He was struck by how stoic the old man was in spite of the pain he must be feeling. He was docile; never speaking; never complaining. Carefully, he and the young girl led the old man into the shallow stream. The young priest performed a short version of the water ceremony, paying tribute to the seven directions and the power of the stream and cleansing properties of the water and then encouraged the old man to drink the decoction. Atselvdi pulled the gourd rattle from his belt and began to shake it and sing the sacred words, "Now Then! Ha! Now you two Thunder Boys have come to listen, you two little wizards from the Nightland where you stay. It is the very thing you two adorn yourselves with. Just a snake that has come to put the important thing under him."

As Atselvdi continued the prayer to the Thunder Boys, he felt the penetrating stare of the young girl causing the hairs on the back of his neck to stir. "They are but ghosts that have caused it. Now then! Ha, now you two have come to listen, you Two Little Men, you two away from here in the Nightland where you live."

His throat constricted making his voice weak and raspy and his face felt clammy. He struggled to finish, "In the middle of the day they have let the important things down. You two have come to take it away as you two come by, to adorn yourselves with it. You two have put it away over there in the black boxes that are kept in the Nightland. It is worthless!"

Atselvdi glanced over at the young girl. Her gaze was filled with admiration, awe, and fascination. Oddly, it made him nervous.

Following his lead, the granddaughter grabbed her grandfather's arm and the two helped him wade out of the stream. Atselvdi gathered up the pot and then they helped the old man back to his house.

"I will return in the morning for the next treatment," Atselvdi explained. "We must do this four times over four days."

The daughter sweetly thanked the priest. She seemed unpretentious and yet shy and respectful. She dressed plainly and let her hair hang naturally. It was the way of the forest people. They were more earthy, innocent, and simple, but possessed a grace and genuineness.

Dusk was approaching as Atselvdi walked out of the house. He had hoped to get to the next patient before dark. The twin sisters were in their familiar spots.

"Where are you going?" One of the sisters challenged.

"Good evening, Grandmother. I suppose I will have to try to find the house of White Fawn in the dark."

"You can't leave!" The other sister protested.

Atselvdi paused.

"See there?" The old woman pointed toward a tree in front of the house.

Atselvdi looked in the direction she pointed. He jumped back and gasped! He thought, for a moment, that he had seen the appearance of an old man with long, flowing hair, covered by a dark cloak perched in the tree. He blinked and looked again. It was a large horned owl, sitting in the tree.

The first old sister challenged, "You saw the witch, didn't you?"

"No, it's just a horned owl." Atselvdi insisted.

"You have your Grandfather's powers. You can see the witch!"

Atselvdi shivered imperceptibly. Was she correct? Had he just seen a witch? He studied the object in the tree carefully. The horned owl stared back at him with haunting eyes. The knowing stare of the tsisgili was unnerving, or was it a tsigili? Perhaps the sister was right. Perhaps he possessed the gift to see witches!

The second twin sister spoke, "If you leave, the witch will put the sickness under him again."

The first twin sister chimed in, "You must stay the night and protect him."

The second twin sister continued, "The witch will not come in while you are here."

Thunder rumbled over the mountain somewhere behind the hut. Heavy, dark clouds were approaching. The thought of traveling in the rain and in the dark to his next patient was not appealing to him. Atselvdi accepted the invitation.

*He was desperately searching
for the very meaning of
life itself in hopes of saving
their fragile lives.*

THE LONG DAY WAS coming to an end for the Tsikohi row-weary canoers. The children playing by the river were a welcome sign for them. Tawodi turned around to signal Wahuhu, but saw that he had also spotted them and was pulling in to the sandy bank where the children had paused to study the strangers. As the long boats aimed toward the children, they scampered into the thick woods. By the time the Tsikohians had beached their boats, a delegation from the village had assembled to welcome them and invite them to a feast in their honor.

The exhausted return party enjoyed the venison and squash as the village youth danced around the billowing fire. Wahuhu listened intently to the village Chief as he related what he knew about the dead Tagwas.

"They arrived as Grandmother Sun was descending to her night place behind the mountain peaks."

The old Chief pointed to the west. He enjoyed his pipe as he remembered the encounter. He shook his head. "They were haughty, disrespectful men that expected grand treatment. The big one claimed to be the son of the Chief of the Ani Tagwa."

The old Chief spat on the ground contemptuously.

"We had a dance ... like tonight. It is our custom. We took them in as brothers ... as friends."

Again, the old Chief spat.

"They became friendly with our daughters—too friendly."

He pressed his palm against his forehead. "Our daughters did not find them appealing."

Wahuhu recognized the reference to the ugly flat heads.

The Chief continued, "Our young men resented their bold arrogance. They soon fought."

The memory was clearly distasteful to the benevolent Chief. "I asked them to leave. They required persuasion."

He handed the pipe to his guest, folded his arms and sat back repugnantly.

Wahuhu tasted the pipe. He decided that he liked the sacred tobacco of Tsikohi better, but nodded his compliments to the proud Chief. After enjoying the pipe for a few moments, Wahuhu inquired, "Do you know where they came from?"

The Chief waved off the pipe graciously as he responded, "They did not say, but we have heard that the Ani Tagwa have split. It is said that the offensive Chief has moved his people near the Tsalagi lands east of the Keowee River."

Wahuhu was familiar with the area. He had fought many battles there against the Tagwa. It was rugged, desolate land that the Cherokee rarely hunted. Few Cherokee made it their home. Prior to the war, a number of Tagwa villages had moved into the no-man's land. In the wars, the Tagwa had been pushed back to the Catawba River where they currently resided. Wahuhu decided that in the morrow they would continue up the Chattooga River and take one of the tributaries to its headwaters, then port over to one of the many streams feeding into the Keowee River.

Grandmother Sun was closing the door to her residence in the west. The Raven Mocker, Kalanu Ahkyeliski, watched the distant cloud light up as tiny fingers of lightning danced underneath. He listened for the rumble of the great Thunder. It drew his mind to the legends of the Thunder Boys, the children of Thunder, and their exploits. He mused about how Thunder Boy had journeyed west to the Nightland in search of his father, Thunder. When he had arrived, his father had tested him by giving him a box filled with snakes. To prove he was Thunder's son, the boy had reached into the writhing snakes and pulled out a rattlesnake and draped it around his neck as a necklace.

The necklace reminded him! His old mentor had once given him a necklace, a beautiful necklace, for the promise to never return. At the time, he was young and naïve and did not understand that the old man was a witch. He was fascinated by his collection of exotic medicines that captured his imagination and held his desire to learn more like a slave held in bondage.

Obsessed, he was compelled to return and learn more only to find the old man and his wife dying from the curse of his first visit.

He remembered his desperate mission to save the old couple from impending death. The lessons the old man taught him and the insights into the nature of life and balance and the dark ways that were the foundation of his great knowledge even today. He felt a warm, good feeling even these many, many years later remembering how he had quickly mastered all that the old man and old woman knew and then pushed that knowledge deeper and farther, searching for the link to immortality. He was desperately searching for the very meaning of life itself in hopes of saving their fragile lives.

Suddenly a strong gust of wind hit him and threatened to blow him off Edoda, his rock throne on the edge of the cliff. The old wizard pulled his bear skin cape around his shoulders and closed it over his rejuvenated body. Tonight he would eat the last of the heart, liver, and marrow he had collected. He already felt young and strong and invigorated. He would not have to visit the Ani Yun Wiya again for many years. But the encounter had been exciting and he realized how much he missed interacting with real people. He wondered if Ali would be so frightened of him if he appeared to her in his current state. He marveled at the strength and courage she had demonstrated against her captors. She was a most beautiful and strong young woman. She reminded him of his long deceased wife: the same dark eyes; the same silky black hair; the same slender frame.

He looked out over the beautiful green forests and saw the Thunder Boys bringing rain. The clouds were heavy and dark. He knew the rain would be coming in sheets so he climbed off Edoda and rushed into the shelter of his small, seven-sided hut he used like an osi— a warm retreat.

*Waya Usti drew his blanket
cape snugly around his
shoulders and fixed
his stare on the window
of his love's room.*

As Atselvdi unrolled his blanket onto the floor and shook out the wrinkles, the wind gusted outside shaking the mattted walls of the little hut. The girl giggled from the bunk above her grandfather and was joined by the giggles of the old twins sitting together on their bunks watching the awkward priest prepare his bed for the night. The old man just snored.

The embarrassed boy-priest sheepishly looked at his audience. He opened his mouth to speak as thunder rumbled above. The old women and the girl howled with laughter. Atselvdi realized that when he shook his mat, the wind had hit and when he opened his mouth to speak, it was as if the thunder had come out of his mouth. It was as if he was orchestrating the weather with his movements.

Atselvdi again tried to speak as the rain suddenly crashed down on the roof and drowned him out. And it drowned out the hoots of laughter but not the sight of the shaking bellies and grimacing faces of his hosts. Atselvdi bravely lay down on his makeshift bed. The show was over. The old women reluctantly crawled into their beds.

Atselvdi stared up at the roof that was glowing orange from the radiating embers of the hearth. He found it amusing that the hoot owl, or witch, or whatever it was, was getting wet. But he hoped the rain would end before sunrise so that he could leave early for White Fawn's house.

Hopefully, he could treat White Fawn and one other before returning for the old man's second session. The wind surged, blowing the rain hard across the roof reminding him that he must stop thinking about what he wanted the rain to do and leave it to do as it wished. His thoughts were just making it angry.

Lightning flashed. The Thunder Boys had arrived as he had requested and would be taking away the thing laid under the old man so he would not dream of snakes biting him tonight.

Atselvdi's eyes were drawn up to the pretty girl's bunk. The glow from the embers was enough for him to see that she was staring at him. The bottom fell out of his stomach and he quickly looked away. His embarrassment forced sweat to bead on his forehead, as he lay paralyzed under his blanket until the light from the embers faded into darkness. Only then could he summon the courage to look back in her direction.

Waya Usti lay in his bed listening intensely. The storm had passed and now the cicadas were singing so loudly he could barely hear his parents snoring in the next room.

Quietly he slipped out of his house and headed down the street toward Ali's house.

Only the billions of distant campfires of the spirits in the sky illuminated the village. In the distance, lightning illuminated the dark storm clouds. He tried to stay in the shadows as he walked and hoped that he would not see anyone nor be seen.

Pockets of damp, wet air held wispy gray fog, remnants of the flash rain storm that had passed as quickly as it had arrived. These pockets felt cool after the long hot day.

The self-appointed guardian sought his favorite dark, quiet spot across from Ali's house. The old, decaying hut had been abandoned for many summers since the old woman who had inhabited it had gone to the Nightland. Since she had no family, no one had bothered to tear it down, and so it had become the perfect base for reconnoitering.

All was quiet in and around Ali's house. Waya Usti drew his blanket cape snugly around his shoulders and fixed his stare on the window of his love's room. It was silly, he knew, to still be guarding her. In his heart, he knew it was just a thinly veiled excuse to be near her.

Adanvdo and Sali sat next to the hearth in Sali's hut. They had not spoken for a long time, each contemplating the dilemma they faced—what to do about the witch.

A voice from the door greeted them with, "Osiyo, Sali."

Sali's eyes popped open and he stared at his priest cohort with alarm. Equally alarmed, Adanvdo mouthed, "Who's that?"

Sali responded to the mysterious visitor. "Siyo, enter."

The two priests turned to see whom Sali had just invited to sit with them. The unknown visitor pulled back the door cover and poked his smiling face through the doorway. The relieved men happily greeted the village keeper of Sacred Days and the Sacred Fire. Stoker stooped to enter and moved across the room to sit by the hearth. As Adanvdo placed a fresh log on the fire, Sali refreshed his pipe, restarted it and graciously handed it to their guest. Sali started the conversation.

"We are pleased that you have come, Stoker, and are anxious to learn the purpose of your visit."

Stoker puffed on the pipe, clearly enjoying Sali's specially blended tobacco. At the point when Adanvdo had decided their guest was enjoying smoking so much that he had forgotten his mission, Stoker glanced at Sali, blinked, coughed slightly and then began. "I have observed a visitor from the Ani Nokwisi!"

Sali stared blankly at the old village astronomer, but Adanvdo could not contain his alarm!

Sensing that Sali was confused, Adanvdo repeated for clarity, "Someone from the Star People has come to visit."

Sali interjected, "Do you mean you, Stoker?"

The old astronomer laughed gaily, then replied, "Oh, not me! I am but a humble observer of the sky. No, priest, I think that one of the stars has come down to visit our village."

Stoker raised his eyebrows. "Are you familiar with the story told by the elders of the men who were curious about two shiny objects hovering over a hilltop? They found two furry, sparkling creatures that glowed like fire at night. After seven days, the furry things flew into the sky to take their place among the stars."

The two priests shifted impatiently.

"I observed one of the creatures flying around our village and hiding in a tree near the center of town recently. And then again, he came and hid in the tree above the Long Man when you were blessing the retrieval party. And then he came back and hid near Adanvdo's house. I knew he was of the Nokwisi because sparks trailed his flight."

Sali's eyes grew large and protruded like mushrooms pushing up through moist ground as Adanvdo's eyes were piercing from his angrily frowning face. The two priests glowered at the happy man, melting his exuberant expression. Adanvdo realized that they had poured water on his fire of enthusiasm.

"We are, of course, surprised by this news, old friend. What do you think the Nokwisi is looking for?"

The deflated man's brow wrinkled as he unfocused his pleading, apologetic eyes. Adanvdo could see that the poor man had not considered this question before.

Sali closed his eyes, smacked his lips and folded his arms nervously. Adanvdo searched for a way to put their guest at ease. "Do not be alarmed, Stoker, these are not things Sali and I are accustomed to ... like you are. I'm sure that something important must prompt a star person to bless our village with so many visits!"

The astronomer stammered, "I just supposed that the spirit world sent their messenger to speak with you, Spirit Dancer."

Sali's eyes popped open and he coughed as he probed Adanvdo's face for his response. The experienced Uku held his composure and responded, "Perhaps that is it, my friend."

Adanvdo saw an opportunity. "Of course, I would be very honored to receive a direct message from the spirits in the sky. It would be a great tragedy to miss such an opportunity, would it not?"

The old astronomer's spirits were perking up again.

Adanvdo continued, "Perhaps the next time you see the Nokwisi seeking me, you could find me straight away so that I can ... make myself available?"

Stoker grinned broadly. "Certainly, Uku."

The priests were not grinning. They looked at each other without words but knew what each was thinking. Stoker had seen the witch and confirmed that the witch was still hanging around the village. Remembering Sali's trick of feeding a dog the witch's tea, Adanvdo extended an invitation. "Stoker, Sali is making some of his delicious tea tomorrow. Would you join us?"

*He aimed the hollow reed
at the wife and started to
blow when "WHAP!"*

Aᴛꜱᴇʟᴠᴅɪ ᴀᴡᴏᴋᴇ ᴛᴏ ᴅᴀʀᴋɴᴇꜱꜱ. The rain had stopped and it was deathly still except for the old man's snoring, yet outside the birds were singing happily. It must be early morning just before sunrise, he guessed.

Silently, he slipped out of his make-shift bed, rolled it up and carefully stuffed it into his backpack. He tip-toed across the room and paused at the door. There was no one stirring.

He wanted to slip away unnoticed and just be gone when the family woke. He did not want to face the pretty granddaughter and haughty twins this morning after last night's embarrassing ordeal.

He stealthily pulled back the door cover and slipped outside. It was twilight. There was a thick fog and the air felt wet, cool and heavy. He breathed in the fresh air and felt invigorated and ready to set off for the dilapidated hut of Little Fawn.

"Good morning, little priest!"

Atselvdi wheeled around to see the twins sitting in their usual spot on the porch grinning at him. His heart leaped as he spotted the pretty granddaughter leaning sheepishly against one of the roof supports. Her large brown eyes stared at him from behind her glistening black streaks of hair cascading down in front of her face. Her slender arms were crossed at her stomach almost hidden beneath her billowing leather blouse. One slender, light brown leg was crossed over the other in a casual pose that intimidated Atselvdi in the most profound and inexplicable way.

"Oh ... osiyo ... I ... uh ... I didn't want to disturb you ... I thought ..."

One of the twins interrupted his awkward babbling. "You're a sound sleeper. You didn't even wake up when we tickled your nose this morning."

Atselvdi's hand reflexively reached up to his nose. His face turned red and sweat beaded on his forehead.

The girl softly asked, "Are you hungry? I could warm up something."

Atselvdi felt numb all over and the world seemed to be fuzzy as he stumbled off the porch. "No ... I'm not hungry ... gotta get to White Fawn's ..."

He hurried into the forest asylum to escape the taunting cackles of the twins and the pretty girl.

It was not a long walk to White Fawn's dilapidated shack. As he strode down the path, he could not get the image of the granddaughter casually leaning against the porch post out of his mind except when the image of her face taunting him from her bunk flashed into his mind. She was the most beautiful, alluring, hateful, disgusting girl he had ever met!

He wished that he did not have to return to treat her grandfather. He would not have to return until the sun was high, but already he dreaded it more than anything he had ever dreaded in his life. Maybe he would just go home. Maybe he would hurt himself someway and have to ask one of the other priests to take over.

The priest toyed with purposefully twisting his ankle on the rough trail. It would be very easy to do. Then he thought about having to hobble down the mountain with a twisted ankle.

He found White Fawn sitting on a stump wrapping a stone flint point on an arrow shaft.

"Osiyo, White Fawn," Atselvdi yelled out.

The young hunter finished tying off the wrapping for the arrow point. "Come with me. She is inside."

Atselvdi followed White Fawn into the shack. His frail wife was slumped over leaning against the hearth. Atselvdi was surprised by the disarray of the room. Clearly White Fawn's wife was not into housekeeping.

Atselvdi stepped over the clutter and knelt beside the distraught woman. Her hand was gripping her forehead and she was leaning against the rocks of the hearth as if she were exhausted. The dark shadows around her eyes betrayed her lack of sleep.

"She has headaches," White Fawn explained.

Atselvdi tenderly asked, "Where does it hurt?"

The agonizing woman put down her hand and glared at him. "My Head!"

Atselvdi touched the crown of her forehead. "Here?"

"Yes."

He moved his hand to her temples. "Here?"

She shook her head no.

He touched the nape of her neck. "Here?"

"Yes."

He touched the base of her skull. "Here?"

She took her hand and swept an arc from her forehead all the way to the back of her head.

Atselvdi shrugged off his backpack, got up and addressed the husband, "I will need a hollow reed ..." He made a small circle with his fingers indicating the thickness of the reed, "... and it should be the length from your wrist to your elbow."

White Fawn darted out of the house. Atselvdi found a small clay pot. "I am going to go fill this with water."

The wife did not respond.

Atselvdi knew just where he wanted to draw the water. He had passed a small waterfall on his way that produced the white water he needed. As he carried the pot down the hill to the stream, the image of the granddaughter flashed into his mind. He tried to remember if there had been any introductions, but there had not been. She had led him straight to her grandfather when he arrived.

He did not even know her name. It would be awkward to ask now. She would jump to the conclusion that he liked her. Which, of course, he did not! He just wanted to associate a name with the girl who had humiliated him.

When Atselvdi returned to the shack, White Fawn had returned also. He presented Atselvdi with a handful of reeds from which to choose. Atselvdi picked one.

He placed his pot of water on the hearth and raked seven glowing coals together. He placed the pot on the coals and then retrieved one of the rabbit fur pouches from his backpack that contained powder of a root. He pinched out a small amount and sprinkled it into the pot.

He then retrieved a large leather pouch full of his grandmother's sacred tobacco. He scooped out a small portion of the tobacco and poured it into the pot. He took one of the reeds and stirred until it mixed.

Then he knelt beside the afflicted woman. He began messaging her forehead, then the top of her head, and the back of her head and neck and then worked his way back to the forehead and started over. As he did so, he chanted, "The little men have just passed by, they have caused relief. The wizards have just passed by, they have caused relief. Relief has been rubbed in, they have caused relief! Sge!"

Atselvdi repeated the conjure while massaging her head four times and then sat back. He reached over and stirred the pot again. He took the short reed, dipped one end into the concoction and then sucked in a mouthful. He aimed the hollow reed at the wife and started to blow when "WHAP!"

The world spun around and he found himself laying flat with his head throbbing. In the haze, he could hear White Fawn's wife screaming and White Fawn calling his name frantically, "Atselvdi! Atselvdi! I am so sorry! I am so sorry!"

*He appreciated the young
hunter's intentions.*

WHITE FAWN HELPED THE bewildered priest sit up. "What happened?" the stunned priest inquired.

"When you aimed the blowgun at my wife I just re-acted. I didn't think. Forgive me, Atselvdi. Are you hurt?"

Atselvdi rubbed his throbbing head and felt a small bump above his left eye in the hairline. His stomach felt nauseous and he realized that he must have swallowed the concoction!

"I think I'm going to lose my stomach!" he said as he put his hand over his mouth. White Fawn grabbed Atselvdi and pulled him out of the hut and dragged him down to the stream. Atselvdi expelled the concoction into the stream while wondering if he was violating a taboo. White Fawn splashed icy water into his face and began apologizing again.

Atselvdi held up his hand to stop him. He realized that the water actually felt good on his face so he dipped his cupped hands in the water and splashed himself.

The nausea lingered on, but Atselvdi could not wait for relief. He had another stop to make before returning for the grandfather's snake treatment. As Atselvdi walked back to the shack, he did a double take and his heart stopped. The granddaughter was leaning against the door jam in that same seductive pose from the front porch. *What is she doing here?*

But then his vision cleared and he saw that it was White Fawn's skinny wife.

"Are you all right?" she asked in a soft voice.

Atselvdi took a deep breath. "Shall we try that again?"

White Fawn's wife took his arm and walked him back into the house. His mind knew better, but his heart was convinced that she was the granddaughter and her warmth and softness was thrilling in a way he was not accustomed. As she knelt beside the hearth and leaned forward offering her head to Atselvdi, he felt strangely embarrassed and hesitant to touch her. *What is wrong with me?*

Atselvdi took a deep breath and tried to control his dizziness. He cleared his throat and started massaging her head and managed to get through the first lines of the conjure by clearing his throat repeatedly.

White Fawn's wife pulled back and looked at him sternly. "Do it like you did before."

Atselvdi was shocked. She tilted her head toward him again. The nauseous, lovesick, kid-priest placed his shaky hands on her head and began to massage tentatively.

"No!" she shouted as she pulled back again and stared at him. "Rub hard, it feels good."

Atselvdi clamped his mouth and raced back to the stream.

White Fawn sat down on a rock next to the queasy priest. Atselvdi splashed more water on his face as he thought, *please don't say anything! I am trying to keep my stomach!*

"Her head is worse."

Atselvdi's stomach convulsed but nothing came out. He quickly splashed water on his face again. He took a deep breath. The taste of vomit was bitter and stinging in his mouth. He cupped his hands and captured some water to drink. He was afraid to swallow it, so he swished it around and spit on the ground away from the stream. "I'll be fine. Just give me some time."

"She says it hurts really bad."

"Okay, but I will need some more time."

White Fawn stood and walked away.

Atselvdi pinched mint leaves from one of his pouches and placed it in his mouth, then inhaled the fresh mountain air and struggled to regain his strength. Slowly he began to feel better.

When he returned to the hut, he found White Fawn trying to massage his wife's head. She was impatiently instructing him where to massage, "Harder, rub harder!"

White Fawn started to move away. Atselvdi waved for him to continue. "Don't stop!" she yelled.

Atselvdi began the conjure. "The little men have just passed by; they have caused relief. The wizards have just passed by; they have caused relief. Relief has been rubbed in; they have caused relief. Sge!"

Atselvdi picked up the hollow reed and instructed White Fawn to move to one side. He instructed White Fawn's wife to sit up straight, lower her head, and cover her eyes. He dipped the reed into the potful of water, tobacco, and root powder and filled his mouth. He glanced to check on White Fawn, then raised the hollow reed to his lips and sprayed the concoction on his wife's forehead. She lurched back and looked at the priest through her hands. Atselvdi instructed her to spin around. He sprayed the back of her head and neck with the concoction.

He motioned for White Fawn to resume the massages and he repeated the conjure. Then he sprayed her with the concoction again.

With each treatment, the young woman became more relaxed, friendly, and chatty. The treatments were working. After four treatments, Atselvdi led the couple to the stream. As she splashed the icy water on her face, Atselvdi recited the prayer for cleansing and asked the stream to carry her pain away. She stroked his arm gratefully.

White Fawn thanked the priest and gave him the arrows he had been working on in payment. Atselvdi accepted his gift graciously. He had no use for arrows, but admired the craftsmanship White Fawn had put into their making. He appreciated the young hunter's intentions.

He thanked White Fawn and headed for his next patient. He was still a little light headed and his stomach was still queasy but he hoped the walk and mountain air would help.

*Atselvdi looked back but the
stranger was gone!*

It HAD BEEN HARD going from the Chattuga River up the tributary and over the mountain, but it had been nice coasting down the widening stream into the broad Keowee River. Grandmother Sun was high in the sky arch when the entourage pulled into the friendly Cherokee village where Wahuhu, called Ocones, was recognized and warmly greeted. The village rolled out and immersed the weary travelers generously with food and drink. It was a very large village, sitting in a most beautiful vale.

The happy Tsikohians were escorted to the center of the village where Chief Attakulla and his comely daughter, Jacossee, warmly greeted them and immediately called for a feast. As in the previous village where they had stopped the night before, the chief and villagers clearly remembered their encounter with the three brazen Tagwas! They too had run them off after they had insulted the hospitality of the villagers. Chief Attakulla felt certain that he knew where the Tagwas had come from and drew a map in the sand. Wahuhu was quite familiar with the rivers he alluded to and was forming a good idea where they would find their village.

Rested and refreshed, the return party ventured on crossing the Keowa Lake and turned up a wide tributary. Wahuhu exhorted his expectant warriors to push hard so that they could reach the last Cherokee village before dark. After that, it would be no man's land until they reached the Tagwa village.

The strange man was hiding behind a large tree. Atselvdi did not see him and almost walked past him when the deep, resonant voice said, "Osiyo, priest."

Atselvdi shrieked and spun around in midair. "What?"

"May I walk with you?"

Before Atselvdi could answer, the mysterious stranger had started walking. Atselvdi could not see his face because of long, black raven feathers flowing out from the bottom of the thick headband decorated with black beads.

Atselvdi had never seen a headdress like this one, not even in any of the many ceremonies he had attended growing up with his grandfather, the Uku. The headdress looked as if the man was wearing it upside down. The raven feathers effectively hid the strangers face. The headdress was complemented by the long, flowing cape covered with black raven feathers. He fell in beside the mysterious man. "Are you a member of the family?"

The stranger was silent.

"I'm on my way to treat Goingsnake. I thought you might be a family member coming to show me the way."

"I can show you the way," the stranger said ominously. "You are Atselvdi, son of Tsi-la, grandson of Kalona Ehlawei of the Ani Gilohi."

"I am." Atselvdi was embarrassed. Where were his manners? He should have introduced himself. Atselvdi thought it not only strange that the stranger knew his name, but that he knew his mother's and grandmother's names. "Did you know my mother?"

"I have known all of your family and I know your great-grandfather, Adanvdo Alsgida."

Atselvdi was finding this stranger a bit spooky. "How do you know my great-grandfather?"

The stranger was silent. Maybe he was remembering or perhaps looking for an explanation. Atselvdi waited. Finally, the stranger asked, "Is he well?"

"Grandfather is well. He is getting older, but still gets around well enough."

"He is a fine man ... and a great wizard."

Wizard? Atselvdi had never thought of his grandfather as a wizard. "What do you mean wizard?"

The stranger thought about it for a moment, then explained, "He is wise. He is very knowledgeable. He is a friend of the spirit world."

The stranger paused again but seemed to still be thinking about his answer. Atselvdi waited.

"His powers are so great ... he belongs with the wizards does he not?"

"How do you know my grandfather?"

"I've known him all his life."

Although Atselvdi could not see the man behind the circle of raven feathers, he did not seem to be old enough to have known his grandfather all his life. The odd couple walked on in silence for a while and then the stranger stopped and pointed. "Goingsnake is up there."

Atselvdi looked ahead. A well-worn trail joined their trail and continued through the thick forest.

"Wado," Atselvdi said. "What is your name? I will tell Grandfather I met you."

Atselvdi looked back but the stranger was gone! Atselvdi looked all around, but there was no trace of the stranger. A coldness passed through Atselvdi and made him shiver.

Grandmother Sun was well past its high point in the sky when Atselvdi finally returned to the house of grandfather Beaver. A twin welcomed him back. "We thought you must've gotten lost."

I'm not so lucky, he thought. "It's been a strange day. How is grandfather?"

One twin answered, "Said he slept good last night."

The other twin added, "The snakes left him alone."

They both cackled loudly.

The girl with the huge brown eyes and long, shiny black hair stepped out on the porch cradling a pot. "Grandfather is ready to go to water."

One twin handed him a basket. "We got your roots."

Atselvdi grabbed the basket. "Go get the pot boiling, I'll help your grandfather."

The twins rolled up on their feet. "You go help Sudalegi, we'll get Grandfather."

"Sudalegi? One Thing?" Atselvdi questioned. So *that's her name!*

One twin explained, "Yeah, One Thing, not two things like us."

The twins cackled as they moved into the hut to get the old man.

Atselvdi found Sudalegi at the stream boiling the pot of water. "The twins call you Sudalegi. Is that your name?"

"That's what they call me." She seemed perturbed.

"What IS your name?"

The girl squatting beside the pot pulled her hair back and looked up at him with penetrating brown eyes. *Oh, no! Now she thinks I like her!* "No one ever comes up here. I guess you can call me whatever you like."

"Oh." Now Atselvdi was really on the spot. "What name did your grandmother give you?"

The girl rocked back onto the ground with her arms hugging her legs and her chin on her knees. She appeared to be sad and distant. Atselvdi felt uncomfortable. It appeared to be a source of pain for her. Finally, she explained, "I don't know what my grandmother named me. I never knew her, nor my mother. They were dead when Grandfather found me. He's not my real grandfather, but he has made me feel like his granddaughter."

Atselvdi did not know what to say ... or do. She seemed so sad and vulnerable that he wanted to hug her, but he felt so awkward. The moment was interrupted by the twins and Grandfather. Atselvdi gratefully stepped back into his comfortable priestly role.

*Atselvdi felt his face burning
as the beautiful Sudalegi
grabbed his hand and
dragged him around behind
the house to the garden.*

ADANVDO WAS ALONE NOW and allowed himself to feel miserable. It had been a long day and he had attended to many requests. He unfastened his belts and pouches and let them fall to the floor, then shrugged out of his cape and vest and allowed them to drop as well.

He unfastened his trousers and pushed them down as he plopped down on his cot, leaving them crumpled beside the bed. As he leaned back to lie down, his head-band was knocked off by the top bunk and fell onto his lap. He brushed it onto the floor and stretched his long, spindly legs on top of the blankets. He rubbed the back of his head to relieve the sting.

He exhaled and began to finally relax. As he stared at the thatched base of the bunk above him—Atselvdi's bunk—his thoughts drifted to his great-grandson. He tried to remember who he was going to see and what their needs would require of him. He chuckled when he thought of Beaver's contrary twin daughters he would encounter, but then he grew concerned.

The twins were obsessed with witches and witchcraft, always convinced that they had seen one or that one was waiting to slip in and lay a spell under them. His stomach tightened with worry that the twins would believe that their father's dreams were the work of a witch!

Normally, he would not be concerned about their harmless visions, but so soon after the brutal murders of Crooked Foot and the Tagwa, Atselvdi would be vulnerable and possibly drawn in by the twins. He would have to remember to talk to Atselvdi about the twins to see what he might need to straighten out.

It would not be easy to dismiss the fantasies of two old women and yet have to explain the reality of the soul thieving witch.

Adanvdo's tired mind began to let go and drift back to his childhood. His brother's laughing face flashed into his mind. He remembered his brother taunting and goading him into doing things he did not want to do. He had both hated and worshiped his brother when they were kids. He had never known a more driven person in his long life. He had never known anyone with more talent and potential.

Adanvdo's heart ached for his brother. But what happened to his brother, how he turned out, was so tragic that Adanvdo had spent his lifetime trying to block it out. Even now, as he slipped off to sleep, his weary mind prevented him from dreaming about the level of evil achieved by his brother.

The information that One Thing had shared with him had completely changed his attitude toward her. He was no longer intimidated by her. When she giggled at his mishaps now, it seemed simple and innocent and he was able to laugh with her and at himself.

He was beginning to feel more comfortable with this odd family. Even the twins seemed more ornery than malicious now. Their cantankerousness was just a façade. Atselvdi was impressed with how well the twins and One Thing worked together to prepare dinner. There was clearly a practiced cooperation and unselfishness in their interactions.

And Grandfather was becoming more docile and friendly as his health improved. It was not hard to understand why he was named Doya. His oversized front teeth and long, thin face did make him look like a beaver.

After dinner, the twins insisted that everyone retire to the porch to cool off. While on the porch, they insisted that Sudalegi show the priest the huge squash growing in the garden. "Maybe the priest knows a conjure to keep the birds from pecking on it."

Atselvdi felt his face burning as the beautiful Sudalegi grabbed his hand and dragged him around behind the house to the garden. He was thrilled to be alone with this amazing girl.

She had not let go of his hand as they entered the garden. This made the young priest a little uneasy, but he had no intention of letting go either.

Grandmother Sun had reached the end of her journey and twilight was fading. Sudalegi let go of his hand and ceremoniously pointed both hands to one side. "Well ... there it is."

Atselvdi was confused. "There what is?"

"The giant squash Sis wanted you to see."

Atselvdi squinted at the ground. Sudalegi giggled, bent over and pointed to a very average sized squash. "See ... right there."

Atselvdi could not help himself, he broke down laughing, which made her laugh. Then he laughed harder, which made her laugh harder. They fell down and held their stomachs and tears flowed but they could not stop.

Only exhaustion intervened eventually to end the hilarity that the poor little squash had caused. It was getting dark now and the light of the moon made the leaves of the squash glisten. Atselvdi sat up and leaned on one elbow. Sudalegi was smiling at him. Even with a silvery sheen, she looked beautiful. For the first time in his life, priesthood and conjures and medicines were not in his thoughts.

*When the Village Chief
viewed the largest Tagwa,
he spat on the corpse.*

KALONA EHLAWEI LAY STARING into the darkness listening to the whispers of a gentle breeze, noisy cicada, and frogs screaming in the distance. She was uneasy but did not know why.

Slowly her eyes adjusted to the darkness and she looked across the room at the bed where her granddaughter lay sleeping. Ali had been comatose since returning from the abduction. Kalona wondered what horrible experience had driven her happy, gentle granddaughter so deep into herself.

When the awful Tagwa warriors' corpses had been brought back to the village, Kalona had forced herself to go view the beasts. She was shocked by the size and ghastly appearances of the three men. She had never seen anything so hideous. She had heard stories told by returning warriors describing the cranial deformation of the Tagwa foreheads and she had tried to imagine what they must look like, but her imagination had fallen short of reality.

Seeing the Tagwas reinforced her doubt about how a fragile little girl like Ali could have done what she was reported to have done to the monsters. The only plausible explanation was that she had been rescued by the Little People. Maybe her lifetime friend among the Yunwi Tsunsdi, Nvwoti Atlisdodi Usdi, had respected her request after all.

Kalona heard something! Something was stirring near Ali. The tired grandmother lay motionless, breathless, peering into the darkness trying to discern what might be lurking there.

A shuffling sound was obscured by the raspy breathing of Ali.

"Nvwoti? Is that you?" she whispered, hoping that her little friend had come to visit her and explain what really happened to Ali and the Tagwas. As a little girl, just thinking about the Yunwi Tsunsdi late at night would bring her little friend to her. When she had told her father about the adventures she had experienced with the Yunwi Tsunsdi, he had waved it off as a dream. But she knew it was not a dream. It was too real to be a dream.

Cautiously, she drew back the bear skin blanket and listened, hearing more shuffling noises. She rose and approached her granddaughter's bed. As she grew closer, she realized that it was Ali that was stirring. Her granddaughter was having a nightmare! Kalona sat beside her granddaughter and stroked her hair. Ali jerked away and began screaming!

"It's okay, Ali, I am here, darling. You are safe now."

Kalona grabbed her granddaughter up in her arms and tried to comfort her. Ali buried her head in her grandmother's bosom and sobbed uncontrollably.

Adanvdo shuffled up beside his daughter, "Ali?"

"She has awakened, Father."

"Asgayagalunlati!" Adanvdo began to chant shaking his fist as though it contained a rattle. The conscious girl and her grandmother cried together.

Nearby, moonlight glistened off a tear running down the cheek of a young boy hiding and listening in the shadows of a decrepit old hut.

After leaving Keowee Lake, there had been a lot of portaging from shallow stream to shallow stream. As Grandmother Sun slowly faded, the Tsikohi contingent pulled into the last Cherokee village before no-man's land.

Once again, the villagers opened up their village to the exhausted travelers. Once again, the Tagwas were quite familiar to them. But this time, the Tagwas had names. When the Village Chief viewed the largest Tagwa, he spat on the corpse.

"Their village is beyond the peak, around the bend in the river in the valley. They moved there last year after the Ani Tagwa expelled them. There is no mystery why they were expelled."

The festive spirit of the village had faltered since the showing of the bodies. The villagers glared at the benevolent couriers. They could see in the villagers' questioning eyes that they could not understand why anyone would show compassion for these three degenerates and their families.

During the evening's dance, Wahuhu learned more details about the renegade Tagwa tribe including the whereabouts of the village and insights into the Tagwa chief and his dissident family. The hosting Chief recommended the bodies be burned and the gallant couriers of Tsikohi return home.

"You will receive no gratitude from the Gihli!"

Wahuhu questioned, "The Dog?"

"The Tagwa chief calls himself Gihli, Dog."

Three figures sat around the hearth illuminated by the low fire streaming out of the glowing coals. Kalona cradled Ali in her arms and rocked gently. The proud old great-grandfather sat patiently staring at the recently awakened granddaughter. She was quiet now and seemed at peace in the arms of her loving grandmother.

"There was a snake!" Ali volunteered.

Kalona glanced at her father. The old Uku looked back at her reassuringly. "Tell me about the snake, Granddaughter."

"It was wrapped around me, pinning me to a tree. Its head was very strange, sort of like a human head, it looked at me and then it opened its mouth ..." Ali sobbed quietly.

Kalona frowned at her father questioningly. Adanvdo shook his head no. Kalona studied her father. He had taught her that dreaming of snakes usually indicated the dreamer had a toothache, or the body was swelling, or the dreamer had eaten something disagreeable.

Obviously, the experienced priest did not believe that this dream meant any of that. This was something new—something Kalona had not encountered before.

Ali was quiet now. The trio sat in silence for a long while, until she slept again.

"What does it mean, Father?" Kalona asked as she returned to the hearth after gently laying her sleeping granddaughter back in bed. She seemed peaceful now.

Adanvdo spoke softly, "It was not a dream. It was a recollection in dream form."

His daughter frowned. "You think there was a giant snake at the campsite?"

Adanvdo did not answer right away. He seemed to be carefully constructing his answer. "Did you see the Tagwa bodies?"

Kalona shifted. She did not want to change the subject. "Yes."

"Did you look at their heads?"

Kalona let her mind remember those horrifying faces. Then, she understood. "The swept back foreheads ... their heads do resemble a snake's head."

"She is remembering." Adanvdo explained. "Hopefully, it will be revealed to her slowly."

44

"He says that it hurts his heart to hear that a Tagwa son is responsible for the death of a Tsalagi daughter. He wants to know what retribution the Tsalagi Chief requires to avenge the deaths."

For Tawodi and the other warriors, this was an exciting adventure into unknown territory. But for Wahuhu and the messenger, Awi Gawonisgv, it was a journey down memory lane, visiting old familiar battle grounds from the wars with the Tagwa years past.

The caravan of boats reached a small tributary. "To the right!" Wahuhu commanded from the center boat. Without response, Tawodi dropped his paddle to steer as his crew switched their oars to the left side of their boat and turned into the small tributary.

Wahuhu explained, "The Tagwa village should be around that bend. We will pull into the beach."

They spotted the beach as they reached the bend. Tawodi counted ten straw huts clustered in the clearing by the sandy shore. The residents did not have the deformed foreheads of the dead warriors in their boats. Three men were working on a boat while ten or more women were cleaning fish or washing clothes by the river or grinding corn by the huts. They seemed harmless enough.

As the dugout canoes rounded the bend, the villagers spotted them and stopped what they were doing to observe the rare occurrence. At first they seemed unconcerned and curious, but as the boats turned and lined up to dock, the women backed away from the shore and the men working on the boat moved to the shore protectively.

Awi Gawonisgv yelled a friendly greeting to the apprehensive men. One raised his hand in a half-hearted wave. Clearly, the men were very wary.

Awi Gawonisgv spoke to them in Tagwan. One of the men answered him and waved for them to dock their boats.

They rowed up to the shore and then the boatmen waded into the water and guided their boats ashore. Awi Gawonisgv began a friendly conversation with the men, but was soon interrupted by a party of ten warriors filing into the clearing from between the huts. Immediately, the women scurried into their huts and the three men guiding them to shore returned to their boat and pretended to work.

It was clear who the leader was. He was a tall, slender, muscular young man with a fierce look and the expected flattened forehead. Awi Gawonisgv rolled out of the boat and waded onto the shore. He shouted a friendly greeting to the leader. The leader and his rough-looking warriors did not respond except to scowl at the strangers.

Tawodi Gvnagei was nervous and placed one hand on his knife, the other on the bow angled across his body. "Move your hands away from your weapons, men," Wahuhu commanded in a low voice as he rolled out of the boat and moved up to stand by Awi Gawonisgv.

"Look peaceful, if you can." Awi Gawonisgv advised.

The Tagwa leader sent a messenger out to greet them. The skinny young man ran up to Awi Gawonisgv and began jabboring to him. Tawodi could only understand bits and pieces. The Tagwa language was similar and shared some words with Tsalagi. But Awi Gawonisgv could speak many dialects and languages. Being fluent in multiple languages had made Awi Gawonisgv a very valuable messenger and assistant to the chief.

Awi Gawonisgv introduced Wahuhu to the messenger and then apparently told the Tagwan about the bodies judging from the startled look on his face and his glance at the boats. The nervous little man ran back to the Tagwa leader.

Tawodi watched the messenger and leader banter back and forth. Several other warriors gave their opinions. Finally, the leader approached Awi Gawonisgv and Wahuhu. Through Awi Gawonisgv, Wahuhu and the Tagwa leader exchanged greetings and then Wahuhu led him to the boats.

Wahuhu allowed the Tagwa leader to pull back the black shroud from one of the corpses. The stench sent the startled leader staggering backward. Tawodi watched the reaction of the Tagwa leader's men. They stood stiff and expressionless until the leader laughed at himself, then they heartily joined in.

The Tagwa leader approached the corpse again and studied the grayish-blue swollen head. He cocked his head one way then the other trying to identify the dead man. Finally, he shouted a name. One of the Tagwa warriors darted out of the pack and ran up to the leader. The leader gruffly spoke to the warrior who obediently looked at the corpse. The poor warrior's eyes grew wide and grief changed his face. The poor man sadly nodded.

The Tagwa leader asked Wahuhu a question. Awi Gawonisgv translated for Wahuhu. "He wants to know what happened."

"Tell him that these warriors attacked our village."

Awi Gawonisgv studied Wahuhu for a moment. Wahuhu maintained eye-contact with the leader. Awi Gawonisgv translated.

The leader squinted and studied Wahuhu for a long while. Wahuhu did not blink. Without looking away, the Tagwa leader shouted to his men and the warriors bounded down to the beach toward the Tsalagi. Tawodi and the other Tsalagi warriors reached for their weapons. Awi Gawonisgv urgently whispered, "Stand still, he has ordered them to retrieve the bodies."

The Tagwas ran past the Tsikohians to the boats and lifted the bodies onto their shoulders. The leader whispered to the distraught young warrior who had identified a corpse. The young man raced off into the woods. The leader snarled a few words at Wahuhu and turned to lead his men from the shore.

Awi Gawonisgv explained, "He has invited us to his village to meet with the Chief."

Three Tagwa warriors waited for the Tsikohians to follow the other Tagwas carrying their dead and then fell in behind them. As they entered the thick forest behind the huts, a drum began to beat in the distance. The Tagwas began chanting what Tawodi assumed must be a funeral march.

What had appeared to be a tiny village turned out to be only a tiny outlier of the actual inland village. The

Tagwa welcoming party took the visitors through the massing villagers to their council house where four elders, the Chief, his translator/messenger, and top warrior were waiting outside. Awi Gawonisgv and Wahuhu seemed comfortable and unafraid, but Tawodi was uneasy. He did not like the odds and the hostile attitude of the young leader.

The Chief and the elders approached the first corpse, paused, and waited. The Chief looked sternly at his petulant young leader. Startled by the reproach, the leader clumsily rushed to his side. The Chief maintained his stare making the oafish warrior edgy and nervous. He was clearly confused. The Chief subtly nodded toward the corpse encouraging the young dimwit to pull back the corpse's shroud revealing the swollen face.

The Chief studied the horrid face stoically, but the elders were startled by the stench and decomposition. The Chief solemnly moved to the next body and allowed his aide to expose the second bloated face. The Chief's face was expressionless as were the recomposed elders. The examining party moved to the third remains. The lout pulled back the shroud. This time, even the Chief was startled. The crowd collectively gasped.

The Chief regained his composure. His face was stern and his eyes piercing. His entourage appeared nervous and edgy; the crowd was hushed. As the young oafish leader replaced the shroud, he got his first glimpse of the corpse. His eyes bulged, he released the shroud, stumbled backward and let out an agonizing, blood curdling scream.

Without blinking, the Chief muttered something urgently through his clenched teeth. The agonizing leader's face expressed disbelief and uncertainty.

Tawodi anxiously searched for an escape path.

The Chief motioned for Wahuhu and Awi Gawonisgv to enter the Council House. Wahuhu pointed to Tawodi and the Chief approved. The four were followed by the elders and the dumbfounded warrior.

Inside, the young leader spoke animatedly to the Chief. Awi Gawonisgv discreetly whispered to Wahuhu, "The young leader doesn't believe that the dead men attacked our village and wants the Chief to force us to tell the truth."

... "Oh, no, one of the corpses is the Chief's son!"

The Chief showed no emotion, and finally dismissed the warrior with a wave of his hand. The warrior controlled his anger but did not disguise it as he left the council house in a huff.

The Chief spoke to Wahuhu and Awi Gawonisgv translated, "He says that his people are grateful to you for bringing home their sons."

Tawodi studied the elders as they studied Wahuhu. Their expressions were contrary to the Chief's words.

Wahuhu responded, "Tell him that the Tagwa are our friends and we have done this out of respect."

The Chief's interpreter translated Wahuhu's words. The Chief invited Wahuhu to sit next to him and signaled to one of the elders who began preparing a pipe. After adding tobacco and getting the pipe lit, he handed it to the Chief. The Chief smoked the pipe thoughtfully and allowed the smoke to lazily drift out of his mouth. Then he spoke. When he handed the pipe to Wahuhu, Awi Gawonisgv translated, "For many years the Tagwas and the Tsalagis have lived in peace. It has been a good thing. The Tagwas would not attack their friends, the Tsalagi."

Wahuhu sucked deeply and slowly on the pipe and let the smoke escape without exhaling. The Tagwa tobacco was bitter, but Wahuhu did not want to insult his host. He then calmly responded, "The Tsalagi also believe that peace with the Tagwas is a good thing. We do not believe that the actions of the Tagwa sons represent the intentions of the Tagwa fathers."

Wahuhu handed the pipe back to the Chief. Tawodi studied the elders and the Chief carefully. The Chief was very calm, but the elders were clearly agitated as they heard the words from the interpreter. The Chief took another long drag on the pipe and again allowed the smoke to escape slowly. His response appeared to be distasteful to the elders. Awi Gawonisgv translated, "We regret that our sons have acted independently. Were there losses among the Tsalagi?"

Wahuhu calmly allowed the smoke to escape from his mouth and then answered, "We have lost two daughters."

The Tagwa translator gasped, and then relayed the message to his Chief. The elders gasped and looked to their leader for his reaction. Tawodi also studied him intensely. He sensed a slight watering in his eyes but otherwise no visible reaction. The Chief accepted the pipe from Wahuhu and immediately handed it to an elder to be restocked. Tawodi read this as a clever tactic by the Chief to regain his composure. As the elder dumped out the used tobacco and added fresh tobacco, another elder opened his mouth to question the Chief, but was stopped short by his raised hand.

The Chief received the pipe from the elder and drew in a long breath of smoke. He looked at the pipe thoughtfully, then blew out the smoke steadily. He spoke and then handed the pipe back to Wahuhu. Tawodi noted that the elders remained in shock and he perceived grave concern in their faces.

"He says that it hurts his heart to hear that a Tagwa son is responsible for the death of a Tsalagi daughter. He wants to know what retribution the Tsalagi Chief requires to avenge the deaths."

Wahuhu took an extra-long draw on the pipe and held the smoke and the suspense even longer. He maintained a grave look on his face and finally blew out the smoke. "I speak for my Chief and my people when I tell you that we do not want more pain. The deaths of your sons are a great loss to you, just as the deaths of our daughters are a devastating loss to us. But more loss will not balance the grief."

Wahuhu handed the pipe back and his translator related the message. The seven elders traded glances. Tawodi detected an uptick in confidence, maybe arrogance.

The Chief laid down the pipe and nodded acceptance to Wahuhu. Wahuhu nodded back and stood. Awi Gawonisgv and Tawodi stood with Wahuhu and the three departed the council house.

Outside they found their warriors and the Tagwa warriors locked in a staring contest. Wahuhu walked quickly but confidently between the two parties and whispered, "We go now."

Tawodi watched the young leader in his peripheral vision. The young warrior seemed conflicted as to what to do. He stormed into the council house leaving his little band of followers uneasy and agitated. Tawodi fell in behind his colleagues and stealthily watched the Tagwa warriors. They were intensely studying the council house. He could see in their eyes that they craved action.

The enraged young leader's voice could be heard coming from the council house. Tawodi ducked in behind a tree and allowed his fellow warriors to continue without him. He surreptitiously watched the council house through the leaves of the tree. He could hear emotional discussion in the council house and then the young leader came storming out. His followers awaited his orders. The young leader grimaced, clenched his fists and stomped off behind the crowd and out of Tawodi's sight. His little band trailed off behind him.

Tawodi caught up with Wahuhu and whispered, "I don't like it. That young leader is a hot head. He wants revenge."

Wahuhu whispered confidently, "The Chief will control his son."

Tawodi was stunned by Wahuhu's revelation. He considered it and then it made perfect sense. The young leader had in fact demonstrated all of the characteristics of a spoiled, power mad offspring. "I'm sure you are right, but I would like to watch him."

Wahuhu stopped and glared sternly into Tawodi's eyes. "The thirteen year peace is riding on our actions."

Suddenly, Tawodi felt the weight of his request. He blinked rapidly as he searched for words. Wahuhu placed his hand on Tawodi's shoulder. "We will wait for you at the headwaters."

Reflexively, he crossed his body with his hands and snatched the arrow from its flight toward his forehead.

Aʟɪ sᴄʀᴇᴀᴍᴇᴅ. Kᴀʟᴏɴᴀ's ᴋɴᴜᴄᴋʟᴇs slammed against the wall as she threw off her covers and struggled to scramble out of her bed. "Ali! It is okay, Ali. Grandmother is coming."

Ali sat up in her bed gripping the sides and staring into space as if preparing for something horrible. Kalona approached cautiously, softly trying to calm her.

"Are you all right, Ali? Grandmother will take care of you."

Gingerly, she embraced her granddaughter and felt her muscles slowly relax. "Tell me about it, dear."

Ali pushed back and pulled her covers up to her neck. "He threw me down ... hard! He wrapped a strap around my mouth. His eyes ... they were huge and protruded out of his head."

Ali buried her face in her grandmother's bosom. Kalona tried to comfort her. "Want to eat something?"

Her granddaughter shivered and then slid back under the covers of her bed, turned her back to her grandmother and slipped quietly back to sleep.

Kalona shook her head. She wanted her sweet granddaughter back, but she dreaded the dreams and memories that would eventually come back to her. It was not fair. If only she could just forget ... just go on as if nothing had ever happened.

The tired grandmother rubbed her eyes. Grandmother Sun's rays were streaming into the room. Kalona had overslept. She stood and stretched her stiff back, slipped on her dress, and headed to the main room.

She found her father nursing the fire. "I heard," he said.

"Is there anything you can give her to suppress the memories? Some potion, some conjure?"

Adanvdo continued to stir the coals as he added more wood, "She must be allowed to heal. We must not interfere. She will not remember more than she is capable of handling. It may take a while."

Kalona rubbed her hands on her dress and clicked her teeth as she glanced about impatiently. She knew he was right. She knew that Ali had to come back in her own way and in her own time. But she just wished that she could spare her the pain. She just wished that she could endure it for her.

Adanvdo glanced up at his poor daughter and tried to shift her attention. "I wonder how Atselvdi is doing?"

Kalona's eyes flashed wide briefly. "Atselvdi! Oh, my, I forgot all about ..."

"I'm sure he is fine. He was capable of administering medicine years ago."

Kalona's memories of little Atselvdi flooded her thoughts. "You remember that time I was sick and you were up the mountain? He was so pudgy and cute back then ..."

Kalona's words trailed off as she remembered. Adanvdo added, "He took care of you, didn't he?"

"Yes, he dragged one of your medicine pouches into my bedroom and said, 'Grama, I bring you messin.'"

The laughter felt good and released the tension.

Tawodi silently ran through the woods in the direction the young leader had gone. He had not gone far when he heard voices so he quickly ducked behind a thicket and waited. The young leader emerged with six angry friends. Tawodi recognized the jest of the conversation even though he did not speak Tagwan. The spirited young men were talking themselves up for a fight.

Tawodi carefully followed the small band of renegades as they headed west toward the river keeping his distance. Soon they reached a rocky cliff overlooking the river. The rocky promenade would provide a perfect setup for an ambush. Tawodi sneaked up stream and hid behind a boulder where he could watch both the Tagwas and the river. It was not a long wait before the boats with his friends appeared. They were rowing steadily along the widening tributary.

Tawodi observed that the Tagwas had also spotted the Tsalagi boats. The Tagwa Chief's spoiled son stood boldly and confidently drew an arrow from his quiver. He was obviously showing off for his friends who were clearly impressed and anxious for a fight.

As the Tsalagi boats approached the rocky promenade, the renegade leader took aim at them. Tawodi could not stand by any longer. He stepped from behind the boulder and screamed, "HI-YEEEEE!"

The startled renegade leader spun around, lost his balance and fell back against a boulder, bumping his elbow and causing him to misfire the arrow directly at Tawodi.

In Tawodi's mind the world suddenly moved in slow motion. Reflexively, he crossed his body with his hands and snatched the arrow from its flight toward his forehead. Tawodi's heart was pounding as he stood unharmed before the amazed Tagwa renegades. He could not believe what he had just done, nor could the Tagwas, and nor could his startled colleagues in the river.

None of the observers had been able to discern in the confusion that the young leader had fired the arrow while falling away and not with full force and velocity. Distracted by Tawodi's yell, all anyone had seen was the end result—a towering giant intercepting a deadly arrow in midair!

Everyone, including Tawodi, stood in shock for an instant. The startled leader dropped his bow and stumbled trying to regain his balance. His horrified followers were frozen in place spellbound by the super-human feat they thought they had just observed. The amazed Tsalagis sat motionless in their boats as they drifted down stream.

Wahuhu was the first to respond. "HI-YAAAAH," he commanded as he began paddling his boat toward the bank under the promenade. His warriors snapped out of their trances and raced after him.

Tawodi regained his composer and straightened up confidently. He held out the arrow, taunting the trembling son. The son's traumatized followers remained completely paralyzed by fear.

Tawodi ripped his bow off his body and slowly strung the arrow. The wide eyes of the Tagwas grew wider as Tawodi drew back the arrow and pointed it at the crouching, cowardly son who held out his hand desperately begging for mercy from the awesome giant. Tawodi sneered at the pitiful coward and then pointed the arrow at one of the followers. The leader fled to the safety of the forest. Like quail, the rest of the Tagwa covey scattered into the forest behind him.

As the Tsalagi warriors raced up and surrounded the cowering son of the Chief, Tawodi walked up to him and glared into his teary eyes. The menacing giant held out the arrow in front of his cringing adversary's face and snapped it in half!

The defeated assailant fell on his face and bawled like a baby.

Wahuhu gave the signal and his men raced back to their boats.

Wahuhu was anxious to put some distance between him and the Tagwas, unsure of what impact Tawodi's confrontation might have on the Chief. He sensed that he was a fair man and that he had firm control over the dissident tribe. But, he had also sensed that he sat alone in his dealings in this matter. He also harbored concern that his instincts about the Chief did not match the description or opinion of the Tsalagi Chief who lived nearby.

Wahuhu's men were of the same mind. They pushed their canoes up the tributary, hustled over the peak with their loads and then continued to paddle rigorously downstream without any encouragement from their leader. Out of courtesy, Wahuhu stopped by the Tsalagi village at the end of the world to update the Chief on their encounter with the Tagwas. He showed grave concern and wished the brave, but in his mind foolish, couriers a safe journey home. As the brave but foolish couriers departed, Wahuhu looked back. The village was lowering its white flag and sentries were reporting to their stations around the barricade.

With darkness approaching, the weary caravan gratefully pulled into the village at Keowa and enjoyed a welcome, festive reception.

*She was not an object to be
possessed but a phenomenon
that can only be admired
and observed.*

Her soft black hair floated in the breeze like happy tentacles dancing around her head. She was leaning slightly forward with her slender arms bent across her lap, one hand dangling to one side, the other raised holding a flower close to her face. She was studying the petals of the yellow flower as if it held some mysterious secret. She twirled the flower between her thumb and forefinger as she shifted her stare into the distance.

All of the people of the forest who had requested his medicine had been attended to, but Atselvdi did not want to return home. He felt warm and content sitting beside One Thing. She was quiet and reserved unlike the girls he knew in the village. She did not chatter constantly or aggravate him. She did not flirt and make him uncomfortable. To be with her was to just be with her: no presumptions, no obligations, no innuendos, no schemes, and no sexual tension.

He wanted to just sit beside her, walk with her, and stare at her. She was beautiful but she did not seem to know it or care. When she looked at him, she seemed genuinely happy to see him. When she walked with him, she seemed genuinely happy to be with him. She gave him undivided attention, yet demanded nothing in return.

Being with her was like being with his sister in many ways. He was comfortable with her and felt like he could talk to her without being judged. He could be himself—free of critical scrutiny. She accepted him; she approved of him; she liked him.

With Sudalegi, there was no rush; time was not important. This was not so for Grandmother Sun. She continued her relentless journey across the sky vault unfettered by his desire for time to stand still. He wanted to stop the sun and preserve this wonderful moment with a girl with a different pace, from a different place where time did not matter. She had no obligations, no responsibilities, no one awaiting her return, worrying over her safety, pushing her to achieve or guiding her life.

Sudalegi was truly free and uninhibited. He had never considered such a state could exist in human form. Only the animals, birds, and insects lived free of commitment, free of accountability, free from the bondage that humans place on themselves.

He wanted her. He wanted her to be with him, to become a permanent part of his life, to share everything with him. But, his thoughts and desires stirred guilt within his heart. How could he have her and not take away her freedom. How could he have her without obligating her; without imprisoning her; without stealing from her the freedom and natural life that he so admired? It was a quandary, an unsolvable puzzle, an impossible dilemma.

Sudalegi raised the flower in the air and released it to the wind. Atselvdi watched it float aimlessly across the clearing, dipping, swirling, as if dancing freely and carelessly to an unknown destiny. Was it a metaphor for their relationship, a sign that he should let her go to float in the wind?

He looked at Sudalegi and she looked back with a gleam in her eyes. As she brushed back her wind-blown hair, she seemed to be answering his question. She was like the flower. She was not an object to be possessed but a phenomenon that can only be admired and observed. She had to be free to exist.

The wild thing cocked her head to one side as if peering through his eyes into his soul. "Why so sad?" she implored of him.

Her happy face was infectious. Atselvdi felt his face slacken and his heart leap, rising above the clouds with her essence empowering him, engulfing him with the excitement of free fall.

He knew the answer to his quandary. You do not possess a flower wild and free. She was that rare thing you enjoy without restriction, like breathing the free air, watching the waterfall, or admiring the eagle soar. You may embrace these things but you cannot possess them.

The shadows had grown long around them. It would be dark before he could get home. Grandmother Sun had stolen the moment from him. As if looking into a mirror, Sudalegi's face reflected his changing mood. Their time together had run out. Atselvdi's demanding world was beckoning. Unlike her, he was not free to linger, he was the prisoner of his obligations.

*Ali's eyes were staring at the
fire, but she did not see
the flames.*

Wahuhu awoke before Grandmother Sun was offering any morning light. He did not have to wake his men. When they heard him stirring, each emerged from various quarters and quietly packed the canoes. No one spoke. They were of a single mind to return home.

Ali stood in the bedroom entry watching her grandmother stir the corn mush in a small bowl she had fixed for herself. The world did not stand still just because someone suffered a tragedy. Her grandfather was probably already out tending to requests. The old woman apparently felt her presence. She looked up.

"Are you hungry, child?"

"Yes, Grandmother."

Ali sat beside her grandmother and let the buffalo skin slip off her shoulders as she grabbed the bowlful of corn mush. Kalona seemed shocked by her appearance. Ali looked down at her frail body to see that there was no fat on her bones at all. Her skeleton was protruding through her pale skin.

Ali quickly devoured the corn mush. Kalona quickly prepared another bowl of the gruel and gave her the second bowl and watched as she made quick work of it as well.

"My, you are a hungry little thing! I am so proud to see you eat again. It is a good sign."

Ali blushed and wiped her mouth. Kalona handed her another bowlful.

"Did you sleep well?"

The recovering girl answered, "Yes. Did Grandfather interpret my dream?"

Kalona seemed taken aback by the question. She thought carefully before answering. "He said that your dream was not an omen and that the sickness has not been placed under you."

Ali set down the unfinished bowl of corn mush. She thought about the answer. She wiped her mouth and chin. "What happened to me?"

Kalona paused before answering. "What do you remember?"

Ali studied the fire in the hearth trying to remember. She shivered slightly and pulled the buffalo skin back over her shoulders. "I remember the cornfield ... it was foggy ... a breeze was coming ..."

Kalona listened patiently as her granddaughter tried to recall more.

"I remember being uneasy ... I remember a raven cawing ..."

Ali's eyes were staring at the fire, but she did not see the flames. She saw the basket sitting beside her feet in the cornfield. She saw the head of corn tumbling slowly from her hand into the basket. She heard the breeze building in the surrounding trees. She heard the dry corn stalks rattling as the wind swept into the cornfield. She heard a raven call. She looked up, the raven appeared to be on fire. Then she saw a huge dark shadow emerge from the fog ...

Ali screamed and jumped to her feet! Her grandmother pulled the trembling girl to her bosom. "It's okay, dear, nothing is going to harm you. You are safe now."

"What was it, Grandmother? What was that shadow in the fog coming at me?"

"You will remember in time, Granddaughter. When you are ready to see it, it will appear. For now, just rest and try not to think about it."

Ali relaxed. She felt safe with her grandmother. She did not want to think about it anymore. She felt full now and wanted to go lie back down. She pushed away from her grandmother, picked up her buffalo skin and draped it over her shoulders. "I'm going to go lie down for a while."

"Maybe later we can take a walk?"

Ali did not answer. Her mind could not let go of the emerging shadow in the fog.

The mood of the flotilla had risen in tandem with Grandmother Sun. Wahuhu allowed his men to laugh and brag about their encounter with the Tagwa. Their elation centered on reliving their encounter with each man's perspective adding to the grandeur of the events.

The tense meeting with the leader and his council highlighted Wahuhu's expert diplomacy. The tension outside the Council emphasized the bravery and steadfastness of the overwhelmingly outnumbered warriors. The angry villains that sought to ambush the returning caravan was embellished until it was a large contingent of the fierce warriors. And Tawodi's perceived super-human feat of stopping the deadly arrow enroute to penetrate his skull and single-handedly defeating the deadly intentions of the fierce warriors capped the day.

Spirits were high and energy abundant as the merry warriors flowed with the current of the widening Chattooga River. Time passed quickly and the confluence with the Long Man arrived as day transitioned into evening. The rest of the journey would be more difficult, having to paddle upstream the long distance to home, but the warriors' chatter ceased, adrenalin took over and the triumphant men pushed their boats homeward.

Adanvdo Alsgida trudged home as the darkness followed the sun westward and into the ground. It had been a long hard day and he had seen many patients. He could hear the whistling of a breeze flowing between the houses behind him. He paused. As the breeze blew against his back, he shivered and gasped not from the chill of the breeze but from the thought that flashed into his head. Kalanu Ahkyeliski, his father, was the only man alive that he knew who could steal a person's souls. Was he the witch that had killed Crooked Foot? Was he the witch that stole the souls of the Tagwa abductor? Adanvdo could not believe that his father was evil like his brother, but his brother was dead and his corpse securely inhumed in stone. So, who else?

As the breeze pushed past, the haunted old Uku shuffled quickly into his house. Somewhere in the distance, a raven called. Sweat beaded up on his forehead. Was it the witch calling or just his fear causing him to overreact? He stood still, holding his breath and listening intensely for any movement outside his door.

A cricket ventured a call to his mate telling Adanvdo that nothing was stirring outside. He pulled back the door cover just enough to peek outside. The distant fires of the spirits twinkled in the sky and brother moon illuminated the houses around his house. He studied the shadows carefully and looked down the street where the breeze had flowed.

Suddenly he glimpsed something move out of the corner of his eye. Was there something or someone standing next to the abandoned house across the street? Adanvdo studied the spot first looking directly at it, then looking just to the side of it, and then just to the other side. Sometimes he had to not look at things in the dark to see them.

Finally, he concluded that the hairs that floated on his eyes had deceived him. He was being paranoid. There was nothing there. The crickets testified to that; they were singing their hearts out now.

The tired old man shuffled across the main room to his bedroom. As he neared the door, he listened for his great-grandson snoring in the bunk above his, but the room was silent. *Maybe Atselvdi will return tomorrow.* Quietly, Adanvdo removed his priestly garb and draped them over the wood chest where he kept his formal dress. Moments later, he was snoring loudly.

In the room next to Adanvdo's, Kalona breathed easier knowing that her father was now home and sleeping. She could hear Ali's breathing quickening and knew she *was* dreaming again! The dutiful old woman sat up and waited for Ali's inevitable screams.

Suddenly, the restless dreamer reached out as if trying to grab something. Then Ali sat up and gasped. Her eyes were blinking rapidly as she looked around her and slowly began to understand where she was. Kalona rushed to her side and hugged her. "You were dreaming, Granddaughter."

Ali began to sob. "Let's go sit by the hearth. I bet you are hungry."

As they approached the hearth, Adanvdo shuffled out of his room and questioned, "Another dream?"

Kalona nodded. He waved his hand toward the hearth. "Let's sit."

Adanvdo whispered, "You look terrible, Grandson.

Dᴜʀɪɴɢ ʜɪs sᴛᴀʏ ɪɴ the mountain forest, Atselvdi realized that he had forgotten about witches and his great-grandfather and even his sister! But the closer he got to Tsikohi the more his mind turned from his fantasies of Sudalegi to the harsh realities awaiting him at home.

His concern for his frail great-grandfather and concern for his troubled sister drove him to overcome his exhaustion and hunger and make the return without stopping. Brother Moon illuminated the stockade as the exhausted priest crossed the shallows of the Long Man. It was a short walk once inside, but it seemed longer that night. Atselvdi paused at the door of his house, took a deep breath and then entered."

"Atselvdi!" his grandmother exclaimed. She ran over to her grandson and hugged him grandly.

Atselvdi could see his great-grandfather sitting by the hearth smiling at him. Across from the old man, a small figure was buried under a large buffalo blanket. Ali did not look around. His great-grandfather implored him, "Sit with us, Grandson."

Atselvdi dropped his backpack and sat at his usual place next to his sister at the hearth and awkwardly stated the obvious, "You are awake, Sis."

Ali was cuddling a bowl of three sisters soup and staring blankly at the fire. Juices from the bowl of vegetables glistened on her chin. Atselvdi looked questioningly at his grandmother.

"She was about to tell us about her nightmare," Kalona whispered.

Ali looked at her brother with tears welling in her sad eyes. "Amadohi and I decided to go swimming in the lake. We were standing on the shore naked when we noticed a weird man in the water looking up at us!"

Kalona sat beside her granddaughter and put her arms around her. Her eyes were wet as she listened.

"His head looked distorted in the water. His face was large but the top of his head was tiny." The image made her tremble.

Atselvdi closed the blanket around her as she continued, "He had two white circles around his eyes."

The face of the dead Tagwa with white circles around his eyes flashed in Atselvdi's mind. Ali explained to her great-grandfather with tears streaming down her grimacing face, "A mysterious shadow passed over him and then, suddenly, blood gushed from his chest and he stared at us with fear in his eyes and slowly started sinking to the bottom of the lake!"

She continued sobbing as she struggled to finish telling the nightmare. "As he sank, air bubbles flooded out of his mouth."

The terrified girl reached out to her grandmother for comfort. "That stare! That horrible stare!" Kalona pulled the devastated girl to her.

Atselvdi noticed Adanvdo's eyes welling up as the thought of what his darling great-granddaughter had gone through broke his heart.

He could not keep from sobbing quietly while trying to comfort his weeping sister. Atselvdi was now completely exhausted. His grieving great-grandfather struggled to his feet. No one noticed as he dipped three sisters into a bowl and cut a large slice of venison off the spit. The kind old man carried the food to his famished great-grandson. He stood patiently waiting until Atselvdi felt him by his side.

"Atselvdi," Kalona whispered. Atselvdi looked at his grandmother who pointed in the direction of Adanvdo. Surprised to find his great-grandfather standing beside him holding out a bowl and a slice of venison, Atselvdi reached out to accept the meal.

Adanvdo whispered, "You look terrible, Grandson."

He was perplexed by his grandfather's jibe. His grandmother and sister jerked their heads around with shock on their faces. Kalona and Ali looked at him and spontaneously burst out laughing. Atselvdi looked at his great-grandfather who was pointing at his shadow on the wall. He glanced at his image and then looked back into his grandfather's eyes and they burst into laughter also.

The normally well-coiffed hair was a tattered mess; it looked like a juniper bush. The two buns that were once affixed neatly on each side of his head were falling down and looking ragged. The braided strands of hair that were normally neatly fed through an ornamental deer bone centered on top of his head were dancing in all directions above his head like writhing worms.

That night, as Brother Moon peeked over the trees to look back on the quiet village, for the sad family, laughter brought them back to a moment of happiness.

So, that's what happened?
Tawodi thought to himself.

Amadohi sat beside her best friend, Ali, sleeping peacefully. Amadohi stroked her friend's coal black hair and thought how pretty Ali looked with her hair flared loosely around her head. It was very rare to see the petite girl without her hair braided or wrapped elaborately.

Amadohi was glad she was not of the Long Hair clan. She unconsciously grabbed the ends of her own free flowing hair and twisted the strands around her finger as her mind wandered. She yawned broadly and deeply. Amadohi had been sleeping soundly when her mother had shaken her awake.

"The men have returned!" her mother had whispered. "I must go to council. Kalona wants you to sit with Ali."

The men are back! She had sat up in bed and rubbed her eyes. It was too soon! They were not expected back for another day or two. She loved Ali and was happy to be watching her, but she longed to be at the Council House near a very tall, massive warrior that she had been unable to get out of her mind.

She had been careful not to disclose it, but she had noticed and admired him ever since his family had moved to Tsikohi several summers past. At first, she had thought him chunky and ugly. But, he had a gentleness about him. And for a giant, he moved gracefully and athletically. Once she had grown accustomed to his size, he had become more handsome to her. She had privately spent many lazy afternoons daydreaming about getting to know him. She had fancied all the ways she could set up a meeting.

But, it had not happened as she had dreamt it. When she actually did meet him, it was nothing like she had planned. The meeting was brief, formal, and without incident. It was right after the return of Ali when Tawodi had exited Ali's house to find her and her mother coming to see the family.

She wondered how she had impressed him. She replayed every second of the chance encounter in her mind over and over trying to imagine how she looked and how she had reacted. She remembered pushing her best smile at him when she thanked him for updating them on the condition of Ali. In her mind, she tried to visualize it. Sweat beaded on her face. She covered her face with her hands. *I must have looked dreadful!* she lamented. *My eyes were puffy from crying. I'll bet my nose was running and my face was red and swollen!*

The love-struck girl clenched her fists and grunted in disgust.

Kalona Ehlawei nudged her father. He had begun to snore and was drawing attention. Adanvdo snorted and smacked his lips as he clamored to awaken. He blinked and looked about. The Council House was packed with curious villagers. He straightened himself and tried to appear unconcerned that some were staring and laughing at him.

Atselvdi and Wananahi entered the Council House together. As Wananahi took her place with the Beloved Women, Atselvdi timidly rushed back to a bench in the back beside his grandmother. Kalona touched his hand and inquired, "Is Amadohi with Ali?"

The modest young priest nodded assuredly and sat down. He was embarrassed by being late and feared everyone was looking at him. He was devastated when he saw so many looking his way and sniggering. He just wanted to disappear.

Chief Waya Gigage stood and waited for the room to get quiet. "Our very brave friends have returned. They have delivered the corpses of the Tagwa rebels to their mothers, family, and tribe in accordance with the decree of the Beloved Women."

Waya paused and looked in the direction of the Beloved Women seated around the sacred fire adding, "And, of course, with the blessings of the Great Uku and War Chief in Katuwa."

The crowd grumbled as he continued, "Wahuhu tells me that it went well and that the peace between our tribes will continue. Wahuhu, will you tell us of the journey?"

Waya sat down and, slowly, the fatigued Wahuhu stood to face the congregation. "When we arrived, we were met by the Tagwa Chief's son and escorted to the council house. The Chief was very cordial despite his clear remorse over the dead sons. In council, he expressed his sorrow to the families of Walelu and Delagalis and his regret that sons of the Tagwa were responsible. He assured us that they were acting independently and did not represent the Ani Tagwa. And he expressed his desire that the thirteen year peace continue between the Tagwa and Tsalagi."

So, that's what happened? Tawodi thought to himself.

The crowd murmured to each other. Wahuhu waited patiently for quiet … "The Tagwa Chief's impetuous son was of a different opinion, however!"

The crowd was roiled again. Wahuhu waited … "He and several of his comrades decided to seek revenge independently."

Once again, the crowd was provoked. Once again Wahuhu waited them out. "Fortunately, we had in our party a very perceptive young man."

Wahuhu waited as the crowd whispered guesses among themselves. "Tawodi Gvnagei read the danger correctly and requested to stay behind to spy on the hot-headed young warrior."

The crowd was quiet now. The charismatic old warrior had their undivided attention. "He managed to follow them discretely to a rock formation overlooking the river where they planned to ambush us as we passed."

The clever storyteller paused to allow his audience to gasp. "What happened next is beyond anything I have ever witnessed!"

Wahuhu paused again and seemed to look each member of the congregation in the eye before continuing, leaving his admirers spellbound. "As the Tagwa warriors drew down on us, Tawodi stepped up alone to challenge them. The Chief's son spun around and shot his arrow at Tawodi. The arrow was dead on track for the center of Tawodi's forehead!"

The crowd collectively gasped as Wahuhu pointed to his own forehead and drew it in to indicate the line of flight of the arrow. Then he faced the very embarrassed Tawodi. "Tawodi, without blinking an eye, snatched the arrow out of the air inches from penetration!"

He enacted the snatching action and held his fist inches from his forehead as he faced the stunned assembly. His eyes radiating the intensity of his words, "This super-human warrior snatched death from the sky and held up the captured arrow in triumph before the cowering Tagwas."

Wahuhu walked through the crowd with his fist raised and an expression of contempt on his face. "And then ... Tawodi defiantly strung that arrow into his bow and aimed it at the Chief's son."

Now he enacted the motions with an imaginary bow and arrow. He pulled back the imaginary arrow fully and pointed at one of the villagers. The villager's eyes bulged and his mouth gaped as he jumped back and fell off the back of the bench. The crowd roared with laughter (and relief).

Wahuhu held the invisible weapon drawn and turned to aim it at several others to the delight of the audience, each time drawing great laughter and applause. Spontaneously the audience began to clap and chant "Ta – wo – di! Ta – wo – di! Ta – wo – di!"

Atselvdi had seen spirit fires flare and then flash across the sky. "So, all of those things were the witch?"

"IT WAS FOGGY AND I was in the cornfield again!" Ali was trembling in the arms of her warm, loving grandmother. "Again, I watched the ear of corn tumbling slowly into the basket. I could hear the wind approaching and I looked up to see a raven fly over and screech. It's tail and wings were on fire."

Adanvdo gasped. Kalona looked at her father with concern as their granddaughter continued, "Then I heard someone running and looked down to see a huge man running at me. He was painted and he was running so fast that it looked like his skin and hair was flowing off his skull! He had this mean, determined look on his face and he grabbed me without stopping and carried me on his hip. I was flopping around and every time he stepped it hurt as if I would break in half! I tried to scream, but his stinking hand was clasped over my mouth. I struggled but he was so strong that nothing I could do affected him. I sensed that there were others like him and other girls like me."

Kalona shifted uncomfortably, and Atselvdi was spellbound as she added, "I tried to see who the others were, but I couldn't. He slapped a strap around my mouth and then slung me over his shoulder! It hurt so bad that I woke up!"

Adanvdo's eyes did not hide his concern. Atselvdi had watched his grandfather react to the words, *a raven flew over ... its tail and wings were on fire!*

As Kalona coaxed the tormented granddaughter to eat, the old Uku stood and headed to his room. Atselvdi perceived that something in his sister's dream had greatly disturbed him. Quietly, the curious apprentice followed his grandfather and paused at the doorway to the bedroom to observe. Adanvdo stooped over and lifted an old wooden box from under his bed.

Adanvdo sat with the small box in his lap. He had never shared with Atselvdi what was in the box or where it came from. Atselvdi had often been curious and, as a child, he had often considered sneaking in and opening the box, but was afraid to. He was afraid that his grandfather would know or that the spirits would tell on him.

Adanvdo laid his arms across the box and gripped the edges with his hands. Atselvdi could see that his great-grandfather was remembering, his eyes staring into space. The curious spy ducked back behind the wall and then slowly peeked around the door again. Adanvdo was mumbling or chanting, he could not tell which. His eyes were closed and there was a sadness on his face.

He finished the chant, then mumbled, "Come sit with me, Grandson."

Surprised that his grandfather was aware of his presence, Atselvdi obediently joined his grandfather on the bed. Without looking at his anxious student, Adanvdo began, "The Raven Mocker can shift his shape!"

"Raven Mocker?"

Atselvdi was excited that his grandfather was finally going to share important information about the witch with him.

"He changes into a raven when he seeks a victim. The energy of his dark powers radiates from him as he flies. Many mistake the energy for fire. Some think they see a star falling from the sky, but they have really witnessed the raven mocker on the prowl."

Atselvdi had seen spirit fires flare and then flash across the sky. "So, all of those things were the witch?"

Adanvdo chuckled. "Oh, no, the spirit fires do fall from the sky sometimes. But the witch's fiery trail is very pronounced. You would know the difference."

The sad old man consoled, "If you see the fiery raven, do not be afraid. You have drunk the witch's tea and you have a pact with the white spirits. The witch will avoid you if he can. Do not be afraid to sit with the sick. He knows that if he enters the room, you will be able to see him as he really is and not in his shifted shape. And he knows that if you see him as he really is, he is doomed. Within seven days his dark powers will erode and his captured lives will escape and his askinas will collapse, leaving him to rot to death."

Adanvdo added, "Families may call upon you to sit with their sick to protect them. Do not back away from this duty. You are one of few who can keep a witch away."

The young apprentice's eyes grew large. Could he summon the courage to face the raven mocker witch? Not only had his great-grandfather illuminated him to the sacred ways to defeat a tsigili, he had validated that tsigilis exist and have incredibly dark powers. Something he had doubted before.

"I may have seen a tsigili, Grandfather, the twins pointed him out to me. Only he wasn't a raven; he was a horned owl."

Adanvdo shook his head and hissed. "Those twins see witches everywhere. That was not a witch. That was just a horned owl. The twins cannot see witches. They think they can and therefore see witches everywhere."

Atselvdi laughed with relief. Adanvdo cocked his head to one side. "What did you do?"

"Well, a storm was coming anyway, so I spent the night with them."

Adanvdo realized now that he would have to explain the difference between a common shaman and the tsigili.

Ali appeared at the door. "Grandfather, what do my dreams mean?"

The two priests looked up. The sadness returned to the old man's face as he bent over and shoved the mysterious box back under the bed. He patted the bed next to him beckoning his beloved granddaughter to come sit by him.

Ali rewarded his kindness with her heartwarming smile and joined him. The loving great-grandfather put his arm around his great-granddaughter and hugged her. "You are remembering, Granddaughter."

Ali thought for a moment then asked, "So the huge man is real?"

"Do not be too hasty to understand the dreams, Granddaughter."

"Why can't you just tell me what happened?"

"You are not ready to know these things."

"How do you know that?"

"If you were ready, would it be hidden from you?"

Ali pondered this revelation. She was certain that no one was smarter than her grandfather and she was certain that no one was closer to the spirits than her grandfather. She did not understand why it was being hidden from her, but she did not doubt that her grandfather was right.

Suddenly, a dark silhouette emerged from the door and strode directly toward him.

It was the morning side of a late night when Tawodi waded through the shallows of the Long Man and crossed the sandy beach to his home village, Tsikohi. The Great Chief at Cherokee capital city, Katuwa, had offered him a place to stay for the night, but he was anxious to return home and show his parents and friends the ceremonial tomahawk he had been awarded for his bravery, diplomacy, and extraordinary physical skills demonstrated against the Tagwa rebels.

His mother would be relieved. She had been very alarmed when the Great Chief's messenger had come to the door and requested Tawodi return to Katuwa with him. *She always fears the worst*, he thought.

Entering the stockade, he had a mysterious urge to detour by Amadohi's house before going home. It made no logical sense. What would he do? She would not be up yet so he would not get to see her. Still, his heart drove him to turn left at the Clan Council House at the top of the hill along the main avenue instead of continuing straight to his house.

It was very dark and quiet in the village and the wispy fog carried a chill in it. He shivered and pulled his cape close around him. As he neared the house of the pretty girl who had captured his attention like nothing else he had ever encountered, his stomach twinged and his heart raced. Sweat formed on his brow and his nerves disintegrated. He stopped in the street and looked around.

Everything was still, yet he felt as if everyone in the village was looking at him; peeking at him from the covered doorways of the houses; hiding behind the trees or the corners of the houses. Just ahead on the left side of the street was Ali's house. His shoulders tightened and his neck withdrew into them like a turtle. Her great-grandfather was the village Uku. Her spooky brother was a priest and her grandmother the Peace Chief. He feared they could sense his presence.

Tawodi decided not to approach the target of his impulse directly. He stealthily darted between the houses to his right and paused to catch his breath and regain his nerve. He could feel his heart pounding in his head and hear himself breathing. He feared that the noise would wake the neighborhood.

Then he heard something else! It was hardly perceptible, but something nevertheless. He pressed his giant frame against the mud plaster of the house and peeked around the corner. He studied the house of Ali. The door cover hung limp and was dead still. Further down the street was a broken down abandoned hut. Someone was stirring inside it! Suddenly, a dark silhouette emerged from the door and strode directly toward him. Tawodi pulled back and waited breathlessly for the silhouette to pass. He could hear the careful footsteps advancing toward him, taking several quick steps and then pausing, then several more and pausing.

Tawodi could tell that the presence had come to the corner of the house he was leaning against and was standing only two steps away! The big youth felt very tiny and inadequate as he gripped the ceremonial tomahawk and slowly raised it into a ready position. He reached across his waist and started pulling his knife from its scabbard.

Suddenly, a tall, slender man entered the space between the houses and pressed up against the wall of the house opposite Tawodi. The man's back was toward him and he was clearly not aware of his presence. Tawodi froze!

The tall man was watching the street anxiously. Tawodi glanced at the street. He could hear someone walking in the street. The tall man pressed his chest against the house. There was something very familiar about him.

Tawodi glimpsed movement in the street and looked to see a wispy, white, ghostlike figure shuffling along. *A woman out walking so late?* He looked back at the tall shadow. In the instant before looking directly at the tall man, his eyes caught a clearer image of the silhouette and he knew that the mysterious man was his cousin, Waya Usti. Tawodi's impulse was to laugh, but he remained silent. The sneaky cousin headed between the houses away from the street. Quickly, he disappeared around the corner.

How pathetic! Hiding in the night just to gaze at his girlfriend's house, Tawodi thought. *He's really got it bad.*

Tawodi chuckled to himself until he realized that he was on the same mission. The proud young man swallowed hard. *How pathetic am I?*

Tawodi looked up the street to spot the passerby. The eery woman in the flowing, long white dress turned left by Ali's house and disappeared down that street. Tawodi started home but stopped. He thought about the old shack that Waya Usti had come out of.

Tawodi checked the street in front of Ali's house again. The coast was clear. The large man tried to make himself invisible as he slipped into the street and headed for the dilapidated hut. As he entered the intersection in front of the hut, he glanced to his right. His hunch was correct, the old hut also provided an excellent view of Amadohi's house!

52

She regripped the claw and pushed her mind to remember more.

W ITH THE RETURN OF the bestowal troop, optimism abounded in the little village of Tsikohi. Anxious to get this bad chapter in their lives behind them, the residents hoped that happiness would soon return.

Ali sat on the edge of her bed and watched her tired grandmother sleeping peacefully. She gazed out the window at the tall pine growing across the street.

She remembered that an old woman used to sit in the shade of that tree and watch her play. Kalona had told her that as a young girl, the old woman had protected the tree while it was a sapling and the grateful mature tree paid her back with shade.

In old age, the tree was the only companion for the old lady since all of her relatives had died. When the old woman died, Ali's grandmother and great-grandfather had tended to her burial. But no one had come to remove her house and it was now rotting and about to fall down. Ali suspected that the old woman's spirit now dwelled in the tree that was still growing taller and stronger.

She had been a little afraid of the old woman and the old woman had never tried to befriend little Ali. She had just sat there weaving baskets and glaring at the little girl and her twin brother as they played.

Ali now wished that she had tried to make friends with her. Now she wondered what the old woman had thought about and what she was really like. She had made special baskets for her great-grandfather and her grandmother. Kalona had visited with her and took food to her and sometimes sat and talked with her. But Grandmother was a friend to everyone and the old woman did not appear to be close to Kalona. Ali made a mental note to ask her grandmother about the old woman.

Ali felt good that morning. She was getting her strength back now. Today, a piece of her wanted to go outside, but a piece of her did not want to leave the security of the house. She walked over to the window to look out and feel the cool air from outside. She looked at the spot where the old woman used to sit. It was empty now. But then she detected movement in the old decrepit house. It was like a shadow moving inside; like the old woman's spirit roaming around in her old house. She searched through the windows and cracks for the allusive shadow, but now the house was still. It made her shiver. It felt as if the old woman's ghost was staring back at her.

For a moment, she thought she might go outside and search inside the old house, but then she returned across the room and lay back down on the bed, curled into a fetal position, and closed her eyes. She did not know why she was so afraid to go out. Something deep within her bade her stay near her bed or the hearth in the next room with her grandmother. Thinking of leaving brought great anxiety to her.

Ali rolled over on her back and stretched out taking in a deep breath. She rose up and forced herself to leave the bedroom. Her body felt oddly light and her head a bit dizzy as she stepped into the main room. Warm embers glowed in the hearth inviting her to sit. She strolled over to the door of her great-grandfather's room and found it empty.

It felt good to be walking about so she wandered into her great-grandfather's room to admire the baskets and pouches full of wondrous things. As a little girl, she had secretly investigated the contents. There were many pretty beads and shells and feathers. There were many plants and roots. She could remember the smell of dirt, the sweet smell of berries, and the pungent odor of some of the roots.

Ali ran her hand over the stiff basket weaves—probably woven by the old woman under the tree. The smell of her grandfather was in the room. She longed to talk with her grandfather again about her dreams, but she knew he would just advise her to let the dreams unveil the gaps in her memories in their own time.

She looked at the corner behind the bunk beds where her brother kept his personal items, stacked neatly, unlike the random piles of her grandfather.

She touched the top bunk where Atselvdi slept. Just a woven mat and a buffalo blanket satisfied her serious and dedicated brother, but she also felt something furry and stiff. It was the ragged rabbit skin that her brother had needed to sleep with at night as a small boy. She suspected he still clutched the skin at night, but no one spoke of it now.

She felt something against her foot. She reached down and pulled out a wooden box. She remembered that her great-grandfather had shoved it under the bed when she came in to ask about her dreams the previous night.

She sat on the bed cradling it in her lap as her great-grandfather had done. It had an unusual handle on the top. She studied it and then grasped it. It was a huge bird's claw!

Images flashed in her head as she touched it—images of a campsite in a canyon. Ali shivered. She drew back her hand, but then she realized that she had been there. The image of the three Tagwa warriors flashed into her head and she could see Delagalis bound to stakes in the ground with a giant warrior sleeping next to her. Ali realized that she was starting to remember.

She regripped the claw and pushed her mind to remember more. She remembered being tied to a tree and the excruciating pain in her arms and wrists and ankles. The images suddenly started flooding back: the brutal stabbings of the other girls; the tormenting Tagwa that slugged her in the stomach; and the nauseating pain.

Then she saw the naked Tagwa angrily swaggering up to her with the huge knife! Ali threw down the box, grabbed her hair and screamed until she passed out.

It was her great-grandfather who found her unconscious on his bed. His heart quaked when he spotted his secret box lying on the floor. He quickly shoved it back under the bed and then sat down beside Ali.

Feeling a sadness that comes when a parent observes a child losing his/her innocence, he lamented, it has all been revealed to her!

CHAPTER

53

"Grandfather says that the droplets show how one drop affects the entire pond just as one man's actions affect all men."

IT WAS COOL IN the shade by the water. The occasional breeze rocked the trees and funneled its way through the canyon carved out by the Long Man. Ali sat next to her twin brother below the beaver dams in silence.

She was amused by her brother's childish playing. He held the trunk end of a small tree branch in both hands, dipped the leafy branches into the water, and watched the ripples in the water. Once the water calmed, he flicked the branch upward sending a spray of water into the air. He quickly moved the branch away to let the droplets fall back into the water and watched the circling ripples mingling with the waves of the disturbed waters as they radiated outward, merging, spreading, calming.

Ali sat with her chin on her knees studying the water. She threaded her fingers into her hair falling across her forehead and pushed the flowing black hair up onto the top of her head, turned her head at an angle and stared at her brother.

"What are you doing?"

Atselvdi jumped as if he had forgotten about his sister sitting next to him. They had been sitting for a long time wrapped up in their individual thoughts and just enjoying a lazy, cool afternoon. It was so peaceful in this, his favorite spot, where he had told her he did his best thinking.

"Grandfather says that the droplets show how one drop affects the entire pond just as one man's actions affect all men."

He submerged the branch tip back into the water and waited for the waters to calm.

"Grandfather told me that this demonstrates how life absorbs tragedies and upheavals. He told me that patience restores the calm; that time maintains the balance; that all things find their place; and that the natural way of things is peace."

She sensed that Atselvdi had been surprised but elated when she had accepted his offer to walk with him. He had tried to strike up a conversation, but she had been reluctant to chat. It had been less than a moon cycle since she had remembered the abduction. The dreadful memories had left her withdrawn and moody and she had only rarely ventured outdoors. As they passed by the old woman's crumbling house, she thought she detected movement inside again. She had gasped and Atselvdi had embraced her to comfort her. She had told him about the ghost she thought she had seen in the old house numerous times. Oddly, Atselvdi had just changed the subject. She found it odd that her brother was not interested in the dead searching for their ancestors in spite of his being a priest.

Ali turned her attention to her brother still studying the water in the pond. He was deep in thought. "What are you thinking now?" she asked softly.

"I was thinking that soon you will find peace. I was thinking that the Tagwa warriors disturbed the peace of Tsikohi, too, and now peace is returning to the village. Just as the waters eventually smooth out, people return to their normal activities, hearts mend, and in time, you will be your happy self again."

Ali looked back at the water, released her hair and wrapped both arms around her legs. *Maybe he was right. Maybe the ripples from her ordeal—more like waves—would soon smooth out like the water.*

Atselvdi flipped the branch up again sending a spray of water into the air, moved the branch to one side and watched the droplets fall back into the water. She wondered if he was demonstrating his theory for her again or if there were ripples in his life right now. She wondered what deep thoughts might be troubling her serious brother. She speculated that he must be pondering issues of the priesthood or perhaps some troubling affliction of one of his patients. She would have been amused by the heavy concerns weighing on his mind: *Was he just a droplet in One Thing's life that would soon disappear from her thoughts? Had the ripples of their encounter already disappeared?*

A noise from the forest caused them to turn to glimpse a vague shadow hiding in the trees. It was a scary shadow that she had seen before! It was the feeling she had gotten looking at the old woman's house across the street ... the feeling that someone was spying on her. She gasped and leaped into her brother's arms. As she trembled in fear, she blurted out, "It's the shadow, Atselvdi!"

Atselvdi looked back and then began to giggle. She angrily pulled away and glared at her insensitive twin brother.

"I'm sorry, Sis," Atselvdi offered, "but I just saw the mysterious shadow you speak of and I know who it is. Wait here."

"I will not!" protested Ali grabbing him again, "Don't you dare leave me here alone."

Atselvdi hugged his frightened sister. "Okay, but don't you want to know who's been spying on you?"

"Spying on me?" the trembling girl quizzed.

"HI YEE! Waya Usti!" Atselvdi shouted. "Come join us!"

"Waya Usti?"

The tall, muscular, bashful young man stepped out from behind the tree and shyly walked toward Ali and her brother. Ali stood. She recognized the young man as the boy everyone kidded because of his shyness and silly name. She had felt sorry for him and had never participated in any of the cruel teasing. As they had grown older, Ali had come to admire the quiet, strong Wolf Puppy.

As Waya Usti approached, much to the anguish of the young man, Atselvdi continued, "When Waya Usti learned about your abduction, he was the first to join the search party. He was first to follow your screams to the Tagwa camp, and he was the one who carried you back to the village."

Waya Usti stared at the ground as if completely humiliated. Ali clasped her hands in front of her modestly, straightened her arms and gently swayed back and forth as she smiled sweetly and studied the bashful young man before her.

Atselvdi was enjoying embarrassing his friend and sister, so he continued, "He has appointed himself to be your protector and has watched over you from the shadows ever since."

Waya Usti clenched his teeth and growled, "Enough, Atselvdi!"

Ali giggled delightfully. She had never taken Waya Usti seriously. She was flattered by his attention. She had also not noticed how he had matured. Suddenly, she realized that the tormented kid she had protected years ago was now a strong, handsome young man.

Waya Usti was blushing and stirring the dirt with his foot. He looked like he might turn and run home to his mother.

Ali wanted to rescue him. "We were just sitting by the beaver dams. Do you want to join us?"

The forlorn young man suddenly appeared to be soaring! "Uh huh!" he muttered dumbly.

Atselvdi glanced up at Grandmother Sun. "Ali, I need to go. Grandfather wants me to help with ball play practice. Will you be all right?"

Ali pouted. "Ball play! Why so soon after ..."

"Grandfather thinks it is time."

Ali hissed her contempt. Atselvdi persisted, "Grandfather thinks it is just what Tsikohi needs to get back to normal."

"I'll be fine. Maybe Waya Usti will stay with me."

The twins looked at their bashful friend who opened his mouth, but no words came out.

Adanvdo finished his inspection and then turned the team over to his grandson and able assistant, Tlomeha Usdi.

Eɪɢʜᴛ ʙᴀʟʟ ᴘʟᴀʏᴇʀs sᴛᴏᴏᴅ before the Uku beside the Long Man. Today, these specially selected young men—Tsikohi's most athletic, most aggressive, most proven and respected—would begin their training for the most important ball game of the year against their long-time rival, the team from Gwalgahi, an old village along the Hiawasee River.

Adanvdo could see it in their eyes; in their faces; in their body language. In a word, it was confidence. Most of the players had also played on last year's undefeated team. They had confidence in themselves and in the Uku. It was the formula for success for a ball team—to believe in and have confidence in themselves and in their leader. As the Uku, it had been Adanvdo's duty to prepare, bless, and coach the village ball teams for many years.

He was proud of his success. He had always felt that the secret to his success was knowing that it was his job to make the players believe that they would win. And it meant that the players first had to believe fully in him. Then, through him, they could come to believe in themselves. And the more they won, the more they believed in themselves and the more they believed in the Uku's powers.

The anetso was arguably the most important activity in a village. It had been so longer than any living memory. It was believed that Ball Play had been invented by the Tsalagi and the Iroquois as a means to end perpetual war between the two, hence the reason it was called anetso or war's brother.

It was said that the Tsalagi and the Iroquois had once been one tribe. But when the Iroquois disrespected the Tsalagi, the Tsalagi broke away and for many years fought a seemingly endless war.

Finally, the two Great Chiefs counseled and decided to settle the dispute through the anetso. Since then, every year the biggest event for the Ani Yun Wiya was the anetso between the two national teams and since then peace had prevailed between the Iroquois and the Tsalagi.

The idea had spread throughout the neighboring tribes and the anetso had become an important activity among all the tribes east of Big River. It did not always keep the peace between tribes, but it had become a great deterrent and the most effective way to settle major disputes between the tribes short of war.

For the villages of the Ani Yun Wiya, the anetso was a major celebration and a chance to get together with friends of other villages in a fierce competition.

Nothing built a priest's reputation quicker than guiding a team to victory. Adanvdo's success with the Tsikohi ball team many years before had been one of the key factors that led to his becoming the village Uku. That was why he had been working with his great-grandson to develop in him the necessary knowledge and confidence so that he could one day take over the Tsikohi ball team.

Adanvdo handed over the players to Atselvdi to take them to water for the first of many times before the ball play. In this ceremony, the priest placed them under strict gaktuntas, or taboos. They learned that they must not eat the flesh of the rabbit because the rabbit is a timid animal, easily alarmed and liable to lose its wits when pursued by the hunter. They must avoid the meat of the frog because the frog's bones are brittle and easily broken. They must abstain from eating the young of any bird or animal and must not touch an infant. They must not eat certain fish that are sluggish when they swim. They must not eat the atunka herb because its stalk is easily broken.

As they emerged from the river, they were greeted by the legendary player, Tlomeha Usdi, who presented each player with two ball sticks. Each stick was roughly the length of a man's forearm and resembled a long wooden spoon. The bowl of the "spoon" was a network of thongs of twisted sinew. The sticks were made of hickory that had been doubled back over itself to form the bowl and then strapped together tightly to form the handle.

Sticks made by Tlomeha Usdi were coveted among ball players everywhere. His sticks were rugged, yet flexible. The bowl was a perfect oval with the netting more tightly stretched to create a shallower bowl enabling the player to fling the ball much farther than sticks with a loose pocket. Although the tighter netting made it more difficult to catch the ball, the players soon attained the knack of trapping the ball between the two sticks through practice—a technique perfected by Tlomeha Usdi when playing for the Tsalagi National Team.

Tlomeha Usdi grasped the neck of the sticks and held them out to each player. The player grasped the end of the handles, snapped them from Tlomeha Usdi's grasp and held them against their chest as a gesture of respect for the renowned ball player. Tlomeha Usdi was the only ball player from Tsikohi to ever make the Tsalagi National Team.

Although he appeared to be too short and too fragile to be a ball player, his quickness, his scrappiness, his persistence, and his single-minded determination had enabled him to not only overcome his shortcomings but also excel in the game. Long retired from the game, it was now Tlomeha Usdi's responsibility to teach the Tsikohi players the skills of the game.

Adanvdo knew that a team could also get over confident and he feared that this team was possibly getting to that point. So, after receiving their sticks, he had the players stand shoulder-to-shoulder so that he could inspect each one. It was a little ceremony he used to sew a small element of doubt and insecurity. Some, he tested their muscles; some, he spread their eyelids and inspected their eyes; he asked questions about their diet or about any taboos they might have broken recently. It was the sixth player who failed inspection. Adanvdo tested his strength then asked, "Did I hear that you are recently married?"

"Yes, Uku!" the player responded proudly. He stood straight with his head held high.

"Is your wife with child?"

"Yes, Uku!" the player beamed.

"You must go. You cannot play this time."

The players gasped. The disqualified player teared up and began to tremble. Adanvdo could see that he wanted to protest but respected the great Uku. Adanvdo explained, "In the creation of the child, you have given much of yourself. More than you realize. Your spirit must be split to provide for the spirit of your child. Part of your energy has gone to the child. Soon, you will be whole again. For now, you do not possess your complete strength, your complete energy, or your complete spirit."

Adanvdo looked at each player with challenging eyes. "To beat the Gwalgahi, every player must possess his ultimate strength, energy, and spirit!"

The devastated player bravely dropped out of the lineup. Adanvdo knew that he was losing a very talented player and one that his teammates greatly admired. He also knew that in a perverse way, his expulsion would inspire his teammates to be at their maximum potential to beat the very able team from Gwalgahi.

Adanvdo finished his inspection and then turned the team over to his grandson and able assistant, Tlomeha Usdi. Today he would stand back and let them handle the preparation and training.

*But to fight the black powers,
a priest had to know how
they worked, where they
came from, and how to
defeat them.*

As Adanvdo watched them trotting off down the meadow toward the box canyon, he thought about the career of his trusted assistant. When he had first taken over the team so many years before, the previous team leader had selected the players for the team based on size. But Adanvdo had felt that they needed finesse, speed, and cleverness to win against teams that were often bigger and stronger. He had seen in little Tlomeha Usdi all of those qualities.

With the addition of his skills and quickness, Adanvdo had managed to turn the team around. With Tlomeha Usdi they went through four seasons undefeated. Their success caught the attention of Katuwa and Tlomeha Usdi was recruited to play for the Tsalagi National Team.

It was a great honor for Tlomeha Usdi, but his size proved to be a tremendous disadvantage at that level of play. Had it not been for the legendary anetso between the Tsalagi and the Kusa, Tlomeha Usdi might have slipped into quiet obscurity.

The villages along the Coosawatti aspired to be part of the Ani Yun Wiya, The Real People, the Tsalagi. But the Kusa Chief insisted they remain part of the Ani Kusa. The villagers secretly sent a delegation to Katuwa to beseech the National Council of the Ani Yun Wiya to allow them to join the Tsalagi Nation and to protect them from Kusa retaliation.

The Tsalagi Council discussed the request and decided to use the annual anetso between the two tribes as a way to settle the dispute peacefully. When the delegations from the Tsalagi and the Kusa met, the Tsalagi delegation made the wager. If the Kusa team should win, the villages along the Coosawattee would remain Kusa. But if the Tsalagi team won, the villages along the river would become Tsalagi.

"At first, the Kusa Chief resisted, but when the Tsalagi Chief questioned his confidence in his team, the shamed Kusa Chief accepted the wager.

When Tlomeha Usdi learned that the fate of the villages were at stake, he went to the Great Uku and pleaded to be allowed to play. At that time, the Uku did not believe that little Tlomeha Usdi had the size and strength to play against the Kusa. So, the anetso began without him in the game. Quickly the Kusas scored a point, then another, then another before the Tsalagi managed to score their first point. The two teams were very evenly matched and the game went on and on. Injuries began to knock players out of the game until finally the Great Uku had no choice but to send in Tlomeha Usdi. The score was ten to eight in favor of the Kusa when the "little bat" entered the game. The Kusa needed only one score to win.

That day, Tlomeha Usdi scored four straight points leading the Tsalagi National Team to victory. Since that day, the villages along the Coosawattee have been part of the Tsalagi Nation. And Tlomeha Usdi has been a hero in not only Tsikohi, but throughout the great nation of the Ani Yun Wiya.

Adanvdo warmed a bowl of stew and sat next to the hearth. Little by little, Adanvdo had turned more and more over to Atselvdi. This year, he planned to let Atselvdi take the ball players to water and later, he would allow Atselvdi to play a major role at the dance and during the game. Slowly, he hoped to build the team's and the village's confidence in Atselvdi and, more importantly, build Atselvdi's confidence in himself. It was one more step toward taking over the most important task of village Uku.

Adanvdo shuffled to his room and sat on his bed. A feeling of dread lay over him as he thought about his great-grandson. All day his mind kept returning to Atselvdi and now he was more resolved than ever that it was also time to introduce Atselvdi to the dark ways of the witch.

Since birth, Atselvdi had seemed gifted. He had learned childhood stories quickly and demonstrated that he could repeat them perfectly after hearing them just once. It was that feat that had earned him the nickname Atselvdi, meaning one who imitates.

He was always a happy and enthusiastic child, especially when tagging along with his great-grandfather. It was during these tag-alongs that Adanvdo observed what only he could see—that the spirits favored Atselvdi. And as Atselvdi grew, his perceptions grew and he picked up on the blessings and cures and his special connection with the spirits gave him a natural healing ability.

Adanvdo could see that the spirits favored Atselvdi not only because of his brilliance, but also for his sincerity, goodness, and innocence. So, Adanvdo had nurtured those qualities and sheltered Atselvdi from witches, wizards, conjurers, and all evil thinkers. And Atselvdi had flourished and was, in his great-grandfather's eyes, the premier priest in the village and on his way to becoming the premier candidate for village Uku. And maybe, someday, even the Uku of all of the Ani Yun Wiya!

One thing stood in Atselvdi's way ... knowledge of the black path. And now with the mutilated victims, Adanvdo knew that time had run out. He could no longer postpone Atselvdi's enlightenment.

Adanvdo was fearful of how the boy would respond to this knowledge. Many fine priests had crossed over when they learned how their powers could be used for self-gain. Adanvdo knew too well the power of the temptations that accompany such weighty knowledge. He had personal knowledge of this black power having seen even priests very close to him succumb and follow the dark path.

But to fight the black powers, a priest had to know how they worked, where they came from, and how to defeat them. To be successful, the white priest had to know more about the black powers than the witch himself. The old Uku prayed that Atselvdi's voracious appetite for knowledge and special connection with the spirits would keep him from being sucked down the black path of witch-craft. For he feared that Atselvdi also had the potential to be the most formidable witch ever known.

*The next part was too
traumatic for either to relive.
They found solace in silence.*

GRANDMOTHER SUN WAS HIGH and short shadows pointed north. Ali and Waya Usti sat quietly staring at the Long Man. They had not spoken much since Atselvdi had left them. Waya Usti felt awkward and inadequate sitting next to the girl he had secretly admired since they were small children. She was so beautiful and petite. Every movement and every pose was feminine and sexy. She was the prettiest girl in the village and, he was quite sure, on all of Turtle Island.

Her legs were arched and her feet pointed in unison to the river. She sat perfectly erect with her delicate hands draped over her knees. Her long, silky black hair flowed partly down her chest, swirling and suggestively hiding her bulging breasts. His face felt hot and his stomach was queasy. He sensed that just sitting there was not enough. He sensed that she expected him to speak.

Ali felt momentary relief from the passing breeze that lifted her hair exposing her hot, sweaty neck. She had insisted her grandmother not coif her hair this morning, but now she felt hot, awkward, and common. She waited patiently for Waya Usti to speak. It had been a very long time and she was getting impatient. She sensed that he was bashful and uncomfortable and tried not to look at him hoping it would help. She had understood his reluctance to speak while in the company of her brother, but what was his excuse now?

He had developed into a very handsome boy: long sinewy muscles; shiny, black hair; dark eyes; narrow face; and broad lips. If he was tense or nervous, his posture did not show it. He appeared to be relaxed and thoughtful.

Ali could not wait any longer. "What did Atselvdi mean when he said that you were the first to join the search party; first to follow my screams to the Tagwa camp?"

Waya Usti was startled and gazed at her with wide eyes. Quickly, though, he composed himself. "Well, Father was summoned by Chief Waya shortly after learning that Delagalis was missing. We didn't know about you at that point. I went along just out of curiosity.

"When we arrived, Waya told us that Walelu was also missing and that someone had spotted some tracks leading out of the cornfield. When we were led to the tracks, we quickly determined that there were three distinct footprints. We followed them a short distance and realized that there were three large men running into the forest, each with a heavy load. Father sent me back to inform Waya. I arrived just as he announced that there were three girls missing—you, Delagalis, and Walelu."

Ali puffed out her lower lip and brought her fists to her hips, "You determined that they were carrying a HEAVY load?"

Waya Usti's eyes widened again. Then the playful beauty burst into laughter. A relieved Waya Usti joined in.

"You weren't exactly FIRST were you?"

Waya Usti blushed. "Well ... no, I guess actually I was last."

They laughed again. It felt good. The tension evaporated. Both relaxed and began to enjoy each other's company and conversation became easier. Waya Usti related to her the story of the search. He told her about his distress over not being able to check out the western trail at the Agusa Jisdu.

"It turns out you were right!" Ali opined.

"I should've kept going. I should've ignored them!"

"You couldn't. Tawodi wouldn't have let you."

Oddly, her observation rankled him! "I could out run that big lug easily."

Ali was surprised by his fervid response! His muscles tensed. Was he jealous of Tawodi? Had she trampled on his male ego? She reached over and touched his clenched fist. "I'm sure you could ... easily. But, at the time, you couldn't know that you were right."

Waya Usti flinched when he felt her tender hand touch him. He had never had an anxiety attack before, so he did not know what was happening to him. His stomach felt as if it had opened up and the wind was blowing freely through it. His face felt as if all of the blood from his entire body had rushed to his head. He could not move his head or his arms or any part of him.

Ali bent around to look into his face. "Are you all right?"

Her concerned look broke the spell. The love struck young man relaxed. The reassuring girl leaned back and locked her fingers around her knees. "So, how far did you go before Wahuhu was sure you were going the wrong way?"

Waya Usti felt reassured and relaxed again. He felt a special excitement as he told the rest of the story. Ali appeared relaxed and interested in him, truly interested, as he spoke. And the more he talked, the more comfortable he felt next to her.

He told her about the night atop the boulder overlooking the Agusa Jisdu and his dream. He was surprised when he felt a bit choked up when he told her the part about her dropping into the water.

She reached for his hand, leaned against his arm and laid her head on his shoulder. "I had a weird dream that night, too. I dreamed a huge snake with a man's head had coiled around me and opened its mouth showing its huge, gleaming fangs. Then it struck and sunk its fangs into my armpits! I woke up and realized that my armpits were stinging from being pressed against the tree trunks I was tied to."

Embarrassed, she giggled at the irony. Waya Usti looked into her eyes and found an insecurity and vulnerability he had not seen before. SHE was looking to HIM for reassurance, for approval. With a newfound confidence and feeling of closeness and familiarity, Waya Usti embraced his pretty sweetheart and held her tight. She did not resist. She hugged him back.

They did not continue with the story. The next part was too traumatic for either to relive. They found solace in silence.

He and Ali had always been able to share things with each other that they could not share with anyone else.

Atselvdi finished the water ceremony and released the ball players for the day. As he trudged home, his thoughts were isolated so deep within that he was oblivious to the world around him. The recent crisis in his life had penetrated his psyche like nothing he had ever experienced. In fact, he had no experience in this area of life from the priesthood. He had never thought about it; he had never considered it; he had never expected he would ever be affected by it.

Certainly, he had heard about these things. It was, he realized, all around him and always had been. But it had never affected him directly. How could something so devastating not be part of his training? How could his great-grandfather leave him so vulnerable?

He especially blamed his grandmother for not preparing him. She had always been his behind-the-scenes protector. She had always been the one person in his life who sensed when he needed something more than great-grandfather could or would provide. They had both failed him. They had sheltered him from the one thing that could completely derail him and turn his life upside down—a pretty girl!

This was the kind of thing that he wanted very much to share with his twin sister. All morning, while sitting with her at the beaver dams, he had tried to figure out how to bring it up. They had such a special bond. It was like no other relationship. He and Ali had always been able to share things with each other that they could not share with anyone else. But, he worried about whether his sister was ready to talk about such things so soon after such a traumatic experience with evil, sex-crazed men. He felt that he needed to be there for her, not the other way around. And so the morning had lingered on in silence until Waya Usti had showed up.

More than anything, he wanted to return to the forest to see Sudalegi. His thoughts and his dreams were saturated with thoughts of her silky, black hair; her brown, seductive eyes; her smooth, hickory skin; her mischievousness; her playfulness; her warmth and caring. His heart was racing just thinking about her.

Nothing else in his life now mattered more than just the mere thought of her. He felt trapped by his priestly responsibilities. Grandfather expected him to help with the ball team, but he did not need his help. What would it hurt for him to get away for a while? It was the Uku that the team looked to and had confidence in. He was just the assistant doing those things the Uku did not like to do—the dirty jobs.

Atselvdi began to hatch a plan to return to see her. Would his great-grandfather believe that he needed to go check on old Beaver again? Maybe he could take medicine to White Fawn's wife or check on Goingsnake. Then, no one would suspect his real reason for returning, and he could just stop in to check on Sudalegi's grandfather.

He thought about how long it had been since any request had come from the forest people. Unfortunately, the forest people were hardy and seldom requested medicine. All he needed was an excuse. Surely someone would need a priest or medicine man soon.

Thunder rumbled behind him. He watched the Thunder Boys throwing lightning bolts from a large, dark cloud building over the mountain where Sudalegi lived. He wondered if the Thunder Boys would remind Sudalegi of him and that night when he orchestrated the storm with his movements. The branches of the trees by the Long Man hissed as they rolled and tumbled responding to a stiff breeze that made him stagger and his clothes flap wildly. Rain was coming and would be there soon.

Waya Usti lay in his bed waiting for the rain to stop and for his parents' loud snoring to reassure him that he could slip out.

The kind eyes and dazzling smile of Ali flashed into his mind. Somehow just the thought of her tickled his stomach. He sucked in the crisp night air to quell this arresting feeling. Being near her had been like nothing he had ever experienced before. It was exciting and scary, a million feelings, any one of which would be tumultuous, and they were all attacking him at once! Still he wanted more. He wanted to spend every moment with her.

Quietly slipping out of his house, he headed down the street toward Ali's house, guided by the glow of the billions of distant campfires of the spirits in the sky. He walked boldly down the middle of the familiar street. It had become his nightly routine. He no longer felt fear, only excitement for his secret mission.

He entered the familiar dark hut and slipped across room in the blackness to his favorite spot. A short journey he had made many times since Ali had returned, but this time the normally clear path was obstructed and he stumbled over some very large obstacle!

"Hi-yeeee!" Waya Usti screeched as he tumbled into the darkness. Stark fear charged the young guardian's adrenalin and he scrambled to his feet and stood ready to defend himself from some mysterious, ominous foe!

From a dark hulking shadow came a familiar voice, whispering, "You are the clumsiest, love-sick fool I've ever known."

"Tawodi?"

"What blind man can't see someone my size? How are you going to protect your little sweetheart if you can't even see a giant right in front of you? What if I had been a bear, or a Tagwa warrior?"

Waya Usti's stomach quaked! Tawodi was right. What kind of protector was he?

Tawodi had been joking with his cousin, but suddenly he realized that his joke had hurt his friend deeply. Now he felt terrible inside. The cruel obstacle pulled himself up to walk over to his distraught cousin but was interrupted by, "So, what are YOU doing here?"

Tawodi coughed. He did not want to admit his purpose but suddenly realized Waya Usti must be thinking that he fancied Ali. "It's not what you think, Cousin."

Waya Usti remained silent. Tawodi waited. He slowly realized that he wasn't going to get out of admitting his purpose. "Okay, come here."

Waya Usti remained silent and did not move. Tawodi sensed that things were worse than he thought. He now feared that Waya Usti might be in a mood to fight.

"Look over there. Can you see that house?" Tawodi pointed toward Amadohi's house. But Waya Usti could not see Tawodi.

Finally, Tawodi realized that he was standing in darkness. Exasperated, the huge man stormed over to his cousin and grabbed his head with the purpose to turn it in the direction of Amadohi's house, but his cousin interpreted the advance in a different way and flew into a furious attack on his hulking cousin.

The two warriors tumbled noisily to the ground and crashed through a rotting wall into the street. Waya Usti was no match for the massive Tawodi but for a short time neither was convinced of it. Tawodi tried to embrace his feisty cousin and restrain him but Waya Usti was wiry and was doing a good job of kicking and slugging his confounded cousin.

The blows stung Tawodi but curiously caused him to start laughing. His mirth made Waya Usti more furious and determined to annihilate his big, fat rival! Finally, Tawodi rolled on top of his skinny cousin and forced his arms against the ground.

"Will you stop?" the giant cousin implored through his laughter. "I came to spy on Amadohi, not Ali, you drumhead!"

Waya Usti stopped struggling and replayed what Tawodi had just said in his head. Then he too burst into laughter as Tawodi released him and rolled over on his back. The two cousins fell into raucous laughter until they realized that there were gathering shadows around them. The glowing stars made the crowd look like white, glowing spirits. A tall man pushed through the crowd. "What is going on?"

Tawodi recognized the familiar voice of Wahuhu who examined the huge warrior sprawled on the ground. "Tawodi? Who is that with you?"

"It's me, Waya Usti, Grandfather."

"Well, what are you boys doing out here?"

"I think they have girl problems," Kalona volunteered as she shook her head disgustedly and returned to her home.

Tawodi and Waya Usti experienced the exact same feeling upon hearing Chief Kalona's remark—absolute and total humiliation.

Then it was the crowd's turn to be engulfed in uproarious laughter. But one member of the crowd was not laughing. One dismayed mother, Wananahi, was dragging her struggling but overjoyed daughter back home.

Deep dread filled Atselvdi as he saw the concern in his great-grandfather's glare. He knew that he had overstepped his bounds.

The morning smelled damp and fresh. After taking the ball players to water, Atselvdi turned them over to Tlomeha Usdi. Little Bat lead them away to start their practice drills. The young priest watched them jog into the box canyon to the secret practice field and then strolled down the Long Man to the point where the trail ended on the north side of the river. He climbed up the steep, heavily forested hill to the point where the river had shaved it off leaving a sheer cliff overlooking the small lake pushing against beaver dams.

He climbed onto a pile of boulders and found a natural chair to sit on and lean back. It was a very cool autumn day and Atselvdi relaxed and stared at the distant colorful forested mountains. He tried to figure out where Sudalegi's house might be. Looking at the area from where he sat made it seem so very far away—far away in more than just distance. The forest people were also distant in the way they thought, lived, and believed.

Atselvdi was despondent. He could think of no great scheme nor excuse for returning to the forest people to see Sudalegi.

"You look ... glum."

Atselvdi recoiled! He turned to see his great-grandfather breathing hard as he sat on a large, flat-topped rock at the base of the pile of boulders. "I didn't ... mean ... to startle you, Grandson."

"I didn't hear you approach, Grandfather."

"I ... followed you. I ... wanted ... to talk," Adanvdo uttered gasping. The steep walk had left him breathless. "Just need to ... catch my breath."

Atselvdi was concerned that whatever his great-grandfather wanted to talk about must be very important for him to tackle the steep hill at his advanced age.

Finally, the old Uku took a deep breath and began, "I've noticed that you have been very ... well, troubled, since the murders by the witch. I know that this event has shaken you."

Adanvdo paused. He seemed to be deep in thought. Actually, Atselvdi realized that he had not thought about witches for a long time now. He remembered how confused and afraid he had been right after they found the mutilated body. And this subject probably would have dominated his thoughts except for One Thing!

"I should have spent more time with you talking about the dark path. I just hoped that it wouldn't be necessary until you had mastered the white path."

Atselvdi wondered what was left to master. He knew all of the conjures and medicines. He felt that all he had learned the last year or two was just subtleties and variations.

Adanvdo continued, "Truthfully, you are a master of the white path and have been for some time."

Adanvdo looked up at his great-grandson. Atselvdi saw something new in his grandfather's eyes. He appeared to be uncertain, or perhaps it was apologetic. Atselvdi was accustomed to seeing confidence or kindness or sympathy in his grandfather's eyes, never uncertainty or doubt.

Adanvdo looked away and studied the staff he held with both hands in front of him. He laid the staff to one side, clasped his hands in his lap and took a deep breath. This was clearly very difficult for him. He appeared to be trying to remember something, or perhaps just searching for where to begin. "There are different types of witches, different levels, that is."

Atselvdi waited for his great-grandfather to continue.

"There are common witches. They engage in malicious conjures. They may lay illness or curses under their victims. They may use medicines for dark or frivolous purposes. And then there are killer witches, like the one who murdered our friend for his askina—his four souls."

Atselvdi contemplated this, then asked, "How do you tell them apart?"

Adanvdo thought about it for a long time before answering. "Sometimes you can't tell a killer witch from a common witch. Ironically, only when the killer witch has shifted his shape can he be identified as a killer witch. And even then, only by a seer. Common witches are very dangerous because they do not look any different from a normal person. The priest must be extra vigilant around a common witch or he will be tricked."

Atselvdi's stomach churned. He felt fearful. He might have been around a witch and did not know it. "Why would anyone want to be a witch?"

Atselvdi perceived that his great-grandfather considered it a good question. He could see that Adanvdo was being careful with his answer. "Perhaps the common witches are harder to understand. Maybe, they think that it is only a minor thing and it sets them apart and commands a certain type of respect or at least notoriety. Maybe they succumb to the pressure from someone who requests a dark potion. They may not realize the consequences of connecting with the dark ways and consorting with the black spirits. Perhaps they have rationalized it somehow."

Atselvdi tried to understand. It seemed like such a high price to pay.

Adanvdo took a deep breath and continued, "For the killer witch, the lure is immortality."

Adanvdo shivered. Atselvdi reasoned that immortality was more important to an old man than a young man. With the end so far in the future, young men did not tend to think of it much. At least he knew he did not. But he could see how an old man might be tempted. Atselvdi sensed that his great-grandfather was waiting for his reaction. "How many witches are there? Do I know, I mean, have I ever seen any?"

"Probably not."

Atselvdi waited for more specifics, while Adanvdo looked down at the ground deep in thought. "You may have seen a common witch or two. They are around. Old women well versed in medicines and cures sometimes step over to the dark path. But I don't think you have ever seen or been around a truly dark witch, a tsigili.

A tsigili? Atselvdi had heard his grandfather use the term and knew it meant witch. But he had never heard anyone else use the term.

Adanvdo clarified, "I call that level of witch tsigili, chee-gee-lee as apposed to Tsisgili."

Atselvdi frowned, prompting Adanvdo to explain further. "There once was an evil witch whose actual birth name was Tsisgili. Over time, Sali and I came to call his kind tsigili."

Atselvdi's mind was spinning with questions. It was hard for him to be respectful and allow Adanvdo to speak at his own pace. It was hard for him to let the truth unfold naturally as he had been taught. He wanted the old Uku to delve into the secrets and share his knowledge.

Atselvdi took advantage of Adanvdo's pause to ask, "How does the witch acquire askinas?"

Adanvdo seemed startled by his impetuous question. He glared at his great-grandson, studying his eyes, searching for something. Perhaps he was searching for signs that Atselvdi was too eager to know the secrets; signs that Atselvdi's intentions were more than healthy curiosity. He hoped that his perceptive great-grandfather would only see the innocence and curiosity he felt.

Deep dread filled Atselvdi as he saw the concern in his great-grandfather's glare. He knew that he had overstepped his bounds. He wanted to beg for forgiveness. He wanted to withdraw the question.

Adanvdo looked at the ground and spoke slowly, "To steal a man's souls is more than a clever conjure. To steal a man's souls is to steal his life, not only from the man, but from his family, his friends, his village, and an affront to the ways of the Ani Yun Wiya, the real people, the

Cherokee. It upsets the balance of all things. No man should know these things until he understands all of the consequences; all of the ramifications. Life is sacrosanct and to steal it is profane."

Adanvdo looked deep into Atselvdi's eyes. "I shall teach you to identify and defeat the witch, not become one!"

Kalanu circled the megalith in the meadow where his evil son was entombed. It was intact; Tsisgili's evil souls were imprisoned there for eternity.

THE OLD RAVEN SAT quietly, shrouded in the leafy darkness of the huge tree. The first light of morning glistened off the wispy fog drifting along the cool waters of the Long Man. One by one, the sleepy villagers filtered out of the stockade and waded into the wide shallows. The low rumble of voices grew steadily louder.

Kalanu Ahkyeliski, in raven form, perked up. *There he is!* His son, Adanvdo Alsgida, shuffled out of the main entrance of the stockade leaning on a long staff and comforted by a full-length woolly cape. His skinny great-grandson trailed along as though sleepwalking. His stout, nurturing granddaughter ushered her pretty grand-daughter. Aside from her sleepiness, the girl appeared to be faring well after her ordeal. It was a proud, loving family and Adanvdo appeared to be quite content with his life.

What a waste! Adanvdo could've been so much more than a simple Uku in a remote and forgotten village. His wisdom and power are far too great to be wasted this way, the Raven Mocker lamented.

The village Uku of Tsikohi was a mystery to the shape-shifted wizard hiding in the bosom of the black oak. *Will he really allow himself to wither away and die when he has within him the power to rejuvenate himself? Will he really reject immortality?*

The utter absurdity of this thought forced the raven into an involuntary convulsion of cachinnation. Some villagers studied the dense tree searching for the cackling raven. Some searched out of curiosity and Adanvdo's stomach quaked! *Could it be? Would he risk it?* He searched the dark depths of the black oak. One glimpse by a seer was all that was needed to abrogate the witch's contract with the dark spirits condemning him to death!

The black eyes of the raven scoured the crowd below. The rest of him remained deathly still. His searching paused on a strange little man standing in the back of the congregation. He was facing in the direction of the raven, but appeared to be asleep. Then, suddenly, from beneath the wrinkled puffs of his face, two eyes popped open and seemed to peer directly at him.

His wings twitched slightly before he could regain control of himself. *Sali!* The black bird hiding in the darkness of the tree shadows glared at the old priest glaring back in his direction. *Does he see me?*

The shape-shifted wizard had no choice but to remain perfectly quiet and hope the wrinkled old seer had not spotted him. The old priest's persistence and patience were maddening. Adanvdo proceeded with the morning blessing, lecturing on the dangers of malicious behavior, and completed a second blessing. Still, Sali peered at the spot in the black oak, at Kalanu Ahkyeliski. Still the raven man stared back at his menacing foe. *Doesn't he ever blink?*

The congregations began to wade out of the Long Man, visiting, laughing, hugging, and cajoling. Adanvdo waded over to his friend who sat fixated on the ancient tree growing out of the soggy bank of the river. "Do you see him?" he whispered.

The glazed eyes of the old priest relaxed and receded a bit as he shook his head no. "But I know he's there."

Adanvdo investigated the black oak one last time and then hooked his arm into Sali's and helped him trudge across the sandy bank. "Why would he risk it? He knows that if we spot him ... What a wasted effort to target us."

Sali appeared unconvinced, but quipped, "We're on our last leg. We probably have nothing to worry about."

As the two old men strolled over to the shade, Adanvdo confessed, "I've begun Atselvdi's training on witchcraft."

Sali paused to look at his friend. "Did you tell him about ... the family connection?"

Adanvdo shook his head. "Not yet, but it was a good talk. He listened intently and I don't think he showed any signs that he might be tempted."

Sali did not respond. Adanvdo continued, "He asked how to steal someone's soul, but I sensed he was just curious. I told him that my intent is to teach him about them, not how to be one."

Sali responded, "To conquer one, you have to know their ways."

"I know, but that can come later."

The old friends disappeared into the stockade.

The raven shook off his stiffness from sitting completely still for so long. *You have nothing to worry about, my son, Atselvdi's heart is pure.*

Everyone had gone inside now and the Raven Mocker was free to take flight. He took the path that would avoid his flying over the village. His soaring heart drove him to climb high above the clouds and float above the world on the soft currents of Mother Earth's breath. He was proud of his family. He and Sakonige had done well by Adanvdo, but they had also given birth to and raised Tsisgili, Adanvdo's twin brother. Tsisgili was pure evil.

Kalanu circled the megalith in the meadow where his evil son was entombed. It was intact; Tsisgili's evil souls were imprisoned there for eternity.

If only Adanvdo could live for eternity.

Then the old witch remembered his leftovers. *Maybe I could leave Adanvdo a gift in the little* box *he keeps under the bed.* Then he chuckled as he thought to himself, *the gift of eternal life!*

This was more like the feeling of actually slipping off the edge and falling into the abyss.

Wananahi walked alongside her friend. "Are you anxious to see a certain chief at the anetso?"

Kalona chuckled, then shook her head. "I don't know. Maybe. It's been a long time since I've seen him."

"Oh, I'm sure he is just as ugly as ever."

Kalona gasped and slapped her friend's shoulder playfully. Unfortunately, there was too much truth in her remark. She did not know if it was because he was from a town named Frog Place, but Chief Waya Nigawisgv reminded people of a frog. He was fat with spindly, bowed legs and short skinny arms with short fingers attached to fat hands. His head was pointed and bald (except for a swatch threaded through a deer bone right on top. His cheeks sagged into bulging, drooping jowls that pulled the corners of his mouth down into a smug frown. His nose was short and flat and pointed up exposing his triangular nostrils. His brow dipped in the center and a deep crease cut up the center of his forehead. His bushy eyebrows partially hid his black, beady eyes. Despite all these physical shortcomings, the brash man was arrogant and overbearing. He had a very high opinion of himself.

Yet, he could be clever and witty and doted over Kalona when they were together. There had not been many men who had showed an interest in her since her husband was killed in war. She knew that she was a tough, no-nonsense woman—not dainty and charming like her peers. She sensed that most men were intimidated by her.

After she lost her husband, she had not really wanted another husband. It had been enough to look after her father and sickly daughter. Then, there had been the twins. And there were the great responsibilities of being the village Peace Chief.

The women walked along quietly until Kalona inquired, "Are you ready for the dance?"

"Oh! I meant to tell you. I finished my dress."

"You did? Let's go see it."

The stout woman and the thin woman throttled up and strode up the street with a purpose in their gate.

Tawodi Gvnagei felt awkward, hulky, and dumb. Sitting on the edge of the precipice made him feel queasy and uneasy. When Amadohi leaned against him, his heart leaped and he leaned back to keep from slipping over the edge!

Amadohi straightened, looked at him curiously and asked, "What's wrong?"

Tawodi tried to act nonchalant, "Nothing, just caught me off guard, I guess."

Amadohi giggled, peered over the edge, looked sideways at the big baby and said, "Oh, look at the tiny trees down there. Aren't they cute?"

Tawodi looked down at the great depth and felt his head spin. Amadohi's eyes sparkled. "Is that a tiny little deer down there?"

Tawodi looked up to the sky. "Maybe we should go see if the Ball Play dance has started."

"I'll bet mother is looking for me already." The devious girl grabbed the apprehensive hulk around the neck and forced his head toward the east. "There's the dance field right down there. Do you see her?"

Tawodi reflexively pushed back, knocking over his tormentor and flattening himself out on the ground. Amadohi burst into giddy, taunting laughter. Tawodi admired his lovely tormentor as she lay on her back laughing with her head bouncing and her breasts dancing and her stomach convulsing as she languished in his misery.

She was beautiful. Tawodi rolled over on his side, placed his arm up, bent his elbow and rested his head on his palm. Her giggling tapered off leaving a delightful smile, gleaming eyes, and graceful repose.

Tawodi reached over and caressed her cheek, gently turning her head toward him. Amadohi looked into his eyes, smiling calmly, confidently, lovingly. Tawodi felt a rush unlike he had ever experienced. He was a fearless warrior feeling fear for the first time. Not even his phobia of cliff edges compared to this. This was more like the feeling of actually slipping off the edge and falling into the abyss.

Amadohi rolled away and jumped to her feet. "I do need to go. I am hoping to coax Ali into going to the dance with me."

Tawodi pushed himself up. "You think she will?"

"Yes, she has come a long way. I think she may be ready."

Atselvdi sat beside the Long Man mesmerized by the flowing smoke rising off the flames from the giant fire inside the village. He prayed the message the smoke carried to the spirits in the sky was positive and would garner their support for the anetso.

He was alone now and cut off from the celebrations inside. It had been a while since the Beloved Women had delivered baskets of food to the players for their last feast before the game tomorrow. Now the Beloved Women and the players were inside and the players were dancing around the bonfire while the village maidens were dancing and singing in a great circle surrounding the players. Musicians pounded on huge water drums, shook gourd rattles and sang the ball play song. It was noisy and festive, but outside, Atselvdi was quiet and distant.

Tomorrow, the Tsikohi ballplayers would be challenged by the Gwalgahi village ballplayers. But tonight all villagers would be gathered around the dance field to watch and dance with the ballplayers, feast, place wagers on the game, or just visit and enjoy themselves. Tonight, as the ball play priest, it was his responsibility to stay outside and pray for victory; to connect with the spirits to bring success to the players; to think about strategy and plan for the game. Many times during the night, he would collect the players and go to water to keep their spirits cleansed.

Atselvdi stared at the tips of the flames and the light dome above the stockade. Strong spirits lived within the flames. All things were the dwelling places for spirits. All things possessed power and the power of all things could be tapped through their spirits. For the first time in Atselvdi's life, he thought about the possibility of someone tapping those powers for selfish use. For the first time in his life, he tried to reason why someone would do this. And for the first time in his life, he feared he could understand why!

Not all things could be understood with the mind. He was learning that many things were only understood by the heart. The heart was a complicated interpreter, though. The heart understood things in ways the mind could not because the heart was not logical and was guided by sometimes unreasonable and illogical factors.

Just learning that such feelings existed had opened up his own dark feelings and it scared him. He needed his great-grandfather's guidance. He needed for his great-grandfather to explain this evil phenomenon that lurked in the darkness and that had been hidden to him for all of his life. Why had Adanvdo protected him from this?

Atselvdi's insatiable appetite for knowledge was consuming him now. He must know everything about the dark world. He must know what made the tsigili work; what potions they used; what conjures they used. But, Atselvdi knew that his great-grandfather would not divulge these things until certain that he would not be tempted by them. Adanvdo might even be offended if he asked. Then, Atselvdi had an idea!

She tried to console Waya Usti. "Want to wait for us by the beaver dams?"

Amadohi led Ali out to the dance field to join the other girls already dancing. The ballplayers were also already dancing around the bonfire. They were dipping and gesturing as if playing ball, showing off their bravado and ball skills. The young maidens were dancing and singing in a circle outside the players, hoping to impress them with their own moves.

Amadohi started singing as she helped Ali strap on the heavy turtle shell rattlers to her shins. The girl next to her greeted her, "Osiyo, Gigahai Utsati!" and then giggled with her friends.

Ali was confused and just ignored them. The haughty girl jeered at her again, "Aren't you going to speak, Gigahai Utsati?"

Ali looked at the girl and frowned. Why was she calling her Much Blood? The girl and her friends giggled all over again. Amadohi stepped between Ali and the rude girls and whispered, "Don't pay any attention to them."

"Ooh! Did we scare you Gigahai Utsati?"

"Who is Gigahai Utsati?" Ali inquired of Amadohi.

"It's nobody, They're nobody, ignore them."

The drummer changed to a rapid drumbeat.

"Don't look back, Gigahai Utsati, the mean old warriors are coming!"

Ali looked at the taunting girl giggling with her friends, scowled and then marched up to her. The girl and her friends screamed and then the girl said, "Oh, please, don't stab me! Please, don't stab me!" This greatly delighted her friends and they all giggled nervously at Ali.

"What are you talking about?" Ali screamed the words into the face of her taunter.

Amadohi grabbed Ali's arm and dragged her off the dance field. "What is going on Amadohi? Why do they hate me?"

"Forget about it, Ali, they're just stupid girls."

Ali dug in and jerked her arm loose from Amadohi. "No! You tell me what is going on, now!"

Amadohi looked at her friend with pleading eyes. "Ali, I can't …"

"It's about what happened to me isn't it?"

Amadohi slumped and reluctantly replied, "Yes, but you should learn about it through your dreams."

"No! I want you to tell me now! You HAVE to tell me now."

Amadohi looked sadly at her friend. "Okay. I'll tell you what I know, but you can't tell your grandmother or she'll cook me and call it four sisters!"

The joke broke Ali's huff and she laughed at her silly friend. Amadohi grabbed Ali by the arm and pulled her friend aside. She helped her remove the turtle shells and looked for a place where they could have privacy. She then led her toward the stockade exit.

As they were about to exit, Waya Usti and Tawodi came running up. "Where are you going?"

"Oh, dear!" Amadohi lamented. "Ali and I have something we have to do alone."

Tawodi and Waya Usti blushed brightly. "Oh … well … sure … we'll just wait here."

Amadohi and Ali giggled. "Not THAT! Just something private we need to discuss."

The boys stood there looking dumbfounded. Ali sensed that they had hurt the boys' feelings. She tried to console Waya Usti. "Want to wait for us by the beaver dams?"

This perked up the boys' spirits and they bobbed their heads up and down.

The girls giggled and ran out the stockade exit and up the river. The boys slapped each other on the back and ran downstream toward the beaver dams.

Kalona Ehlawei sat with the other Beloved Women on the benches reserved for them beside the dancing grounds. Kalona loved these gatherings. There was always lots of gossip and delicacies to eat. Kalona bit into a strawberry. "Mmmmm. Oh, thank you, Unelanunhi," referring to the story about how the great Apportioner, who took pity on the first man when his wife left him, gave him strawberries to lure her back.

The women chuckled. One laid her hand on Kalona's arm. "It's good to see Ali getting out. I was so afraid she would never let a man touch her again, but I see she has recovered!"

Kalona frowned. "What do you mean?"

The old gossip pointed in the direction of the stockade exit. Kalona saw Amadohi and Ali talking to Tawodi and Waya Usti. Suddenly, the two girls dashed through the exit and then the boys followed.

Kalona gasped!

"Oh, dear, Kalona, you better lock that girl up."

The old women cackled, but stopped short when Kalona did not laugh with them. Kalona looked at her best friend and Amadohi's mother, Wananahi. "Shall we go prepare the fire for venison?"

It was the tradition that a young man would present a deer he had killed on the doorstep of the young woman he wished to marry. If the grandmother approved of the marriage, she would cook the venison.

"It's not venison I'm thinking about cooking!" Amadohi's mother retorted glaring in the direction of Tawodi.

The Beloved Women laughed loudly.

Atselvdi peeked around a hut and stared at the dilapidated old clan house. It was large for a clan house and had been built by the Ani Gotegewi, the Wild Potato clan. But when the clan dwindled, it had fallen into disrepair. Then, when the old priest, Sali, claimed it for his home, no one had objected.

The light from the great fire at the dance was blocked by many huts, shrouding Atselvdi in darkness. And the singing girls and yelping players were distant echoes that Atselvdi's pounding heart drowned out. With the game tomorrow, Atselvdi knew that he should be by the Long Man praying and strategizing, since this was his first game to be in charge of the team. It would soon be time to take them to water to cleanse their souls and connect them with the spirits. But the dance would last all night and he would take the players to water numerous times. He rationalized that he would not be missed for a short time.

Atselvdi was conflicted about deceiving his great-grandfather. Adanvdo had always been his single source for counsel and had taught him everything he knew about being a priest. And Adanvdo had always been right; he had never steered him wrong. So, Atselvdi felt very guilty to be thinking about consulting another priest, especially this priest, his grandfather's best friend, Sali.

Feigning shyness, she strolled back toward the clearing. Waya Usti took a deep breath and followed.

AMADOHI SAT ON A large rock next to the Long Man and invited Ali to join her. She took a deep breath and began, "You remember being in the cornfield?"

"Yes."

"What else do you remember?"

"It was foggy, a breeze was coming and rattling the cornstalks. Someone ran at me from the fog."

"That someone was a Tagwa warrior."

"I remember his ugly, deformed head. At first, I thought he was running so fast that his skin was swept back on his head."

The two friends laughed half-heartedly.

"He and two of his buddies kidnapped you, Walelu, and Delagalis and took you up into the canyon of the Agusa Jisdu."

"Yes, I remember the camp and seeing Walelu and Delagalis tied to trees, like me. I remember tormenting one of the Tagwas and making him so mad that he punched me in the stomach. It hurt so bad I vomited in his face."

"You did? Oh, that's great! I bet he was really mad."

I don't remember much after that, just crazy images from my dreams. They don't make much sense. Do you know what happened?"

"No one knows. They found Walelu tied to a tree. She was naked and had been slashed to death! Delagalis was tied to the ground and she had been stabbed repeatedly. The three Tagwa warriors were floating in the stream and they had been stabbed to death, too!"

Horrific visions flashed into Ali's mind. Tears welled up in her eyes as she shared her memories with her best friend. "I remember feeling my hands come free from the ropes, and the awful Tagwa approaching me flicking his privates with the flat part of the blade to torment me. I remember grabbing the knife and shoving it into his crotch! I remember his screams of pain. I remember finding the knife in my hands and plunging it into his chest. There were hundreds of Little People flooding into the campsite like ants swarming over an ant bed. The Tagwas were swinging their fists and kicking at the miniature warriors. I attacked the Tagwas, slashing and stabbing them with that huge bloody knife!" she paused as she recalled the surge of rage in her as she slashed them and thrust the knife into them. "I remember the horrified looks on their faces as I stabbed and shoved them into the stream."

Then she remembered the strangest part. "A huge, black birdlike shadow descended over me and the Tagwa ..."

Ali jumped back and screamed. Amadohi tried to hug her but was pushed away. She remembered the consuming fear that she had felt that night in the midst of a raging, life-or-death battle, stabbing anything and every-thing that approached her. The trembling girl burst into tears and grabbed her dear friend for comfort. Amadohi sobbed quietly as she hugged her tormented friend, trying to comfort her.

It took a long time before Ali regained herself and as she wiped her wet face with her hands, she asked, "So, what were the girls at the dance referring to?"

Amadohi sniffed and rubbed her nose with the back of her hand. "Well, when Wahuhu saw the bloody, dead Tagwas floating in the stream, Walelu and Delagalis ... and you ... he was overwhelmed by the carnage and muttered mama gigahai utsati.

"Water with much blood. The girls were calling me Bloody One."

Ali separated from her friend and was silent for a long time while pondering this new ripple in her ordeal. "So, everyone thinks that I am a blood-thirsty warrior woman?"

"Only morons."

They giggled. Amadohi touched her friend's arm. "Speaking of morons, we have two of them waiting for us by the beaver dams."

Two slumping shadows sat next to the Long Man. The big slumping shadow spoke, "Well, we really fell for that one, didn't we?"

The humiliated hulk punctuated his disgust by skip-ping a flat rock across the surface of the pond. The thinner, muscular shadow replied, "You don't think they're coming?"

Tawodi was silent. He felt sorry for his poor love-sick cousin. "Maybe they're lost. Girls are terrible at finding places."

Waya Usti felt his gut tighten. "We should go look for them!"

Tawodi jerked his head around to look at Waya Usti. Visions of Tagwa warriors flashed into his mind. They jumped to their feet and raced back up the river fearing the worst. As they reached the bend in the river, Tawodi threw his arm across Waya Usti's chest and slid to a stop. "Listen!" Tawodi whispered as he pointed at two silhouettes approaching.

Waya Usti recognized the tall slender silhouette of Amadohi and the shorter petite silhouette of Ali strolling along slowly and talking. Their soft voices echoed off the rock wall on the opposite side of the Long Man. The young men ducked into the bushes to hide and listen.

"Everyone thinks that I stabbed the Tagwas to death?"

"I don't know. Wahuhu does."

Ali persisted, "Do you?"

"It's pretty hard to believe, but what else could've happened? Isn't that what you remember?"

The girls strolled along in thought until Amadohi added, "Your grandmother has a different idea. She thinks the Little People saved you."

Amadohi laughed and Ali chuckled obligingly, but shuddered as the memory of Nvwoti Atlisdodi Usdi whispering to her as he untied her hands and feet flashed across her mind. Finally, she asked, "How do you know about that?"

Amadohi chuckled. "Your grandmother told my mother and I can get anything out of her."

The girls laughed and grabbed each other's hand. Amadohi's mirth transitioned into concern. "Are you going to be all right, Ali?"

Ali shrugged. Amadohi inquired, "You up to joining the guys?"

Waya Usti and Tawodi strained to hear the answer, but there was just silence. The two guys grew tense with anticipation.

Amadohi broke the silence with words of encouragement for her friend, "They're kinda cute."

The kinda cute guys beamed. Ali responded, "You think they're still waiting for us after all this time?"

"Of course! They can't believe their dumb luck."

The two confident girls giggled happily and continued toward the beaver dams.

Waya Usti started to race back but Tawodi grabbed his arm. "Let's teach them a lesson," he whispered.

They waited for the girls to pass and then carefully followed from a distance. When the girls reached the beaver dams and discovered that no one was waiting, their hearts sank. They stood in the clearing searching all about, then Ali sadly turned back. "I guess they didn't wait."

Amadohi grabbed her forlorn friend's arms. She was worried that this was the last straw for her depressed friend. "We did make them wait a long time."

Amadohi could see that tears were trickling down Ali's cheeks and tried to offer encouragement, "I'll bet they went to look for us."

Ali wiped her tears and then continued back toward the trail. Amadohi sighed and caught up with her. She put her arm around her dejected friend to comfort her.

As they stepped out of the clearing onto the trail, Ali screamed. Startled, Amadohi looked up to see two silhouettes standing in the trail!

Together they realized that it was Waya Usti and Tawodi standing with their arms crossed.

"What are you doing?" Amadohi scolded. "You about scared us to death!"

"I'm sor ..." Waya Usti blurted out but was stopped by a sharp jab from Tawodi's elbow.

"Well, good evening, girls. What 'dumb luck' for us to still be here after all this time."

Amadohi gasped! "You were following us! ... You were listening to us!" Amadohi attacked Tawodi, punching and kicking him violently.

"Ow, ouch, stop! You're hurting me!" Tawodi complained playfully.

Waya Usti and Ali laughed at the mock fight of their friends as Tawodi grabbed Amadohi's wrists, twisted them causing her to spin around, then wrapped his arms around her and pulled her back against him. Amadohi couldn't believe how easily the strong giant incapacitated her, but she loved it.

"Are you okay?" Waya Usti asked Ali sheepishly. She wiped her face quickly. Feigning shyness, she strolled back toward the clearing. Waya Usti took a deep breath and followed.

*Beads of sweat popped out
on Atselvdi's face and he felt
utterly ridiculous.*

THE MOON HAD LONG since set behind the cliffs west of the village. Kalona Ehlawei sat quietly staring at the village entrance. Ali and Amadohi had not returned and Kalona was very worried. She scanned the dancers hopefully just in case she had missed them when they returned, but her granddaughter was not among the girls dancing around the great fire. She scanned the crowd, but realized that Ali was too short to find in a crowd and she doubted that she would be able to find Amadohi either.

"Do you think we should be concerned?" Wananahi whispered to Kalona.

It startled Kalona, but she realized that Wananahi must be just as worried about Amadohi as she was about Ali. Kalona tried to act nonchalant. "Surely they are safe with Tawodi and Waya Usti."

Wananahi forced a grin. "Like rabbits are safe with wolves guarding them!"

Kalona smirked, but neither woman disguised her concern. Kalona looked toward the drummer where her grandson Atselvdi would be standing waiting to take the ball players to water. Atselvdi was not there! Kalona's heart sank. "Can you see Atselvdi?"

Wananahi jerked her head around to scan the area around the big fire. "Is it time to go to water already?"

"Probably not."

Wananahi glanced around the area behind the players, but then returned her stare to the village entrance. "He couldn't help us anyway. Maybe we should go look for them on our own."

"What if we find them?"

Wananahi looked at Kalona puzzled. Kalona smirked slyly. Wananahi got it. "Oh, that would be awkward!"

The old women giggled.

"What are you two giggling about?" asked one of the Beloved Women.

Kalona realized that she had not listened to nor participated in the nonstop chatter of her friends for quite a while. She had been so concerned about her granddaughter that she had even forgotten anyone was around. Wananahi was at a loss for words and looked at Kalona expectantly. Kalona raised her chin defiantly and answered, "What do you think we're giggling at?"

The woman checked her hair. "I have no idea!"

Kalona reached out to her fragile friend. "Not at you, dear." Kalona lowered her voice to a whisper, "We're wondering what our children are up to."

The old woman accepted Kalona's hand and raised her eyebrows. "Best not to think about that."

The three feigned laughter and then pretended interest in the ongoing conversation of the other Beloved Women. Kalona glanced at Wananahi. The two looked at each other knowingly and quietly slipped away from their friends.

Sali was so strange and mysterious that Atselvdi feared he might even be a witch! So Atselvdi just stood and stared at the clan house wrestling over whether to go forward or not.

"Come sit with me," a quiet raspy voice murmured in the darkness. Atselvdi shrieked, jumped up and spun around causing his braided hair, which was sticking up through a deer bone on the top of his head, to flare out like propellers while he was spinning and then dance back and forth wildly when he stopped. Atselvdi's eyes slowly adjusted and he began to make out a faint outline. Frozen and unable to speak, he imagined the beady eyes of the scary old priest popping out of their cavernous pits beaming at him. He wanted to run, but his legs were dead. He could not hear the drums continuing to beat the slow, rhythmic beat of the dance. He could not hear the cherub like voices of the girls singing the song of the ball play dance echoing in the distance. He could only hear the heavy silence of Sali waiting patiently for a response from him.

"Sali?"

Sali chuckled and started walking toward his hut. Beads of sweat popped out on Atselvdi's face and he felt utterly ridiculous. Now he had no choice but to follow the ancient man into his clan house.

The small room had seven sides and was dark save the red hue provided by the dying hearth embers centered in the room. *Sali must have been away for a while.* Sali handed Atselvdi several logs for the hearth and picked up another to carry himself.

Atselvdi placed the logs on the hearth and blew carefully on the embers to reignite the fire. As Atselvdi sat down, Sali tossed his log carelessly on the others and the fire ignited and flamed up with a loud whoosh!

Atselvdi fell back in amazement and studied Sali for a moment. Sali calmly sat beside the hearth. The old priest seemed indifferent. Atselvdi sat beside the old priest and desperately searched for the words to begin.

"You are troubled?" Sali prompted.

Atselvdi looked at the collection of wrinkled blobs that was Sali's face. He could not make out where Sali's eyes, nose, or mouth might be. *How* can *he tell I'm troubled,* he thought.

"Witches," Atselvdi blurted out.

Sali was silent for a long time. "There are some who claim to be witches. There are some who are suspected of being witches, but few that really are," Sali answered.

Atselvdi respectfully waited to be sure Sali was finished.

"The one who visited our village?" Atselvdi questioned. He could not detect any reaction from Sali. He waited anxiously for the answer.

Finally, he detected movement in the lower quarter of the wrinkled mounds. "He was more than a witch."

Sali was silent again but the movement continued as if he were chewing something nasty, then he spit out his words contemptuously, "He was a tsigili!"

Sali said the name again in a slow, rasping whisper, as if he despised the name but feared that the evil witch might hear him.

After a long pause, Atselvdi ventured a question, "Who is he? Where did he come from?"

Sali breathed in deeply and exhaled slowly. Even though Sali's wrinkles seemed to effectively mask expression, somehow Atselvdi sensed deep grief in Sali.

As Atselvdi waited for Sali's measured answer, he glanced around the old clan house. The glow from the crackling fire made the grotesque artifacts hanging on the wall appear ghostly and scary. The room was sparsely furnished and meticulously neat.

A smacking sound got Atselvdi's attention. He studied the wrinkled face of the old man. Unconsciously, Sali was rolling his tongue around making a round bump that moved back and forth, up and down on his cheek like a mouse burrowing around in his mouth. Atselvdi perceived that Sali was remembering. He waited.

Finally, the eyes of the old man popped open and stared at the startled Atselvdi. He cursed to himself for falling for that old trick again. Sali always did that to startle his audience, and it almost always worked!

"I am not the one, Grandson, with the answers you seek.

Sali held his intense stare on Atselvdi. His bulging eyes searched the rude young priest as though punishing him with indignation. Then his chin trembled and he whispered, "No one knows more about tsigili than Adanvdo Alsgida. You must ask him these questions."

Sali closed his eyes. Atselvdi stared at the fire and wondered if his meeting with Sali would get back to his grandfather and make him angry. He felt a pang in his stomach as he thought about the possibility.

Sali added, "You should focus on the anetso tonight. The tsigili has gone and will not likely return."

And with that, the old man's face transformed into its usual blobs of wrinkles. The conversation was over.

"If your reflexes are so quick, how was I able to sock you on the forehead? I'm certainly not as fast as an arrow!"

THE SOUNDS OF THE village dance echoed faintly through the forest and cliffs along the Long Man. Ali had blocked out the festive sounds and was listening to the splashing water trickling through the beaver dams. She kept remembering that night at the Tagwa camp, and tried to remember more about what happened.

A lazy breeze passed by leaving her chilled. She shivered and Waya Usti cradled her close. She felt so safe in his arms and even though she was freezing, she did not want this enchanting evening to end. The embrace triggered another memory that had been lost in her trauma. Now she remembered Waya Usti trying to comfort her at the campsite. And she remembered how scared she was, so scared that she fought everyone and everything as if her life depended upon it.

She looked up at Waya Usti sympathetically. She wanted to tell him she was sorry for fighting him. She wanted to tell him that now she knew that he had just tried to rescue and comfort her. But, instead, she closed her eyes and buried her face in Waya Usti's shoulder.

She and Waya Usti had not spoken for a long time. Just being with him was enough now. And Tawodi and Amadohi had not stopped chattering. Tawodi had explained every detail of his trip to the Tagwa village to return the bodies of the Tagwa warriors. At first, Amadohi had punched him and reminded him that, Ali was present. Poor Tawodi had buried his face in his hands with shame.

Ali did not know why, but she wanted to hear about the journey and about the Ani Tagwa. "No, please, Tawodi, it's okay. I want to hear all about it, really."

"Are you sure, Ali?" Amadohi cautioned.

"I am sure, Amadohi."

So Tawodi began his version of his legendary journey and triumph over the Tagwa Chief's son and his little band of cowards. Strangely, hearing the story and being with her friends made her feel normal again.

"And he shot his arrow straight at me. I swear it was heading straight for my forehead!" Tawodi pointed at his forehead and drew his finger in as if it were an incoming arrow. Amadohi gasped, but Ali realized that she wasn't listening and forced her mind to replay Tawodi's last sentence. She leaned forward to look at Tawodi.

Tawodi continued, "Before I even realized it, I reached up and grabbed the arrow and stopped it in midair!"

Amadohi slugged him on his arm. "No you didn't!" she laughed.

"Yes, I did!" Tawodi said, pleadingly.

"That's not possible," Amadohi argued.

"I would agree with you if I hadn't done it myself," Tawodi countered.

Waya Usti defended his cousin. "It is true. Wahuhu told the same story at the Council House after we returned."

"No, you two are just telling stories!" Amadohi persisted. "You must think we are the dumbest girls in the village."

"I think it's true," Ali volunteered. "I heard Great-Grandfather telling it. He didn't know I could hear him and I didn't know what he was talking about then. I didn't know it was you, Tawodi."

"Now do you believe me?" Tawodi boasted.

Snap! "Ouch! Why did you do that?" Tawodi exclaimed rubbing his forehead.

"If your reflexes are so quick, how was I able to sock you on the forehead? I'm certainly not as fast as an arrow!"

The four friends laughed heartily and their laughter carried across the waters and up the trail toward the village where two old women were hiding and desperately trying to muffle their own giggles.

"Is anyone else freezing?" Ali suddenly asked.

"Yes!" Amadohi agreed, "Let's go back to the dance and get warm. Besides, I know a couple of Beloved Women who'll be out searching for us if we're gone much longer."

Two Beloved Women glanced at each other from their hiding place while their children laughed innocently in the distance and rose to head back to the dance. Frantically, the old women tried to duck down behind the bushes, but as they squatted, their knees popped, echoing through the trees!

"What was that?" questioned a startled Amadohi.

Tawodi and Waya Usti tensed and searched the darkness for the origin of the sound. Ali hugged Waya Usti tightly. In a vain attempt to comfort her, he suggested, "Probably a deer."

"Yeah, yeah, probably a deer," agreed Tawodi.

No one believed it was a deer, but no one had a better explanation. "Come on, let's get back to the dance," Amadohi insisted. "It's probably Mother and Kalona trying to hide in the bushes."

Nervous laughter enjoined the guilty children as they headed up the path to the village.

Pain and discomfort engulfed Kalona and Wananahi as they crouched in the bushes waiting for their children to pass by. They would later find humor in their situation, but not right then. Finally, the voices of the happy couples faded enough for the two old women to pull themselves up and stretch their aching muscles.

"If we cut across the fields to the east entrance, we might make it back before them," reasoned Kalona.

Wananahi asked, "Don't you want to go check on Atselvdi since he wasn't there when we went by?"

Kalona smoothed her dress down around her hips and grumbled, "He had probably gone to get the players to take them to water."

Wananahi pursed her lips. "Yes, of course."

The women rushed up the trail to where the fields stretched out along the east side of the village. It was difficult walking through the soft fields and the old women were quite winded when they reached the entrance to Tsikohi.

"Halt!" a voice from above shouted. Kalona and Wananahi shrieked and jumped back looking guiltily all around them.

"Is that you, Peace Chief?" the voice challenged.

Kalona now realized that the voice was coming from the guard platform. It had been peacetime for so long that the platform was rarely used. But, with the ball play scheduled for the next day, guards were in place to make sure the opposing team did not try to sneak in and deliver some dark spell on the local team.

"Yes, it's me," Kalona answered in a huff.

"You may pass through," the guard allowed.

Kalona grumbled as she hustled through the entrance switch back with Wananahi in tow. As Kalona emerged on the other side, she pulled up short and was bumped by Wananahi, then whispered, "Quiet."

Wananahi peeked around Kalona's shoulder in time to see a very tall, very skinny, person rush across the street and disappear behind huts lined along the right side of the street.

"Was that Atselvdi?" Wananahi inquired.

"I think it was!" Kalona exclaimed.

*Even at her age, her father
still could unnerve her.*

THE FIRST LIGHT OF morning illuminated Tlomeha Usdi's frowning face. The ball play had been the most important thing in his life and he had played in enough games to know that the priest was the key to success in the anetso. He knew the blessings by heart and he knew when the priest was inspiring the players. And he knew that if the priest's spirit was down, it would bring down the players as well. Something was wrong with Atselvdi so he feared that today would be a disaster for the Tsikohi team.

It was obvious to Tlomeha Usdi that Atselvdi was distracted. The players seemed subdued also. He knew he had to do something. As the last player waded out of the river and Atselvdi followed, he saw his chance and slipped up beside Atselvdi.

"Are you feeling well, priest?" Tlomeha Usdi whispered.

Atselvdi was startled and seemed puzzled by the question. Tlomeha continued, "It must be strange for your great-grandfather to be absent. Would you like for him to be here? I can go fetch him."

"Oh, no, that's not it. I mean, I am fine. I just forgot part of the blessing but I am fine now."

Tlomeha was not so sure. "Maybe you would be more comfortable if he was just ... around?"

"No!" Atselvdi snapped and stomped off.

Tlomeha shook his head. The team was in trouble. Their priest was in trouble. Then he remembered. "Oh! Atselvdi!" he yelled.

Atselvdi stopped to face the little man.

Tlomeha Usdi raised his hand to signal stop. He ran up to the skinny, dejected boy priest. "Someone was looking for you last night while you were away."

Atselvdi flinched. *Great-Grandfather came to check on me! What will I tell him?*

Tlomeha surprised him. "Some forest people ... old man, twin daughters, young girl with a funny name ... came visiting. I forgot to tell you when you got back last night in your rush to go to water."

Adanvdo sat under the porch fidgeting as the first light of morning was appearing. He sensed that something was not right. The daylight was not crisp like it should be. The smell of the earth and the wood of his house and the grass growing beside the house and the dry straw woven for the walls all smelled dull and not sharp like they should in the morning air. Adanvdo rolled two beads in his hand trying to decide if he should ask the spirits for guidance.

Kalona stepped out wiping her hands on a cloth. "Are you hungry, Father?"

Adanvdo replaced the beads in his medicine pack. Kalona helped him stand and walk into the house.

"Ali had another nightmare," Kalona whispered as she helped her father sit beside the hearth.

Adanvdo glanced up. It had been a while since his great-granddaughter's last bad dream. She was definitely recovering, but he knew that she still had a way to go. The dreams would recur from time to time, but not so much to reveal lost memories now, rather more to deal with the suppressed emotions and pain.

"Last night at the dance was a big night for her," Kalona continued. "Being around so many people may have been a little too much."

Adanvdo asked, "You came home early, then?"

"Oh, yes. I just felt that staying out all night would be too much for her. And she didn't protest so I think she was tired."

"It may have been overwhelming for her," Adanvdo mumbled.

Kalona handed her father a bowl of mush and sat beside him. "It is so sad that such a sweet girl should have had to go through such a horrible experience."

Adanvdo was silent and reflective as he ate. He did not seem to notice that Kalona was sitting quietly, patiently hoping he would share his thoughts. Finally, Adanvdo finished his breakfast, set the bowl on the hearth and declared, "Game day."

Kalona was surprised and a little disgusted. Adanvdo noticed Kalona's reaction. "Ali will be fine, and today is Atselvdi's debut! How was Atselvdi last night?"

Kalona's eyes grew large and she seemed edgy. "Well, actually I was so busy watching out for Ali, that I only saw him once."

Adanvdo looked at her with critical, penetrating eyes. Even at her age, her father still could unnerve her. She blurted out, "We saw him near Sali's hut!"

Adanvdo appeared to be surprised. "He wasn't at the Long Man or with the team?"

"Well, not at that moment, but I'm sure he got back in time to take them to water." Kalona felt very guilty.

"Why were you over there?" Adanvdo asked.

Kalona smoothed her dress nervously. "Wananahi and I went for a walk in the fields and were returning."

"Did Atselvdi say why he was at Sali's?"

"Well, no, he didn't see us. I don't know for sure he was at Sali's. He was just coming from that direction."

Adanvdo's stomach churned. He knew why Atselvdi had visited Sali. If Atselvdi was so obsessed with learning about the dark ways of the tsigili, he would not be his best for the team. Just thinking about the dark ways could contaminate his thoughts. The team needed to be inspired to win.

Kalona gathered up the bowls. "I think I'll check on Ali."

As his daughter left for Ali's bedroom, Adanvdo struggled to his feet and headed out the door.

He entered into the switchback at the northern entrance of the village and hid behind the exit wall to surreptitiously observe preparations for the game beside the Long Man. The players had stripped for the game and Tlomeha Usdi was moving from player to player scratching them with the kanuga.

Usually reserved for very special occasions when extra powers were perceived to be needed, Adanvdo could see that Tlomeha Usdi had chosen the comb-like kanuga with seven rattlesnake teeth!

The seven parallel scratches running down the player's arms, legs, and back and the large "X" across their chests were cut deeper than usual. As Tlomeha Usdi plunged the kanuga into the shoulder of the player and pulled it down the length of his arm, he was talking incessantly, apparently trying to pump them up for the game.

It was not the Little Bat's nature to give pep talks in these final moments before the game, but Adanvdo could see that today Tlomeha Usdi was desperate. Something was terribly wrong. The players should be displaying courage and confidence, but were complacent instead.

He searched for his grandson, but Atselvdi was not there. Adanvdo was engulfed by a great sadness, because he knew that for him to step in would only make matters worse.

*Atselvdi? How selfish of me,
Atselvdi is facing failure and
all I can think about is that
arrogant chief and poor Ali.*

THE GROUNDS AROUND THE ball play field were filling with the citizens from Tsikohi and Gwalgahi, Town of Frogs. It appeared that everyone had turned out. Even mothers with small babies and the frail and elderly had somehow managed to get to the game. West of the field, atop the mound and in front of the Council House, two red thrones reserved for the War Chiefs of Gwalgahi and Tsikohi sat proudly next to a white throne for the Peace Chief. On a modest bench next to the thrones, the old wizard Sali sat with his arms crossed, slumped like a round mound seemingly uninterested in the opening pomp and ceremony of the anetso.

The grand procession had begun led by Tsikohi's two chiefs and Uku. Ball play counselors followed who would be advising the anetso priest, Atselvdi, of any signs or taboos they might observe to help him with strategies or conjures, followed by Tlomeha Usdi marching proudly beside Atselvdi. Finally, the players marched in with their netted sticks held up to their chests which provoked proud, boisterous cheers.

As the Tsikohi procession turned to march along the east side of the field, the Gwalgahi procession was allowed in. One thing that almost all Tsikohians shared was their distaste for the Gwalgahi Chief, Waya Nigawisgv. There was not much to like about the arrogant Whining Wolf.

After the procession, the teams, their priests, and advisors huddled on the sidelines while Chief Waya Nigawisgv and Chief Waya Gigage climbed up onto the mound to sit beside each other as rivals. The two chiefs bowed politely to each other but then sat and stared at the field.

Four women with tump baskets on their backs marched in and placed their loads at the base of the mound. The baskets were filled with corn, beans, and squash and represented the Gwalgahi wager. Four Tsikohi women joined them with matching portions of corn, beans, and squash in their baskets. With this, the citizens of the villages began their lively individual wagering on the sidelines.

The ball players lined up facing each other in the center of the field and placed their sticks at their feet. They stood at attention and jeered at each other.

Two players from Gwalgahi did not have a Tsikohi player opposite them so they were required to remove themselves so the teams would be even. A basket of balls from Gwalgahi was presented to Chief Waya Gigage for his inspection. He examined and approved them.

The basket was delivered to the "driver" who chose a ball and marched to the center of the field where the players were maneuvering for position. As some rowdy gamblers continued to haggle on the sidelines, the rest of the onlookers hushed when the driver stood in the midst of the players and enthusiastically tossed the ball high into the air. The crowd cheered as the players battled for the ball. The game was on!

Kalona Ehlawei stole a glimpse of the exuberant chief from Gwalgahi. She fingered the beautiful turquoise necklace that he had given her several years before at the annual meeting of the two teams. She wondered if he was wearing the medicine pouch necklace she had made for him. She didn't notice when the Gwalgahi team got the first three scores, but she noticed that he had avoided looking at her. She also noticed that Ali and Amadohi were standing with Waya Usti and Tawodi.

When the Tsikohi team scored for the first time, the Chief briefly glowered at her and then looked away. It was clear that Waya Nigawisgv was still very angry with her for declining to sit with him this year. Kalona felt miserable. How could she have possibly thought that her rebuke would bring him humility? It had brought him humiliation, not the same thing at all.

The Gwalgahi team quickly scored four times more. Chief Waya Nigawisgv gloated and harangued the chiefs of Tsikohi. Kalona was pale and weak and felt sick. *It is my fault! I have angered the spirits with my vindictive prank against Waya Nigawisgv.*

Although the Tsikohi team managed another score, it was now seven to two and the Tsikohi players and their supporters were looking dejected. Kalona looked at Wananahi and vaguely remembered her trying to talk. *I have been so rude!* Kalona thought. Now she needed a favor and how could she ask her best friend after treating her so curtly. Kalona leaned over and touched Wananahi gently on her shoulder. I am dreadfully sorry that I have been so distracted."

"I understand, Kalona. This is such an important day for Atselvdi ... so much riding on it and so much pressure!

Kalona gulped! *Atselvdi? How selfish of me, Atselvdi is facing failure and all I can think about is that arrogant chief and poor Ali.*

Across the field, Adanvdo stood on the sidelines. He had stayed on the sidelines to serve as one of the seven counselors. He looked up at the mound and noticed that Sali was staring at someone slipping in through the north exit adjacent to the Council House mound. She was a wispy woman, frail and demure. Her long grayish hair hung from her head past her waist unattended, tangled like dry corn silk. It blended with her ragged, tarnished, once white cloth dress that covered her feet. With her pale skin, she was ghostlike in her appearance and in the way she glided slowly along.

Adanvdo watched her when she paused momentarily as if getting her bearings next to the mound. Then she floated dreamlike, oblivious to the raucous crowds and brawling ball play. Her face and her stature haunted him. He felt that he should recognize her, but his memories were vague and hollow.

He and Sali looked at each other with the same questioning look ... *do we know her?* When they looked back, the ghostly woman had disappeared.

Kalona swallowed hard, rubbed her dry mouth, and looked across at Waya Nigawisgv. It was time for her to show some humility of her own and apologize to the poor man. She would not be able to live with herself if she did not clear things up. With watering eyes, Kalona removed the turquoise necklace given to her by the arrogant man. She handed it to her confidant, Wananahi, and whispered her wishes. "Show this to Waya Nigawisgv and say to him that the humble possessor pleads for his forgiveness."

Wananahi gave Kalona a look of bewilderment. "Say what?"

Adanvdo looked at his great-grandson. Atselvdi hung his head as his team floundered against the formidable team from Gwalgahi. The Gwalgahi supporters roared as their team scored again! It was now nine to five. Adanvdo could sense that the Tsikohi team, like its team priest, Atselvdi, were dejected and had lost their confidence. *Something must be done!*

THE RAVEN MOCKER, KALANU Ahkyeliski, sat on the stone throne that he had named Edoda staring across the top of the canyon at the autumn colors starting to appear in the surrounding forests. The wizard felt very good. His body had metabolized the four souls, the askinas, of his victim and he felt rejuvenated. His senses were at their peak again. He could smell even distant and subtle smells. He stuck out his tongue and feasted on the treats drifting in the wind. He gazed with clarity on faraway peaks. He laid his head back and gazed at the clouds.

An image flashed in his head. He closed his eyes and tried to capture it, but it was fleeting. He slowly opened his eyes again to find the cloud that had prompted the image. It was a round, puffy cloud among other cumulus types. He focused on the center of the cloud until there was a blue circle with a yellowish border. Then he closed his eyes and waited for the image to materialize.

A curved, thick line, a half circle, materialized as a fuzzy white against a black background. On one end, spikes flared out. The other end divided into two crooked shapes. *What could it be?*

Then he realized it was a forlorn priest in Tsikohi. It was Atselvdi, his great-great-grandson! The wizard rolled off Edoda and rushed into his hut to retrieve a special mixture of root and herbs and his crystals. He poured the mixture into a steaming bowl of water and gulped it down as he disrobed and carried the heavy crystals to the sterile pond.

He stepped into the icy waters and waded up to the chute of water pouring out of the cliff face into the pond. The gelid waters took his breath away but he did not hesitate.

He gripped the crystals firmly, pushed the crystals into the crashing waterfall, and sang the chant for vision quests. Standing beside the pounding waters he focused on the spires of the clear crystals. The pounding water splashing over the crystals and the hallucinatory effects of the root and herb juices combined to produce dazzling images.

He shivered uncontrollably as he began to discern the images dancing in the crystals. He could see the despondent priest sitting beside the ball field while two ball teams fought violently to control the small deer skin ball. He closed his eyes and allowed the feelings of the priest to enter his heart. He felt Atselvdi's desperation, his debilitating depression, his utter sense of hopelessness.

Atselvdi was feeling failure, contempt, and helplessness. He could feel that Atselvdi was descending into a dark place. There was no time to waste!

The master wizard crashed through the frigid waterfall and waded to the rock ledge behind to stow his crystals. He dove into the water and swam under the waterspout to the center of the pond. As he emerged, he began shape-shifting into a hairy, silky, black-skinned, fiery creature and flittered skyward!

Wananahi slipped up behind Waya Nigawisgv. She touched his arm gently. Stunned to see her standing behind him, he gibbered and looked away.

The nervous messenger cleared her throat and stammered, "Chief, uh, I bring a message from Chief Kalona Ehlawei."

The humiliated chief pushed out his lower lip and tilted his head back defiantly. Wananahi waited impatiently. She felt her jaws tighten. *This is ridiculous! The old grump doesn't deserve Kalona's apology.*

"Well?" the old grump grunted, "give me the message."

Wananahi straightened her dress and fidgeted before continuing, "It's about the seating. Well, Kalona, uh, feels terrible about it."

Waya Nigawisgv turned with interest to look at the stammering woman.

"Oh! She told me to give you this turquoise necklace and tell you, uh, the humiliated owner of this begs you to forgive her. ... oh no, that's not it ..."

The prideful man could not hold it in any longer and burst into giddy laughter that made his plentiful belly shake. Wananahi did not know whether she should stay or run. But finally, the grotesque chortler gained control of himself and handed the turquoise necklace back to the incompetent messenger. "Tell Ka ... the Chief she is forgiven."

Unnerved by the tragedy unfolding on the field, Atselvdi lowered his head to call upon the white spirits for help. After a heartfelt plea, Atselvdi received an epiphany!

Suddenly, he knew his own lack of confidence was manifesting itself in the team. They had lost confidence because he was not confident. Atselvdi beamed at Tlomeha Usdi and waved him over. He yelled to the team, "Look at me! I have received a special message from the spirits and we are going to win!"

Atselvdi had their attention so he continued, "The spirits have sent the Little Bat to help us."

Tlomeha Usdi's eyes grew wide.

Adanvdo listened to his grandson yelling at his players. He watched Tlomeha Usdi's eyes grow bright, his energy build, and his chest puff out. He heard the team shout and raise their arms triumphantly. What was Atselvdi up to?

Whatever the plan, it was clear to the proud great-grandfather that the team was inspired. *Maybe he has done it!*

The crowd cheered as they watched Tlomeha Usdi trot onto the field to join the Tsikohi team. The crowd from Gwalgahi gasped and chattered animatedly. The Gwalgahi team leader on the side of the field stared dumbfounded at the frail old man headed out to join the team. He huddled with his counselors and then selected a player to cover the added Tsikohi player.

Adanvdo reached out and shouted, "No!"

He watched Tlomeha Usdi get into position. He had to stop it! The old man would be killed! He rushed up to his grandson to plead for him to recall the old hero.

Finally, Adanvdo asked the question that was burning in his heart, "Has he turned?"

THE EXPERIENCED OLD BALL player stood back away from the ball toss hoping to catch a deflected ball. Gwalgahi's biggest bruiser followed him and stood threateningly at his back. It reminded him of a game years ago, when in a similar situation, the player had whacked him on the head. Tlomeha Usdi knew that he would need all of his quickness to keep away from this behemoth but he was confident. He felt like the young "Little Bat" once again.

The ball was tossed and the players converged as the ball came down. The ball disappeared temporarily in the mass of clashing bodies and then popped out. Tlomeha Usdi snagged it in his stick's netting at a dead run and headed for the goal, but the uncatchable speed of his youth just was not in his feet anymore.

Once tackled, the whole of the Gwalgahi team piled on him, burying him beneath their grabbing, kicking, and slugging bulk. The ball players from Tsikohi dove on and the entirety of both teams writhed in a flailing, tangled heap.

The Tsikohi crowd suddenly gasped! Was this the end of their little hero? They pointed and shrieked, "Look! Beneath the pile, what is it?"

A small, black fluttering creature crawled out from under the pile and took flight with the ball clenched in its claws. Its erratic flight left no doubt that it was a bat, a tlomeha!

The bat carried the ball through the poles and dropped it for a Tsikohi score. The crowd stood dumbfounded for a moment and then shouted triumphantly! Heads of the stilled masses in the pile on the field stared in awe at the ball lying on the ground past the poles.

Adanvdo stood silent amid the celebrating crowd. The bat returned to the pile, the jubilant Tsikohi fans danced and shouted along the sidelines. Slowly the pile broke away and lying beneath was the bruised and battered body of Tlomeha Usdi. Adanvdo held his breath while the players lifted their Little Bat to their shoulders. The tiny old man was jabbing his fists into the air triumphantly. *He survived!*

Atselvdi was jumping up and down shouting to his players, "We can't lose. Don't you see?"

Ali had been standing next to her best friend. They were holding their breath in anticipation and concern for Tlomeha Usdi, when the black object emerged from the pile of ball players. When it launched off the ground, the crowd launched to their feet. Ali gasped, "The Raven!"

She tried desperately to get a better view, but too many people were standing in front of her. Amadohi, being much taller, was standing on tiptoes with her head bobbing back and forth trying to spot the mysterious black creature.

"Can you see it? Is it a raven?" Ali cried frantically.

Amadohi looked down at her friend. "Raven? You saw a raven?"

"I think so ..." Ali replied tentatively.

She grew quiet. She had only glimpsed the black object. The image of a raven had flashed into her mind, but she wasn't sure what she had seen. She closed her eyes and tried to visualize the pile of players and the thing that crawled out.

Images of a flaming raven flashed into her head. She tried to focus on the images. She envisioned a large flaming raven standing at a campfire. It was not just any campfire. She saw the bodies of Delagalis and a hideous Tagwa lying in front of the campfire. The Tagwa jumped up in fright as the raven spread its fiery wings.

She was jarred from the memory by loud arguing. It was an old man yelling at Amadohi, both were red-faced and angry.

"It was a tlomeha?" Amadohi yelled.

"Yes," the old man insisted, "Tlomeha Usdi."

"A little tlomeha?"

"No, Tlomeha Usdi!"

"Oh! No! Not him! I'm asking what was the little black thing?"

"Tlomeha Usdi!"

"A little bat?"

"No!" the old man insisted, "Little Bat himself!"

In disgust, Amadohi exclaimed, "I don't know what it was, Ali."

The Tsikohi players inspired by their hero, the Little Bat, Tlomeha Usdi, and convinced that the spirits had granted him great and mystical powers, were now confident that they were destined to win. How could they lose with the spirits on their side? And the event left the Gwalgahi team shaken and questioning their own confidence.

As Adanvdo left the field, Sali stood waiting for him. Adanvdo paused and looked curiously at the old sage. The old sage of short stature queried, "I couldn't see it, could you?"

Adanvdo was apprehensive, Sali continued, "Some said that they think they saw Tlomeha Usdi turn into a bat and carry the ball through the poles?"

Adanvdo nudged a tall spectator. "What did you see?"

"I saw Tlomeha Usdi disappear beneath the pile and then a bat crawled out with the ball and carried it away for a score."

Sali considered this. "An actual bat or Tlomeha acting batlike?"

"I saw an actual bat fly out of the pile."

Sali's wrinkled face showed distress. Adanvdo looked toward the ball field. The crowd was ecstatic. Tlomeha Usdi was being carried off the field on the shoulders of his teammates. Atselvdi was reveling in their success. This reaction deeply concerned Adanvdo. It bore the mark of witchcraft!

Adanvdo returned to the sidelines. He did not believe that Tlomeha Usdi was a witch. He looked at Atselvdi. No, Atselvdi could not have done it. *But how?*

The crowd roared as Tsikohi scored again. They now had the momentum and confidence. He watched in awe as Atselvdi commanded his team to score and score again until Tsikohi scored the winning point.

As Adanvdo Alsgida approached the clan council hut, he could smell the sweet odor of sacred tobacco smoke. He paused to sample the familiar aroma of Sali's special mixture. "Sali?"

Sali called out to Adanvdo to come sit with him, "Edoda."

He found the old priest sitting in the hut beside the hearth. He had prepared a proper fire so that the smoke could connect with the spirits. Gratefully, Adanvdo knelt to sit beside the old sage and asked, "What brings you to the Council House of the Ani Wodi clan, my friend?"

Sali sat motionless with his eyes closed, puffing on his pipe. Adanvdo crossed his legs to sit and reached for the pipe he kept on the hearth. He placed the pipe in his mouth and reached for his personal tobacco pouch. Sali, without opening his eyes, handed his own pouch to his friend. Adanvdo graciously accepted.

It was rare that he had the opportunity to enjoy Sali's special tobacco. He had always wondered what secret ingredient Sali added to get that wonderfully sweet taste. Adanvdo opened the pouch and scooped the delicious tobacco into his pipe bowl. He handed the pouch back to Sali who unconsciously took the pouch and laid it in his lap. Adanvdo tamped down the tobacco and lit a splint.

As he sucked on the pipe to get it started, Sali removed his own pipe from his mouth. Adanvdo recognized the gesture that meant Sali was about to speak.

"Tlomeha ... most curious."

Adanvdo agreed that the appearance of the bat was very curious. "Witch?"

"Who?"

Adanvdo was silent. He had his suspicions, but wanted to get Sali's opinion. Adanvdo bated his wise priest friend with, "The witch's purpose is perplexing."

Sali raised his pipe to his lips. Adanvdo perceived that the old priest would consider this carefully before speaking. The two old priests sat quietly smoking and thinking. Why would a witch that only recently murdered an innocent, good man for his souls now use his powers, at great risk, to help the Tsikohi team win?

There was the possibility that the witch was actually sabotaging the Gwalgahi team. But, still, it was a seemingly trivial matter for a witch to risk so much. It just did not make sense that a witch with such prowess would use his great talents because he was a big fan of the anetso.

There had to be an alternative reason. Adanvdo responded, "We can rule out Tlomeha Usdi."

Both knew him well enough to know that he had never demonstrated any signs of witchcraft. It was also very doubtful that he had befriended a witch that might come to his rescue in a ball game.

Sali removed his pipe to suggest, "Atselvdi?"

This revelation startled Adanvdo. He choked on the smoke in his lungs. It was not the suggestion that Atselvdi might be the reason behind the appearance of the witch—

Adanvdo also believed that Atselvdi was somehow behind the incident—but he was surprised that Sali had so quickly and confidently come up with Atselvdi as being involved.

As Adanvdo continued to cough the smoke from his lungs, Sali continued, "The young priest has developed an interest in the dark ways."

Adanvdo cleared his throat. Sali returned to his pipe. Adanvdo struggled to speak with a congested voice, "What do you know?"

Sali removed the pipe. "He came to me with questions."

Adanvdo cleared his throat again and returned to his pipe. The two smoked quietly and thoughtfully for a time. Finally, Adanvdo asked the question that was burning in his heart, "Has he turned?"

Sali coughed softly, but continued to chew on the pipe. After a thoughtful moment, he pulled the pipe away to answer, "No man can turn and learn that much without help. He was not the tlomeha."

Sali was right. Atselvdi was not the bat. The bat was someone with wizardly powers. Besides, Atselvdi was in plain sight while the bat was in flight. "You think Atselvdi has found a mentor?"

Sali sucked on a dry pipe. He removed the pipe from his mouth and dumped out the ashes on the hearth. Both experienced old priests watched the actions of the ashes as Sali dipped the empty bowl into his tobacco pouch. Adanvdo dumped his ashes beside Sali's ashes. Sali handed him the pouch without turning his gaze from the two piles. Satisfied that there were no significant signs in the ashes, Adanvdo took the pouch and dipped his pipe bowl for a refill.

Sali re-lit his pipe and sucked to stimulate the fired tobacco. Once satisfied the pipe was lit, he responded, "Perhaps a mentor has found Atselvdi."

On one hand, Adanvdo was relieved to hear this. Perhaps there was still time to save Atselvdi. But, now, perhaps it was a race, a contest. Adanvdo would be battling against an accomplished wizard for Atselvdi's heart. Adanvdo pondered this for some time before realizing that his conversation with Sali was back to where it had started. Adanvdo removed his pipe. "Who?"

Sali faced the Uku. His sinister eyes bulged and stared into Adanvdo's eyes. "Who else could it be?"

Kalona watched the enraged chief of Gwalgahi stomp off, leaving without even an acknowledgement. Wananahi touched Kalona's arm lovingly. "Don't let him get to you, Dear. He's just confused and humiliated by the defeat. You deserve so much better than …"

Kalona clutched Wananahi's hand. "I know you are right. He only thinks of himself. There is no room for someone else in his life."

She turned for home and added, "Truthfully, there is no room in my life for him either … or any man at this point in my life."

As the memories began to flood back, Ali screamed and covered her eyes.

Aᴌɪ ꜰᴏᴜɴᴅ ʜᴇʀ ᴛᴡɪɴ brother sitting in his favorite spot beside the Long Man just below the beaver dams. Atselvdi was dipping a leafy branch in the water. She remembered his analogy of the way disturbed waters slowly calm themselves.

"Siyo, Brother."

Atselvdi turned to see his sister standing at the edge of the clearing. "Hi, Sis. Come sit with me."

The grateful sister joined her brother. She pulled her shawl close under her chin to warm her chilled throat and chest. "The air is brisk this morning."

Atselvdi looked around as if he were unaware of this fact. "Yea, it will be getting colder now."

"Congratulations! The anetso was a triumph."

Atselvdi did not respond. Ali could see that something was deeply concerning her brother. As a twin, they had a special relationship. She could often feel his feelings and he could often feel hers. She could now feel that whatever was troubling Atselvdi was very profound. She waited for him to speak.

Atselvdi raised the branch and dropped it back into the water sending myriads of waves rippling out from the submerged branch. As he watched the ripples, he spoke, "Did you see the bat?"

"I thought it was a raven, but I learned later it was a bat."

"A raven?"

She laughed at herself. "Sometimes my eyes deceive me."

Atselvdi seemed inordinately concerned about her comment. He questioned, "What do you think it really was?"

She was struck by this question. "You don't think it was a bat?"

Atselvdi appeared to be searching for an answer. Finally, he explained, "There is so much you don't know, Sis. A lot has happened since ..."

He paused and glanced at his sister. Ali was surprised. Of course, life had continued since her abduction. Atselvdi remarked, "We really have not reconnected since your ... ordeal with the Tagwas. Maybe it is time we caught up."

His face expressed deep concern. "Ali, do you remember when Crooked Foot was found dead after Grandfather treated his granddaughter?"

Ali looked at her brother blankly. His eyes widened. "Oh, no, that happened while you were being abducted."

He told her about how the old man had come to their house and asked Adanvdo to look at his granddaughter. He told her about how their great-grandfather had hated the old man's barking dog and how he had transferred the sickness to the dog to get rid of it. They both laughed at how cantankerous their great-grandfather could be. It felt good to be sharing things with her brother again. They were so much alike in the way they saw things.

Atselvdi then told her about the next morning when the old man's wife had thrown rocks at their house and accused their grandfather of killing her husband. He told her about going to see the corpse with Adanvdo and the deceased's face locked in a look of horror. He told her about the askina that the witch had stolen. He told her about his discussions with their great-grandfather about witches.

As he spoke, Ali began to realize that the description of the witch Atselvdi was describing sounded a lot like the raven-man she had seen at the Tagwa campsite.

"I think I have seen the Raven Mocker!" she suddenly interjected.

Atselvdi stopped with his mouth open in mid-sentence.

"At the campsite in the canyon a flaming raven swooped in. He was huge and scary. I remember now that he ferociously attacked one of the Tagwas."

As the memories began to flood back, Ali screamed and covered her eyes. Atselvdi leaped over to her and hugged her. "I'm sorry, Ali, I didn't mean to trigger the memories. It's okay; everything's okay now. You are safe, Ali!"

Ali looked into her brother's eyes. "It is all so weird, Brother. I'm not really sure whether I dreamed it or it really happened."

Atselvdi looked at his despairing sister, then looked at the calm waters. "You may never know for sure, Ali. But something really horrific occurred at that campsite.

Perhaps you were so scared that you imagined the witch helping you, and in a frenzy, you summoned the strength and courage to defeat your abductors."

Ali looked at the calm waters and thought about her brother's conjecture. Perhaps he was correct. Would she ever know for sure?

Adanvdo sat alone in his darkening room clutching the small box with the claw of a giant Tlanuwa bird attached to the top like a handle. It just did not add up. He knew only two witches that could shape-shift into a bat. One was his evil brother, Tsisgili, who was securely entombed in the stone spire in the meadow. That just left Kalanu Ahkyeliski! But why would his father get involved in a ball play and risk being seen by a seer. He would have to know that both he and Sali would be in the crowd. And for what benefit?

Adanvdo shook his head. *That's just nonsense.*

The baffled Uku rotated the box, unwrapped the leather strap, and raised the old lid slowly. A putrid stench escaped and burned his nostrils. Adanvdo reflexively slammed the lid closed. How many years had it been … fifty summers? *How could the stench last fifty summers? … It couldn't!*

Adanvdo threw open the lid. He gasped and his eyes burned but he forced himself to look in. The box was not empty! Crusted blobs lay beside a yellowed rib bone! Adanvdo looked up and sadly closed the lid. The dried blobs were the remains of a human heart and a human liver. His father had left him a gift!

Adanvdo inhaled deeply, shook his head and protested, *Father!*

It was not the first time his father had tried to save his life. It had been the point of contention between them that had finally driven him to stop climbing the mountain to visit the old man. He knew that his father meant well, but just could not seem to understand that he had chosen the white path.

But his father's kind heart did not just extend to him. He suspected that his father was behind Ali's rescue. He shook his head, and now had his father risked all just to help Atselvdi save face? How could such an unselfish, kind man cling to the black path?

Adanvdo stood to go dump the contents of the Tlanuwa box. Perhaps he should visit his father again.

Kalona stepped outside to refresh herself with the chilly morning air. She absent-mindedly patted her tightly coiffed hair as the breeze teased with it. Out of the corner of her eye, she spotted a strange, white cloud floating down the street. Under closer examination the cloud proved to be an old woman with cotton-white hair and a yellowing white dress flowing down to her ankles.

Determining that the old woman was a stranger, Kalona greeted her cordially, "Osiyo, are you looking for someone?"

The old woman seemed startled by Kalona's approach, placed her withering fingers over her mouth and drew back a few steps. Kalona waited for her reply. "Oh! I was looking for the Tomb of the Witch. I heard that it is in Tsikohi?"

"Yes, well, it is not in Tsikohi. It is just west of the walls in the meadow. If you go back up the street and cross the avenue, you will see the west entrance. Go out there and you will see a tall, thin stone spire sticking up out of the meadow."

The timid woman pointed up the street with questioning eyes. Kalona offered, "Shall I help you find it?"

The old woman's eyes grew large. "Oh, no! I'm sure I can find it."

Hurriedly, the wispy woman strode up the street. She appeared to almost be floating with the breeze blowing her cloth dress and nappy hair behind her. She was a most curious creature to Kalona and she debated about following her.

As the ghostly woman disappeared behind the rise in the street, Kalona made her decision. She clinched her fists and strode up the street in pursuit of the curiosity.

When she reached the western entrance, she cautiously slipped through the switchback and paused to peer around the wall into the meadow. She watched the old woman touching the stone spire tenderly. She appeared to be weeping as she walked around the base of the spire dragging her hand along the multi-faceted grooves and surfaces of the stone. At last, she collapsed to her knees and sobbed into her hands.

Kalona's eyes squinted as she tried to read the reason behind the old hag's actions. *Who would weep over the grave of that witch?*

Kalona wiped her hands on her dress, shook her head and headed home. As she approached the porch, her father stepped out and apparently noticed the concern on her face. "What is it, Daughter? Have you seen a spirit?"

Kalona stopped and replied, "Perhaps! There was a ghostly old woman asking about the Witch's Tomb. ... very curious."

Adanvdo's eyes squinted. "I think I may have seen her at the anetso. Do you know who she is?"

"No. She is a stranger. Just passing through, I suspect."

"I think I may know her from somewhere," he rubbed his chin in thought, "but I cannot recollect how I know her."

Kalona paused and then suggested, "Come in. I have some venison on the spit."

The old man looked down at the box in his hands. "I will be in shortly."

*"Sending a National Force
could trigger a war with
the Kusas. Anyway, it is
not certain who is behind
the raids."*

An elated Waya Usti stepped outside into the cool morning air. The thrill of the anetso dance and being with Ali was still fresh in his mind and heart. So much had happened since that humiliating night when he and Tawodi had fought in the street and woke up the entire village. Since then, his visits with Ali by the Long Man and their leisurely strolls had pushed those bad memories away. He looked toward the general direction of her house wondering if he would get to see her again today.

His ebullience was interrupted by a loud commotion coming from the north side of the village. He listened intently to determine exactly where. The sounds echoed off the houses of the village, but he was certain that the sounds were coming from the ball field. He ran toward the field to see what was happening.

When he arrived, he found a number of his friends playing the popular game of Chunkey and standing near the large, round, polished stone. Several arrows were buried in the sand scattered around the stone. All had penetrated at an angle and all had been shot from roughly the same spot. But one arrow stood almost straight up with the rock nudged up against it. Standing proudly beside the vertical arrow was his big cousin, Tawodi. He was being taunted by his fellow Chunkey players when Tawodi spotted his cousin and hailed him to join them.

"They think it is luck! Tell 'em, Cousin." Tawodi implored.

One player protested, "He just shoots straight up and it always comes down where the stone stops! He's the luckiest dumb giant I've ever seen."

Waya Usti laughed. "It's not luck. It's not even a mystery."

"What?" the disgusted player replied.

"He's just hurling the arrow up to the spirit world and letting them place it for him."

The player threw down his bow and tackled Waya Usti prompting the other players to throw down their bows and pile on forming a mound of writhing, fighting, shouting, laughing wrestlers. Tawodi slung his bow across his body and started grabbing waist belts and pulling flailing young men off the pile one after another until he reached the original two protagonists.

Without the help of his friends, the player who started it all was quickly pinned by Waya Usti. Tawodi lifted up his triumphant cousin to receive the mock praise of the others.

"How do you really do it?" the downcast player asked from the ground resting on his elbows.

"Roll the stone and I'll show you." Tawodi jeered.

The young men laughed and gathered up their bows for another round. The defeated player heaved the stone across the ball field. Tawodi raised his bow above his head keeping his eyes on the ball and released the arrow, shooting it, as before, apparently straight up.

The other players raised their loaded bows and shot their arrows straight up imitating Tawodi. They all stood quietly watching them sail high into the sky, pause, then start backing up, flip over and race back to earth. Suddenly, they all shrieked and scattered as the arrows rained down on them.

Narrowly escaping disaster, the players rolled on the ground laughing happily. When they regained their senses, they noticed Tawodi standing next to the rock that was leaning up against his vertical arrow. The big man proudly said, "See, just like that."

The incensed young men jumped to their feet and plowed into Tawodi. They were like bees attacking a bear and Tawodi brushed them aside accordingly. Not giving up, the pesky warriors fought on pushing Tawodi across the field, through the stockade exit and finally into the Long Man.

Sitting, exhausted, in the cool shallows of the Long Man the players laughed and chided each other until they noticed Wahuhu exiting the stockade and marching purposefully toward them. Tawodi jumped to his feet and stood erect to greet his warrior leader. The others followed suit.

"We've gotten word that Kusas have attacked an out-lying village on the Coosawattee. Chief wants to meet in the Council House."

With that, the stern old warrior marched back into the stockade.

"Gotta go, guys," Tawodi explained as he waded out of the water and headed for the Council House.

Waya Usti had been waiting outside the Council House long enough to watch Grandmother Sun travel four fists across the sky vault. Suddenly, the warriors began exiting the Council House and Waya hailed his oversized cousin. "What did you learn at council?"

Tawodi glanced about and then whispered, "We may be sending a force to the Coosawattee."

Waya Usti shook his head. "I suspected that."

Tawodi led his cousin to the side of the stockade for privacy. "The Chief and Wahuhu are going to Katuwa to meet with the National Council."

"What's to discuss? Surely we will defend the people of the Coosawattee."

"Sending a National Force could trigger a war with the Kusas. Anyway, it is not certain who is behind the raids."

"You don't believe it is the new Kusa chief?"

"Sure I do. And so does about everyone else. But, he is clever. He has been sending small raiding parties with non-descript war paint."

"What does he hope to accomplish with small raiding parties?"

Tawodi thought about this. He shook his head. "Well, I don't know. He can't send his National Force for the same reason we hesitate sending ours: It would definitely trigger war."

"But, he can't win the villages of the Coosawattee with raiding parties. He can only anger them and turn them against the Kusas."

"Actually, there are a lot of old Kusas living there among the Tsalagi. It has always been that way. That was why it was a problem in the first place. Some felt allegiance to the Kusa, some to the Tsalagi, but within the villages, they lived in peace. That's why an anetso worked. Most of the people of the Coosawattee did not care whether they were Kusa or Tsalagi. They just wanted peace. But, it may be that Kusa Chief, Little Feather, hopes that the raiding parties will stir up dissension and turn neighbor against neighbor. Once a Tsalagi kills a Kusa, he will have an excuse to send in the Kusa warriors to defend the Kusa villagers."

Waya Usti was enlightened. Tawodi's analysis made sense. "What can be done?"

Tawodi slapped his cousin on the back. "That's why they've called a council, little cousin."

*He knew how he felt about
it personally and he sensed
that most of Tsikohi was in
favor of sending warriors
to help defend the people
along the Coosawattee.*

THE COUNCIL HOUSE WAS filled with noisy, curious, and in some cases, furious Tsikohi citizens. The word had gotten out. The Great Council in Katuwa had decided to not send the National Warriors to Coosawattee to protect the villagers from raiders.

The Tsikohi warriors, clan priests, Beloved Women, Peace Chief, Uku and his assistant were all present waiting for the War Chief and his Principal Warrior and messenger/ assistant to arrive. Messenger/assistant Awi Gawonisgv entered the council house followed by Wahuhu, and then Waya Gigage. The Council House grew quiet as the three took their places in front of the tall-backed red thrones. Chief Waya remained standing as his colleagues took their seats.

He bowed to the Peace Chief and Uku before speaking. "Friends of Tsikohi, I bring news from Katuwa. The Great Council has made a decision concerning the recent malicious raids on the villages along the Coosawattee River. Since the raiders do not appear to represent any nation, it would not be appropriate to send National Warriors to defend them."

The Council House erupted! Jeers and shouts represented the contempt of the citizens for this decision. Someone yelled out, "Who's going to protect the Tsalagis along the Coosawattee?"

Waya Gigage raised both hands pleading for order. Slowly the citizens took their seats and quieted down to allow him to speak. "The Council decided that each village shall decide whether they want to send warriors to help the people of Coosawattee."

The citizens exploded again clearly disgusted with the suggestion. Waya raised his hands again and waited for the crowd to settle down. "Friends, I understand your impatience with this decision, but hear me. The villages along the Coosawattee are a special case. There are both Kusa and Tsalagi living side by side. They have lived peacefully with each other for over a generation. Tsikohi played a major role in obtaining that peace. Some of you are old enough to remember and I expect that the rest of you have at least heard about the great anetso that placed the Coosawattee under the Ani Yun Wiya."

The Citizens looked toward the bench where Tlomeha Usdi sat. The notorious old ball player looked down humbly. They voiced their approval of the Little Bat that had played so magnificently in that fateful anetso.

Waya resumed, "The Council felt that the goal of the raiders is to get the Kusa and Tsalagi to turn against each other and start fighting among themselves. If this happens, it would put the Coosawattee back in jeopardy and give the Kusa an excuse to get involved again."

Waya Usti looked at his cousin. Tawodi had assessed the situation perfectly. The Chief was repeating him almost word for word.

The Chief continued, "Now the great people of Tsikohi have been asked to help the Coosawattee people once again."

The Tsikohi citizens voiced their support loudly and enthusiastically.

The wise Chief recognized the window of opportunity. He exited the Council House with Wahuhu and Awi Gawonisgv trailing behind along with Peace Chief Kalona, Uku Adanvdo Alsgida, his assistant, Sali, and his apprentice, Atselvdi. Everyone knew that they were headed to Waya Gigage's house to officially discuss the matter in private. Decisions on war were ultimately decided by the War Chief.

Some remained in the Council House while others congregated outside to exchange opinions on the matter. Of course, there were those who kept their feelings to themselves. Kalona, Adanvdo, Sali, Atselvdi and Awi Gawonisgv left the house of Waya Gigage after only a short time. They had given the War Chief their opinions and pledged their support. However, it would ultimately fall to Waya Gigage to make the final decision.

The War Chief and his Principal Assistant were alone next to the hearth. Wahuhu thought he knew how Waya would go. He knew how he felt about it personally and he sensed that most of Tsikohi was in favor of sending warriors to help defend the people along the Coosawattee. His place was to support the War Chief no matter what he decided.

Waya Gigage puffed on his pipe absently, his mind deep in thought. At last he shared his thoughts. "We have been at peace for a long time. Most of the young warriors don't know how to fight. They have never actually been in a battle. They are fine young men and very willing. No doubt, Wahuhu, you could lead them through it, but most of our warriors are getting old and war is not for old men. If something happened to you, who would lead in your place?"

Wahuhu sat patiently gazing into the glowing embers. He offered his opinion. "Tawodi is an exceptional young man. One day he will take my seat in the Council." He wondered what could be taking Waya so long to decide. It seemed to him to be an easy decision. "The people of the Coosawattee need help. They are our brothers. The citizens of Tsikohi have voiced support." *What else was there to think about?*

Waya resumed, "The raiders most likely aren't independent! They are probably acting on behalf of the Kusa Chief Ugidahli Usdi. All he has to do is to have one of them discretely kill a Kusa villager and it starts war. Our warriors would be on the front lines against the Kusas until our National Warriors could arrive. They would have little chance! Many would be killed!"

Wahuhu could feel his anguish. He admired the man and his compassion. Still, the decision seemed simple to him. Their brothers needed help. They should provide it.

Amadohi sat next to Ali beside the hearth waiting for word from the Council House. They had been reflective until Amadohi broke the silence. "Well, there's no doubt that Tawodi will have to go!"

Ali reached for her friend's hand. "Waya will be needed as a scout, I'm sure."

Amadohi tried to reassure her friend. "Not necessarily. Waya Usti hasn't any experience as a warrior. I'm sure the National Warriors have plenty of scouts."

Ali tried to think of something to comfort Amadohi. "Maybe Tawodi will be left behind to guard the village."

"Against what? We're too far away to really be in danger. If the Kusas attacked, they probably would head for Katuwa."

The girls heard the door cover ruffle and turned to see Wananahi enter. She stopped just inside the door, rubbed her cold hands and stared at the two fretful girls sitting by the fire, holding hands and anxiously waiting for her to speak.

"The decision from Katuwa is to not send warriors."

The two girls beamed.

"Before you start celebrating, each village is to decide for itself if it wants to send warriors to help."

The exuberant faces transposed into frightful faces.

"Chief Waya and Wahuhu are in his house. I'm sure they will decide something soon."

Amadohi blurted out, "Will they come tell you?"

Wananahi felt sorry for the two girls. "If he decides in favor of sending warriors, he will go outside and shake his gourd rattle and do a little dance to announce it."

The anxious girls looked at each other in a panic and Ali spoke, "We can't hear that from here!"

Amadohi exclaimed, "Your house is closer, Ali!"

Ali considered it. "Still too far away. Chief Waya lives next to the Council House!"

"Waya Usti's house is closer."

"He's across from the Clan Hut, might as well go there."

Wananahi felt compelled to intervene. "Girls, girls, calm down, word will spread fast. Why don't we go over and wait for news with Kalona."

The girls did not wait for her to finish the sentence. They were up, grabbed Wananahi by the hand and rushed to wait with the Peace Chief.

Tawodi stood with his arms crossed, feet apart, back straight stoically staring at the War Chief's house from behind the Council House atop the mound. He was surrounded by a dozen young admirers and want-to-be friends. The towering titan enjoyed almost hero status among his peers and younger boys. The boys jockeyed for Tawodi's attention and approval.

One boy quipped, "How long does it take to say war?"

The other boys giggled nervously.

"Maybe it's his naptime!" another rejoined.

Another boasted, "We could've whipped 'em and been back by now!"

The boys continued their bantering but Tawodi was not amused. He feared that going to defend the Coosawattee was a trap. *This approach affectively divides the Tsalagi forces. The renegade Kusa Chief can easily start a skirmish so that he has an excuse to send in his forces. They could easily defeat the small inexperienced forces of the village volunteers and then march against the reduced National Forces. Think it through, Chief Waya, this is a bad idea!*

Waya Usti ran up the stairs of the mound and spotted his oversized cousin. He chuckled at the sight of the doting admirers flocked around the disinterested Tawodi. He glanced at the Chief's house. It was still quiet. He wormed his way next to his cousin. "What's the word?"

Tawodi shook his head. Waya Usti glanced around the anxious crowd. "Looks like everyone is ready for war."

Tawodi cursed under his breath. The perceptive cousin challenged him for his thoughts. Tawodi looked around suspiciously then decided to just shake his head futilely.

Waya Usti looked at his cousin with alarm. He whispered, "You don't think we should send support?"

Tawodi looked around, grimaced, then whispered back, "It's for the Chief to decide."

Waya Usti looked at his cousin. "Why do you not approve of sending warriors from Tsikohi? I know you are not afraid to go to war. Surely you don't want to leave the Tsalagi of the Coosawattee defenseless."

Someone declared, "The Chief!"

Tawodi spotted several people pointing. The crowd got louder as the War Chief came out of his house and began shaking his gourd rattle, dancing, and shouting the war whoop! This meant that he had made his decision. Tsikohi warriors would go to aid their brothers along the Coosawattee.

The crowd cheered and began bailing off the mound to gather around his house, essentially volunteering to join the Tsikohi forces. Tawodi's little fraternity scrambled down the mound falling over each other, fighting to be first. Tawodi could not believe it. It looked like everyone, even the old men and little boys were flowing in and around the Chief's house.

Tawodi looked at his cousin. Waya Usti asked, "What do we do?"

Tawodi shrugged then reluctantly headed for the Chief's house.

*He certainly had not
anticipated the anguish
that he saw in her face or
felt in her words when he
told her of his decision.
Now, he felt distraught, but
he could not back out.*

So many had come forward to join the war party that the War Council had to meet to make choices. The oldest and the youngest were eliminated immediately, which left mostly young, inexperienced warriors. Warriors were selected based upon skill level and positions needed to form a war party. Some exceptions were made. Several boys, warriors under the age of twenty, were allowed to go.

Atselvdi was too young to be a warrior or to participate in a war party. But, because all of the other priests were too old, he was chosen to be the company priest and would carry the ark containing coals from the sacred fire. He would also be responsible for handling the spiritual ceremonies, conjures, and to make sure all traditions were observed. A village kuni-akati was chosen to help him treat the wounded.

The village army would need three principal leaders. Chief Waya appointed Wahuhu to lead the company in his place since this was not a declared war, just a defensive action. In this position, Wahuhu would assume the title of Raven. Tawodi would carry the flag of Tsikohi. In this role, he would be considered equal in authority with the Raven should he fall. Finally, Awi Gawonisgv was selected as the Skaliloski, the chief speaker.

Waya Gigage decided to only send four of his seven counselors. To assist in the traditional dances and ceremonies, he chose one of the village drummers, an experienced singer, and several cooks.

Waya Usti along with three others were chosen to do any tracking and to serve as scouts for the army.

Kalona Ehlawei was asked to organize the preparation of food for the war party. She would enlist helpers to prepare corn cakes for each person to carry individually and then prepare baskets of provisions so the cooks could prepare meals in the field.

There was much to do to ready the army. Each warrior provided his own weapons including his personalized shield, war club, axe, knife, lance, bow, and arrows. Wahuhu and the war counselors organized last minute training and strategy sessions. Elders, council members, and priests all visited the warriors to give them inspiration. Adanvdo took the warriors to water and prayed sacred war prayers.

For four days and nights the warriors would be expected to fast and to refuse anything given to them. Gifts, food, anything to be given to the warriors had to be dropped in front of them and not passed to them directly. But no other taboos were enjoined.

Ali sobbed quietly beside the man she had just come to love. Waya Usti was trying to understand and absorb what she had shared with him. She had confessed to him that she needed him in a very possessive way. Something she had never experienced before. She felt safe with him. He was the doorway that had led her out of the horrific world that the Tagwa warriors had forced her into. She felt normal and whole again with him.

She shared that she could no longer be the happy, innocent, confident girl she had been. Now, she needed Waya Usti in her life. She felt dirty and abused around everyone else. Everyone else pitied her and their eyes betrayed their pity. She knew they meant well, but she hated the way it made her feel. Wolf Puppy loved her unconditionally. When he looked at her, it was not with pity or sympathy but with admiration. He loved HER, not what happened to her. With him, nothing had changed. With him, she could escape and be the new Alihelitsidasdi.

Waya Usti stared into the flowing waters of the Long Man conflicted. On the one hand, he was excited about going to the Coosawattee to help the people fight the raiders. Though, he understood Ali's concern. He tried to comfort and assure her that nothing would happen to him. The fact was, it had not occurred to him that the mission would be dangerous or that he might get hurt or even killed! All he had thought about was the sense of pride and honor he had felt joining his friends in volunteering to represent Tsikohi. It had seemed the right thing to do—the ONLY thing to do. He had not hesitated.

He had even been excited to share his brave decision with the girl he loved. He expected her to be impressed and proud of him. He certainly had not anticipated the anguish that he saw in her face or felt in her words when he told her of his decision. Now, he felt distraught, but he could not back out. And he could see that Ali could never share his enthusiasm and excitement. The glory was gone. Even Tawodi seemed doubtful! The mission tasted sour now.

Waya Usti stood. "They are calling us to water. I have to go."

Ali put her arms around him and kissed him tenderly. Waya Usti was thrilled by her action. He wrapped his arms around her and hugged her gently. She felt delicate and soft against him. He did not want to leave her. He wanted to hold her forever.

As they separated, Ali smiled with quivering lips and whispered, "I have something for you."

She reached into the pouch she had carried with her and pulled out the corn cake she had made him for his journey. She started to hand it to him and then remembered and placed it at his feet.

As she stepped back, Waya Usti reached over to pick it up. As he did, Ali pitched something to the ground in front of him. It was a medicine pouch made of deer skin with red beads sewn on and a leather strap. He hesitated and then picked it up. The significance of it panged his heart. It meant that he was the one, her special someone. It was for protection. He placed it around his neck, raised it to his lips and kissed it while staring at his special someone, Ali, the girl whose name meant Happiness and who signified to him his own happiness. Without her he could never be happy.

Kalona helped Atselvdi pack. As the priest for the war party, he had a lot to pack. "Don't forget your bear skin cape. Winter is near."

He took the warm fur from her. "Wado, Grandmother."

She just wanted to hug him, but it made him uncomfortable since he had gotten older. She brushed the back of his neck instead. Atselvdi was concentrating on what all he needed. She could tell that his mind was going through a mental checklist. She waited.

Finally, Atselvdi straightened. She could read his mind. He was satisfied that he had everything! He became very serious. *Perhaps reality is setting in!* she thought. Atselvdi noticed his grandmother. Kalona smiled back, maternally. Atselvdi lifted his packs off his shoulders, set them on the floor, and embraced his grandmother.

"I'll be fine, Grandmother."

Tears filled the old woman's eyes. "I know you will, Grandson."

She helped him lift the heavy packs and slip the wide straps over his shoulders. She was afraid his skinny legs would buckle under the weight. The fragile little priest crossed the living room and Kalona rushed ahead to hold back the door cover while he slid through.

Kalona stepped outside smiling to herself. She could see that Atselvdi was proud. She believed that she was many times stouter than her skinny grandson, and wanted to carry one of the packs, but she would allow him his manly pride. She would walk with him to the Council

House where he would store his stuff until the next morning.

Grandmother Sun had disappeared behind the western mountains leaving very little light. Atselvdi stopped short as he stepped into the street. Kalona looked at Atselvdi and saw that he was looking up the street. About fifteen paces in front of Atselvdi, a slender silhouette stood facing him with long flowing hair that seemed to be gently dancing in the light breeze. *Who's this?*

Atselvdi looked surprised, even shocked. "Sudalegi?" he whispered.

The shadow reached up and brushed her hair from her face. "I heard about the war party."

"How?"

She smirked, "We hear things in the forest."

Atselvdi was completely stunned. Kalona stepped back into the doorway but kept an eye on the girl. The mystery girl began to sashay up to Atselvdi. "Aren't you glad to see me?"

"Uh huh." Atselvdi stammered.

He likes this girl! Kalona detected.

"I looked for you at the dance. Your assistant said he would tell you when you got back."

"He forgot. He told me the next day."

The girl was close enough and Kalona's eyes had adjusted enough that she could now tell that this little stranger was very plain but very pretty. She could also see that she was very taken with Atselvdi. *He doesn't have a chance!*

The impish girl stood close in front of the priest. "Where are you going?"

"Oh ... I am taking my packs to the Council House. We leave from there in the morning."

"Can I come with you?"

"Sure!"

The enchantress lifted one of the packs off Atselvdi and slipped it onto her shoulder. Kalona sighed as the two walked up the street together. *Atselvdi called her one thing when he saw her? What does that mean? Why one thing? I'm going to have to look into this!*

He would never begrudge his village's peaceful times, but he was a warrior at heart. This was how his life was meant to be.

T AWODI SLAPPED HIS NOSE and then retorted, "Ouch!"

He awoke to find Amadohi laughing so hard that there was no longer any sound coming out of her mouth. She was doubled over holding her stomach and tears were streaming from her eyes. In her hand, he saw the answer to what had just happened. She was holding a feather. Tawodi jerked off the buffalo skin that was covering Amadohi, exposing her to the chilly morning. Amadohi grabbed the blanket and tugged, but she was no match for Tawodi.

"I'm sorry! Please, I'm freezing!" Amadohi playfully punched Tawodi and then pulled on the blanket and then punched and then pulled and then kicked until Tawodi relented.

Amadohi rolled over on her stomach and placed her chin on Tawodi's chest. "I just couldn't resist. You were sleeping so peacefully."

Tawodi looked up at the dark blue-black sky. Grandmother Sun would soon appear to the east. He realized that he and Amadohi had spent the night on the precipice west of the village, which afforded incredible views of the country surrounding Tsikohi. It also afforded a bird's eye view of the village. The north side of the formation was a long, gradual incline making the ascent an easy hike. But the south side was a sheer drop sticking up out of the meadow like a huge, stone knife blade.

Tawodi raised his head and tried to look down at Amadohi. "Have you been awake all night?"

"What choice did I have with your snoring?"

Tawodi dropped his head back in disgust. Amadohi giggled and continued, "Besides, this is the last chance I'll have to see you for a long time. I wanted to study your face so that I won't forget it. Sort of like forcing myself to have a nightmare!"

Tawodi chose to ignore her gibe. "Today's the day!"

Amadohi turned her head and laid it on Tawodi's chest again. She wished that this night would never end. It had been magical. Tawodi was a good man. He was kind and gentle despite his massive size and quite thoughtful—for a man.

He looked past her down on Tsikohi. Warriors were starting to arrive at the Council House. Amadohi's angelic face faded into a frown. Tawodi looked into her eyes and sadness engulfed him as well. Nothing had ever been as perfect as that night. Tawodi rolled over to embrace his love one last time.

The Tsikohi company of warriors strutted westward along the winding path through the mountain forests and grassy valleys that would eventually lead to the headwaters of the Coosawattee River.

Atselvdi marched in front carrying the ceramic pot containing the sacred embers from Tsikohi's sacred fire. When Wahuhu had seen the skinny priest try to move along with all of his heavy baggage, the normally solemn old warrior doubled over laughing which touched off the rest of the company. Wahuhu then appointed two warriors to help carry Atselvdi's heavy packs. They trudged along behind the skinny priest.

Wahuhu strode stoically in the lead just behind Atselvdi and his helpers with his right-hand man, Tawodi Gvnagei, at his side holding the Tsikohi flag. Following the ridgeline to their right were their scouts and Waya Usti. Their counterparts reconnoitered on the left flank.

The first day was a long day. They had to cross the many mountain ranges and tributary streams that Tsikohi was nestled among. Wahuhu hoped to cross this difficult part of the trip before nightfall and camp at the base of the mountain ranges. Tomorrow their journey would be easier, crossing the wide valley that would lead them to the mountain range to be crossed to reach the Coosawattee. That mountain range was the eastern continental divide where the rivers on this side flowed east. The rivers on the other side flowed west. The troop's spirits were high and they were filled with energy and enthusiasm. Wahuhu was proud to be leading a war party again after so many years. He would never begrudge his village's peaceful times, but he was a warrior at heart. This was how his life was meant to be.

Amadohi had spent the morning catching up on her sleep while Ali had spied on her grandmother's secret mission to learn more about Atselvdi's mysterious visitor.

As Grandmother Sun was beyond the crest of her day's journey, Ali and Amadohi sat in the shade of the porch that extended along the south side of Amadohi's house. They had not spoken to each other except to say hello since Ali had come over. They did not need to speak to each other. They just needed to be with each other to share their misery.

Amadohi sighed. "Where do you think they are now?"

Ali thought about it and tried to picture the western trail leading out of Tsikohi toward the valley. "I think they were hoping to reach the valley tonight."

Amadohi huffed. "Why do men love war so much?"

Ali shook her head. "It is part of them. We love babies; they love war."

Amadohi laughed. "Why can't those people along the Coosawattee defend themselves? It's just a little raiding party."

"Good point. I guess no one even thought about that."

Amadohi nudged her distraught friend and looked toward the street. Ali looked over to see her great-grandfather shuffling along. He appeared to be in a hurry. They watched him disappear between the houses south of them.

"Someone has called for the Uku." Ali surmised.

The curious girls moved to the street to get a better look. Adanvdo turned back east and disappeared again behind a house.

"Come on!" Amadohi challenged as she trotted stealthily between the houses and stopped to peek around to see where Adanvdo had gone. Ali slipped up behind her.

"He's standing in front of Sali's hut," Amadohi reported in a whisper. Then she led Ali back to the street and ran to the stockade wall. The two girls slid secretively behind the hut and hid between it and the stockade wall. They placed their ears against the wall of the hut to listen.

Adanvdo asked, "You think the Owlman that raped her was Tsisgili?"

"Osiyo!" Adanvdo called from outside Sali's hut.

After a moment, Sali peeked out. "Adanvdo?"

Then Sali pulled back the cover and invited the Uku inside. They sat down by the hearth and stared at the glowing embers. The room was very hot. Adanvdo pulled off his cape while Sali repacked his pipe, started it and passed it to his guest.

Adanvdo started the conversation. "I have been thinking about the bat. I agree with you. It had to be Kalanu Ahkyeliski. But it was risky appearing as a bat knowing he might be seen by you or me."

Sali added, "We didn't see him but he must have known we were there."

Adanvdo questioned, "Why would he do it? What did he hope to gain from it?"

Sali closed his eyes. "... for Atselvdi? Your father has a kind heart sometimes. He is an enigma"

Adanvdo was relieved to have Sali agree. "Perhaps, love of family ... concern for his grandson. It worries me, though. Will he try to turn Atselvdi to the dark ways as he has tried to turn me so many times?"

Sali took a deep breath. "Did he try to TURN you? Or did he try to PRESERVE you?"

The question was spot on. His father had never really tried to turn him away from the priesthood. He just could not understand why Adanvdo would allow himself to die knowing how to attain immortality.

"I cannot be sure he will not do the same with Atselvdi."

"No, you cannot."

Adanvdo shifted nervously, this was only part of what he had come to discuss with his friend. There was something that to him was even more mysterious. They sat in silence for a long time before Adanvdo changed the subject.

"I saw that you noticed the wispy woman at the anetso. She asked Kalona about the Tomb of the Witch. I feel as though I know her, but I cannot remember how."

Sali removed the pipe from his lips. "I felt the same thing."

Adanvdo felt a little surge of excitement. "Someone we both know?"

Sali resumed smoking as Adanvdo strained to place the face to a memory. Sali removed the pipe again. "She is interested in the tomb of Tsisgili? Perhaps she knew him."

After a long pause, they faced each other with eyes widened by the enlightenment and whispered in unison, "Saloli. She has returned!"

Memories flooded into Adanvdo's brain of the timid girl that was his wife's sister. It had been so long since her disappearance that he had essentially forgotten that she existed. Perhaps he had wanted her to cease to exist. The years had not been kind to her. She looked as if she had aged two years for every one.

Saloli, Squirrel, had suffered a traumatic event around the time he had met her and she had moved in with his wife-to-be, Wadulisi. She hid in the darkness as if frightened by even her own shadow.

His cousin, Big Elk, was living with him at the time. Saloli was a pretty girl and the big, gentle man with an even bigger heart was instantly infatuated by the seemingly helpless, fragile girl. He managed to bring her out of her shell for a time, but more visits by someone she called Owlman left her with shifting and sometimes violent moods.

Sali mused, "She was his wife."

Adanvdo asked, "You think the Owlman that raped her was Tsisgili?"

Sali did not answer but Adanvdo knew that Sali had always suspected that Adanvdo's evil brother was the horror in Saloli's life. He remembered that when Tsisgili appeared on the day Wadulisi was giving birth to little Kalona, his appearance had induced Saloli to give birth prematurely on the spot.

It was the day that no Tsikohian could forget. It was the day that his father battled Tsisgili in a life-and-death explosive battle in which his father's powers prevailed and left the evil brother entombed in the stone megalith.

The encounter left Wadulisi in a coma and Saloli in the clutches of a mental breakdown. Strapped with two babies to nurture, the deranged Squirrel snapped one night, dumped the babies in the river and disappeared.

Fortunately, Big Elk discovered her missing shortly afterward and a massive search party discovered little Kalona Ehlawei sleeping peacefully on the river bank. Sadly, Saloli's baby's blanket was found downstream, but the baby was never found.

A bewildered Amadohi stepped back from the wall of Sali's hut and looked at Ali. Ali pulled her head back but was expressionless as she was rolling over in her mind what she had just heard. Amadohi nudged her. The two spies followed the stockade wall to the street, turned right and exited through the stockade's east exit into the cornfield.

"Who is Kalanu Ahkyeliski? He mocks ravens?" Amadohi inquired.

Ali tried to remember where she had heard the name but could not. "I don't know, but I think I've heard the name before."

Amadohi remembered the first part of the conversation. "He must be a witch."

"Why?"

"Adanvdo asked Sali if Tlomeha Usdi was a witch, remember?"

Ali answered thoughtfully, "Yes, you're right."

"Why would your grandfather think Tlomeha Usdi was a witch?"

"Well, he DID turn into a bat at the ball play, didn't he?"

"Ooh! That was freaky, wasn't it?"

Ali remembered her talk with Atselvdi. She wished she could talk to him now. He would be interested in this piece of news. She wondered how he was doing so far away. And she wondered how a certain young warrior-scout was doing. "Do you think they're there yet?"

"Adanvdo and Sali?"

Ali laughed. She realized how far from the subject her mind had jumped. "No, I meant ..."

"You can't think of anything else can you?"

Ali shoved Amadohi playfully. "I guess you've forgotten all about that big ol' chunk, Tawodi?"

"Who?"

The two laughed and strolled through the tall pines on a bed of soft needles, they paused to watch a squirrel scamper across their path, stop, shake its tail as if taunting them, then bound up a tree.

Amadohi remembered the conversation they had overheard. "Do you know the squirrel?"

Ali laughed. "Oh, sure, I call him Walnut."

Amadohi was puzzled. "Walnut?"

Ali frowned. "No, I don't know the squirrel, do you?"

Amadohi glanced at the spot where the squirrel had paused, then giggled. "Oh, no! Not that squirrel, the woman your great-grandfather and Sali were talking about. The one that asked your grandmother about the Tomb of the Witch."

"You mean the wispy woman?"

Amadohi studied her friend. "Yes. Did they say that she dumped your grandmother in the river?"

Ali frowned. "Yes."

Amadohi then asked, "Had you ever heard that before?"

"No. Grandmother nor Grandfather, for that matter, ever talk about that time. I knew that it was difficult for Grandmother because her mother, Wadulisi, died when Kalona was born. But I never knew about the witch or any of that."

Amadohi shook her head. "I thought the Tomb of the Witch was just some old myth. Do you think there really is a witch in that spire?"

"Evidently he was Saloli's husband!"

Amadohi shivered. "Ooh! How creepy is that?"

Ali had an idea. "Let's go look at it!"

Amadohi's eyes grew large. "Absolutely not!"

Kalona Ehlawei dragged herself into her house and collapsed in her bed. A tentative voice called to her from across the room, "Grandmother?"

"Yes, dear, it's me." Kalona paused to catch her breath, "I'm sorry I woke you, go back to sleep."

"Where have you been?"

"Oh, I just needed to visit a friend in the mountains."

Ali rolled over onto her side and stared across the dark room. "That's what you said when you left. What do you think of Sudalegi?"

"You knew?"

"Not at first, so I followed you."

"You followed me?"

"Not all the way. When you had to stop, I started to come to you to help, but Sudalegi beat me to it."

They both laughed. "She knew I was following her all along. I couldn't believe she came back to help me!

"Kalona mused. "She's actually a very sweet girl. We had a good visit."

"She's very pretty."

"Oh! Yes, she is! And those twins are a hoot!"

"Did they tell you why they call her Sudalegi?"

Kalona realized that she had not found the opportunity to ask how she had gotten the name One Thing. "No! I meant to ask her about that."

"Atselvdi said that the twins named her One Thing because she's not two things like them!"

Kalona cackled and then realized that Ali had talked to Atselvdi about her! "When did you talk to Atselvdi?"

"The night before they left, Waya and I were down by the beaver dams and she came strolling up and asked us if we knew a young priest named Atselvdi. I about fell over! Waya and I led her into the village and when we topped the hill and started to turn to head for the house, we saw Atselvdi stumbling out the door with all his packs and stuff.

Waya and I went on to his house to pick up his packs and then met Atselvdi and Sudalegi back at the Council House. Atselvdi was very embarrassed, but we made him introduce her and spent some time just talking. She's definitely a forest girl, but she's very nice and I can tell that Atselvdi likes her a lot."

Ali lay silent reminiscing about that night, the last night with Waya Usti. Parting had been so difficult.

Her thoughts were interrupted by her grandmother's snoring. She rolled out of bed and pulled covers over her exhausted grandmother who had always been there for her and her brother!

"He was also very angry and has disappeared along with several sympathetic warriors. I fear he will come here seeking revenge."

Chief Waya Gigage stepped through the door of his house into the crisp chill of the autumn morning. He sucked in a deep breath of the brisk air. It felt good in his lungs. He pictured the Tsikohi company of warriors rising and getting ready for another day's march toward Coosawattee. He hoped that they had made it to the base of the mountains on the first day. That would put them on track to reach the rally point and join with the other Tsalagi village volunteers in four days. He reasoned that they would be assigned to an important village—probably Ustanali—because of Wahuhu's prestige and experience.

He turned toward the Council House and was startled to see four silhouettes standing on the mound looking down at him. They were not fellow villagers. They were not Tsalagi. *Tagwas!*

His heart began to pound. One was wearing the headdress of a chief. He glanced around and spotted a dozen or so more standing next to the Council House. *I should have deployed sentinels! We are completely vulnerable!*

He glanced around the stockade wondering if there were more Tagwas. *They could be all over the village!*

The Tagwa Chief raised his hand, then entered the Council House, followed by his three companions. Waya Gigage rushed back into his house to send his wife to roust his interim principal assistant, interim messenger, the Peace Chief, the Uku, and then to alert the elderly warriors to assemble around the Council House. He quickly explained that a Tagwa delegation had come to meet with them, hoping not to alarm her. But she was alarmed.

The Tsikohi War Chief rushed back outside, composed himself and marched up the mound steps. He paid no attention to the Tagwa warriors standing guard around the Council House and they appeared to pay no attention to him.

When he entered, he found the four Tagwas seated on the benches around the hearth. The fire tender was bringing up logs to add to the fire. Waya Gigage could see the fear in Stoker's eyes, but the old man bravely tended to his duties.

Waya Gigage calmly walked to his throne to fetch his pipe and tobacco and then returned to sit on the bench across from the Tagwa Chief. He took his time preparing the pipe. His interim principal assistant entered, followed by his interim messenger. They took up seats next to him.

Waya puffed on the pipe to get it started then handed it to his assistant to deliver to the Tagwa Chief. He wondered how they would communicate. His translator, Awi Gawonisgv, was with the warriors headed for Coosawattee. He knew a little of the Tagwa language. Many words were common to both but the Tagwa dialect made understanding difficult.

The Tagwa Chief seemed to be enjoying the sweet cultured tobacco that was uniquely Tsalagi. Peace Chief Kalona entered with Adanvdo Alsgida holding on to her arm. The stern, brave Beloved Woman glared at the Tagwa delegation while the stoic Uku ignored them as they took up seats behind Waya and his assistants.

The Tagwa War Chief began, "Our hearts are broken. Our renegade sons have shamed us."

Waya was shocked! He spoke perfect Tsalagi. The Tagwa Chief returned to the pipe thoughtfully. "We are grateful for your kindness. Your actions have gained our respect and we now consider you our brothers."

Wahuhu had been very impressed with this chief. He had reported that he considered him to be an honorable man of peace. Waya could see why Wahuhu was so impressed.

An assistant delivered the pipe back to Waya Gigage. Waya respectfully accepted the pipe and then answered, "We are proud to be your brothers and you are welcome in our village."

He sent the pipe back to the Tagwa Chief. The Chief took his time smoking the pipe. He seemed to be searching for words to express his main purpose. "I am aware of an incident between one of your warriors and my son."

Oh, dear, here it comes! Waya thought to himself, *Tawodi has shamed the Chief's son.*

The Tagwa Chief continued, "I would like to meet this warrior. ... And I would be honored to see the warrior I spoke with that day again."

Waya accepted the pipe and ordered it to be refilled. He did not want to admit to the Tagwa Chief that Tawodi and Wahuhu, and nearly all of Tsikohi's most capable warriors, were a day's journey away. He definitely did not want him to know that Tsikohi was virtually defenseless!

Kalona shifted uncomfortably on her throne behind him. She usually trusted the judgment of Waya Gigage, and she was sure he would not trust a Tagwa Chief. However, she would caution him to be careful what he admitted to him. *No doubt the Tagwas have seen the red flag flying in front of the Council House showing we are at war. So, they probably suspect we are virtually defenseless!*

His assistant handed Waya the refreshed pipe. He enjoyed the pipe and then explained, "Wahuhu Adawehi and Tawodi Gvnagei both have expressed great respect for you."

He sent the pipe back to the Tagwa Chief. He thought he might have heard Kalona sigh behind him.

The Tagwa Chief took the pipe. He smoked it calmly for a moment and then continued, "I am very ashamed of my son's behavior."

He took a deep breath and a couple more draws on the pipe. "He was also very angry and has disappeared along with several sympathetic warriors. I fear he will come here seeking revenge."

Waya thought he might have heard Kalona gasp behind him. He observed the three Tagwas beside the chief. Their faces were of stone.

"Your village has suffered enough from my village. We have come to stand between you and my son and his renegades."

Waya thought he might have felt Kalona's shock! He studied the Tagwa Chief looking for signs that he was sincere. His face showed no emotion; his eyes were steady. There were no clues to judge the veracity of the man.

"She's in her house. She's scared out of her mind. She thinks she has a knife and that they are coming for her again."

Aʟɪ sᴀᴛ ᴜᴘ ɪᴍᴍᴇᴅɪᴀᴛᴇʟʏ wide awake! She remembered where she had heard the name Kalanu Ahkyeliski. When Atselvdi had told her about the old man that was killed, he said by a Raven Mocker witch. He had told her Kalanu Ahkyeliski was the worst, the highest level. He was a witch capable of shape-shifting into a raven or other critters, like a bat!

She threw on her dress and fur cape, slipped into her fur boots and raced out of her bedroom. Curiously, no one was home! She wondered where her grandmother and great-grandfather could be so early in the morning. Yet she was glad that she did not have to explain where she was going.

She knew that Amadohi would still be asleep this early. As she rounded Amadohi's house, she found Wananahi sitting on the porch wrapped in her bear skin blanket waiting for sunrise. "Ali!"

"Osiyo!" Ali pulled her cape tight and sat next to her.

"It is the most beautiful part of the day, don't you think? The clouds are so colorful, the air is so crisp, and it is so peaceful."

Ali took note of the clouds, the air, and the quiet, but her mind was on witches. "I don't suppose that Amadohi is up yet?"

"Oh, no, it will be a while before she stirs."

"I want to talk to her. Would it be all right if I ..."

"Of course, it would do her good to see this part of the day once in a while."

It took some coaxing, but Ali managed to drag her sleepy friend out of bed, into some clothes, and out for a walk. They headed for the dance field where they could talk in private. As they strolled past Ali's house, she noticed that it still appeared empty.

"I remember where I heard the name of the witch," Ali blurted out.

Amadohi yawned grandly and rubbed her nose with the front collar of her fur cape. "What witch?"

"Kalanu Ahkyeliski! You remember when we spied on Sali and Great-Grandfather. Well, Atselvdi told me about ..." Ali stopped short! Amadohi trudged on a few steps, then stopped to see what happened to her friend. "Ali?"

Ali was frozen in place. Her eyes were wide, her face pale.

"What is it?"

Amadohi looked to see what Ali was staring at. She could not believe her eyes. Tagwa warriors were lined up along the north wall of the stockade behind the ball field.

Amadohi grabbed her traumatized friend and dragged her back to Ali's house. "Kalona! Adanvdo!" she yelled as she hugged her friend and led her to the hearth. She helped Ali sit and covered her snugly with her cape.

"It's okay, Ali. Talk to me."

"Tagwa!" she yelled. Her eyes turned from shock to fury. Suddenly, before Amadohi even knew what happened, Ali leaped to her feet and whirled around. Her fist was raised as if she had a knife in it and she was ready for combat.

Amadohi tried to hug her and reassure her, but the girl warrior slung her off, sending her sprawling across the floor. When Amadohi looked up, Ali was backing into a corner of the room threatening imaginary combatants with the imaginary knife!

Amadohi was scared, really scared, fear like she had never felt before! How did Tagwa warriors get into the village? They were real. She saw them with her own eyes. Had they come for Ali again? Were they ghosts ... vengeful spirits of the Tagwas that Ali had brutally slaughtered?

Amadohi raced to the doorway, pushed the door cover aside and peeked out. Carefully, she slipped out on the porch and looked around the corner of the house, down the street to where the ball field lay. The Tagwas had not moved. Amadohi raced across the street to her house and fell into her mother's arms. "Tagwas! There's Tagwas at the ball field!"

Wananahi hugged her panicked daughter. "What? Tagwas? What are you talking about?"

Amadohi implored her to look around the corner of the house. Wananahi shrieked! "Ali! Where's Ali?"

"She's in her house. She's scared out of her mind. She thinks she has a knife and that they are coming for her again."

Wananahi broke loose from her daughter and raced to Ali's house. She burst into the house and found the horrified girl curled up in the corner sobbing. She ran and threw her arms around her, but Ali stiffened and shoved her away, then she said, "Amadohi?"

"Yes, it's me Ali. You're fine. It's okay!"

The terrified girl looked at Wananahi sprawled on the floor in front of her. She jumped up to help Wananahi stand. "I'm sorry! I thought ..."

After the council, Waya privately invited Kalona and Adanvdo to his private residence. They found Waya's wife sick with fear lying beside the hearth. Waya rushed to her side to comfort her and was quickly joined by Kalona. "It's going to be fine," Waya promised. "Believe it or not, the Tagwa Chief says he is here to protect us from his son's vengeance."

"Why would he do that?" she demanded.

The fearless diplomat explained, "He says they are grateful for our selfless return of their boys."

"Pshaw!" she huffed.

Kalona tried to support her colleague. "It is true, my dear, strange as it may seem."

Adanvdo knelt beside the woman. "Drink this. You will feel better."

The Uku handed her a bowl with an odd mixture steaming in it. As she took a sip, he began whispering a chant and shaking his gourd rattle. The two chiefs slipped away to sit together by the hearth. As Waya prepared a pipe, Kalona asked, "Do you think it wise to let them bivouac on the ball field ... inside our walls?"

Waya blew out smoke. "I don't think we have a choice. If the Chief is telling the truth, it would be better for them to be inside so as to not be detected by his son and his band of renegades."

"Yes, if he is telling the truth. Do you trust him?"

Waya shook his head. "Again, I don't think we have a choice."

"Shouldn't we send a messenger to call back our warriors?" questioned Kalona.

"I asked my messenger to see if he could slip out. But, it could take him two days to catch up to them so it would be three or four days before they could get back. Until then, we must try to keep everyone calm and come up with a contingency plan."

"What do you make of him insisting that only HIS forces be involved in any fighting? Do you accept his explanation that it is a family matter ... for them alone? He's correct in saying the village of Tsikohi has not done anything at this point to warrant retribution. So by not being involved in any fighting, there should be no reason for something to develop with us."

"We can only hope."

"Your idea to insist upon having our sentries since they would be visible to the outside and would not tip off the renegades was good."

"And I think your refusal to evacuate the village was wise."

"Oh, I don't really trust the Tagwas to protect us as I argued, but I do believe we would be completely vulnerable if he has troops outside waiting for us."

Adanvdo joined them. "Let's hope the messenger got out."

To celebrate the success of the coexistence, the chiefs decided to have a dinner.

SEVERAL DAYS PASSED IN Tsikohi without incident. The Tagwas, much to Kalona's surprise, turned out to be very humble guests. The Chief was not only wise and peaceful, but also quite charming. And he saw to it that his warriors kept to themselves and were not rowdy or disruptive.

Chief Waya Gigage made sure that the citizens were polite and stayed away from contact as much as possible. And Chief Kalona saw to it that the young girls of the village were kept away from the Tagwa warriors. They were not to be on the streets without escort and were not allowed to leave the stockade under any circumstances. They were allowed to congregate in the Clan Council Houses for social contact during the day, but were to be closely guarded.

All village volunteers were to meet near the head-waters of the Coosawattee where they would be assigned to the different villages along the river. Because of the rugged mountain ranges that the company of warriors from Tsikohi had to traverse, or in some cases go around, it was noon on the fourth day before the weary warriors topped the last peak and looked down on the Tsalagi camps set up around a small lake.

As the Tsikohi warriors approached, they were met by their messenger Awi Gawonisgv, Talking Deer, who had gone ahead to announce their arrival and acquire instructions.

He ran up to Wahuhu and explained, "Katuwa has sent a war council to coordinate the assignment of the war parties. They have set up a temporary council house near the center of the camps. I will show you our camp."

He escorted them to a clearing along the river below the lake where they could set up camp. They learned that most of the village forces had already been given assign-ments and some would be leaving for their destinations the next morning.

As he had done each night of the journey, Atselvdi supervised the construction of the campfire, carefully gathering small chunks of wood for the sacred ark and stoking the embers to provoke a small fire in the canister. He poked a dry stick after it was burning well and trans-ferred a piece of the sacred fire from Tsikohi to the new campfire. He would take the company to water after they returned from Council.

In the meantime, Wahuhu and Tawodi supervised setting up their makeshift shelters and stowing away their provisions. Tonight the drummers would set up around the fire and they would dance and pray.

With camp coming together Wahuhu, Tawodi, and Atselvdi headed for the Council House to get their assignment from the National War Council.

Waya Usti sat alone atop a rocky ledge. It provided him with a good view of the camp's northern perimeter. He was very tired from the trip, but he would be vigilant until his partner relieved him at sundown. His heart directed his weary mind to the morning of their departure and his last sight of Ali. It ripped out his heart to walk away from her: distraught with sad, red, puffy eyes; trembling lips; teary, wet cheeks; slumped shoulders; and toiling hands. It was as if his heart was bound to her and parting meant leaving his heart behind. The image made tears well up in Waya Usti's eyes.

Below him, a disturbance drew his attention. The warriors were rising in anticipation of the return of Wahuhu, Atselvdi, and Tawodi. All of the camp engulfed them and besieged them with THE question: Where were they to be assigned? Waya Usti strained to hear, but voices echoed in the clearing distorting the words. Then he picked it out—*Ustanali!*

Ustanali meant a natural barrier of rocks across a stream and was a prominent village just above the confluence of the Coosawattee and Conasauga Rivers in the heart of the Coosawattee territory. Because of its location and size, Ustanali was a key community. They were being honored by the assignment.

The arrangements between the Tsikohi villagers and the Tagwa visitors seemed to be working and there had been no known incidents—aside from Ali's episode. To celebrate the success of the coexistence, the chiefs decided to have a dinner.

Kalona and Adanvdo sat with the Tagwa Chief and Waya Gigage at a special table atop the mound overlooking the ball field. Below the Tagwa warriors were enjoying a feast prepared by the grateful Tsikohi citizens.

Kalona felt very uneasy having all of the Tagwa warriors inside the village walls. They were completely vulnerable. And she was still suspicious of the Tagwa Chief although she had to admit he was very charming. The conversations they had each evening had been cordial, even enjoyable. She was beginning to like the witty man.

The witty man spoke, "Chief, do you ... Oh, excuse me," he acknowledged Chief Kalona, "Chief Waya Gigage, do you expect Wahuhu to return soon?"

Waya glanced at Kalona. She frowned expressing her apprehension. Waya did not have to be reminded that he must be careful with his answer. "I expect him at any time."

The Tagwa chief raised his eyebrows. "I look forward to seeing him again."

He drank from a clay pot, wiped his mouth, then remarked, "I was hoping you would include your warriors at this dinner."

Waya glanced again at Kalona. Her eyes betrayed her concern. Waya started to respond but was saved by the

Tagwa Chief adding, "Of course, I agree that there is no need to risk a squabble at this point."

Waya added, "Perhaps at another time."

The sun had long descended behind the mountains surrounding the lake and headwaters of the Coosawattee. Campfires were raging creating orange domes over the trees. Drums echoed all along the river and around the lake. Waya Usti could hear yelps from the dancing warriors. Below, the warriors from Tsikohi were doing likewise. It was almost dark now and his duty relief was climbing up the rocky escarpment. He acknowledged his replacement and headed down to the camp.

As he entered the clearing, he spotted Tawodi sitting up against a boulder staring at the night sky and joined him.

Tawodi looked up at him. "I think we are heading into a trap that we don't have a chance of winning."

Waya Usti sat down next to his huge cousin. "But the raiding parties are small and we should have no problem quelling them."

"The raiding parties aren't going to attack one of our companies."

"I don't understand."

"I'm not worried about the raiders. I'm worried about the Kusa National Warriors."

Waya Usti was confused. "But we are not at war with the Kusas. We're just here to protect the Coosawattee region from renegade warriors. Isn't that why the National

Warriors weren't sent—to avoid provoking the Kusa warriors?"

Tawodi leaned forward and looked at his confused cousin to explain, "Okay, consider this. Half of the Tsalagi forces are here and will be deployed in small autonomous groups strung out along the Coosawattee River."

Waya Usti frowned. "Half of the Tsalagi forces? None of the forces are here. These are all village volunteers, aren't they?"

"If we were to go to war against the Kusas, would we only send the National Warriors?"

"Oh, I see. All of the village volunteers would deploy with the National Warriors."

"Correct. The forces that are here would be combined with the National Warriors and would be a formidable force. But, what if the Kusa Chief could divide the Tsalagi forces in half? Then he would have a very good chance of defeating them, wouldn't he?"

"Yes, probably."

Tawodi leaned back. "So, what if after the village volunteers get deployed, and essentially broken up into dozens of small forces far away from the Tsalagi National Warriors, the Kusa Chief figures out a way to stir up the Kusa and the Tsalagi villagers and some Kusas get killed?"

"Then he would have an excuse to move in to protect them."

"And what if he has already readied the entire Kusa Warriors, including all of the Kusa Village forces?"

Waya Usti sat up. "Then he could easily take out the Tsalagi Village forces! We would be vastly outnumbered."

"He could destroy us before we could organize and before the Tsalagi National Warriors could get here. Then he would only have the Tsalagi Regular National Warriors, essentially half of the Tsalagi forces, to fight."

Waya Usti sat back stunned. "Have you discussed this with Wahuhu?"

"Not yet. It's only a theory."

"You've gotta tell him about this! Come on, let's see what Wahuhu thinks!"

The movement of the air drew his attention back to the lips of nature preparing to speak again.

Wananahi and Amadohi carried baskets of food to the ball field. "Take yours over to that table and I will distribute these here."

Amadohi carried her baskets to the empty table at the corner of the ball field. As she unloaded the food onto the makeshift table, Amadohi sensed one of the Tagwa warriors staring at her. She glanced up to see a tall, slender, handsome young warrior confidently smiling at her. He did not have a flattened Head like so many of the warriors. He looked quite normal and even gentle. Amadohi smiled back. Wananahi was busy straightening dishes and removing lids and did not notice.

The young warrior moved closer and whispered, "Osiyo."

Amadohi's heart raced. She looked away and whispered, "Siyo."

She tried to ignore the forward young warrior. Kalona had been very clear that there was to be no interaction between the Tagwa warriors and the young girls. But the charming young man persisted, "We are all very ashamed that our cousins attacked your village."

Amadohi busied herself arranging food on the table. He continued, "I understand two girls were killed?"

Amadohi nodded.

"Was anyone else hurt?"

Amadohi moved further down. The pleasant warrior moved with her. "Who?"

Amadohi ignored him. He continued, "Will they be okay?"

Amadohi glanced up at him. He studied her for a moment. His dark eyes seemed kind. She sensed that he was genuinely concerned. He asked, "Were you hurt?"

"Oh, no, it was my friend."

The curious young man continued to study her. She felt flattered. "She was getting better until she saw you, I mean all of you, in the village."

"How was she hurt?"

"She wasn't so much hurt physically. It was just having to watch those men brutalize and murder the other two girls."

The warrior was quiet and then he commented, "That must have been very traumatic for her."

Amadohi looked down.

"I hope that we will be able to rectify the injustice some way."

Amadohi glanced back up at him—at his eyes. He seemed sincere. "We don't expect anything of you. We just want to move on, and forget."

"How do you forget the loss of family? How do you not want the wrong rectified?"

"We want to follow the white path."

Wahuhu had listened to Tawodi and Waya Usti without comment. The three were standing beside the river and gazing across at the darkness on the other side. The two young warriors waited impatiently for Wahuhu's reaction.

"It's an interesting hypothesis," he allowed.

Tawodi beamed proudly but remained quiet. After a moment, Wahuhu continued, "If you are correct, they will wait until we are all deployed to determine our positions."

Waya Usti interjected, "They will probably pick a village that is not guarded. Do you know which villages were assigned and which will be unoccupied?"

Wahuhu shook his head. "No. We only learned of our assignment."

After a moment, Wahuhu suggested, "We must talk to the delegation from Katuwa."

Atselvdi stretched out under the fur skins and breathed out a long aaahhhhh as he relaxed. As if imitating him, as his whisper subsided the breath of the breeze picked up the sound as it moved through the trees, aaahhhhh, moving the limbs of the trees in a lazy roll. The unseen mouth of nature pushed its breath through the leaves making them hiss, shhheeeee.

Moving into the clearing, the breeze released to blow a low whispered hleeeeewwww. With the trailing end of the wind rattling the leaves again, shhheeeee, like falling rain. The young priest mused and repeated with his own breath, aaahhhh-shhheeeee-leeeewwww-shhheeee. He sat up with alarm! Nature was calling his name, calling to him to get his attention, saying: "Listen, listen young priest." So, he listened.

A stronger breath flowed through the loaded branches pushing them in a gentle sway, sssssseeewww, then changed to a hollow, haunting like breath deep in nature's throat, daaaahhhhh. Then, she inhaled to suck the leafy branches back in, hleeeeeee and then breathed out through rattling leaves sssshhhhhggggeeeee.

Seeww-daaahhh-hleee-shgeee! Atselvdi repeated, breathing the name of One Thing that he missed more than any other thing. The woman whose absence left him empty and wanton, Sudalege: soft, smooth, brown skin; twinkling, almond eyes; wispy, floating, shiny black hair.

Seeww-daaahhh-hleee-shgeee! He loved the way the wind pronounced her name in a lazy, lush, hushed, breathy manner. The image of her mischievous, taunting eyes and her smirking soft lips flashed before him. She was simply leaning casually against the porch post. Her flowing hair caressed her cheek and then fell over her breasts to hide them seductively and draw his attention to the bulge and swell of what was left exposed. The power of her attraction, the lure of her features captivated him seemingly so unintentionally and innocently. Yet feeling the stares of her twin sisters gave him a guilty feeling as if gazing upon her with his eyes was as sinful as touching her with his hands.

The movement of the air drew his attention back to the lips of nature preparing to speak again. She hissed through the leaves cheeeeeeesss and then, with a following breath that rolled over the weaker hiss to say geeeeeee and spray her droplets of spit onto him as she clicked her tongue on the roof of her mouth and abruptly ceased with hleee.

Scheeess-geee-hleee! Atselvdi repeated as he pulled his furry hides up close around his neck. "Tsigili! Witch!"

A wide and powerful swell of wind moved across the whole of the forest surrounding the river basin and vulnerable camp. As it moved past, the flames of the fire fluttered and danced with excited frenzy. Light and unattached objects tumbled or skidded briefly across the ground. Atselvdi held his covers tight. He felt like unprotected bait for the witch, easy picking for the soul-hunting butcher with an appetite for his souls.

An owl hooted in the distance. It made his heart quake and his stomach churn. Atselvdi had never been so far from the security of his home, his grandfather, and his grandmother. He longed to be near his sister who would sense his anxiety and vulnerability and comfort him.

He heard his name called in the distance, "Atselvdi," and then again, only much closer.

It was not a name whispered in the wind, it was clear, distinct, pronounced by a human. Atselvdi rose up to find Waya Usti running toward him. "Atselvdi, Wahuhu wants you to join us. We are going to request a council with the delegation from Katuwa."

The Tagwa Chief finished his meal. It had been a very pleasant evening. He had shared his sadness over his son's rebelliousness and his remorse over having to stand against him. He explained his belief that he had a responsibility as the Chief of the Tagwa to set an example. But he also had a responsibility as a father. He never dreamed it would mean having to turn on his own son. Kalona had been touched by his candor and sincerity.

The Chief sat back and looked at Kalona. She could see that his thoughts were turning away from the distasteful subject of his son. He appeared to be considering whether or not to speak to her.

"You want to ask something, Chief?"

"I was wondering if you would consider calling me by my name?"

Kalona gulped. She realized that she did not know his name. She had just called him Chief. She was embarrassed. "Oh ... you have a name?"

He laughed heartily and then stared at her in earnest. "Yes, I do."

Kalona looked down shyly. He leaned forward and whispered, "Would you believe it is Gihli?"

Kalona's mouth fell open in surprise. "Gihli? But that is a Tsalagi word!"

"I thought you would be amused. One other thing ..."

Kalona looked at him curiously. "Yes?"

"Would you walk with me? My legs are getting stiff from sitting."

Chief Gihli rose as did Kalona. "It would be nice to walk."

Amadohi had explained that she was uncomfortable among all the warriors and wanted to leave. Wananahi had brushed her arm sympathetically and told her that she could leave, of course.

Amadohi turned in front of her house but instead of entering, she continued past the house next to hers and ducked in between it and the next house. The Tagwa warrior was leaning against the wall. Amadohi glanced around nervously. "You found it!"

"Is one of these your house?"

Amadohi took a deep breath. "No. They are both abandoned."

The warrior surveyed her. She could not catch her breath. He looked into her eyes. "You seem nervous. Do I make you uncomfortable?"

Amadohi looked down at her hands, busy trying to rub off tension. "Yes," she said meekly.

"I'm not going to hurt you." He paused and then laughed. "If I did, my chief would chop off my head."

Amadohi expelled a brief, involuntary chuckle. The warrior smiled gratefully. "That's better."

In the darkness, she felt his soft hand stroke her arm. It felt tingly, exciting, in a naughty, forbidden way. She moved away hoping he would stop, but afraid that he would. The handsome man moved closer, his bare skin touching her almost imperceptibly. Her lungs felt empty, her stomach airy as if it had stolen the wind from her lungs. He pressed closer. "Tell me about your friend."

*"My grandmother laughs
about my name, too!"*

W̲AHUHU ADAWEHI HAD A reputation throughout the Ani Yun Wiya as a wise and competent warrior. When the delegation from Katuwa learned that he was urgently seeking their counsel, they were quick to oblige.

The small, make-shift, seven-sided council house, which had been quickly constructed to accommodate the delegation from Katuwa, sat atop a natural mound in a long, oval-shaped clearing bordering the lake. The council house faced east and overlooked the large campfire and dance field set in the center of the clearing between the lake and the mound.

As the four petitioners from Tsikohi walked up the slope to the Council House, Wahuhu coached his colleagues that the War Council Raven would be the one in charge. He had requested Tawodi, Atselvdi, and Waya Usti to join him. They were announced as they entered the council house.

Four red thrones stood prominently in the back of the room. The sacred fire burned in the large, round hearth in the center and two rows of red benches encircled the fire with a wide aisle down the middle. It was like a smaller version of the council house in Tsikohi without white benches or plain benches for the public.

Wahuhu walked past the hearth and stood facing the Katuwa delegation. Tawodi led Waya Usti over to sit on the benches. Tawodi had been there before and knew the routine. Atselvdi followed and sat next to Tawodi.

Wahuhu stood before the delegate from Katuwa smoking the pipe assuming he was the Raven. The Raven gazed at Wahuhu sternly. He held the pipe close to his lips as he spoke, "Wahuhu Adawehi, you have requested our counsel."

It was not a question. The Katuwa Raven passed the pipe to the Tsikohi Raven. Wahuhu smoked the pipe briefly, then spoke, "Tawodi Gvnagei and Waya Usti have come to me with grave concerns. Their perspectives are quite original and I feel we should discuss the possibilities and contingencies."

The Katuwa delegation nodded in unison. Wahuhu handed the pipe to Tawodi and sat down. Tawodi gulped and stood. He walked up to face the imposing dignitaries. Despite his superior size, he felt quite inferior before them. He started to speak, then remembered the pipe. He puffed on it nervously, then spoke, "I am concerned that we may be marching into a trap!"

He remembered the trick he had observed of using the pipe for time to think and construct one's words. He jammed the pipe into his mouth and inhaled. He then began a coughing fit. Despite all his efforts, he could not stop the little hacking coughs. From some unknown place, someone handed him water to drink. He had never been so humiliated in his life—except for maybe that night when he and Waya Usti woke up the village fighting over Ali.

Tawodi drank the water slowly and carefully, then composed himself and continued, "In the normal course of things, if we were to go to war with the Kusas, all of the village forces would be called to Katuwa and merged with the Tsalagi National Warriors. I'm sure the Kusas would not expect to prevail against such a force. But if the village forces were drawn out and split up into small companies and isolated too far away for help from the National Warriors, they would be no match for the Kusa National Warriors."

The Katuwa contingent looked at each other with alarm. Tawodi continued, "I think we all suspect that the raiders are not independent renegades but agents of the Kusa Chief. If that assumption is correct, they have successfully drawn out the desired result—the separation and isolation of the Tsalagi village forces!

"We will soon be in a perfect setup to be conquered. All the Kusa Chief will need is an excuse to launch an attack. With the full power of the Kusa warriors, he could attack and destroy each individual village company of warriors in quick order. He would probably suffer only minor losses. Having easily defeated half the forces available to the Tsalagi Nation, he could turn his warriors north and engage a substantially smaller Tsalagi National force."

The Katuwa War Council delegates leaned in from their thrones and engaged in tense whispered dialog. Wahuhu stood and walked up beside Tawodi. He gently took the forgotten pipe from his hand and presented it to an assistant to refill and restart as he motioned for Tawodi to return to his seat. He waited for the pipe while the Katuwa delegates slowly wound down their discussion. They appeared disquieted.

Wahuhu puffed on the pipe for a moment and then began, "Waya Usti is our ..." There was sniggering among the Katuwans over the name Wolf Puppy. Wahuhu paused. The Katuwa contingent cleared their throats and shifted in their seats and composed themselves.

"Waya Usti is our scout and tracker. He possesses a clever mind and has proposed an interesting angle on this possible dilemma."

Wahuhu handed the pipe to the scout with the childish name. He took the pipe. As he stood, it was as if he pushed up into a dim layer of atmosphere that turned his face very pale. He timidly approached the Katuwans with his hands hanging down in front of him clutching the smoldering pipe. "My grandmother laughs about my name, too!"

The whole Council laughed warmly at the humorous young man. Since his grandmother probably gave him his name, the comment was doubly clever.

The laughter made Waya Usti feel a little more at ease. He began, "I put myself in the Kusa Chief's place and tried to imagine what I would do. I think I would wait until all of the Tsalagi village forces are assigned and in place and then look for the weakness—a small mixed village with no protection."

The War Council Raven frowned, leaned forward and raised a finger. Waya Usti paused and waited for his question. "Mixed?"

Waya Usti clarified, "A village where Kusa and Tsalagi live together."

The Raven raised his eyebrows and sat back. Waya Usti continued, "It would only take one or two assassins to slip in, kill a Kusa and make it look like a Tsalagi murder."

Grave concern embraced the faces of the Katuwa delegation as Waya Usti added, "It would be the excuse needed by the Kusa Chief. With a ready force, if I were that Chief, I would attack the Tsalagi forces in the center, split my forces and work outward, quickly overwhelming the villages and wiping them out, or at least scattering the village companies. Then I would send the two contingents north, one up the Hiawasee, the other up the Conasauga to intercept the Tsalagi National Warriors at the confluence of the Hiawasee and the Tanase."

The Raven reached for the pipe. Waya Usti had forgotten that he had it. He lunged forward to hand the pipe to the Raven who accepted it graciously. He studied the barrel and found it dormant, so he handed it to an assistant. "Your plan is a good one. We are grateful you are not the Kusa Chief!"

Everyone laughed convivially. One of the council members laid a hand on the Raven's arm. He paused as the others leaned in to secretly discuss something. The group bantered back and forth and then the Raven proposed, "We wonder what you would do if you were the Tsalagi Raven?"

Waya Usti started to speak when the assistant held out the pipe to him. He held up his hand to refuse the pipe and began, "I think ..."

There was a stir and low murmurs around the room. Waya Usti looked around to see concerned faces. The

Raven spoke up, "It is not required to HOLD the pipe while speaking!"

This evoked a round of chortles.

Waya Usti realized that he had committed an indiscretion by refusing the pipe. His face felt hot and beads of sweat popped out on his forehead. "I apologize, Raven, I am not informed on these matters."

The kindly Raven intervened. "It is not important. Please continue, Wolf Puppy."

Waya Usti shifted trying to remember where he had stopped. Then he realized that he hadn't started. "If I were ... the Tsalagi Raven ... I would want to turn the Kusa Chief's plan around to my favor. I would first send a messenger to Katuwa requesting the National Warriors advance immediately. While waiting, I would locate the Kusa forces. Such a large army should be difficult to hide. Once our National Warriors were within a day away, I would deploy as planned. I would discretely distribute messengers among all villages along the Coosawattee so that as soon as the provocation occurred, all companies could be alerted and as soon as the Kusa forces moved, all companies could be warned."

The council members sitting beside the Raven were leaning forward studying the clever young strategist's words. The Raven motioned for him to continue.

"Well, assuming that the Kusas attack the middle, I would have the companies pull back and only feign contact. The points of contact could lure the advancing Kusas up ... or down ... the Coosawattee while the other companies could set up an ambush. Our National Warriors could then move in on the divided Kusas and wipe them out!"

*"If we proceed with the plan
we have suggested here today,
then if we are wrong and
the Chief's intentions are
honorable, there is no
harm done."*

THERE WAS SOMETHING WARM and even a little exciting about walking alone with Chief Gihli. This complex man clearly ruled his village with an iron hand and had complete control of them, and yet he seemed so gentle and refined. Kalona had never met anyone like him. Could it be that he was so different in the Ani Tagwa world that their admiration and respect drove them to such loyalty?

Kalona ventured a question, "How is it that you speak such excellent Tsalagi?"

The Chief looked down seriously. "I lived in a Tsalagi village for a while when I was young."

Kalona was taken aback. A Tagwa child might be adopted by a Tsalagi family if, in war, his parents were killed. Children could also be kidnapped and raised as slaves. In this case, they would be chained outside the house with the dogs. "Oh, I see ... hence the name?"

Chief Gihli looked at her sternly. The look shocked her, but the sternness quickly melted into kindness, even perhaps shyness. "Yes, hence the name, Gihli, Dog."

Not wanting to let on her suspicions concerning his status as a child, she questioned, "That must have been interesting. The Tsalagi and the Tagwa have always been enemies. Did your family get along with their Tsalagi neighbors?"

"I did not know my Tagwa family at that time. I lived with a Tsalagi family. They raised me. I returned to the Tagwa ... after my Tsalagi family was killed."

Kalona sensed that this episode in Gihli's life was painful, so she did not press him for more, although the implications concerned her.

Chief Gihli changed the subject. "Tell me about you. You must have led a very interesting life to have risen to be Peace Chief."

With the conclusion of Waya Usti's presentation, the four representatives from Tsikohi had been excused so that the War Council could meet privately.

Outside the council house, the Ravens from the other villages were huddled around waiting to learn the nature of the council requested by Wahuhu. Wahuhu explained briefly their concern that the raiding parties could be secretly acting on behalf of the Kusa Chief and that he was worried that he might have a more sinister plan. He did not elaborate beyond that but it was enough to prompt a great deal of discussion and argument among the Ravens. Wahuhu shook his head in dismay that none of these *leaders* seemed to have gotten the point and the discussions centered on whether the new Kusa Chief would honor his father's commitments or not and whether or not another anetso was in order.

Atselvdi approached Wahuhu with something that was obviously bothering him. "Throughout the council, the Katuwa Raven has done all of the talking. Isn't it curious that the Raven is not sitting in his traditional position? Shouldn't the chair to the far left be for the Raven's right-hand man? Then, to his left, the Raven; then to his left, the speaker, then the messenger? But, in this council, the Raven is sitting in the third chair from the left instead of the second—where the speaker should be sitting. When we came for assignment, the Raven was sitting in his usual chair—one from the left."

Wahuhu appreciated the young priest's attention to detail, and naiveté. "The War Council members are co-equals. All four are part of the Great War Chief's counselors. I don't suppose it matters where they sit. It is only a formality that one has been designated the Raven."

An assistant stepped out of the council house and summoned the Tsikohians to come back in.

Atselvdi, Tawodi, and Waya Usti sat down as Wahuhu approached the War Council. This time the pipe was held by the delegate to the supposed Raven's right. He spoke, "What if you are wrong?"

Wahuhu was surprised, but held his composure. He accepted the pipe and smoked thoughtfully before replying, "Wrong about the raiders?"

The counselor clarified, "About the Kusa Chief's intentions."

Wahuhu was not prepared for this question. He smoked thoughtfully for some time before answering.

The counselor grew impatient. "Perhaps the Hawk or the Puppy have considered this possibility?"

Wahuhu offered his colleagues the pipe, but their faces expressed the dismay that Wahuhu felt. "If the Kusa Chief has no plan and the raiders are what they seem, then our precautions are not necessary. But if we proceed on that assumption and we are wrong, it could be a disaster. If we proceed with the plan we have suggested here today, then if we are wrong and the Chief's intentions are honorable, there is no harm done."

Wahuhu handed back the pipe. The counselor persisted, "No harm done? Your plan would have us sit here for four days waiting for National Forces to deploy. The villagers of the Coosawattee have already suffered three raids since the council in Katuwa. Wasn't the reason for your coming here to protect the Coosawattee brothers? Or was your intention to defeat the Ani Kusa?"

Wahuhu accepted the pipe and forced himself to remain calm and smoke the pipe before answering. "We came here to protect our brothers, but we must also protect ourselves and our families."

The pipe was passed to another counselor. "What evidence do you have that the Kusa Chief has sinister plans?"

Wahuhu did not like the direction this was going. He sensed that for some reason the council members were uncomfortable with Waya Usti's suggestion. He wondered what part actually made them uncomfortable. "We have only reasoning. The raiders are suspicious because they do not wear the paint of any known tribe or village. They do not appear to be very interested in looting since they have only taken insignificant items. Their raids appear to be more aimed at disruption than any-thing else."

Wahuhu paused but held onto the pipe, puffing on it thoughtfully before continuing, "I think it is reasonable to be wary of the new chief. It is no secret that he was against the anetso and that he and his father were very much at odds over the decision. At one time, he was quite vocal in support for war against us."

He smoked some more and then added, "And I think it is reasonable to be cautious for caution's sake."

He continued to hold the pipe before concluding with an attempt at compromise. "If the Kusa Army is out there, we should be able to find it. And then we would have the evidence."

Wahuhu returned the pipe. This time the presumed Raven accepted the pipe. He looked at his colleagues. They shook their heads. He addressed Wahuhu, "It could take several days to find the Kusa Army, if it is out there. It would take two to three days for a messenger to return to Katuwa. The Great War Chief may or may not agree with you and therefore may or may not deploy the National Warriors. While all of this is happening, the villagers of the Coosawattee are defenseless. If we keep our forces at camp for many days while the villagers are ravaged by the raiders, the villagers might turn away from the Tsalagi and turn to the Kusas for protection. We could lose the Coosawattee region without a fight."

Wahuhu understood now. Unfortunately, he could not think of a counter. He declined the pipe. The delegates bowed and the Raven ended the council. "There will be no change in our original plan."

*The Katuwa delegation was
bound by their orders, but
he was not.*

Adanvdo Alsgida and Waya Gigage sat alone at the table and watched the festivity on the ball field. Adanvdo spoke, "Do you trust the Chief?"

Waya deduced that Adanvdo did not trust the Chief based on his comment. "You do not?"

"Four times I have consulted the beads. Four times it has been the black bead."

The beads! As a child, Waya Gigage had doubted the beads. He watched the priests use the beads and had been convinced that they used the beads as a con, not a conjure. He had even tried the beads himself, but had never been able to feel anything. But, Adanvdo Alsgida and Sali were not con men. They were the real thing. So when Adanvdo believed that the beads were telling him something, Waya felt that he should be wary. "That could be a grave portent for the village."

"Do you have a contingency plan, Waya?"

Waya's stomach churned. He was a no-nonsense, down-to-earth rationalist. His primary responsibility, his purpose on earth, was the safety of his village. And with his best warriors gone to defend the villages along the Coosawattee River and the Tagwas firmly entrenched within the walls of Tsikohi, his options were very limited.

At one point, they could have evacuated the women and children. The Tagwa Chief had offered to let them do so, but Kalona was against it. She feared they would be walking into an ambush and he had to agree. If the Chief's son and rebels were out there, they would not be able to get past them.

So, what were his options? He had a small contingent of old warriors available to him. He had met with them already and found them to be eager to pick up their rusty war clubs to defend their village if necessary. But they would be out-numbered and overpowered by the young battle-ready Tagwa warriors.

There were a number of younger men who were fairly adept with the bow and arrow, but they too would be quickly routed by the Tagwas. He knew that the old warriors and young boys were willing to fight to the death, but they were of no use in a direct attack on the Tagwa.

Sadly, their only option at this point, in his mind, was to hope that the Tagwa Chief was sincere and that his purpose for coming to Tsikohi was just as he had stated. If not, the old warriors, young men, and even some of the women and girls would have to take up arms and try to hold off the Tagwas long enough to evacuate the women and children out the east entrance, through the fields to the forest beyond. There were many caves and other places to hide up in the mountain east of the village.

He had kept the Uku's question waiting too long. Adanvdo broke into his thoughts. "A wise warrior once told me that 'A well-crafted plan is a deterrent. The lack of a plan is an invitation.'"

Waya Gigage recognized his own advice given years ago to the Uku. "It is too late for deterrents. We are left with only surprise."

Adanvdo was silent and Waya could see that his answer was flippant. He continued, "The walls of Tsikohi were built to keep the battle out of the village. But, if the battle is waged within the walls, the walls serve to contain the battle."

He could see that Adanvdo was interested, but it was unclear to him. He added, "If we could localize the battle ... if we could concentrate our forces in a corner of the village, we might be able to defend it for a while."

Adanvdo's eyes widened indicating he understood.

As the dejected delegation from Tsikohi returned to camp, Tawodi was bewildered. "Was that the same delegation that we talked to before the break?"

"Why were they so angry?" Waya Usti asked.

Wahuhu took a deep breath. "Only the Raven spoke in the first session. It was his place, I suppose, to hear our concerns. But, evidently, our arguments were not convincing."

"They were agitated that I did not know how to properly address them!" Waya Usti lamented.

"No, that was not it. I think they were actually amused by it and liked you. I think that the shift in attitude was borne out of the difficulty of the decision they had to make. Deep down they may be very concerned that we are right, but they are under great pressure. Perhaps they were worried that changing the plan without consulting the Great War Chief would be disobedient. The Great War Chief can be very harsh when it comes to disobedience. And, of course, as they said, it would take days to consult him about altering his plan."

The rationale of Wahuhu provoked thoughtful silence. What he said made a lot of sense. The delegates were put in an impossible dilemma. They could not accept a new plan when they were under orders from the Great War Chief.

But Tawodi could not let go. "What are we going to do?"

The wise, experienced old warrior took a deep breath. It was clear that he was conflicted. The young, impetuous warriors waited respectfully albeit impatiently.

Wahuhu could not let go either. It was too important for him to withdraw and do nothing. The Katuwa delegation was bound by their orders, but he was not. He saw that only he could organize a contingency. He knew what he would have to do and he was willing to accept the risk ... and the consequences.

Wahuhu looked at his young assistant, Tawodi. "Tonight, you and Waya Usti are going to start the search for the Kusa National Forces! I think I know where to look. I suspect that we shall soon get the word that we are all to deploy in the morning. I intend to stop at each village assigned and visit with each Raven. I want to at least establish an emergency line of communication between us and a contingency plan of action. If ... when you discover the Kusa forces, join us at Ustanali immediately and we will sound the alarm."

*"Hmmph. They believe
that Tagwas have come
to save them from Tagwas?
Ridiculous!"*

Aᴌɪʜᴇʟɪᴛsɪᴅᴀsᴅɪ ʟᴀʏ ᴏɴ ʜᴇʀ bed staring out the window at the moonlit clouds. She absolutely could not understand how they could let the Tagwas camp in their village after what had happened. And what was worse, tonight they had prepared a feast for them! Worse yet, she sensed that her grandmother was beginning to trust them ... her grandmother! She had hated the Tagwa most of her life. Ali could not remember her grandmother ever having anything good to say about a Tagwa.

Ali believed with all her heart that the Tagwa had come for revenge. What she could not understand was why they were waiting. They could annihilate the village anytime, so why go to the trouble and time of making friends and building trust. *It doesn't make sense!*

"It sure doesn't!"

She looked around the dark room. "Who said that?"

"Oh, it breaks my heart that you have forgotten me so easily after all I've done for you!"

"Little Medicine Bowl? Is that you?"

"Who else stands by you when everyone else abandons you?"

It was good to have her friend from the Little People visit her again. Her grandmother had warned her that the Yunwi Tsunsdi only visited little children. Ali was no longer a child. She feared that one day Nvwoti Atlisdodi Usdi would stop visiting her.

"Thank you for helping me against the Tagwas."

"You remember that, do you?"

"Well, not everything yet, but I do remember you untying my hands and feet."

She could hear the Yunwi Tsunsdi shuffling across the floor and plopping upon her grandmother's bed. "What kind of grandmother leaves her granddaughter all alone with Tagwas around?"

He's reading my mind! She thought. "She's the Peace Chief. She had to be there."

"Bear poop!"

"Oh, don't be silly, you know you love Grandmother."

"Panther poop!"

Ali snickered. Her little friend was always so cantankerous. "So, what are you going to do about these Tagwas? I suppose you expect me to save you!"

"What can I do? There's too many of them and besides, the whole village thinks that they are here to protect us."

Nvwoti gasped in disgust, "Hmmph. They believe that Tagwas have come to save them from Tagwas? Ridiculous!"

"I agree with you, but no one is going to listen to me."

"So, you're just going to sit here and whine about it?"

The little man's words hurt. "That's not fair!"

"Wah, wah! Do you really believe the Chief's son and a band of delinquents are hiding outside the village waiting to attack?"

She was surprised by his question. Not because it was an improper question but because she realized she had not even thought about whether the Tagwas were lying about the outside threat. She started to speak when she realized that the little man had disappeared. In his place a menacing knife lay on the floor. It looked strangely familiar but her mind forbade her from remembering that it was the knife she had used in the Tagwa camp!

Waya Gigage could not sleep. Adanvdo was right, he needed a better contingency plan. He could not afford to accept the reassurances of Gihli on face value. He remembered that when Wahuhu had journeyed to the Tagwas to return the corpses, the Tsalagi Chief closest to the Tagwa village had painted a very different picture of him. They did not trust him. They had said that he had been ejected from his tribe.

As Chief, Waya had to act with two hearts. For the sake of their safety, he would have to assure Chief Gihli that he believed him. Yet he could not allow himself to trust the Chief completely. He must always be prepared to defend the village from ill intent. He could not lose sight of the possibility that the Tagwas were there for revenge!

How would they survive an attack from inside the stockade with Tagwa warriors guarding every entrance and encircling the village?

They had little choice for evacuation. The main exit was out of the question. The warriors were camped on the ball field. It was too open for anyone to be able to sneak up to that exit. The west exit was less guarded, but once through the exit the huge hill forced them to either head for the Long Man, which would be suicide, or funnel into a wide valley, completely exposing them to attack.

That left the east exit. It was less guarded and once outside there was the cover of the cornstalks all the way to the forest. However, rounding up everyone and ushering them to the exit would set up a massacre. The citizens needed to be ready. No, they needed to be more than ready. They needed to be near the exit and ready to move instantly!

Waya Gigage bolted out of bed. He had a strategy. *There are plenty of houses clustered around the east exit to house all the women and children of the village. They must be discretely moved there so that they can quickly escape once the exit is secured. We have enough forces to secure one exit for a while.*

He woke his wife and dressed. The night would provide cover for him to get with his fellow villagers. *We must start tonight!*

The glistening light from the moon helped Tawodi and Waya Usti see the rocks and rapids in the river. But soon, Brother Moon traveled west and the trees along the river cast long, dark shadows. They found themselves bumping into even large boulders in the stream and hanging up in shallow rapids.

And then it happened. They blindly plummeted over a waterfall and crashed into a deep, churning basin. They had been launched out of the boat in the fall and found themselves fighting and scrambling in a roaring cyclone of water that finally spit them out in the midst of a swift chute before carrying them into a wide, shallow stream.

Coughing water and exhausted, they dragged themselves onto the shore and collapsed. The boat and their provisions were gone! They would have to travel the rest of the way on foot in the dark. But after stumbling around and realizing how difficult it would be and how long it would take, Waya Usti had a better idea. "Was that a log we just fell over?"

"I think so. It was too big to be a Kusa."

Waya Usti was too tired for the joke. "Help me drag it to the river. We can float down with it."

"Great idea."

As twilight began to spread its light across the Coosawattee, two battered and beaten young warriors floated toward the confluence Wahuhu had directed them to. After being dumped off numerous logs, they continued to believe that it was better to float down the river than to try to navigate alongside it on foot. It was certainly faster, and as the river had broadened, the hazards had lessened. Waya Usti suggested, "What we need is a fallen tree with branches."

Tawodi glared at his cousin. Waya Usti explained, "So we can sit on it without it rolling. We cannot just float up the tributary; we will have to row."

With the growing light, they found a suitable tree and made a couple of oars. But the drag from the branches made it almost impossible for the haggard warriors to paddle against the current.

Finally, Tawodi hurled his oar into the water and lay back on the trunk of the tree exasperated. Waya Usti drooped dejectedly. Slowly the tree stopped, reversed and then picked up speed until soon they were flowing back into the Coosawattee. Reluctantly, the two fell off the tree and paddled toward the shore.

An island in the river appeared and the current swept them to the right side of it. "Look!" Tawodi shouted. Waya Usti saw their battered boat was beached on the shore and the pouches with their provisions were scattered around it. Invigorated they swam to shore and collected their provisions. They were so hungry that they ate the soggy corn cakes without comment.

This piece of good fortune gave them renewed energy and purpose. They repacked the boat and set off back to the tributary. What a difference the sleek boat made.

*Thoughts of Sudalegi
provided the young priest
respite from weightier
thoughts like the threats
to mortality, of war, or
of witchcraft.*

KALONA AWOKE WITH A sparkle in her eyes and a smile on her face. She lay in bed and stared at the morning rays from the sun shining through the window. She watched the fuzz and particles dance in a ray of light. She felt like a child again. She had had the most wonderful night of her life!

She would have never guessed that she could like someone so much, especially a Tagwa! Gihli was like no other man she had ever known. He was not selfish and self-centered or arrogant. He was kind, generous and humble. They had spent the whole evening talking about her! What a refreshing experience to meet a man who was genuinely interested in her ... everything about her.

She had slipped in quietly hoping not to wake her granddaughter. She had heard her father snoring as she tiptoed across the living room with the aid of the hearth's low glow. She felt a pang of guilt. Her father still did not trust the Tagwas.

She knew that he had been chanting prayers of safety and that he had consulted the beads. And poor little Ali!

To have the Tagwas in the village after what she had gone through was very hard on her. She had refused to venture outside the house since discovering them in the ball field. If only her father and granddaughter could know Gihli like she knew him. She was certain that they would trust him, too.

Amadohi awakened from a nightmare, her heart pounding, sweating, feeling fear and remorse, the emotions of the dream lingering. Light was flooding into the room and her mother's bed was empty as it usually was when she awoke in the morning. Her mother always got up before sunrise, even when she was up late the night before.

Amadohi rolled over and curled up into a fetal position. She was ashamed of the previous night, but craved to be with the handsome young Tagwa again. She had never met a boy so unselfish and kind, someone so genuinely interested in her and not constantly boasting about himself. She tried to make Tawodi fit her model of a boasting, selfish boy, but could not. He was not like that either. But Tawodi was childish and immature, not like the confident older Tagwa.

She worried what her mother would think. She worried about coming in after her mother had gone to bed. What would she tell her? How would she explain where she had been? She would have to lie to her mother. Would Ali cover for her? But how could she tell Ali about her tryst with the Tagwa? She could not. She would have to come up with something else.

She pulled the cover up over her head and tried to push her thoughts out of her mind. If only she could just go back to sleep.

By the time the night skies began to lighten, the Coosawattee was filled with Tsalagi boats. Wahuhu and the Tsikohi warriors were not the first to launch. Wahuhu had been up all night secretly meeting with Ravens of other village troops. Partly because of his reputation and partly because of the logic of his argument, his contingency plan was well received. Wahuhu was feeling better about the prospect of dealing with a possible Kusa trap. Because of his illicit meetings, the call to break camp for the Tsikohians came late.

In the boat behind Wahuhu, One Thing occupied the mind of Atselvdi. He tried to concentrate on his primary duty—keeping the sacred fire alive in the portable canister. His boat was half-filled with wood chips for feeding the fire and he routinely dropped chips into the canister, but his conscious thought was preoccupied with how impressed Sudalegi might be with his important position in the troop. *If only she could see me now in my priestly dress, tending to the sacred fire, tended to by dedicated servants, heading bravely into imminent danger!*

Thoughts of Sudalegi provided the young priest respite from weightier thoughts like the threats to his mortality, of war, or of witchcraft.

Tawodi and Waya Usti crawled up the rocky hill and looked carefully over the peak at the large, grassy meadow. Just as Wahuhu had described, the valley was large enough to accommodate 1,000 warriors. The stream that meandered through the meadow would supply plenty of water and fish and the surrounding forest was thick with game.

Tawodi rolled over on his back disappointed. "The valley is empty."

Waya Usti gazed out across the meadow and then scoured the surrounding hills. "Now where?"

"Wahuhu suggested the next tributary to the west. It is only a small stream, but boats could cruise unobstructed to the Coosawattee."

"Sge! Look!" Waya Usti whispered urgently.

Tawodi rolled over and looked again. Hundreds of warriors had begun flowing into the meadow from between the hills opposite the scouts. Waya Usti pointed to where the stream entered the forest below their perch. Tawodi saw movement. His eyes focused on several men racing through the tall meadow grass. At first glance, Tawodi said "hunters" as they were quickly disappearing into the forest.

"Wrong weapons."

"You are right. They are carrying war clubs and shields! Let's go!"

Wananahi pulled her buffalo robe tighter. Autumn mornings were getting very chilly. A thick fog was flowing through the village. Soon Grandmother Sun would rise above the mountain and bring warmth and burn away the fog. *Is there someone moving out there?*

She leaned forward and squinted. There was definitely a shadow moving along the street coming from the east entrance. Wisps of fog passed first hiding and then revealing the person. *It's a girl!*

The petite young girl walked directly in front of Wananahi's house. Wananahi's eyes widened. "Ali?"

The startled young girl stopped and looked around. Wananahi realized that it was not Ali, but who? The girl was dressed very plainly, like the forest people. The girl looked her way and then at her. *She's spotted me!*

The girl waved as a thick patch of fog covered her. When the fog cleared, she was gone. *Where did she come from? How did she get past the sentinel?*

Wananahi looked to the sentinel station above the eastern entrance. It appeared to be empty! Had he gone to sleep? Pulling her robe up so she could walk without tripping, she headed down the street toward the entrance, keeping an eye on the sentinel station. The fog wafted by and made it difficult to tell with certainty, but it did appear to be empty! *That's curious!*

Suddenly, two Tagwa warriors' heads popped up in the guard tower. Wananahi walked briskly back toward her house. *Something is wrong!*

She dashed into her house and roused Amadohi. "Amadohi, wake up! Wake up! Something is wrong! We need to go to Kalona's house."

KALONA WAS COOKING BREAKFAST at the hearth when she heard the door cover ruffle. She turned around to find Sudalegi standing at the door, smiling.

"Sadulegi! Where did you come from?"

"I live in the mountains over there," she said pointing northeast.

"No, dear, I mean how did you get past the sentinel?"

"What sentinel?"

A familiar voice called from outside the door. Waya Gigage stepped inside. He raised his hand apologetically. "I'm sorry to burst in on you Kalona, but there is something very important we need to discuss."

"Come in and sit, Waya."

The War Chief frowned at the strange young girl. Kalona introduced her and then explained, "... she is a friend of Atselvdi."

Waya Gigage studied her curiously. "Have you been here since Atselvdi left?"

"No. I came this morning."

Waya frowned. "How did you get past the sentinel?"

"What sentinel?"

"Didn't you come in through one of the entrances?"

"I came in through the east entrance, but I didn't see a sentinel ... or anyone."

Waya Gigage and Kalona exchanged glances. Waya whispered to one of the warriors standing by the door to go check out the east entrance.

Then he asked Kalona. "Could you wake Adanvdo? I need to speak to both of you."

"My! What's going on?"

Adanvdo appeared in the doorway of his room. "Waya?"

"I want to discuss our contingency plan."

As Adanvdo shuffled over to the hearth and retrieved the pipe and began preparing it, Waya filled them in on how he had secretly moved the citizens of Tsikohi to the houses clustered near the east entrance.

Kalona pulled the pot from the fire and set it on the hearth stones. "Are you hungry?"

Waya thought for a moment. "Actually, I am starving. It has been a long, busy night."

Adanvdo handed his friend the pipe while Kalona mixed up bowls for her father, Sudalegi, Waya, and his guard. The door cover ruffled again as Wananahi and Amadohi rushed in. Wananahi blurted out, "Oh! Osiyo, Chief!"

She looked at Sudalegi, "You?"

Kalona quickly introduced Sudalegi and ushered them over to the hearth. "Now what brings you and Amadohi here so early in the morning?"

"I came to tell you that someone ... her ... had come in. I went to check on the sentinel and ours is gone and there are two Tagwas guarding the exit!"

Waya looked at Sudalegi. "Did you see any warriors near the stockade when you came in?"

Sudalegi shrugged. "There was no one."

Ali stepped in from outside. Kalona gasped, "Ali! Where have you been?"

"I slipped out last night and I have been searching for the Chief's son and his band of renegades that are supposedly out there ready to attack. I searched rabbit meadows, up by the waterfall, the box canyon, the fields along the north trail, behind the village. I even climbed up to the Precipice. There are no campfires and no sign of any warriors anywhere."

Ali's face turned sad. "Chief, I found your messenger dead in the meadow. He had been stabbed."

Grave concern showed on Waya's face. "How did you get back in this morning?"

"I tried coming in the west entrance first. The sentinel was gone, but there were Tagwa warriors collecting around it so I went around to the east entrance. Two Tagwas were in the tower looking inward enabling me to slip into the switchback. I managed to duck behind a house and work my way here."

Waya jumped up. "We must hurry!"

"Remain seated, Chief!" A handsome Tagwa warrior entered the room with six other warriors.

Kalona exclaimed, "What's going on?"

Amadohi looked up to see the young Tagwa warrior she had rendezvoused with the previous night. She started to smile, but then caught herself. He was not wearing the pleasant demeanor and easy manner now. This time he was stern, powerful, and challenging.

"Good morning, Peace Chief. Did you enjoy your little walk last night?"

The warrior's tone was sardonic. Kalona was confused. She did not answer.

"Well, my father enjoyed it very much. It was very enlightening. And your version corroborates the information I gleaned from a very helpful young girl," he looked at Amadohi. "... and the information my warriors picked up from various people at the dinner. It appears that my brother was killed by ONE person, Alihelitsidasdi, your granddaughter!"

Looks of shock engulfed the Tsalagis as they glanced around at each other. Kalona gritted her teeth. "He kidnapped her! He and his buddies brutally murdered two other girls. Ali simply defended herself!"

Ali stood quietly in shock. Her hand unconsciously fingered the knife she had tucked into her belt after her encounter with her little friend. Images began flashing in her mind: violent images of vicious faces; of desperately stabbing them; feelings of desperation and rage that she had felt at the climax of the abduction.

Chief Gihli's son smirked at Kalona. "So, which one of the pretty girls is Alihelitsidasdi?"

Kalona glared defiantly at the Chief's son. She did not know what to think. How could this cold blooded Tagwa be related to the man who had shone her such a pleasant evening?

The Tagwa took a deep breath. "Very well, we shall have to figure it out."

The warrior looked in the direction of Amadohi. Wananahi glanced at her daughter and gasped. The warrior walked up to the trembling Amadohi and peered down into her eyes. "Which one is your friend, Amadohi?"

"What?" Amadohi was stunned. She did not understand.

Wananahi grabbed her daughter's arm and pulled her away from the ghoulish Tagwa. The warrior approached Sudalegi who stuck her chin up and challenged him to a staring contest. The son was amused.

"You clearly aren't Alihelitsidasdi. No Long Hair would dress so plainly."

Sudalegi swung a fist at the insulting Tagwa. He grasped her wrist and slung her to the floor! Then he approached Ali and declared, "So, you are Aliheli ... auugh"

The chief's son gulped, choked, and grasped his chest. Blood gushed through his fingers. Suddenly a bloody knife blade swished across his neck. The warrior's eyes rolled up as he collapsed to the floor.

Before the room full of shocked onlookers could grasp what was happening, Ali leaped over the dead warrior and plunged the knife into his stunned assistant. The Tagwa guards were frozen in shock. Waya sprang into action and joined Ali. Together they took out two more Tagwas before the others could scramble through the door shouting in Tagwan.

Waya shouted to the others, "Follow me!"

*Tawodi pulled on the
arrow again but the shaft
pulled loose leaving the
tip embedded.*

The two scouts worked their way carefully down the hill to where the warriors had disappeared. Waya Usti began tracking them. Tawodi followed close behind keeping vigilant watch so his cousin could concentrate on the trail. He was certain they were on the path to finding the raiders.

The trail led over a high ridge overlooking a narrow canyon. Smoke drifted up from below. "Campfire!" Tawodi whispered pointing to the smoke.

They crept to the edge to look down upon a dozen scrubby warriors lounging around the fire. As they lay in the cover of the rocks on the cliff's edge trying to reconcile what they were seeing, three warriors entered the camp. Tawodi gasped, "Tagwas!"

Waya Usti glanced at his cousin and then back at the three warriors. There was something very unsettling about their appearance. It was their heads—their flat heads! "Tagwas!"

"The one in the middle is the Chief's son, the one who fired an arrow at me!"

"What's he doing so far ..."

"The raiders!" Tawodi interrupted.

Waya Usti's mind whirled. *Raiders? Yes! Of course!*

Tawodi pointed back toward the trail and crawled back away from the cliff's edge. Once the two were far enough away from the canyon, they found a good place to hide and talk.

Waya Usti spoke first, "If we kill them, there will be no more raids and the Kusas won't have an excuse to attack."

Tawodi listened patiently and then seemed to be considering the proposal. Finally, he shook his head, "There's something wrong."

"What?"

"I don't know for sure, but it just doesn't add up."

Tawodi continued to contemplate the facts. Waya Usti joined his cousin in thought and began turning the facts over in his mind. Tawodi was right. Why and how did the Kusas employ Tagwas for the raids? "Why Tagwas, right?"

Tawodi gave a passive nod. "It's not only that. What's in it for the Tagwas?"

Tawodi had a good point. "An alliance?" Waya suggested.

"That would make sense. Maybe the Tagwas plan to attack from the east while the Kusas attack from the south."

"If we kill the Tagwa raiders, we give the Tagwas an excuse to attack."

Tawodi's eyes widened. Waya Usti was right. They could not attack the raiders now. No one knew that the raiders were Tagwa. It would look like Tsalagis had attacked innocent Tagwa hunters. "Wait! Yes we can! The Tagwas have no reason to be down here. They are deep among the Kusa. There could be no other explanation but that they are the raiders."

Way Usti snapped his fingers, "If they are with the Kusas, why did they run and hide when the Kusa forces flooded into the valley?" Waya Usti grinned slyly. "If we follow them on a raid and then kill them, there would be no doubt!"

Tawodi thought about it. "It could be days before they raid again."

"What do we do?"

Tawodi looked back in the direction of the raiders' camp, then back toward the meadow where the Kusas were setting up. "Well, we know where they both are. They appear to be setting up for a long stay. We should go to Ustanali and tell Wahuhu what we've discovered!"

Atselvdi's stomach quaked! He felt fear and anxiety for no apparent reason. He looked to the forest alongside the river, scouring for signs of danger. He saw nothing. He looked to the left and right, but nothing, and behind him nothing but Tsalagi boats. He checked the sacred fire canister, but the sacred fire was fine. There was no reason for his anxiety attack. ... *Ali?*

He knew this feeling. He had had it when Ali was abducted. Atselvdi looked back in the direction of Tsikohi. *Ali is in trouble!*

Waya Gigage led Kalona and her father, Wananahi and her daughter, and the stranger from the forest stealthily down the street to a vacant house no longer vacant. It was filled with women and children rounded up quietly by the Tsikohi warriors and others. Waya implored them, "Wait here. We are going to attack the east exit. When we secure it, everyone must move out quickly and scatter into the cornfields and then into the forest. Once there, make your separate ways to our neighbors down the Long Man. We will try to slow them down and lead them away from you."

Kalona gasped, "Where's Ali?"

Waya glanced around. She was gone! "Don't worry, Kalona, I will find her. I need you to coordinate the evacuation."

Waya rushed off toward to the east exit with his small band of warriors.

Tawodi and Waya Usti found their boat and set off down the tributary to rejoin the Tsikohi forces and inform Wahuhu that they had found the Kusa forces just where he had said they would be and that they had also stumbled upon the raiders. The two were extremely proud of themselves. Not only had they correctly prophesied the trap that the Kusas had set for the village forces, but they had found the evidence. And, with Waya Usti's clever plan, they stood a fighting chance of defeating the Kusas, but what about the Tagwa contingent? How did that figure in?

Suddenly, Tawodi heard a swish followed by a thud! An arrow was lodged in Waya Usti's back with the shaft vibrating! Waya Usti looked back at Tawodi curiously and then rolled out of the boat tipping it over and spilling his cousin and all their provisions and most of their weapons into the stream.

Tawodi grabbed his wounded cousin and began swimming toward the bank. He became aware that arrows were raining down into the water around them. Tawodi cried desperately, "Waya! Are you okay?"

"What happened? My back is stinging!"

"You've been hit. You've got an arrow in your back. Kick, cousin, we've gotta get to shore fast!"

The swift stream carried them beyond the range of the arrows and they were finally able to reach the shore and drag themselves into the cover of the forest.

Tawodi put Waya Usti on his stomach so he could look at his wound. The arrow had hit at an angle and lodged in the shoulder blade. Tawodi pulled on the shaft. Waya Usti screeched in pain. "Quiet, Waya."

Tawodi looked around. He had to assume the raiders had spotted them. It was only a matter of time before they caught up to them. Tawodi pulled on the arrow again but the shaft pulled loose leaving the tip embedded. He grabbed his cousin and urged him to flee with him.

But they were too late! Six raiders converged on them!

*His other two sons were,
he would admit only to
himself, quite worthless.
He blamed their mothers.*

Waya Gigage raced between houses toward the east exit. He signaled for his troops to attack. Dozens of warriors bailed out of houses around the exit and attacked the Tagwas. He caught a glimpse of Alihelitsidasdi being hauled off by several Tagwas but not without a fight! He could see at least three dead Tagwas lying around her.

The Tsikohi warriors quickly secured the exit while others set up a defensive perimeter using the houses as cover. Waya waved the citizens out and motioned for them to file through the exit switchback but there were so many! He worried that they would not be able to hold off the Tagwa forces long enough.

He saw Kalona pull her grandfather out of their hideout and head for the exit surrounded by so many other villagers. *The exit isn't wide enough!* he thought. He watched Kalona implore Wananahi and Sudalegi to help Adanvdo and then raced ahead to the exit. Someone needed to supervise the exodus. As Peace Chief, she assumed the role.

But the panicking villagers were not in a mood to exit orderly. She had to yell harshly at her friends and neighbors.

Waya raced to the front line. The Tagwa forces were flowing in from all over the village. It seemed like there were thousands of them! But the Tsikohi forces fought bravely and effectively stopped the initial wave. The Tagwas pulled back and regrouped around neighborhood houses. Waya glanced back to see how the villagers were doing. Only half were through the exit. Kalona was desperately trying to merge the masses into lines, but the people were frightened and hostile.

The second attack was launched, this time from behind nearby houses. Many of the Tagwas were dropped by a wall of arrows, but many got through while the Tsikohi forces were reloading. Now there was a lot of hand-to-hand combat. Chief Waya threw himself into the fray deftly swinging his war club while parrying with his shield.

Only a handful to go! Kalona waved and shouted for the remaining few to push their way into the switchback. She glanced behind her to see that the Tsikohi forces were getting beat back. There were so many bodies lying in the streets. Before Kalona could get the last few through, the Tagwas busted loose and converged on the helpless villagers. Kalona projected herself in front of her fleeing friends but the Tagwas clubbed her, sending her crumpling to the ground. Tsikohi forces collapsed against the stockade walls and battled valiantly.

Waya battled his way to the exit and led a small band through hoping to catch up with and protect the lucky ones who had escaped. But they were violently overrun.

Waya fought feverishly but was overwhelmed and left trampled on the ground.

Bound at their wrists and elbows, Tawodi and Waya Usti were dragged into the Raiders' camp and presented proudly to the Tagwa Chief's cowardly son. The young warrior stood and glared at Tawodi. "YOU!"

Then his glare transformed into delight ending with a devilish laugh. "This is going be VERY delightful, Tsalagi!" He spit the word as if it were a piece of spoiled fish.

An older warrior sitting next to the young degenerate whispered something. The young warrior looked at him like a small boy denied his childish request. He waved them off. Tawodi and Waya Usti were escorted to the center of the camp and tied to two trees. Their arms were forced over two branches and their hands tied behind the trees. Their feet were bound to the bases of the trees.

Waya Usti's memory flashed to the Tagwa campsite where he had found Ali. He remembered that Walelu was bound in the same way and hacked to death by the Tagwa abductors!

They watched the Tagwa son and the elder arguing animatedly. Finally, the warrior son stormed out. Tawodi smirked. "Reminds me of the first time I met him!"

"What do you think they're going to do with us?"

"I don't know. Eventually kill us, I suspect."

Waya Usti's back was stinging fiercely. His position on the tree squeezed his back muscles against the arrowhead lodged in his shoulder blade. Tawodi, seeing that he was in pain, cried, "You gonna be all right?"

"Evidently not!"

Tawodi chuckled. "I mean with your wound?"

"It stings, but it is bearable. You just figure out how to get us out of this."

Tawodi perused the camp, noting each raider and appraising their strength and demeanor. His mind appeared to be racing strategically. "If only we could get free, we might have a fighting chance!" he declared.

Suddenly, a raider raced in and approached the elder and the Chief's son with an alarming message. The two argued for a moment and then the son stood and shouted a command in Tagwan. Waya Usti recognized the word Kusa and questioned, "What's happening?"

"Something about the Kusa. They look surprised, even frightened!"

Chief Gihli sat alone in the Tsikohi Council House on the red throne of the War Chief. He was waiting for his middle son, Falcon, to bring him the killer of his youngest son. Only his middle son had ever shown any promise as a leader. His other two sons were, he would admit only to himself, quite worthless. He blamed their mothers. Ironically, Falcon seemed to have no desire to be a leader while his other sons were driven by ambition. Falcon was like himself: cold, calculating, and cool under pressure.

He heard far away shouting in the village. Chief Gihli rushed out of the Council House and stood at the edge of the mound looking out over the village toward Kalona

Ehlawei's house. He saw people running through the streets and disappearing between the houses.

Fighting broke out at the east exit. His troops looked to him and he pointed and waved for his warriors to attack. He could see that the Tsikohi War Chief had secretly put together a plan. He was trying to evacuate his people. The Tsalagi warriors had secured the east exit and now old men, women and children were flowing toward the exit.

He'll never be able to get them out before we crush his weak reserve forces! At best, they are warriors too old to go to fight on the Coosawattee!

He glimpsed a gang of his warriors carrying a fiercely struggling young girl. They were running through the streets toward him. *Ali*, he surmised.

"Tie her!" he demanded.

Warriors encircling the Council House jumped off the mound to the aid of the gang. They threw the girl down and tried to constrain her. She was like a ferocious animal, like a trapped panther! Gihli had never seen anything like it. Her eyes were wild and crazed. She had the strength of four, maybe more, strong warriors.

"Bring her inside!"

He grabbed the arm of one of the warriors. "Go find my son and have him bring in the troops. We're leaving!"

*Waya Usti wanted to ask why
the raiders had not killed
them, but he did not want
to give them any ideas.*

SHINY CIRCLES WERE SPINNING around inside a glowing hole. The circles began to slow and fill with color. Slowly an image, maybe a face, began to materialize. Wrinkled blobs filled the widening hole. Was it a giant chipmonk peeking in?

Kalona blinked and rubbed her eyes. She opened them to find Sali staring at her. Tiny eyes were protruding and gazing at her intensely.

"Sali?" she ventured.

"Good to see you again, Kalona!"

Kalona tried to remember what happened. Slowly she recollected the battle and trying to defend her friends from the attacking Tagwas. "Is this the upperworld?"

Sali laughed heartily. "No, you're too hard-headed to die from a blow to the head!"

"Where are we?"

She looked around her. She could see that she was still lying beside the stockade exit. She tried to rise up but sharp pain knifed through her head and left her dizzy.

Sali put his hand behind her head and helped her to lie back down. "Just relax, Kalona, you're going to need some time."

"Where are the Tagwas?"

"They've gone."

She didn't understand. "They've gone?"

Someone nearby said, "They crushed us and then moved out."

"Who's that?" Kalona asked.

Sali leaned over into her face. "That's Chief Waya. He's beat up pretty badly, but he'll make it."

"How many ... will make it?"

Sali shook his head and sat back. "I'm afraid many won't. We lost many brothers and sisters. But the ones who made it out of the stockade are okay. The Tagwas didn't pursue them."

Kalona was somewhat relieved. She knew that her father, Wananahi, Amadohi, and Sudalegi were among the first to get out. "Ali?"

There was silence.

"Sali!" she demanded, "what about Ali?"

Sali spoke sadly, "They've taken her."

Kalona tried to jump up, but the pain was intense and her head began to spin as she fell back and passed out.

Tawodi and Waya Usti now were strapped to two long poles and carried like slaughtered deer on the shoulders of raiders. It took four to carry Tawodi, Waya Usti just two. Waya Usti dropped his head back and tried to get a peek at Tawodi being carried ahead of him. Tawodi was dangling from the pole limply. *Could he actually be sleeping through this?*

They were carried roughly over hills and through forests and meadows to a wide river. A dozen boats were tethered in a cove. The two Tsalagi prisoners were carelessly dumped in two separate boats. The raiders boarded their boats and towed the boats of the two prisoners behind them. The sun was starting to get low in the sky as the small fleet floated swiftly along.

Waya Usti could not see where they were going, only occasional overhanging trees or tall cliffs passing by. "Tawodi?"

"Yeah, Waya, you okay?"

"Yeah. You?"

"Yeah."

It sounded like Tawodi's boat might be right next to his. "Where we going, can you tell?"

"I'm guessing we're headed for the Coosawattee. Most tributaries around here flow into it."

Waya Usti wanted to ask why the raiders had not killed them, but he did not want to give them any ideas.

Atselvdi swayed in his boat whispering the prayer for bad dreams, "Listen! White Beaver, from the head waters of the stream; quickly thou hast arisen, facing us. The evil one has apportioned evil for her. But now, you take it away. The evil which has been apportioned for her, release it! Scatter it among the living who care about her ..."

A raven squawked from an overhanging limb of a tree. Atselvdi jumped and shrieked! Thoughts of the witch flooded his mind. Images of Crooked Foot's mutilated face flashed before him. Ali's stories of the giant raven that ravaged the Tagwas, ripping out a heart and liver, made him shiver.

Reflexively, the unnerved priest grabbed his gourd rattle and began to chant loudly, "Wicked ones! The Black Yellow Mockingbird has just brought down your heart! Black Yellow Mockingbird, you have just leaped upon his heart! Red Thread, you have just come to wrap around his heart!"

Wahuhu looked back at the chanting priest. "You okay, Atselvdi?"

Nearby warriors laughed. Atselvdi seemed unfazed as he continued his chant.

Wahuhu shook his head and turned away. Again the warriors laughed.

Ali lay alone bound and gagged in the bottom of a boat being towed. The sky was covered in a film of cold, gray clouds. Occasionally, a light, like a spirit campfire would appear far overhead and then disappear. She kept her eyes trained on the spot. It was curious because it was not dark enough yet to be seeing spirit campfires in the night sky.

It appeared again and she watched closely. It was twinkling like a fire only it was much larger than any spirit campfire she had ever seen.

She heard the swish of the boat bows sliding up on the shore. She felt the bump as her boat landed and then it was hoisted upward and carried through the forest. She guessed that they were probably going around some rapids.

The boat brushed through thick trees and bushes and then broke out into a clearing. Suddenly, the boat was dropped to the ground! Several ugly Tagwa faces peered over the edge of the boat to check her briefly, then disappeared.

Time passed by. Ali could hear the sounds of the Tagwas busily building a campfire and setting up camp. As the shadows grew long and the sky darkened, she could hear the crackling flames and see the glowing smoke rising. She smelled venison cooking and realized how hungry she was, not having eaten anything since the previous day.

Tagwas appeared over the boat again. This time they reached in and lifted her out. She did not fight. They carried her to a spot near the campfire. Chief Gihli was seated across from her. The flames reflected in his menacing eyes that were fixated on her. His face was grim and his mouth turned down dejectedly.

She scowled at him in her most hateful manner. She wanted to leap up and tear his heart out. His lips quivered and then he spoke, "You have murdered two of my sons!"

Ali spit on the ground. The Tagwa warriors lurched toward her but backed off when the Chief waved them away.

"Where does a delicate girl get such evil?"

"From Tagwas!" she countered.

Gihli squinted at her. He seemed to be analyzing her. Perhaps he was deciding what to do with her. Ali did not care. She despised him with every fiber of her body. *You better kill me before I kill you!* she thought.

No one noticed the raven squawk in the tree above the Tagwa Chief. No one noticed the squirrel-like chatter in the surrounding bushes. Except for Ali.

They had placed sentries around the perimeter, and the renegade son kept climbing to a rocky peak and checking something.

WAYA USTI LEANED HIS head over so that he could scratch his nose with his hand that was bound to the pole. As he did, he noticed that the ropes that had come into contact with the pole were fraying. He felt the pole and found that the bark was very rough, so he began to rub the ropes across it. The pole spun around. He tried holding the pole with his knees and it worked better. He finally found that he'd have to grip it with his feet and knees, steadying it with his head. But the rough bark definitely was chewing through the ropes.

Four warriors stood guarding Ali, pointing their lances at the dangerous girl while she gnawed the meat off a deer leg bone. She appeared unbothered by them. Chief Gihli was amused at the spirit of this delicate-looking wild animal. He wished that his sons would have had the spirit and intelligence of Alihelitsidasdi. They might still be alive today. Two were gone now and he feared it was only a matter of time until his hotheaded eldest brought on his own demise.

Ali finished off the meat and hurled the bone at the Chief. One of the guards tackled her and she rolled him off like throwing off a blanket. The Chief had ducked so the deer leg struck the elder sitting behind him on the nose. Other elders tried to tend to the wounded elder, while Chief Gihli roared with laughter and commanded the guards to hold their positions.

Gihli had visions of taking Alihelitsidasdi into his family to replace his dead sons. But he was beginning to doubt that he would ever be able to tame the little hellion ... if only he had gotten her when she was younger. He was not looking forward to killing her, but at this point, he could not let her go and still maintain the respect of his men. Perhaps he could keep her as a wife. Their children would be incredible! Gihli smiled at her. Ali spit at him!

Then, he had a devious idea! <u>Gihli!</u>

As a child, he had been possessed by Tsalagis who kept him tied to their house with the dogs, thus his name! *Alihelitsidasdi shall become my gihli!*

The thought brought him a great exaltation. What perfect justice for the travesty bestowed upon him as a child by the Tsalagi to now take a Tsalagi child and make her his dog.

"Tawodi!" Waya Usti whispered urgently.

There was no answer. He tried again, "Tawodi! Can you hear me?"

Waya Usti pulled himself up enough to see the boats ahead. The sun had gone down, but there was still twilight. The raiders were staring ahead and cruising with the stiff current. "Tawodi!"

Still nothing! *The big lug has gone to sleep!*

The frustrated captive searched the bottom of the boat and found a pebble. He picked it up and chunked it into Tawodi's boat. He glanced at the raiders. They were still looking away. A confused and groggy giant peeked over the edge of his boat. Waya Usti checked the raiders and then raised his fists showing that he had successfully sawed the rope in half.

Tawodi glanced forward checking the raiders and then looked back at Waya Usti. "How?" he mouthed.

Waya Usti demonstrated sawing motions. Tawodi looked down, then looked back before disappearing in the boat. Waya Usti started working on his feet, keeping an eye on the raiders.

The nose of Waya Usti's boat jerked to the right. He looked over the bow to see the raiders turning into a cove to land. He quickly lay back down and gripped the pole, hoping they would not notice that he had severed the rope. A few more knots and his feet would be free too. He hoped Tawodi was able to saw his loose, but doubted that he had had enough time.

He felt his boat bump against the bank. Two raider warriors appeared, lifted the pole, and hoisted him out of the boat. They set the pole ends on their shoulders and headed into the woods. Tawodi was being hauled out of his boat as well. Waya Usti wondered if he had made much progress on his ropes.

The Tsikohi losses could have been worse. Only eight were dead but thirty were wounded and some might die of their wounds. Chief Waya sent messengers to neighboring villages requesting help and seeking information on the Tagwa warriors and their precious captive, Alihelitsidasdi.

Adanvdo and Kalona, in spite of her severe head wound, began tending to the wounded. The Council House was enlisted as a central point for the injured as well as coordinating communications.

Waya, himself badly wounded, had begun almost immediately putting together a search party to go find Ali. He suspected that Gihli would take her back to his village, unless he was planning to kill her as retribution for his two sons she had killed.

Every warrior and every citizen that remained in the village capable of dragging themselves to the Council House volunteered to join the search party for Ali, even young women, children, and old men. Waya picked twenty of the most competent. Sali quickly took them to water. There was no time to fast or prepare. Everyone agreed that the search party should leave immediately.

While the raiders made camp, Tawodi and Waya Usti worked on their bindings. It appeared the raiders were not setting up for an extended stay. Tawodi guessed they were planning another raid. They had not bothered to un-tether them from the poles, nor had they built a campfire.

They had placed sentries around the perimeter, and the renegade son kept climbing to a rocky peak and checking something.

Completely free of his bindings now, Waya Usti nudged his big cousin and raised his free leg! Tawodi started sawing harder, but the noise prompted him to back off. He looked knowingly at Waya Usti. They began the difficult task of shifting around so that Waya Usti could surreptitiously work on Tawodi's ropes.

Hearing something nearby, Tawodi looked over to see a raider stretched out snoring. He elbowed Waya Usti and whispered, "Knife!"

Waya Usti saw the knife and his eyes got wide. No one was paying any attention to them, but it would be very risky. He shook his head no, but Tawodi insisted.

Waya Usti took a deep breath and scanned the camp again. No one was looking. He rolled over again ... and again until he was lying next to the sleeping raider. Carefully, he slid the knife from its scabbard. The sleeping raider snorted, smacked, and rolled away from Waya Usti! He looked at his hand ... the knife was free.

Waya Usti rolled back over to join Tawodi when he heard a raider yell. He had been spotted. He chopped the binding off Tawodi's wrists. Tawodi grabbed the knife and screamed, "Run!"

Waya Usti froze as Tawodi sat up and chopped the ropes loose from his ankles. The raiders were descending upon them. Tawodi screamed again, "Run, Waya!"

Waya Usti sprinted out of the camp into the woods. Tawodi rolled right as the first attacking raider plunged his lance into the ground Tawodi had just vacated. Tawodi rolled left plunging his knife into the raider. Two other raiders tangled with each other as they tried to spear the rolling Tawodi. Tawodi kicked their spears sending them tumbling into more oncoming raiders.

Tawodi sprung to his feet pulling a lance out of the ground and plunging it into a raider attacking from the side. The following raiders learned from their foiled counterparts and halted. They fanned out around Tawodi pointing their lances and knives at him. Tawodi stood his ground threateningly.

The spoiled son of the Tagwa Chief swaggered up smiling grandly. He pulled his bow from his body and slowly loaded it with an arrow. The eyes of the raiders sparkled. The arrogant Tagwa pulled the arrow back until the base of the arrowhead touched his knuckle. Tawodi braced. His adrenaline pulsed.

Swiissssh!

From out of the woods an arrow whizzed by Tawodi and plunged into the forehead of the Tagwa leader! He reflexively released his arrow as he slowly fell backward. Tawodi reached for the arrow and missed as it flew past his head, but no one noticed. The stunned raiders were looking at their leader in shock.

Tawodi dashed into the woods.

With the arrow in flight, they kept their eyes on the Kusa leader. The arrow plunged down into the top of his head.

THE TAGWA WARRIORS DANCED late into the night. Every time that Ali tried to lie down or nod off, Chief Gihli instructed the guards to poke her with their lances. Her hatred and fury grew with each prod.

One of the Chief's assistants approached her. "The Chief wants you to dance."

"No!" she said without hesitation.

"The Chief did not ask if you WANT to dance."

"No!" she answered quickly.

"You MUST dance for the Chief."

Ali glared at the assistant defiantly as he pulled his knife and pointed at her nose. She was undeterred. He moved closer and knelt down in front of her always keeping his knife blade pointed at her.

Slowly and carefully he started cutting the rope binding her feet. Ali watched the man contemptuously. Suddenly the rope snapped and Ali kicked the assistant in the face with all her fury. He screeched and grabbed his nose as blood gushed down in two thick, red streams. Ali rolled onto her feet and dashed for the woods.

The guards raced after her, pummeling her with their lance shafts. Other warriors closed in on her from the front and back. She furiously butted, kicked and bit them.

A raven in the tree above the Chief began squawking loudly and incessantly. Gihli looked up into the tree above him. In the dark shadows of the tree, a spark grew into a flaming fireball that came rolling out of the tree toward him. He gasped and threw his arms up defensively as he dropped to his knees. The blazing raven buzzed him and flew into the brawl over Ali.

Huge, sharp talons snatched one of the warriors and the fiery raven carried him high into the sky before releasing him to windmill down crashing, flipping, tumbling through the branches of a tree.

Suddenly, hundreds of scurrying creatures emerged from the bushes carrying war clubs and chattering like angry squirrels. The Tagwa warriors were at a loss how to battle the tiny men with ferocious energy and determination. The Little People were clubbing the warriors on their knees and feet and when they doubled over, whacked them with powerful uppercuts. They were like ants pouring over the eggs of the queen. The warriors were screaming and swinging wildly to no avail.

The raven snatched another of the warriors off Ali and she burst free wielding a bloody knife. Sliced ropes hung from her wrists and elbows like bracelets of glory. She slashed and stabbed her way through the bewildered warriors in search of Chief Gihli. As she waded through the little Yunwi Tsunsdi warriors, they pointed toward a large black walnut tree where their colleagues were swarming the Chief and trapping him against the tree.

As Ali approached the Chief, the flaming raven grew large and black behind her like a perverse shadow. Gihli began screaming in horror. Ali did not hesitate. She powered through the little warriors and plunged her knife into his chest!

Immediately the raven morphed into a black robed wizard that swooped in over Ali to capture Gihli's last breath!

Ali stood in shock as she watched the witch plunge his hand into the bloody chest of the dead body of Chief Gihli and pull out his heart. Then he plunged his other hand in to retrieve the liver.

Nvwoti Atlisdodi Usdi and a dozen of his little friends gathered around Ali and herded her away.

The little man pronounced, "Ali, the living Tagwas have fled!"

Another Yunwi Tsunsdi exclaimed, "We chased them all away!"

Ali did not respond; she was dazed. The horrible images of the witch kept flashing in her mind!

As they approached the campfire, the Yunwi Tsunsdi were setting up their drums and rattles and singers for a celebration dance—what they loved more than anything! Nvwoti Atlisdodi Usdi led Ali to a spot on the perimeter to sit.

Quickly the dancing began. Slowly, Ali began to come around. Who could be glum watching the Little People jumping and whirling and stomping.

Nvwoti Atlisdodi Usdi encouraged Ali to clap and sing and before long, he was able to coax her into dancing. And the revelry carried on late into the night and for the first time in a long time, Ali felt truly happy and carefree.

Tawodi and Waya Usti reached the cove by the river. They hid downstream listening intently for pursuing raiders, trying to control their breathing. Tawodi whispered, "Hear anything?"

"No, do you?"

Tawodi listened in all directions. "All I can hear is the splashing of water against the bank."

Waya Usti frowned. He looked up into the trees. Tawodi looked up. "What is it?"

"There's no wind!"

Tawodi was confused. Waya Usti examined the river. "The river should just be flowing, not splashing!"

As their eyes adjusted to the light from the full moon, they could see an armada of boats approaching from upstream and they realized that what they were hearing were the oars paddling in the water. Waya Usti gasped, "The Kusas!"

Tawodi grabbed the bow and quiver that Waya had acquired and quietly drew an arrow and strung it in the bow. He aimed it almost straight up. Waya Usti looked up then asked, "What are you doing?"

"Chopping off the head of the serpent!"

Waya Usti looked up again. "There's a snake up there?"

Tawodi whispered, "No, the Raven."

Waya Usti looked up again. "A raven?"

Tawodi released the arrow. "No, THE Raven!"

Waya Usti realized that Tawodi wasn't looking up, but at the armada. *Oh! That Raven—the Kusa leader!*

With the arrow in flight, they kept their eyes on the Kusa leader. The arrow plunged down into the top of his head. He slumped and then rolled out of his boat. Four Kusas dove into the water to rescue him. The other Kusa warriors paused and started looking around. The arrow had seemingly dropped out of the sky giving them no clue where it had come from. The flag bearer handed off the flag and directed warriors to the left and right of the river. The Kusa Warriors deployed immediately.

Tawodi grabbed Waya Usti's arm. "Let's go!"

They dashed into the woods away from the Kusas but shortly ran into the raiders. They quickly reversed with the raiders in pursuit. Ahead the Kusas were flowing onto the shore. Tawodi shot an arrow at the Kusas, grabbed Waya Usti's arm and leaped into a thicket. The Kusas attacked the raiders in a one-sided engagement resulting in the quick slaughter of all the raiders.

Wahuhu shook the unresponsive priest violently. "Atselvdi, wake up! You are having a nightmare."

Atselvdi was disoriented. He slowly realized where he was. "I'm good. I was just ... praying."

Wahuhu stepped back. "Forgive me, priest. I didn't ..."

Wahuhu felt his stomach stir. Had he poisoned the priest's conjure? Would this bring bad fortune upon the troop?

Atselvdi felt an unusual happiness inside. "All is well now."

*Wahuhu sent scouts to
secretly watch the Kusas and
report back when there was
any sign of movement.*

Tawodi and Waya Usti secretly followed the Kusa armada to a point where the river fed into the Coosawattee. The huge army crossed the Coosawattee, landed their boats along the north side of the river and silently disappeared into the woods. Tawodi and Waya Usti beached their boat downstream from where the Kusas landed and then crept through the dark forest and climbed a hill for a good view. Morning twilight was just beginning and a fog was rolling in, but they were able to see that the Kusas were setting up camp in a large valley bordering the river.

"We must find Wahuhu!" Tawodi exclaimed as he backed away from their viewpoint. The spies rushed back to their boat and raced their boat down the Coosawattee to the village of Ustanali to join up with Wahuhu and their fellow Tsikohi warriors. They found that their colleagues had only arrived the previous evening and were up early busily establishing their camp on the ball field of Ustanali. Grateful villagers were engaged in helping their new guardians.

When Wahuhu saw the two haggard explorers enter the stockade, he greeted them and took them to the Council House where they met the Ustanali War Chief. He welcomed them graciously and ordered food be brought in.

As the two famished scouts devoured their breakfast, they detailed their story. They told of finding the Kusa warriors streaming into the valley where Wahuhu had expected them to be. They told of spotting and following raiders back to their camp. Wahuhu was surprised when Tawodi told him the Tagwa Chief's son was the leader!

They related how they had been captured and taken down stream. How Waya Usti had figured out how to saw his ropes and how they had managed, finally, to escape when Waya Usti shot the raider leader with an arrow.

They told their engrossed audience how they had run into the Kusa Armada and how Tawodi had killed their leader with an arrow. And how they had tricked the Kusas into believing that the raiders had done it and how the Kusas slaughtered the raiders. Finally, they told them where the Kusa Warriors were setting up camp.

By the end of their story, the two warriors were rejuvenated, excited, and very proud of themselves. But their pride and enthusiasm hid from them the deep concern on the faces of Wahuhu and the Ustanali Chief.

Wahuhu looked at the Chief. They shared some secret acknowledgment. Wahuhu questioned Tawodi, "You are sure the raiders were Tagwa?"

Tawodi shrugged, "At least some of them were. I know the leader was. I couldn't forget what he looked like after he tried to kill me when ..."

Wahuhu interrupted, "But you don't think the Kusas knew them?"

Tawodi grew pale. Waya Usti's eyes grew large. Tawodi stammered, "I ... I ... didn't say that ... I ..."

Wahuhu interrupted again, "But they assumed that the raiders had killed their leader?"

Tawodi and Waya Usti looked at each other. They were confused. The Ustanali Chief looked at Wahuhu. "It doesn't make sense."

Tawodi and Waya Usti gulped. They realized, too, that it did not make sense.

The Ustanali Chief persisted, "What do you think is going on?"

Wahuhu challenged the two bewildered scouts, "What makes you think the Tagwas are the raiders?"

Tawodi and Waya Usti looked at each other desperately, then timidly at Wahuhu.

Wahuhu took a deep breath. He stood and spoke to the Chief. "We'd better warn the village forces."

As they departed, the Chief implored, "What should we tell them?"

Wahuhu shook his head as they disappeared out of the Council House.

Tawodi and Waya Usti sat stunned. They had lost their appetite.

Messengers raced up and down the Coosawattee with news of where the Kusa National Warriors were camped and with warnings to prepare for a possible attack. The village Ravens had been coached by Wahuhu and were prepared to work together to draw in and set up ambushes when the attacks began. The villages were encouraged to evacuate the citizens for their protection. Messengers were also sent to Katuwa and back to the headwaters hoping to notify the Great War Chief's counselors, although most doubted that they could get a message to Katuwa in time.

The Ustanali Chief called his people to council and it was decided that they would evacuate to their host village on a tributary off the Coosawattee. By the end of the day, the village of Ustanali was packed and ready to leave the next morning.

Wahuhu met with the Tsikohi forces to go over strategy. The next morning, the bulk of the forces would move to the high ground leaving only a token force in the village stockade to engage the Kusas. The idea was to put up a mock defense and then draw the Kusas down the river where the other Tsalagi forces could ambush the pursuing Kusas.

Wahuhu had explained to the other Ravens that since they would not have enough forces to take on the Kusas, their strategy would be to ambush the Kusas inflicting as much damage as possible and then retreat to set up the next ambush. Once the Kusas had pushed to the main rivers leading north, the Tsalagi village forces would double back to reunite in Ustanali and head north to join the National Warriors.

Wahuhu sent scouts to secretly watch the Kusas and report back when there was any sign of movement. With all preparations made, it was time to wait.

Kalona remembered. "It was as if she just snapped and became a super warrior."

KALONA SAT DOWN NEXT to Waya. The War Chief was exhausted, battered, and bruised. He watched her wiping her brow and taking a break from tending to the many wounded lying or sitting around the Council House. Waya touched her on the shoulder. "How is Ali?"

"She's doing amazingly well. She wanted to come help tend to the wounded, but I made her go with Adanvdo for the cleansing ceremony."

"She is truly the most amazing girl I've ever known, Kalona. She possesses the spirit of the panther and the gentleness of the rabbit."

"She is as connected to the spirits as her great-grandfather, or her brother, but in her own way."

Waya agreed. Kalona let out a long breath and then shook her head. "I so misjudged Chief Gihli!"

Kalona looked at Waya curiously. "I guess you know where he got his name? I only learned it the night of the party. He told me that he had lived with the Tsalagi as a boy. That's why he spoke Tsalagi so well."

"That explains a lot!"

Kalona inquired, "It does?"

Waya realized that Kalona did not understand, so he explained, "In the old days, when children were kidnapped from another tribe, they were treated like gihlis. They were tied up and left outside. They were fed with the dogs. They weren't considered to be real people until they somehow proved themselves. The practice probably lingers in the outlying villages where hate is strong among rivals."

Kalona looked into space. "I can just picture the poor little Tagwa boy growing up as a gihli. The hate he must have harbored for us."

"No doubt, it often backfired for the families that practiced it. If the gihlis found an opportunity, they would massacre their captors and flee back to their own kind."

Kalona raised her eyebrows knowingly. "He said that he returned to the Tagwa after his Tsalagi family was killed!"

"Probably by him."

Waya examined her face. She had not asked about what the search party had found when they had located Ali. He somehow knew that it was coming.

"Waya," she asked with much reservation, "what do you think really happened?"

Waya knew that Ali had told a wild and fanciful story about Little People and a Raven rescuing her. It was a similar story to the one she had told about her battle with the Tagwa abductors. "I don't know what to say, Kalona. She's the only one who truly knows what happened. But I can tell you that there was no sign of Little People. No tracks or anything like that. There were also few dead bodies compared to what she remembered. I suppose they might have carried off some of them."

Kalona put her hand on Waya's knee. "You know what I think?"

Waya waited for her version. "I think that she was so scared and so traumatized, that it is part dream and part reality. A tiny little thing like her would have to be out of her mind to do what she did."

Waya chuckled. "I know when she attacked those Tagwas in your house it was amazing."

Kalona remembered. "It was as if she just snapped and became a super warrior."

Waya shook his head. "I hope I never cross her."

The past two days had dragged by in the vacated village of Ustanali. Wahuhu had spent the morning checking his forces stationed along the Coosawattee. With the villagers evacuated, only the small contingent of Tsikohi forces remained. When he returned to the almost empty stockade, he encouraged the small force to stay alert. The Kusa forces would have had time to prepare and could attack at any time.

One of the scouts he had sent to spy on the Kusas raced into the stockade. Breathlessly, he warned Wahuhu that a small contingent of Kusas was coming up the Coosawattee toward Ustanali. Wahuhu looked at the scout curiously. "A SMALL contingent?"

The sentinel at the west entrance shouted and waved that someone was coming. Wahuhu signaled for his troops to take their places. He ran up to the lookout station and was perplexed by what he saw. The Great War Chief from Katuwa and his seven war counselors and the Great Uku had landed downstream from the village and were headed for the entrance surrounded by only about twenty warriors.

The sentinel at the east entrance yelled and waved. Wahuhu could see that a Kusa delegation was coming from downstream. *What is going on?*

A messenger entered the stockade and asked for Wahuhu. Wahuhu bounded down the stairs to greet him. He recognized the messenger from Katuwa. He spoke, "The Great War Chief of the Ani Yun Wiya has arrived and soon the Great War Chief of the Ani Kusas will be here for a council between the two great nations. You are instructed to stand down."

Wahuhu acknowledged and waved to his forces to stand down. Wahuhu could not believe what was happening, nor did he understand it.

The Tsalagi delegation entered the Ustanali stockade and assembled in front of the Council House to greet the Kusa delegation entering the stockade through the east entrance. The introductions were formal and the two great chiefs were stern and stoic. The delegations moved inside.

Wahuhu recognized the Raven from the Katuwa Council at the headwaters of the Coosawattee approaching him. "Wahuhu!"

Wahuhu greeted him.

The Katuwa delegate began, "You must be wondering what this is all about?" The delegate motioned toward the ball field, "Shall we walk?"

The two men strolled across the ball field as the delegate explained, "I'm sorry I could not share this with you the night you and your enthusiastic assistants came to us. Your analysis and plan were alarmingly accurate. It surprised us and we were, quite frankly, at a loss as to what to do. You see, the Great War Chief and his counselors had already come to the same conclusion. Even as you were suggesting it, the National Warriors were setting up north of the Coosawattee and prepared to attack if the Kusas invaded. You can see our dilemma?"

The delegate stopped and looked at Wahuhu as if waiting for a response. Wahuhu realized that he had come very close to upsetting everything. Now he understood why the Katuwa delegation had been so contrary!

The delegate resumed the walk. "We could not divulge the secret without consulting with the Great War Chief and his counselors. We just hoped that you would deploy as instructed and ... well ... trust us."

Wahuhu studied the ground. He suspected that he was in grave trouble.

"When the Great War Chief heard of your proposal, he was impressed, but... well ... perplexed."

The two walked in silence a few steps before the delegate continued, "When we learned that you had ... gone rogue ... and shared your plan with the other ravens, the Great War Chief was, at first, furious, but then realized that it was a perfect complement to his plan!"

Wahuhu breathed a sigh of relief.

The delegate continued, "In the meantime, the Kusa Chief had sent a messenger explaining that the raiders were renegades and that he was concerned about the presence of so many Tsalagi warriors on the Coosawattee. He explained that he was sending his brother with a large force as a defensive measure."

Wahuhu gulped. Tawodi had killed the brother of the Great War Chief of the Kusa! The delegate stopped and studied Wahuhu. "I sense that I have said something that alarms you."

Wahuhu grappled with what to do. Should he protect Tawodi? Who would know? The Kusas probably believed the raiders had killed the brother. Then he remembered that the Ustanali Chief had been present when Tawodi had revealed it. "I'm afraid I need to share something that may be very explosive!"

The delegate frowned. "Yes?"

"It is a long story, but one of my warriors has killed the brother of the Kusa Chief!"

The delegate gasped! They had crossed the ball field and there were log benches where the drummers had set up for dances. The delegate motioned for Wahuhu to sit and he joined him. "I guess I need to hear the long story!"

Wahuhu related the details of Tawodi and Waya Usti's adventure. The delegate, although sympathetic, was deeply concerned. "This could change everything!"

Wahuhu rubbed his face with his palms. "Tawodi was acting on my orders. I am responsible for this. I will offer myself for retribution."

Wahuhu sadly drew his knife. The delegate grasped Wahuhu's wrist. "No. Tawodi did exactly the right thing, considering what he knew at the time."

The delegate sat back in thought. Finally, he commanded Wahuhu, "Send Tawodi away. I will counsel with the Great War Chief."

The delegate jumped up and headed for the Council House, but then stopped. "And send the knife away!"

*"You could hide in Katuwa
until the Green Corn Festival
and then seek forgiveness."*

Aʟɪ ᴡᴀs ɴᴏᴡ ᴀ hero of legendary proportions. Most did not believe her story about witches and Little People helping her. Most now believed that she alone annihilated the three Tagwas that abducted her. Chief Waya Gigage and others had witnessed Ali kill the Tagwa Chief's son among others before being captured. So, when she was found dancing happily all alone around a campfire surrounded by more dead Tagwas including the Chief himself, most were convinced that Alihelitsidasdi had done it again!

The exceptions were Adanvdo and Sali with Kalona on the fence. She could accept that the Yunwi Tsunsdi had helped her granddaughter. But, Adanvdo and Sali believed that there was more to it. The Yunwi Tsunsdi may be fierce and may have special powers, but they would not have horrified Chief Gihli. Adanvdo and Sali believed that Kalanu Ahkyeliski would try to rescue his great-great-granddaughter because they had seen him battle his own son when he had threatened his family years before. Tsisgili was now entombed in the stone megalith thanks to Kalanu Ahkyeliski. Adanvdo and Sali believed that it had happened exactly as Ali had told it.

But something did not fit. Why would his father attack and brutally mutilate Crooked Foot, a defenseless old cripple with but a few years of life left? It did not fit the pattern. There was only one way to clear up the mystery. He would have to confront his father personally.

Adanvdo searched for the cave entrance that led to the path to Kalanu Ahkyeliski's cliffside hideout. So much had changed in the many years since he had been there. Some trees had grown up and some had died; rocks had slid down the cliff face; and erosion had exposed others that weren't there before. Much had changed.

As Grandmother Sun neared the end of her journey, Adanvdo reluctantly headed for home.

It was nightfall when Adanvdo rounded the turn in the trail back to Tsikohi just past Rabbit Meadow. The orderly shapes of the southwest corner of the stockade were now visible in the shadows. To his left the stone megalith, the tomb of his brother, jutted upward into the sky. He thought he heard something and paused to listen. It was a rustling sound coming from the stone shaft.

He could feel in his chest the rush of blood accelerating to fill his body with adrenalin to handle the emergency detected by his senses. His alert eyes searched the moonlit megalith and despite its vagary, detected the ghostlike appearance of the wispy woman, Saloli, clinging to the tomb's base.

Adanvdo found her action repulsive and yet poignant. His brother had raped her, tormented her, and tried to steal her baby. He was sure his brother had never shown her any semblance of affection or concern. And yet, there she was clinging to his tombstone; clinging to his memory; clinging to a wish, a dream that could never be fulfilled.

He could not forgive the deranged woman for attempting to murder not only his daughter but also her own. But, in spite of his contempt, he could not help but feel pity for her pathetic sorrow.

He wondered where she got the gall to return to a village where only hatred and disdain awaited her. How desperate she must be to search for the source of her misery in the twilight of her years. Had she never found happiness? Was this the pathetic measure of her life?

He heard rustling again, but Saloli was still, immovable in her prostration. Someone was walking behind him. He turned to see the silhouette of a giant approaching!

The giant raised his hand and showed his palm. "Siyo, Grandfather."

Adanvdo recognized the voice of Tawodi. He waited for the warrior to catch up. "Where are the others?"

Tawodi placed his hand on the old man's shoulder. "All is well. They will be returning soon."

"You are a messenger now?"

"No, Grandfather, I have been sent to hide until a grave matter is settled."

Adanvdo was confused. "What is this grave matter?"

Tawodi was tired and did not want to have to tell his story twice. "Come with me to see the Chief and I will explain."

Adanvdo glanced back to the tomb of his brother. Saloli was gone.

Waya Gigage invited Adanvdo and Tawodi into his house. They sat around the hearth and listened to Tawodi explain the complicated grave matter that was, hopefully, being settled in Ustanali.

Waya was worried. He knew that the Kusa Chief was hotheaded. He might demand retribution. He also knew that if retribution was demanded, his principal assistant and close friend, Wahuhu, would try to offer himself in place of his warrior.

Adanvdo broke the silence. "You could hide in Katuwa until the Green Corn Festival and then seek forgiveness."

Tawodi had not considered that option. In fact, hiding was distasteful to him. He had wanted to stay and face whatever fate might be handed down, but Wahuhu had commanded him to return to Tsikohi. "No, Grandfather. If the matter cannot be resolved, I will offer myself to the Kusa Chief."

Waya and Adanvdo glanced at each other. They shared their unspoken understanding that Tawodi was naive and did not understand that matters were out of his hands.

Ali sat beside the hearth watching the low flames rolling over the embers. She thought about Atselvdi's ripples in the water analogy of how life calms over time and wondered when or if calm would settle over her again.

She felt her body shiver involuntarily. She was not cold, but she pulled her grandfather's old buffalo blanket snug around her shoulders and slumped over bowing her head. She heard someone enter the room and turned to see her great-grandfather shuffle in.

He looked tired and distraught. "Are you hungry, Grandfather?"

Adanvdo looked at his great-granddaughter. Her eyes were dark and sunken. She appeared to be cowering under the huge blanket. *With all that she has been through, the dear girl is worried that I might be hungry!*

"Just a little something would be nice." He moved over to the hearth and sat in his usual spot on the west side and reached for his pipe. Ali had dropped her blanket and was mixing something in a pot.

"How have you been today?"

Ali placed the pot over the fire and added a log. "Okay."

"Have you been out at all?"

"Amadohi came over and we stared at the fire for a while and then she left. She is very upset. She misses Tawodi."

Adanvdo sucked on the pipe to start it. "Well, if that's true, she'll be happy when she finds out he is back."

Ali spun around and her eyes sparkled. "They are back?"

Adanvdo looked up at the excited young woman and wished he had not said anything. "I'm sorry, child, just

Tawodi is back, But he said the others would be returning soon."

"Why just Tawodi?"

Now Adanvdo really hated himself for saying something. Could he tell her? Would it make matters worse? "Well, it's complicated."

"Spit it out Grandfather! What has happened?"

He realized now that he had to tell her or she would imagine something even worse. "Tawodi and Waya Usti were sent to find the Kusa National Warriors, which they did. They also found the raiders, or thought they did. In a brave attempt to end the war before it even started, Tawodi killed the Kusa Raven and made it look like the raiders did it."

Ali was confused. "That sounds like a good thing."

"Yes, well, it turns out the Kusas weren't planning to invade, they were just providing defense. The raiders weren't a Kusa ploy, as we originally thought. The raiders were actually Tagwas, led by one of Chief Gihli's sons."

Adanvdo smoked the pipe a moment before adding, "I expect Chief Gihli sent his son to stir up trouble knowing that it would draw our warriors away."

His granddaughter removed the pot from the fire and filled a bowl for her great-grandfather.

Adanvdo took the bowl and finished his story, "So, Tawodi provoked war instead of deterring it."

"How did he do that? Don't they think the raiders did it?"

Adanvdo shifted uncomfortably. "Well, Tawodi was so proud of himself that he told about it. This was, of course, before he knew the Kusas weren't planning to attack."

Ali gasped and put her hand over her mouth. "He's on the run?"

"Well, yes, but the Katuwa delegate sent him away as a precaution."

Tears welled up in her eyes. "They will seek retribution."

"We don't know yet, maybe not."

"What about Waya Usti? He was with him, wasn't he?"

"Yes, but he didn't engage the Kusas in any way."

The distraught girl rushed to her room and collapsed on her bed.

Would this nightmare never end? Would she never find peace and happiness again? How much more could she endure?

As Grandmother Sun climbed above the horizon, Kalona Ehlawei rushed home from a council meeting. She found her granddaughter lying on her bed depressed. "Ali! Good news!"

The girl turned her sad eyes toward her grandmother. She had been crying, perhaps all night. She looked terrible.

Kalona sat down beside her and lifted her up in her arms. "The warriors are coming home. They'll be here in two days!"

Ali pulled back with anticipation. "Tawodi?"

"Tawodi has been forgiven. The Kusa Chief will not seek retribution. The Kusa and Tsalagi are still at peace!"

Ali hugged her grandmother gratefully. It was a new day!

*Tlomeha Usdi, the wise old
hunter, winked at the
befuddled priest.*

Tlomeha Usdi slipped quietly through the tall grass approaching the woods south of Rabbit Meadows. Waya Usti moved up behind him quietly. He could tell that his father had spotted a deer, or smelled it, or however he did it, there was a deer somewhere up ahead.

Tawodi crashed forward snapping branches and crunching the frozen grass while he pulled an arrow from his quiver and knocked it on his bow. Tlomeha stood with an expression not of alarm, but more of disbelief. Waya Usti suppressed his strong desire to bust out laughing. He put his hand on his giant cousin's shoulder. "Tawodi, you're going to have to be quiet. You've just alerted all of the creatures on the mountain that we're coming!"

Tawodi whispered the prayer of forgiveness to the Deer Spirit. "Sorry, Awi Usti."

After giving his apologies to the spirit deer who watches over all deer, he pulled back the arrow and fired into the air. Tlomeha Usdi dived for cover. Waya Usti jumped back and watched the arrow sail high into the air and then plummet down intercepting a deer leaping across the meadow.

The huge man held up his arms in triumph and then bounded across the meadow to where the deer fell. Waya Usti helped his father back to his feet. Tlomeha Usdi shook his head and said, "Never again!"

The old hunter dusted himself off and beamed at his son. "Let's go get yours."

"Shouldn't we help Tawodi?"

The fragile little man shook his head. "He is beyond help."

Wananahi burst into the bedroom! "Amadohi! Get up! You're going to want to see this! Hurry!"

Amadohi drug herself out of bed and trudged into the main room. Her mother was peeking through the door, hiding behind the door cover. Amadohi frowned and grumbled to herself, "Not another silly sunrise."

She reluctantly joined her mother and peeked out the other side of the cover. Tawodi was coming down the street with a tiny deer wrapped around his neck. The legs hung down across his chest and he grasped the ankles as he walked proudly up to Amadohi's house, stood for a moment, then lifted the deer over his head and laid it in front of the house.

He paused for a moment and then started walking away, glancing back over his shoulder.

Amadohi stepped back from the door in shock. Her mouth hung open, her eyes wide with amazement. Wananahi giggled beside her with her hands over her mouth. They looked at each other smiling grandly, grabbed each other's hands and began dancing about the room. Tawodi had just made a formal proposal of marriage!

Wananahi joked, "Care for some venison this evening?"

Amadohi giggled and replied, "Yes! Yes! Yes!"

Kalona sat down between her father and Ali in her usual place. She smiled broadly at her grandson sitting across the hearth from her. "It's so good to have you home again, Atselvdi."

"It's good to be home, Grandmother."

Ali sat quietly. It was good to have her brother home again but her thoughts were somewhere else. She was hoping that Waya Usti would come calling.

They heard a commotion outside. Kalona stared at the door. "What's going on out there?"

Atselvdi jumped up and ran to the door. Kalona struggled to get up. Ali helped her get to her feet and steadied her. Kalona held her head and waited for the dizzy spell to go away.

Atselvdi reported, "The commotion is at Amadohi's house. I can't tell what's happened, but the neighbors have gathered. It must not be serious. They are laughing and cheering."

Kalona and Ali rushed to the door and looked out. Kalona whispered, "Wananahi?"

Ali whispered, "Amadohi?"

Atselvdi locked arms with his sister and grandmother. "Come on! Let's go see what's happening."

Adanvdo shuffled over to the door and watched them rush down the street. He was not sure he cared to go, but his curiosity would not let him stay back. He stepped through the door and started toward the commotion when he heard someone grunt and fall down. He looked up the street and saw Waya Usti getting up and struggling to pull a huge deer up on to his shoulders while a small crowd stood watching and laughing.

Adanvdo looked back toward Wananahi's house and shouted, "Ali! Kalona!"

Ali broke away from Kalona and Atselvdi to look at her great-grandfather. He was waving for her to come back. Kalona and Atselvdi stopped and looked back. Kalona whispered, "Oh, Ali. Go help your grandfather."

Ali dutifully ran back to her great-grandfather. "I'm coming, Grandfather. I'm sorry we ran off and left you."

As she reached out to take his arm, he pointed up the street.

"What?" she asked confused.

She looked up to see Waya Usti with an enormous buck draped over him. His legs were buckling and the hooves of the deer drug the ground with each step. Her determined young fiancée trudged down the hill toward her house. He looked up from underneath the massive belly of the deer and saw her.

She put her hands over her mouth, shrieked and ran into her house. Kalona came back as fast as she could, glancing up the street as she passed by Adanvdo to join her granddaughter in the house. Adanvdo laughed with delight at the spectacle.

"What's happening, Grandfather?" Atselvdi questioned as he ran to the side of his great-grandfather. Adanvdo chuckled and replied, "Get ready to eat some venison, Grandson!"

"I'm not hungry, Grandfather."

Atselvdi looked up the street at the struggling boy then noticed that his great-grandfather was shuffling into the house and had not heard his response. Atselvdi suddenly understood what was happening! Waya Usti was about to offer his sister a deer. He was proposing marriage to his sister! He looked toward Amadohi's house and realized that Tawodi had just proposed to Amadohi, too!

Atselvdi's eyes were drawn to a familiar figure among the reveling crowd. As he focused, he recognized Sudalegi staring at him. He gasped! Reflexively he looked back at Waya Usti. Again, his eyes focused on another familiar figure among the revelers surrounding Waya Usti. Tlomeha Usdi, the wise old hunter, winked at the befuddled priest.

Adanvdo's heart leaped when he saw the pure delight in his daughter's and great-granddaughter's eyes. Balance and harmony was returning to Tsikohi and happiness was being restored.

*Everything a raven needs
to know about survival he is
born with. Ravens break out
of the egg and are equipped
with the traits and skills
for life.*

Aᴅᴀɴᴠᴅᴏ'ꜱ ʜᴇᴀʀᴛ ᴄʀɪɴɢᴇᴅ ᴡɪᴛʜ an old feeling remembered from the days before his brother's demise. It
was a recurrent thought, dredging up and refusing to go
away. Why did his father murder poor old Crooked Foot?

His father might be a witch and capable of robbing
a man of his souls, but picking on an aging cripple was
not in character. It just did not add up and Adanvdo's
sense of fairness and justice would not let it go.

He got up early, driven by a new plan to find his
father's hideaway. He would start in the meadow and try
to retrace his steps from the first time he had found the
cave years before with the help of his cousin, Big Elk, an
expert tracker.

The trail through the woods took him to the same
area where he had searched several days before. He was
certain the cave entrance was nearby, but it had changed
so much since Big Elk had helped him find it so many
years before. He remembered that the crack in the rock
slab was obscurely positioned along the mountain base

and he was determined to search every inch if necessary to find it.

As Grandmother Sun climbed above the trees and lent her bright rays to his quest, he was startled when a raven squawked and flew into a small pine tree. Perhaps it was a sign. Perhaps it was his father! He searched the tree and was not surprised to find the tree empty. Instead, he found a split in the rock face behind the tree. He pushed behind the tree and squeezed through the narrow crack that allowed him to enter. Once inside, a grand cave opened up with a trickling stream running down the middle. To his left, a pile of boulders and stones provided a natural rock stairway ascending to a hole in the roof of the grand cavern.

At the top of the rock heap, he found the path that followed the side of the mountain leading around to a wide rocky crag overlooking the canyon of the Agusa Jisdu. In the center of the flat shelf on the side of the mountain, a familiar water spout was still flowing out of the rock face into an icy pond. Beside the pond, a weathered old seven-sided hut set nestled in the shrubs. His father would be waiting inside the hut.

Adanvdo ducked to enter through the low entrance. Once inside, he rose up to look at the spot where he knew he would find his father sitting by the fire in his usual place. He looked remarkably well!

"Osiyo, Father."

"Siyo, Ugugu." Adanvdo chuckled. No one had used his birth name since he had run away from home as a young boy. "Come sit by the fire; we shall smoke."

Adanvdo shuffled over and clumsily lowered himself beside the fire. As he watched the familiar motions of his father preparing the pipe, a warm feeling flushed through him, filling him with memories of a time when he was a young admiring son. Finally, Adanvdo said, "I came to thank you for saving Ali."

His father tipped his head. "She is family."

Adanvdo looked at his father's face. He had not changed in forty years. In fact, he looked better than the last time he had seen him. "It's been a long time."

"I haven't lost touch. ... I have watched you live a good life. ... You seem happy."

"It has been a good life. I am happy. I have a good family."

"Yes, we have a beautiful family. They should not have to pay for my transgressions."

"Nor mine."

"You look old, do you feel well?" Kalanu inquired.

"I feel okay. You look good. Eaten anybody lately?"

Kalanu Ahkyeliski looked stunned and then chuckled and tried his hand at humor. "I have a little someone for you! ... if you like gihli meat."

Adanvdo laughed. He had never understood why his father held on to the dark ways. He was, in his heart, a good man. Adanvdo had tried many times to convince him to reject the dark ways and return to the Ani Yun Wiya to walk the white path again. But Kalanu Ahkyeliski could not let go. Maybe he just had too much invested. At this point, he probably would not be able to adjust to living in a village with the Real People.

Adanvdo responded, "I found your last gift dried and shriveled in the Tlanuwa box."

"There has been plenty of Tagwa to go around." Then his father got very serious. "Ugugu, my son, your time is nearing. If you do not consume askinas, your life will expire. How can you let that happen when you have it within your power to prevent it?"

"Father, I have chosen the white path." Adanvdo was very frustrated having to rehash this old argument. Kalanu shook his head in disgust.

Adanvdo glanced around the hut. "Would you have me live like you?"

The lonely old witch flinched. Adanvdo felt remorse. "I'm sorry, Father. That was inappropriate."

A tear trickled down Kalanu's cheek. He was quiet for a long time before saying, "You are right, Adanvdo. I do not have a life."

Then he chuckled at the irony. "I have no life, but will live forever. You have the perfect life but ...! Where is the fairness in that?"

Adanvdo shook his head. It was true and yet neither was willing to change their path. Adanvdo's heart was heavy as he struggled to build his courage to ask the critical question that was tormenting him, "Father, why the old man with the crooked foot?"

Strife fell across Kalanu's face. His sad eyes turned away from his son. Adanvdo felt his father was grieving. Kalanu shook his head side to side. "I failed him."

Adanvdo frowned. He did not understand. Kalanu glanced at his son and continued, "He is his father's son."

Adanvdo was even more confused. He had not known Crooked Foot's father and could not believe that Kalanu had known him. Kalanu tried to explain, "Kalona was not my only grandchild born that day."

"Uwohasvgi!" Adanvdo whispered. He had always suspected that Saloli's baby was the son of Tsisgili, his twin brother and Kalanu's other son. So, that would make Saloli's baby Kalanu's grandson.

Kalanu continued, "When Saloli placed the babies in the pond, I could not let them drown."

Kalanu turned to Adanvdo with pleading eyes. "Even though he was Tsisgili's son, he was my grandson. He was innocent and did not deserve ... I left little Quiet Raven for you to find, and carried Uwohasvgi home with me."

Adanvdo was astonished, when they found his little daughter washed up on the bank, they had assumed that Uwohasvgi had not survived. All they ever found was his blanket downstream. It had always been assumed that he drowned and was washed to sea by the Long Man's currents. Kalanu continued, "I brought him here and raised him myself hoping that I could teach him a better way—maybe even the white path. I thought I could correct the mistakes I made with his father."

Kalanu shook his head as he relived the memory. "But he had Tsisgili's heart."

Adanvdo looked into the fire and sat quietly until his father felt like resuming. "For a long time, I thought it would work. He was a very sweet child, very smart, quiet, and respectful. He had a pleasing, happy face ..."

Kalanu looked at Adanvdo. "Like yours. He was a lot like you when he was little."

Kalanu returned his gaze to the hearth. "But, as he matured, he changed. His happy little round eyes became menacing, hiding under a heavy brow. His easy smile changed into a thin, arrogant smirk. His soft, pudgy body matured into a hard frame. More and more I felt that he was interested in manipulating me rather than learning from me or working with me. Over time, he came to even look like his father, and act like his father."

Kalanu took a deep breath and looked into Adanvdo's eyes. "I never understood why you and Tsisgili turned out so differently. I rationalized that maybe Tsisgili was closer to his mother and influenced by her. After she took the potion, she became aloof and not of her own heart. I thought that maybe Tsisgili was affected by that."

Kalanu glanced at his good son. "I thought that maybe you were influenced by me. You seemed to look at the world the same way as me. I understood you. I understood your reasoning."

Kalanu stirred the fire unconsciously. "I believed then that we are products of our environment. When we are born, we are all raw clay to be molded by our upbringing."

Kalanu jabbed the fire with a long stick, irritating the coals and sending sparks scurrying into the air. "But I was not looking at you with clear vision. Tsisgili's aloofness was not from his mother. It was different. It was an independence devoid of concern for others. He was like my father, a man he had never known."

Kalanu stared into Adanvdo's eyes to see if the significance registered. "His selfishness and deviousness came from his uncle, and his attraction to witchcraft was like that of his aunt."

Kalanu resumed playing with the fire. "He knew none of those people and yet he was influenced by them."

Adanvdo tried to relate to what his father was saying. His own daughter, Kalona, had always seemed so different from either him or her mother. He had always assumed it was because she had to raise herself and developed her own ways. But, he had often noticed how much she reminded him of his mother, especially after his mother was released from the spell—when his mother was her real self.

Kalanu continued, "And you are more than me and more than your mother. You are like your grandmother. You have many of her little anomalies, peculiarities. You speak with the cadence of her voice. You reason like her."

The old man shifted. "And yet, you never knew her. You did not pick up her idiosyncrasies by being around her."

Kalanu got to the point. "See, I thought that I could take Tsisgili's son and mold him like clay; shield him from the influences that made Tsisgili evil and devious; and raise him to follow the white path, like you."

The old man shook his head as if accepting a new reality. "But, I was wrong. I should have remembered the raven. Everything a raven needs to know about survival he is born with. Ravens break out of the egg and are equipped with the traits and skills for life. They know how to fly; they know how to hunt; they know how to mate; they know how to build a nest and provide for the nestlings."

Adanvdo distracted his father briefly by shifting and rubbing his nose. His father's revelations were resonating with him. They were opening up thoughts he had sensed but never really pondered or studied. It was a new way of thinking for him. It was a new subject he had not fully thought about or reasoned out. It was a paradigm shift and he knew that his father was correct.

"Nothing I could have done would have changed what Uwohasvgi received in the womb, i.e., his heredity, the gifts handed down to him from his ancestors that make him who he is, whose influence is stronger than any influences after the womb."

Adanvdo felt nauseous as he stared at the fire. He whispered, "So, Tsisgili is back? He has come back to occupy his son's body and resume his evil life. Tsisgili's powers have transcended his tomb and he has figured out how to conquer death itself!"

Adanvdo asked Kalanu, "Father, where is he now?"

Kalanu shrugged. "He left me many years ago to search for his father."

Kalanu's face was grim. Adanvdo could see the pain he was feeling. "When Uwohasvgi was very little, he started asking innocent questions, as little ones do. Who is my father? Where is my mother?"

Kalanu glanced at his son. "I did not want to tell him about Tsisgili, his true father, so I told him that his father was a big man with a raven tattoo."

Adanvdo felt a flush swelling his body. Big Elk was a big, lovable, gentle man who had courted Saloli until she had smothered him with her obsessive dependence and then tried to drown the babies and disappeared.

Kalanu shook his head as he gazed into nothingness. "When Uwohasvgi left to find his father, I kept an eye on him. I knew it would not go well. ... and it didn't. Big Elk knew that Uwohasvgi was not his child, so when he showed up claiming Big Elk was his father, it shocked Big Elk and he denied Uwohasvgi. The young man demanded the truth, but he was not prepared for the truth."

Kalanu turned his sad eyes to face Adanvdo. "He understood immediately the implications of his drowning. He demanded to know why his mother would go to such extremes. Big Elk, of course, knew the relationship Saloli had with Tsisgili."

Kalanu bowed his head and Adanvdo could see he was grieving. He respectfully waited. He glanced around the small hut. The once vacant walls were now decorated with signs of the child: small blankets, trinkets, toys, a blowgun.

Kalanu resumed, "After he left Big Elk, he returned demanding the truth, demanding to know about his mother and his father. It became his quest. I watched him through the crystals. He spent his life searching: for his parents; for his roots; for meaning. He was a man without family or purpose."

Kalanu shifted, picked up a stick and jabbed at the coals again. "Several years ago he picked up Saloli's trail in Hiawasee. She had landed there after she left Tsikohi and floundered living a wild, licentious life that never gave her purpose or grounding. Over time, age robbed her of beauty, spirit, and appeal. She wandered direction-less drifting from one village to another.

"Uwohasvgi tracked her easily. Wherever she ventured, people noticed her and she was not easily forgotten.

"When Uwohasvgi found her he confused her. She thought Tsisgili had returned to her."

Kalanu sniggered. "And she confused him. He thought his father might be alive. When she traveled to Tsikohi, he followed expecting to find Tsisgili. Instead, he found you ... and the old man."

Kalanu stirred the fire as he reflected. "I don't know where he learned to transfer the askina. I did not teach him, but he had a quick, devious mind. He never seemed to be interested in what I taught him, but his clever mind absorbed it all."

The remorseful old wizard tossed his stick to the side of the hearth and rubbed his face with his palms. "I had told him about the four souls of a man. He must have put it together when I consumed the saliva, heart, liver, and marrow of a raven."

He shook his head. "I didn't know he saw me. The raven provided me with a way to spy on my family, a way to get close without arousing suspicion, and a way to stay connected."

Adanvdo felt his father's anguish. For all of his life, his good intentions had turned on him. He had become a witch in order to save his mentors. He had accidentally given his girlfriend a love potion, but the deceit had cost him her love. He had used his great powers to help the village of Tororu, his village, to conquer the evil cannibal witch Nunyunuwi only to have the people turn on him and condemn him along with the evil witch. His attempt at retribution in a remote village where he tried to raise a family and provide his medicine also ended in condemnation and exile.

Despite it all, his father had never stopped watching and protecting his family.

Adanvdo shivered. The calm and the peace he had found in Tsikohi after the death of his brother was over. The fear he had lived under for the first half of his life was back. Tsisgili was reaching out of his grave and through his son, returning to haunt him.

He was too old for the battle. He looked at his rejuvenated father. How accomplished was his grandson? Would he be able to save his family one last time?

About the Author

Courtney Miller is the multi-award-winning author of the acclaimed Cherokee Chronicles, a 7-book series on the Cherokee following a fictional family through the ages from antiquity through relocation. His celebrated cozy mysteries and geezer-lit novels, The White Feather Mysteries, pit a Cherokee elder against a rural Sheriff's office in the Wet Mountain Valley of Colorado. He has also authored over 200 articles on the art, archaeology, astronomy, history and cultures of Native America and is considered an expert on ancient Native American cultures. He currently resides near Westcliffe, Colorado. Visit him online at CourtneyMillerAuthor.com.

www.ingramcontent.com/pod-product-compliance
Lightning Source LLC
Chambersburg PA
CBHW031730180726
48283CB00005B/1442